W9-CZA-105

The Lying Club

The Lying Club

Annie Ward

THORNDIKE PRESS
A part of Gale, a Cengage Company

Thorndike Press, a part of Gale, a Cengage Company.

Thorndike Press® Large Print Core.
The text of this Large Print edition is unabridged.
Other aspects of the book may vary from the original edition.
Set in 16 pt. Plantin.

LIBRARY OF CONGRESS CIP DATA ON FILE.
CATALOGUING IN PUBLICATION FOR THIS BOOK
IS AVAILABLE FROM THE LIBRARY OF CONGRESS.

ISBN-13: 978-1-4328-9651-5 (hardcover alk. paper)

Published in 2022 by arrangement with Harlequin Enterprises ULC

Printed in Mexico
Print Number : 1 Print Year : 2022

For my family, friends and two decades
of great teammates.
"WE. ARE. THE. WOLVES."
— *Wolfpack* by Abby Wambach,
US soccer Olympic gold medalist

Prologue

The necktie of her ex was still clasped in her hand when Natalie woke. Her head was pounding, and her mouth tasted bad, like she'd fallen into bed without brushing her teeth. She had a horrible, cloudy feeling that she'd done something regrettable, but in that moment, she couldn't remember what it was.

She wasn't at home. Instead, she was upright, a seat belt crossing her chest. In front of her was the windshield of her own car, coated in a sheet of frost, and her I LOVE COLORADO! key chain was dangling from the ignition.

Natalie realized then that she'd blacked out. It had happened before, when she was much younger, and the memory of that awful awakening hit her with an electrifying jolt. After a frantic inspection, she concluded that all her clothes were on and nothing seemed torn or altered. She slipped the tie into her coat pocket.

Yanking the rearview mirror toward her face, she saw that her hazel eyes were huge, the pupils tiny pinpoints, and her mascara was smudged. A chapped crack ran down the bottom of her lower lip, but there were no other bruises or cuts. It didn't appear that she'd crashed into a building or a tree. There were no sirens.

She rolled down her window, and a thin wall of ice collapsed into the car, dampening her plaid skirt. It was almost dark outside.

Work. She was at work. Across the snowy parking lot, she could see the back door to the east wing of the private school where she was an administrative assistant in the front office.

Pulling on her stocking cap and opening the car door, Natalie noticed footprints, slightly softened by snowfall, leading from her car to the rear exit of the school's gym. Another set of identical prints returned from the door to the car, but not in a straight line. They zigzagged, and there was a large compression in the snow, just about the size of a small person like her. Gingerly, she lowered one boot into the first of the prints to make sure it was a match. It was. It seemed likely that the body-shaped spot in the snow was an indication that she'd fallen, and a quick pat down of her coat confirmed that it was wet.

Natalie stepped out of her car and squinted into the wind. Her legs felt weak, as if she'd just returned from one of her longer runs.

She retraced her own tracks, leading to the school. The sky was changing color from a grayish stormy dusk to night, and it struck Natalie, who loved art, that the swirling white flurries between her and the stars resembled a monochrome Van Gogh painting. Snow-capped peaks surrounded her on all sides. Down the mountain was the town center. Lights twinkled. Houses, vacation condos, and old-timey shops were piled like Christmas gifts on top of one another alongside a dark and twisting river.

The heavy back door was ajar. When she tugged on it, it groaned, scraped, and opened. Heart pounding, she went in.

During school hours, the sports pavilion would have been filled with the sound of bouncing basketballs, laughter, whistles, and sneakers squeaking on the gym floor. Now, there was distant, droning pop music playing up on the mezzanine, but no one was singing along or dropping weights to the floor with a crash.

Natalie walked with slow, hesitant steps over to the double doors that opened onto the basketball courts.

Normally those doors stood propped open by gray rubber wedges. Now they were closed, but each had a rectangular window. Natalie curled her hand and made a cup for her eyes.

It took a second to see anything at all. The court was dim, aglow only from the small green emergency lights situated over the doors and in the corners of the room. Her eyes were adjusting. Something was there.

She jumped away from the door as if the glass had burned her skin. Her hands flew up to cover her mouth. A scream almost escaped, but she stopped it in her throat with a choking noise.

Not far from the door was what looked like a crumpled pile of clothes and broken body parts, motionless in the middle of a spreading pool of blood.

What the hell did I do?

The security lights in the Falcon Academy parking lot flickered. It was early Monday morning and still dark. A beat-up Pathfinder left tracks in the snow as it swerved into a spot reserved for employees.

Harry Doyle climbed out and used his

heel to squelch a cigarette into the ground. He grabbed a battered baseball cap from the dashboard and plopped it on his head, holding down what little was left of his hair. After slamming the driver's door shut, he looked up at the sky, which was turning pink and orange to the east. An enormous blanket of fluffy white covered the parking lot. Last night had been the first big storm of the season, and some parents would call their kids in sick so they could hit the slopes with their friends.

The sixty-eight-year-old custodian shuffled towards the rear entrance of the sports pavilion. The automatic fluorescents in the back hallway glowed a sickly yellow. He hummed as he plodded down the hall to the boys' changing room, where he put his lunch and jacket away in his locker before going to the storage closet. Harry grabbed the fiberglass handle of the deluxe wet mop and hauled it, and the bucket, out into the corridor toward the basketball courts. Pushing past the double doors, he activated all nine light switches with a swipe of his hand. The bulky, caged gymnasium overheads burst to life with a buzz.

"What the hell?" he exclaimed, dropping the mop.

The handle clattered against the maple

wood planks. "Oh dear God." The words came out strangled.

Harry scrambled for his phone in a zippered compartment of his slacks.

"Hello?" he managed to say, after dialing 911. He was having trouble breathing. "The Falcon Academy. Off Highway 70. Just west of Blackswift. Oh Jesus. Jesus Mary and Joseph. We need help. There's a lot of blood."

KBEV 16 Breaking News:

"Melissa O'Hare here, coming to you first on the scene as a major situation is unfolding at one of our local schools. What we know so far is that, not long ago, the sound of sirens shattered the early morning tranquility here outside Big Elk Estates. As you can see behind me, there's a massive police response at the Falcon Academy, a private and well-respected institution in a safe and affluent community. While authorities have declined to comment on the identities of the two people carried out of Falcon Academy several hours ago, one spokesperson for authorities indicated that an investigation is already underway. A person of interest has been identified and detained for questioning. Sources at Colorado Mountain Medical say that the next twelve hours will be key in determining whether the police are dealing with an accident, aggravated assault, or homicide. I'm Melissa O'Hare, and I'll be keeping you up-to-date as this story unfolds."

Six Months Earlier

1

A Honda Civic was waved into the Big Elk Estates gated community by a young security guard, who looked at the car with interest for two reasons. First, this was a Lexus, Hummer, Rover kind of neighborhood, and the Civic wasn't just a cheap old car; it was sporting some paint damage and dents. Second, the twentysomething woman driving it was attractive, with bobbed auburn hair, bright red lips, and fun, oversized sunglasses. She waved at him, and he waved back enthusiastically. Every other car that had entered the estate that day had been driven by frowning retirees in sun visors.

Natalie parked in front of the open house along with a dozen other cars. It was a breathtaking, sprawling, contemporary mountain mansion with huge windows and a beautiful rock garden speckled with ochre- and coral-colored stones. She stood on the immense front lawn for a second, just taking in the magnificence while the breeze caused her drop-waisted dress to flutter around her thighs.

She unzipped and removed her ankle boots in the foyer and stood there barefoot for a moment, enjoying the feel of the cool marble floor while looking up at the stained glass window over the front door. The artwork depicted a doe nuzzling a fawn in a field of yellow flowers with a forest in the background. Natalie pulled out her phone and snapped a quick photo. Then she grabbed a pair of the little sock booties that were required to walk around the house, slipped them on, and began to explore.

Upstairs in the master bedroom, a short, curvy brunette with thick, long, dark hair was describing the distinctive antique chandelier to a small group of visitors. Natalie was familiar with the real estate agent, Asha, after showing up at her open houses on and off for a few months. Asha had a son and daughter at Falcon Academy, Oliver and Mia. Oliver had never been in trouble, but Mia was outspoken, opinionated, and confident. She was described by some teachers as "a girl who took no shit" and by others as "a pain in the ass." Natalie liked Mia.

"Notice the bronze has a patina of copper, gold, green, and ivory," Asha was saying. "Which coexists so beautifully with the view of the mountains through the floor-to-ceiling French doors."

Asha had begun rapturously describing the teardrop crystals hanging down above everyone's heads when she caught sight of Natalie and paused. Midtwenties and dressed more suitably for a concert than a tour of a nine-million-dollar home, Natalie was conspicuous among the well-heeled potential buyers.

A split second later, Asha continued her presentation. The way she moved her hands was so graceful and expressive, it was almost as if she were dancing. She waved hello to an elderly man and woman who were re-entering the master bedroom from the adjoining bath. "Excuse me for a minute," Asha said to her captive audience. "Please. Explore." She inhaled with delight, as if to suggest that the aroma of the house alone was enough to make everyone fall in love. "Take it all in."

Asha steered the elegant, aging couple towards the spectacular view and stood between them, chatting about how blessed they all were to be able to live in the Rockies.

For the next half hour, Natalie took her time meandering about the soon-to-be-sold home of a certain Falcon Academy parental power duo. They were unpleasant people, so Natalie was surprised to find that they had excellent taste in art. The missus had probably hired an interior decorator from one of the coasts. Natalie was somewhat sure that they had been unhappily married, because Yvonne, her friend and coworker in the front office at Falcon, had told her a story about being out for drinks in town and running into the husband. Yvonne said a pleasant hello, and he put a hand against the wall to keep her from advancing to the restroom. "I've always had a thing for Asians," he'd said, and Yvonne had ducked under his arm and walked quickly away.

With a husband like that, it came as no surprise to Natalie that the wife, though having cleaned out most of the bathrooms and closets, had left a few errant Xanax pills scattered at the very back of the bathroom drawer in the guest en suite, along with a wine bottle opener, a lighter, and half a pack of Marlboro Lights.

Natalie pocketed only the pills.

Five minutes later, she sat on the bottom step of the main staircase, tugging the elastic booties off her feet. Asha appeared on the staircase above her and said, "Are you heading out?"

"I am," Natalie said. "I've got some plans."

"Anything fun?" Asha asked, sinking to a seat on the step beside her. There were hardly any people left. The house was closing in a few minutes.

"I'm going to see my brother and take his dog for a hike."

"Good weather for it," Asha said. "I'm going to my daughter's soccer game."

"Mia, right?" Natalie asked.

"Oh, you know her?"

"Of course I do. She's the soccer star."

"That's very kind of you to say." Asha nodded in a humble way. "Yes, Mia's quite good. No thanks to me. I can barely walk and chew gum at the same time. But my husband was sporty. When he was younger."

"I thought the school soccer season was in the fall."

"It is," Asha said. "But some of the girls play year-round. Indoor in winter and club teams in the spring."

"You have a son as well, don't you?" Natalie asked. "Oliver? In sixth grade? Plays the trombone?"

"Yes, I do," Asha answered. She regarded Natalie with a puzzled tilt of her heart-shaped face. "You've been to several of my open houses now."

"Six total." Natalie checked her phone for

notifications. "And I've been to a few of your competitors' too. Yours are way better usually. You do a really good job."

"Thank you for that." Asha paused. "May I ask you something?"

"Ask away."

Asha fiddled with the back of one of her earrings hesitantly. Natalie expected the question to be, *Why, exactly, are you here?* But after a second, she said, "You like art, don't you?"

"I do," Natalie answered, putting her phone away in her purse and hoisting the strap up on her shoulder, indicating she was ready to leave.

"I've noticed you spend a lot of time in front of the paintings."

"Sometimes I just like to be around beautiful things." *And take stuff. And pretend for a minute that this is my life too.* Natalie stood and walked towards the door to retrieve her shoes.

"Who doesn't like beautiful things?" Asha asked, in a rhetorical way. Rumored around the school to be related to some long-dead maharaja, Asha came from money and worked only for pleasure. "Did you like this house?"

What a dumb question. No, every inch of the luxurious ten thousand square feet is of-

fensively uninhabitable. "I did," Natalie answered. "But you know what? I like them all. They're more fun to look at than the four walls of my studio, that's for sure."

"Oh. Well," Asha said in a tone that lacked her earlier warmth. "With some luck, you'll find the right one eventually. Fingers crossed."

Natalie paused, sensing that there was an insinuation, however nicely veiled. Dropping her sunglasses over her eyes, she said, "I'll keep my fingers crossed for you too."

"Excuse me?"

"Your daughter's soccer game." Natalie punched the air. "Go Falcons."

"Oh. Right. Of course." Asha made a face and then swiftly covered her mouth with her fist.

"Everything all right?" Natalie paused to ask.

"Yes, thank you. My stomach. Probably just nerves about the game. After all these years, I've still never gotten quite used to how stressful this sports stuff can be."

"Umm-hmm," Natalie said, unconvinced. As she walked out of the house, backlit by the bright sun, she called over her shoulder, "It will be fine. I'm sure you'll win big. Seems like you always do."

2

"Beautiful," Brooke Elliman said under her breath as she watched her daughter, Sloane, maneuvering down the soccer field, faking this way then that, dribbling around the other team's players with a speed and agility that were truly rare.

Brooke was filming her daughter's performance through her new Panasonic high-definition camcorder, and the quality was amazing. She could zoom in on Sloane to see the concentration on her face and the muscle definition in her strong legs. The camera captured everything from the leaves rustling in the trees on the far side of the field to the flecks of sweat staining Sloane's jersey.

Sloane had a breakaway. Brooke's hand shook a little with excitement and nerves while she filmed, and she leaped to her feet, careful to avoid the REI luxury pop-up canopy she was seated underneath. "It's all you, Sloane! You've got this!"

Sloane crossed the ball to a teammate in the center who took the shot. The ball went over the goal, and the two girls backpedaled away to wait for the opposing team's goal kick. Brooke stopped recording. She irritably spun her wedding band around in circles on her right ring finger, where she'd moved it after Gabe had left. Her engagement diamond was at home in the safe.

Standing on the sideline was Nicholas Maguire, who, in a somewhat unorthodox but dedicated role, coached soccer not only for the Falcon Academy varsity team but also for several local club teams. He was clapping his hands and shouting, "Nice pass! Good work! Almost!" He darted a look in Brooke's direction and gave her a quick wave, which she quickly returned. She began mentally composing a text to send to him after the game.

Glancing towards the sidewalk, Brooke saw that Asha Wilson had finally arrived. Asha's daughter, Mia, had been playing club soccer with Sloane since they were first graders, and they were the only two freshmen to have been selected for the varsity team. Asha and Brooke weren't close friends, but they had spent many enjoyable hours seated next to each other over the years, cheering on the girls. They often commiserated about the many injuries their daughters had incurred and had spent a dozen or so weekends together in random hotels across the Midwest for travel tournaments. On several such occasions, they'd met in the bar and had a few drinks. Brooke had once told Asha that she wished they could get to know each other better. Brooke didn't have any good female friends.

She had tried to nudge the friendship with Asha along by inviting her and her husband, Phil, to dinner, but the well-intentioned invitation had backfired. Asha had not been happy that Brooke kept refilling Phil's wineglass until he was slurring about the stock market and investment opportunities in Telluride. Neither was Asha happy when she found the two of them sharing a joint on the back patio by the pool after Phil had excused himself to use the bathroom.

It had been back to soccer-mom-only friends ever since.

Brooke waved Asha over and patted the empty chair.

"Hello!" Asha said, sinking into the seat with a slight groan and her hand on her stomach. She scanned the field. "Where's Mia?"

"She's on the bench right now."

Asha looked concerned. "Really? Why?" Even though they were the youngest players on the team, Mia and Sloane were already the best.

"Not sure," Brooke said. "But it looked like maybe she was limping a little."

Asha slapped the arm of her chair. "It must be the shin splints."

"That doesn't sound too serious." Brooke appraised Asha's outfit. "You're awfully dressed up." She herself was attired in the color-coordinated mesh athletic ensemble that she'd worn earlier to her advanced cardio kickboxing class. "You look great. I can't be bothered anymore to put on makeup for soccer." This was less than truthful. Brooke did care about looking good for games, because the two men she cared about most were in attendance: her husband, Gabe, and Coach Nick. Her keratin-treated hair hung down over her torso in a sleek Demi Moore curtain. Though she did appear to be free of makeup, she had eyelash extensions and filler-plumped lips and still looked stunning.

"I usually can't be bothered either," Asha responded. "But I just came straight from a showing."

The referee blew the whistle. "Halftime," Brooke said, reaching down to the ground to retrieve a clear plastic tumbler of iced green tea.

Asha suddenly sat up and pointed down at the ground by Brooke's feet. "That's a nice video camera."

"It is. I'm loving it. Have a look." She handed it to Asha, who held it up to her eye. "I got it so I can start filming for Sloane's highlight reel. Coach Nick told me most parents just use iPhones, but I wanted to make sure the quality was top-notch."

After sitting quietly for a while, Asha asked, "I guess you're talking about the videos you send to college coaches for the whole recruiting process? Isn't it early to be thinking about that?"

"No, actually. Coach Nick told me that most of the Division I colleges have filled their rosters by the end of the girls' sophomore years, so I've got to get busy sending emails and planning visits soon."

Asha made a funny noise, similar to the groan that had escaped as she'd sat down in the camp chair.

"Are you all right?" Brooke asked.

Asha didn't answer.

Brooke put a hand on her arm. "Do you want to talk about it? I'll drop it if that's what you prefer. But you can tell me anything."

Asha thought about it for a second and

then whispered, "I've got the weirdest feeling I might be pregnant."

Brooke had not expected this. "Oh my," she responded, bewildered.

"Yeah," Asha said. " 'Oh my' wasn't my first reaction. Mine was more like, 'Oh my God, what the hell is going on with me?' "

After a second, Brooke grinned. "Well, congratulations then!"

"But . . ." Back to rubbing her stomach, Asha said softly, "Phil and I are having some issues."

"No, not you two. I'm so sorry." Brooke waited, but Asha just chewed on her lip and didn't speak. "Whatever it is, it can't be worse than what's going on in my life, right?" Brooke laughed. "Look over there. See Gabe with his little Broncos sun umbrella and aviator sunglasses? He's sitting on the other side of the field so he doesn't have to talk to me. Your husband hasn't moved out and started sleeping with his Spin instructor, has he?"

"No. No, but . . ." Asha shook her head. "Lately he's working a lot more than he used to, and when he's home, he just wants to go to bed. I mean — and *not with me.* Just by himself. Go down to the basement bedroom where it's quiet, turn off the lights and get under the covers and sleep. And when he's awake, he's in a terrible mood. I've tried everything. Talk more. Talk less. Touch him. Leave him alone. Cook him something he likes. Don't cook anything because he's not hungry." Asha buried her face in her hands.

"Oh no, that's got to be hard," Brooke said. "But, you know, if you've got a baby on board, something must still be working between you two." Brooke gave her a mischievous side-eye. "Unless . . ."

Asha sat up, dabbing at one eye. "I wasn't with anyone else. I wouldn't. But the last time with Phil was like two months ago."

At a loss for what to say, Brooke was saved by the referee, who took to the field and blew his whistle, summoning the teams. "Oh!" she said, obviously relieved. "Look. Halftime is over. Here we go."

"Let's go, girls!" Asha yelled, sounding more exhausted than excited. "God, I could use about a hundred naps. I'm sick to my stomach, tired, and so forgetful lately. I lost my favorite bracelet today."

"Was the bracelet insured?" Brooke herself didn't own a single item of jewelry that wasn't worthy of its own policy.

"No."

"That's too bad." Brooke clapped lightly as the girls began to take the field. "Where did you lose it?"

"At the open house."

"Someone stole it," Brooke said in an end-of-story way. "That's what happened. When Gabe and I sold our second home, someone who came to see it took a very rare and valuable old book off the shelf in the library. The thief was only caught when he tried to sell it."

"I guess it's possible," Asha said. "I went to the Sherwoods' house last night to finish staging it for today. I took the bracelet off and put it in this little decorative dish on the kitchen counter and then forgot about it. I remembered it this afternoon when I was about to close up, and it wasn't there." Asha looked sadly at her wrist. The missing bracelet was her favorite. After a second she said, "Do you think it's strange that the front desk girl comes to a lot of my open houses?"

"What girl?"

"The front desk girl from the school. The headmaster's assistant."

Brooke frowned. "The Korean girl with the stud in the side of her nose?"

"No. The other one. There's two. They sit side by side."

"Oh," Brooke said. "I know who you mean. The redhead with the Bettie Page bangs who always looks like she has somewhere better to be."

"Her name is Miss Bellman. Natalie Bellman."

"Why should she be looking at multimillion-dollar houses? She's probably the one who stole your bracelet. Oh look. Go time. And Mia's back in." Brooke hooked her fingers into the sides of her mouth and whistled. "Come on, ladies!" She switched on her camcorder and started to film.

The two girls wore their hair the same way for games and had done so for years. It was parted in the middle in French braids, with the pigtails hanging down their backs. They were playing right wing and left wing, and after kickoff, Mia took the ball and ran with it. Sloane was sprinting down the opposite side, and the girl playing in the center was yelling, "You've got time, you've got time!"

Mia reached the corner, maneuvered around a defensive player, and crossed the ball. Sloane jumped up and used her forehead to drive the ball towards the upper right corner of the goal. It was perfect.

Brooke recorded a few seconds of applause and then pressed Stop on her camera. She dropped it behind her into the chair and screamed, "Good job, girls!" On the other side of the field, Coach Nick was looking in her direction. Brooke placed both of her hands against her mouth and blew a big congratulatory kiss. She fell into her seat, happy. And then she had a thought that sent an icy shudder down the back of her neck. It was just a casual gesture, that kiss, not open to interpretation. No one in the crowd could find anything wrong with a simple gesture like that . . . except Gabe. Had Gabe seen?

Brooke looked across to where her husband was seated by himself. His aviator sunglasses still covered his eyes, and one ankle was still crossed casually over the opposite knee, as if he hadn't reacted at all to their daughter's goal.

"Brooke? Brooke?"

"Sorry. What?"

"Did you get that?" Asha asked. She was beaming. "Tell me you got that great play!"

"I sure did," Brooke answered, trying to forget the stupid blown kiss. "The whole awesome thing."

"Is there any way you could send it to me?"

"Of course, I'd be happy to. I have your email."

"Great. Thanks. I guess I need to get to work on Mia's highlight reel."

"Wait," Brooke said, swiveling in her chair to face Asha. "Are you looking at Division I now? I thought you said you wanted to keep Mia close to home."

"I did. I still do. But she's got other ideas. She changes her mind every other day. One second it's a private liberal arts college and a psychology degree. The next it's finding a program that offers a semester at sea because she's going to be a marine biologist. Recently, she's been talking about bigger schools with good film programs. In California. I can't keep up."

"In California?" Brooke echoed. She didn't look happy.

"Yes. Why is it that so many kids have their hearts set on California?"

"Because it's amazing, beautiful, and exciting."

Asha laughed. "I forgot. You went to college in California, didn't you?"

"UCLA," Brooke answered. "I'm a Bruin."

"That's the school Mia keeps talking about the most."

"If so, that would be because she's heard Sloane talking about it."

Brooke's aggressive tone was lost on Asha, who answered, "Probably. Anyway, I appreciate you sending me the clip. I'll get my own video recorder this week."

Brooke nodded. "Right. Sure. Absolutely."

Asha's phone rang, and she stood up, mouthing, "Offer!" She walked away to take the call. When she came back, the game was almost over. The two women didn't speak again until they said their goodbyes.

"See you soon, Brooke," Asha called. "Take care!"

"You too," Brooke answered coldly, without looking up from an agitated struggle to fold up her camp chair and shove it into its bag.

Sloane seemed like she was in a bad mood when Brooke walked across the field to give her a post-game hug. "Great job, sweets," Brooke said.

"Thank you."

"Where's your dad?" His chair was gone. She shaded her eyes and looked around. Gabe should have been waiting on the sidewalk.

"He left."

"What? He was supposed to be taking you out to dinner."

"I asked him if he minded if we did a rain check. I'm not really in the mood."

"Okay," Brooke said. "No worries. Should I go ahead and make us a reservation at

Café Provence? You can bring a friend. Ask Mia."

"I don't want to ask Mia." Sloane was looking off into the distance and waved at a tall, broad-shouldered boy with tousled bangs slouching against the goalpost. "Can I just go hang out with Reade?"

Reade was an older boy Sloane had been talking about for months. They had recently started to seem like they were a couple. Brooke said, "You know what, why don't I take you and Reade to dinner? I can get to know him a bit better. That would be fun."

"What?" Sloane shook her head. "No. Ugh. I'd rather go on my own if that's okay. Reade's waiting. Please, Mom?"

"But it would be so nice if —"

"Mom! No, it wouldn't." The look on Sloane's face was the clincher. She was not going to come around.

"All right then," Brooke said. "Go ahead."

Sloane turned to leave, and Brooke glanced about self-consciously to see if anyone had heard their conversation.

No one was listening, so Brooke called and waved with a pleasant look on her face. "Great game! Okay then. See you later! You two have fun."

Brooke watched her daughter join Reade, and there was something she didn't like about the way the boy grabbed her around the waist and pulled her into his body so they could walk hip to hip. Reade was two grades above Sloane. A couple of years earlier, Brooke had taken a yoga workshop with his "free-spirited" mom, Linda. The two women had tea once together, after class, and exchanged numbers. Still, for all intents and purposes, Brooke was letting her daughter walk off with a stranger. A distant memory tugged at her. Linda, at that yoga class, crying, telling the instructor about the unexpected death of one of Reade's friends. Brooke hadn't been able to hear much of the conversation and had continued to stretch on her own in the corner. She didn't really know Reade's mom all that well, and Linda stopped going to yoga after that. In fact, she'd gone off the local radar almost completely.

As Brooke lost sight of her daughter over the top of the hill, she hoped that Reade was doing okay. It would be hard, she thought, to move on after the unexpected death of a classmate.

Police Video Excerpt,
Falcon Academy Conference Room
Interview: Bellman, Natalie Marie
1:25 PM

The video pans quickly across a room with a big table in the center and a bookcase at the back, followed by an extreme close-up of fingers moving in front of the lens. A young woman's voice can be heard asking, "You're going to film me?"

Another woman, Detective Beth Larson, answers, "Yes. Give me one sec to adjust the phone on the tripod."

The camera stops shaking. Detective Larson's fingers pull away.

In the frame now is Natalie Bellman, seated catty-corner from Detective Ken Bradley. On the table in front of him are a pen, a pad of paper, his cell phone, a bottle of water, and a little brown can of Double-shot Espresso.

Natalie has nothing. Her elbows rest on the arms of her chair, and her hands are clasped, held close to her body. Her chest is moving up and down visibly, but she is breathing through her nose.

Detective Bradley looks up. He calls to Detective Larson, "Is your phone all set?"

"Good to go," she answers. "Recording."

Detective Bradley places a stack of papers on the table, held together by a binder clip. "There's the photocopy of her Winnie the Pooh planner, if you want to get started reading, Beth," he says. He emphasizes the words *Winnie the Pooh* and gives Natalie a sarcastic smile, as if he finds it amusing, or perhaps just plain bizarre.

Natalie avoids eye contact with him in a way that suggests he's managed to embarrass her.

Detective Larson ducks swiftly in and out, scooping up the document.

Natalie's chest rises and falls even faster. She narrows her eyes in a way that is open for interpretation. Hostility? Suspicion? Terror?

"I'm Detective Ken Bradley," the man says for the purpose of the recording, "and I'm in the Falcon Academy conference room with my partner Detective Beth Larson. Both of us are from Denver Major Crimes." He points at Natalie. "Can you go ahead and confirm your full name and address?"

"Natalie Marie Bellman, 11846 Blacktail Mountain Road, Apartment 12."

"And your title here at Falcon Academy?"

"Administrative assistant."

"Can you please tell us again — and in more detail this time — what you were doing in the sports pavilion yesterday afternoon and again later that evening?"

"I was looking for —"

Detective Bradley drops his big hand down on the conference table with an exasperated sigh. The plastic Poland Spring water bottle falls over.

Natalie twitches and goes quiet.

"Sorry," he says. "Go on."

"I told you once already. I was looking for my earbuds that I had misplaced the previous day while I was working out on the mezzanine, and which I eventually found behind the treadmill."

It sounds rehearsed. She is a bad actress.

Detective Bradley shakes his head and cracks open his canned espresso. "You're going to stick with that story for now? Fine. We've got a long day ahead of us, Natalie. What really happened?"

"I told you. If you'd like me to, I'd be happy to tell you again."

Detective Bradley turns to face his partner, standing back behind the camera. "Beth, do you get the impression everyone around here is full of it, or is it just me?"

From behind the camera Detective Larson responds, "Not just you."

Natalie sighs and looks away.

"It's called lying, Natalie." Detective Bradley leans in, close enough to be intimidating. "Look at me."

She does.

He points a finger in her face. "I think you are lying."

3

Natalie's job as a front office administrative assistant was not exciting. That was just a fact.

Over the course of the day, she would answer phones, type newsletters, send emails, cut out decorations to hang in the hall, rifle through the lost and found looking for name tags sewn into jackets, chat with Yvonne, and drink several cups of chamomile tea.

She'd had plenty of jobs that weren't as sedentary. Bike messenger. Grubhub driver. Instructor at a paint-while-you drink-wine franchise in Denver, where her specialty had been a Saturday afternoon "Paint Your Pet" class. She still made a little money selling her animal portraits on the Etsy website.

It wasn't that she was unhappy, really, with the job at the school. Her weekends and evenings were her own to hike, bike, paint, read, and watch television, and she preferred being deeper in the mountains to the traffic, construction, and flat urban sprawl of Denver. It was also fun to be close to her brother, Jay.

At first, a year and a half earlier, when Jay had asked her if she was interested in coming out to help him recover from his biking accident, she'd been hesitant. Yes, he could compensate her nicely, thanks to his arrangement with the rich, drunk old man who'd run him down, but Natalie had her own life: a handful of friends, their mom, and at that time, a summer job she liked as a server at the rooftop terrace bar of the Le Méridien downtown.

Jay said fine, no problem, but a week later he was asking again.

"I know you're making good tips at the hotel bar, Nat," he'd said. "But my settlement is pretty big. Look, I should be able to walk in a few months. It's not forever. And the lady from care.com is a sweetheart, but if I'm going to pay someone twenty bucks an hour to get my groceries and empty my bedpan, I'd rather it be you."

"Gross," she said, but in the end her answer was yes. She and Jay had been close their whole lives, especially after their dad left when they were kids.

Four months later, Jay was able to walk

with a cane and required less assistance from Natalie. She'd considered going back to Denver, but Jay still needed a lot of help, and truthfully, she liked Falcon Valley better than home. Her mom was conflicted about it; she missed having Natalie close, but she liked the fact that her kids were looking out for one another. Ultimately, Natalie decided to stay in Falcon Valley and randomly applied for jobs until she landed the position as Headmaster Dilly's assistant.

She soon learned that, due to the affluence of the surrounding suburbs as well as the sky-high tuition, Falcon students were of a certain ilk. They were almost all filthy rich. A lot of the kids began to exhibit signs of entitlement around fifth grade, but the little ones were adorable and fresh as apples. Unspoiled and sweet.

No job was perfect, of course. Natalie accepted the fact that she would be blamed if a child's expensive misplaced Patagonia parka was not located in the lost and found. She didn't like it, but she learned to live with it. After work sometimes, she and Yvonne and a couple of teachers would get together and talk and laugh behind the parents' backs. That was satisfying.

Natalie was a little disappointed that her life had become so predictable, since she had always thought great adventure lay just around the next corner. She wanted to see the Sydney Opera House, the Sagrada Família in Barcelona, and the Great Wall of China. To own a loft with enough space for a real art studio in Chicago.

But there was something to be said for a sense of security. Having health care was important, as was a steady paycheck and an employer who was decent. Occasionally, she dated. There were nights out with Yvonne, fulfilling her need for laughter and girl gossip. Natalie and Jay binge-watched Netflix on Friday nights, ordering in nachos and chicken wings. When she began to feel nostalgic, wronged, and unhappy about what had happened after her dad left, and she went off the rails for a while, she could always take one or two of Jay's Vicodins and paint in a dreamy ebb and flow of contented numbness until the bad feelings and memories of the things she'd done were completely forgotten.

She didn't yet know that this mostly peaceful life of hers was soon to change.

It was a rainy spring afternoon in the mountains. All after-school sports at Falcon Academy had been moved indoors. Natalie's workday had ended at four. Thirty minutes later, she entered the sports pavilion with her earbuds, her phone, a towel, and a bottle of water.

This was a first for her. She'd only recently been told by Lars Jaeger, the school athletic director, that she was welcome to use the state-of-the-art fitness equipment in the sports pavilion after school and on weekends.

As she walked towards the stairs leading to the mezzanine training area, she passed Nicholas Maguire. Parents and teachers called him Mr. Maguire, but the kids called him Coach Nick. He was working with a dozen girls at the far end of the basketball court. The collective sound of all of them breathing heavily as they ran shuttle sprints filled the auditorium.

"Let's go, ladies," he yelled, pacing back and forth. "If you aren't here to do your best, you're wasting my time and yours."

Natalie paused at the edge of the bleachers to watch. The girls were pink-faced and panting, beads of lotion-scented sweat dripping onto the court. One girl, Mia Wilson, stopped running and bent over with her hands on her knees.

Coach Nick blew the whistle that hung around his neck. "On second thought, let's take a little water break." He ran over to

Mia and crouched down in front of her. They talked quietly, and eventually he led Mia over to the bleachers, where she sat, hanging her head between her knees. Coach Nick stayed beside her.

Natalie walked over and extended her water bottle. "Sometimes when you're tired, the fountain is just too far away."

Mia looked up and took the water bottle. After taking a few sips, she returned it to Natalie and said, "Thank you, Miss Bellman."

"Yes," Coach Nick said. "Thank you. I'll take her to the trainer for a quick visit. No such thing as being too careful." Nick stood up and extended his hand, and Mia took it, pulling herself to her feet.

"Feel better, Mia," Natalie called.

Natalie knew about him, of course. Nicholas Maguire was a popular fixture at Falcon. In his weathered face was a hint of his formerly chiseled bone structure, and his eyes were an attractive shade of blue, though there were many creases at the corners. His body defied time, Natalie thought, watching him walk away with Mia. Even in his nerdy khaki shorts and tucked-in collared Falcon coaching polo, his muscles were clearly carved to perfection.

Falcon parents, who were hard to impress

since they all considered themselves one step away from royalty, liked to brag about him. At school events, Natalie had overheard conversations such as:

"Did you know Coach Nick played four years for the UCLA men's soccer team?"

"I did! My husband told me he also played the inaugural year of the Major Soccer League for the San Jose team."

"Isn't he dating some famous model?"

"No, he's been in a long-distance relationship with a Canadian actress for the last couple of years. She was on that show *Degrassi.* I don't think she's done anything worth mentioning since."

Apparently Coach Nick's personal misfortune had been a gift to the world of amateur athletics. During his first year of playing professional soccer, he tore his ACL. He was never able to go back, and so he began coaching.

He was well-liked by Falcon dads because he was quick to give them fist bumps and pats on the back. He was a guy's guy. The moms liked him because he was easy on the eyes but tough on his athletes. He had high expectations. There were always a few parents who were hoping for their children to get into prestigious colleges without the necessary grades, and in his twenty years of working around the country, Coach Nick had a notable record. Dozens of his athletes had been accepted to and played for UCLA, USC, Pepperdine, and Loyola Marymount. He was extremely well-connected in his home state of California.

Natalie exited the gym and took the stairs up to the mezzanine, where a handful of students were having personal training sessions with various coaches. She marked her territory at a treadmill by hanging her towel and putting her water bottle in the holder. Instead of pressing Start, she walked to the railing that looked out over the courts. Coach Nick had returned without Mia and was busy placing orange cones, balls, and mats around the gym to create an obstacle course.

Natalie watched as he ran up and down the court, offering encouragement. She felt strangely drawn to him. He was supportive and instructive. For the next ten minutes, while she did more than her normal amount of stretching by the balcony, her eyes never left Coach Nick. As Sloane Elliman-Holt, one of the best athletes at the school, won a race, Coach Nick yelled, "Bravo, speedster! Way to hustle!"

Natalie was overcome with a sense of longing and emptiness that she hadn't felt in years.

At home that night, she wondered if she should get a cat. Maybe she should call her mom. She did. No answer. Consideration was given to creating an account on the new "outdoorsy" dating app called LuvByrd, but she was too nervous. She wondered who her ex-boyfriend in Denver was dating and spent some time thinking about her dad. It had been a long time since a damp envelope of cash had arrived with a scrawled return address from somewhere in Nevada.

She made plans to visit Jay the next day after work, and then settled down into bed to finish her book about a solitary, troubled woman in Scotland who found love with an unlikely match. A happy ending for the lonely lady.

For Natalie, it was a two-Vicodin night.

4

The restaurant table was covered with a red-and-white-checkered tablecloth. In the center was a large, old-fashioned glass decanter filled with olive oil and floating heads of garlic. The song "That's Amore" was playing in the background. It was just Asha and the kids. The fourth chair was empty.

The server approached, pulling a pen from behind her ear. "Okay. Now are you ready?" She'd been by twice already.

Asha gave her an apologetic smile. "Could I just give my husband five more minutes? He should be here any second." The benches up by the hostess station were packed, and in the bar, there were people milling around, waiting for tables.

The server forced a smile. "No problem. I'll check back shortly."

Oliver was playing a game on a rubber-encased iPad underneath the table, and Mia slouched silently, using her straw to suck up an inch of her iced tea and then squirt it back into her glass.

"Dad will be here soon," Asha said unhappily, fishing her phone out of her purse on the floor. She texted Phil.

Honey, where are you? The kids are starving.

Did you not just go ahead and order?

No. We were waiting for you.

Please don't make everything about me. Nearly there.

Asha put her phone away, took a sip of water, and said to Mia, "I think he's pretty close." She felt like she should say more, but she had no energy. Truthfully, she wanted to turn her brain off to avoid thinking about anything at all. Earlier that day, she'd emptied the little trash can in her husband's office, and a hotel key card had fallen out. It was from the Le Méridien in downtown Denver, and the last place Phil had traveled for work, as far as she knew, was Phoenix.

Fifteen minutes later, Asha finally saw Phil

standing in the entrance to the dining room, looking this way and that. Asha wasn't the only person who'd noticed him. A few men and women had turned in his direction. He commanded attention. A former college basketball player, he was still a big, powerful, fit man. He had aged well and was always nicely dressed. Mia had gotten her athletic prowess from him. Oliver was more like Asha. A little on the soft side.

Asha stood up and waved Phil over. As much as she wanted to open the conversation with a complaint about how late he was, she said, "Yay, you're here."

Phil gave Asha a quick peck on the forehead and said, "Sorry." Then he ruffled the hair of both kids and said, "You guys are starving, huh?"

Mia shrugged and said, "Not really."

Oliver didn't even look up. "I could eat."

So she'd lied about the kids starving. Phil often accused her of being passive-aggressive, and he was right. She couldn't help it. It was how her mom had been with her dad, and Asha still felt it was better than being openly confrontational. The look that Phil gave her made it abundantly clear that he was displeased with her.

"Long day?" she asked, hoping to turn the

tide, as he removed his sports coat and took a seat.

"Yeah." He unfolded his napkin and placed it across his big lap. "How about you?"

"So-so," Asha answered.

Picking up the menu, Phil said, "Okay, kids. Devices away." Mia turned her phone facedown, but Oliver continued to play. "Put your iPad away, Oliver. Now."

"I just want to finish this level, Dad."

"I told him he could play until the food gets here," Asha said.

"Well," Phil said. "The food's not here, but I am, and I want him to put it away."

Oliver stood up and obediently handed his iPad to Asha so she could hold it for him. At that point, all three of her family members fell silent as they attempted to decide what they would eat.

Asha quietly observed her husband: the military-style hair, the ruddy complexion, and the thick, muscular neck. They'd been together seventeen years. Asha's parents had wanted her to marry a soft-spoken engineer whose parents were also from a small town outside of Mumbai, but Asha had already developed a huge crush on the big white hunk in her marketing ethics course at the University of Colorado. She still found his all-American masculinity appealing, but she couldn't help but wonder what would have happened had she gone with the gentle engineer who, unlike Phil, had appreciated an aromatic saag paneer. She loved her husband, but something had changed. She was now married to a man who she was nervous — no, afraid — to tell that she was pregnant. A man who had in his possession a key card to a room in a swanky, sexy hotel ninety minutes away. Had he totally lost interest in her, as it had lately seemed? And if so, what would he think of her late-in-life pregnancy? In her worst moments of anxiety, Asha imagined that Phil might believe she'd been aware of his wandering affection and had decided to find a way to hold him down. It wasn't true, exactly, though she had grown a bit lazy about taking her birth control pills on time, occasionally even missing a day or two. She hadn't been too worried about it, thinking she was getting old.

The server appeared and was visibly relieved to find the empty chair now filled. Asha ordered first.

"You're not having a glass of wine?" Phil asked.

"Not tonight."

Mia was immersed in what Phil called her

"great vegetarian experiment," and she ordered the eggplant parmesan.

Oliver was still looking over the menu. "Can I get the Tour of Italy, please?" he asked finally, blinking up at the server.

"Of course," the young lady answered cheerfully.

Probably pleased that the eleven-year-old ordered the most expensive thing on the menu instead of something off the kids' menu, Asha thought. She could have cared less about the money, yet her expression was pinched and disapproving.

Phil cleared his throat in a way that indicated exasperation. "Something wrong?"

"Maybe Oliver doesn't need the Tour of Italy."

"Why?" Phil asked.

Asha looked at her son as he vigorously masticated a piece of bread dripping with peppery parmesan olive oil from the bowl next to his plate. She half expected him to grab the bowl and upend it into his mouth. "I just mean. You know. That he could just choose one favorite. Quality over quantity, I like to say."

"So, no Tour of Italy?" the server asked, looking at husband, then wife, and then back at husband.

"Let him get what he wants." This from

Mia, who was back to scrolling on her phone.

"I agree with Mia," Phil said, and Asha forced herself to turn away so he wouldn't be further incensed by her look of annoyance.

After the server left, Asha inhaled deeply and changed the subject. "So, Mia," Asha said. "I was wondering if you'd like to go with me to Best Buy next weekend and help me pick out a camcorder. I know you've been showing a lot of interest in photography lately."

"Like, to make videos?" Mia asked.

"Yes. Exactly."

"I can make videos on my phone," Mia said, holding it up.

"I know. But you can make even better ones with an expensive video camera. I think you could have a lot of fun with it."

Mia considered it. "True. I'm definitely interested in filmmaking, so that might be cool."

The server slipped Asha and Phil's salads onto the table, and Phil picked up his fork. Instead of eating, he turned to Asha. "Where did this idea originate?"

As Asha salted her tomatoes, she answered, "Brooke Elliman had a camcorder at the last game. The game when you were . . ." She looked at him pointedly in the eyes and said, "Out of town in *Phoenix*. She let me try it. It was really something. Great quality. She got it specifically to make Sloane a highlight reel for college recruiters."

Phil seemed unfazed by Asha's Phoenix reference, but then again, he had no idea she'd found his discarded key for a hotel in Denver. He glanced at Mia and then back at Asha. "What? Already?"

"That's exactly what I said," Asha answered. "They're freshmen! But Brooke said it's not that early after all. Coach Nick told her a lot of Division I schools fill their upcoming team rosters while the girls are sophomores. Which means we would need to have our whole package ready early next year."

"Package?" Phil asked, after a sip of wine. "What's in the package?"

Mia began ticking off items on her fingers. "Highlight reel. About five to eight minutes of me on the field with my best plays. Photos. A personal essay. Transcripts. Recommendation letters. A list of tournaments and camps that I'm planning to attend so I can be scouted. I'll need to have all the coaches' email addresses and phone numbers so we can —"

"Asha," Phil said, interrupting Mia. "Were you aware of all this? It sounds like a lot of work."

"It wasn't until recently that Mia started to consider some bigger, out-of-state Division I schools, so it's all kind of new to me too."

"All right," he said. "Why Division I? What changed?"

"Because Coach Nick told me I'm Division I material. Me and Sloane. We both are."

"Okay," he said eventually. "And you're sure about this out-of-state idea?"

"Well, no," Mia said. "I'm not one hundred percent sure. But I can always change my mind, right? And stay in Colorado. But if I don't prepare for what I might want, then I won't even stand a chance."

Phil nodded. "Yes, that's absolutely right." He shifted his attention to Asha. "I'll come with you to look at those video cameras."

Asha smiled at him. "Great."

"I guess you have your work cut out for you, helping her with this."

"Actually," Mia said, "I can get extra help from Coach Nick, if that's okay. Sloane and Reade Leland and Jeremiah Solomon and some other kids do private training sessions after school and on the weekends. He makes videos of emerging skills and helps with essays. He also knows a lot about the colleges and coaches and what they're looking for, so he can be pretty helpful in, you know, narrowing down which are fallback schools and which are reach schools."

"Hmm." Phil was thinking as he chewed. "Your grades aren't great."

"I know, Dad. I'm not thinking of like, Stanford or Harvard."

"Well, what are you thinking?"

"My fallbacks are Colorado State and Boulder, and my reach school is UCLA."

Asha put a hand on Phil's leg. "That's where Sloane wants to go too. Supposedly, Mr. Maguire has some pull there."

"I think I knew that," Phil said. "Brooke talks a lot about it doesn't she?" Asha nearly asked him when, exactly, he'd been spending so much time talking to Brooke. As far as she knew, the two of them had done no more than sit several chairs apart at a soccer game for years. But Phil went on, "I'm not an expert, but I can hypothesize that pull or no pull, Coach Nick's not going to get UCLA to take two girls the same age from Falcon Academy."

The food was arriving, and Mia picked up her fork and knife. "For once, Sloane may not get what she wants."

Asha nodded in agreement. "Brooke won't like that."

Phil moved his hand underneath the table to where only Asha could see it and extended his middle finger. He mouthed, "Fuck Brooke."

The smile on his face was a little sneaky, and Asha didn't like it. Occasionally she had an unpleasant flashback to the night she and Phil had been invited to Brooke's house for dinner and Asha had walked out onto the patio to find her husband and the hostess huddled together, smoking a joint and laughing by the swimming pool like teenagers. It suddenly occurred to Asha that Phil had started disengaging with her at home just about the same time that Gabe had informed Brooke he didn't consider reconciliation an option.

Asha gave Phil's hand a little good-natured swat with her napkin. Brooke was her friend, and though she could be difficult at times, to mouth "Fuck Brooke" wasn't funny. Asha didn't respond out loud but what she was thinking was, *You probably want to.*

5

Brooke Elliman stood outside the bullet-resistant glass door of the school, holding up her driver's license to the camera. She wore a knee-length suede vest with a hood, and cream-colored equestrian riding tights with leather accents. With her long, straight hair spilling down to her waist, she looked powerful and wild, like she might have just arrived straight from the steppes, having galloped in bareback on one of her purebred Arabians.

Natalie stood up and went over to the window facing the parking lot. "Yvonne," she said out the side of her mouth. "Shit. I thought so. It's Mrs. Elliman."

They both knew Mrs. Elliman was not at the school to drop off some canned goods or old clothes. None of her frequent visits were anything short of electrically charged.

Outside, Mrs. Elliman pocketed her driver's license and waited, arms crossed, one pointy Western riding boot tapping on the sidewalk. Every visitor was vetted by Rex, the security guard, before being buzzed into the atrium. In Mrs. Elliman's case, Rex would simply be going through the motions. Everyone knew her. She was the sole heir to the Elliman Baked Goods fortune and had retained her maiden name after marrying Sloane's dad, Gabe Holt. Brooke had always enjoyed the esteem that came along with her family's reputation, and had insisted that Sloane use the hyphenated Elliman-Holt surname to ensure that her daughter received the same immediate recognition, and befitting respect, that she herself had been shown her whole life.

Rex buzzed her through the front door, and a second later, she entered the office, accompanied by a gust of cool air and the barely-there woodsy hint of a jasmine perfume.

"Good afternoon, Mrs. Elliman," Yvonne said brightly. "Will you be needing a visitor's badge for the campus?"

"I don't think that will be necessary," she said. "I'm just here to see Mark." She was one of a handful of parents who didn't call him Headmaster Dilly.

On Natalie's desk was an apple-shaped nameplate that said *Miss Bellman* in cursive script that she'd been given upon hiring, a small, framed watercolor of Jay's dog, Rocky, and a whimsically painted coffee mug filled with pens. She produced a sign-in log, opened it, and smoothed the pages out. "Can I just get your autograph and the reason for your visit?" Natalie asked.

"I already said so. I just need to speak to Mark."

"Okayyeee," Yvonne said. "Let me just make sure he's available. He probably is. For you. But I'll just check. Be right back."

"Thank you." Mrs. Elliman sighed and ran her hands through her tremendous amount of hair. Then she consulted her silver-and-turquoise watch.

Natalie asked, "Can I get you anything to —"

"I don't want anything to drink, thank you," Mrs. Elliman answered loudly, and somehow the *thank you* came across as *fuck you.*

The headmaster emerged from his office. "Mrs. Elliman!" he said warmly, as if her visit was a wildly appreciated treat. "Hello! What can I do for you?"

"I need to talk about S—" She cut herself off before saying *Sloane.* Natalie and Yvonne both politely averted their eyes. "Something important," Brooke concluded.

"Say no more," Mr. Dilly responded. "Come into the study, won't you?"

The door to his office actually had a sign on it that read *The Study.* Mr. Dilly didn't like to call students, teachers, or parents into his office. He said that "Headmaster's Office" sounded pejorative. It was comfortable in the study, with books, photos of his two Welsh corgis, his overflowing ferns on the windowsill, and the smell of the leather polish that the cleaning staff massaged routinely into the matching ottoman and armchair.

Mr. Dilly closed the study door. A short time after, a slightly flushed Mr. Maguire came walking quickly down the hall and into the office. He wasn't wearing any sort of cap, but he pretended to doff one anyway, saying, "Afternoon, ladies!"

He was dressed in his usual getup of cargo shorts and a light blue Falcon polo, accessorized by his ubiquitous whistle on a rope. Natalie didn't realize she was smiling at him until he returned it enthusiastically. "Nice to see you again . . ." He touched her apple nameplate and said, "Miss Bellman. Thank you for your thoughtfulness the other day when one of my athletes was a little under the weather."

"You're very welcome, Mr. Maguire,"

Natalie responded.

"I would love to stay and chat with the two of you, but I'm afraid I've been summoned to the study, and I get the impression I better not *dilly*dally."

He had never before said more than a few words to either of them when he came to see the headmaster. "Well," Natalie said. "Whatever you do, don't dillydally." Natalie gestured around. "This is a top-speed area only. Please. We don't tolerate dilly-dallying here in the front office."

Yvonne covered her mouth to hide a giggle.

Mr. Maguire shook his finger at Natalie. "That's not fair. I'm a coach *and* a gym teacher. I'm not used to people making fun of me."

Natalie was about to quip back when Mr. Dilly buzzed. "Can one of you find out what's taking Mr. Maguire so long?" he asked in a strained voice.

"See?" he whispered. "I told you. I dillydallied because of you. It's all your fault. *Miss Bellman.*" He then passed behind them into the study.

Yvonne leaned sideways towards Natalie and whispered, "Mrs. Elliman is on the warpath. Looks like some shit is going *down.*"

■ ■ ■ ■

At four o'clock, when Natalie was done with her work and the office was quiet, she grabbed her backpack and headed over to the sports pavilion. In the girls' locker room, she changed into shorts, running shoes, and an old tie-dyed tank top she'd had forever. Her blunt-cut auburn hair hit an inch above her shoulders. It was too short for a proper ponytail, but she pulled it back off her face into a little tuft above her long neck.

It was surprisingly empty up on the mezzanine. Usually there were at least a few coaches and students, but on this afternoon, there appeared to be just the head of the custodial staff, an older man named Harry Doyle. He was using an electric screwdriver to affix some sort of lock onto the training room door, and it was loud. Natalie shouted, "Hi, Harry!"

He turned off his drill long enough to say, "Hello there, Natalie!"

"It's empty up here, isn't it?"

"Lots of away games today," he said, firing his tool up again.

It was nice having the whole place to herself, so Natalie wasn't particularly pleased to see Sloane Elliman-Holt walk in from the staircase, drop her backpack to the ground, and look around expectantly.

Many girls at the school were extremely smart. Half a dozen were uniquely physically talented. Almost all of the students at Falcon, except for a few on scholarship or whose parents worked at the school and paid lower tuition, were wealthy. Sloane had it all, though her grades didn't show it.

She was also a mean girl. Most of the time.

From what Natalie had discerned from her voyeuristic position behind her desk, there was only one girl who Sloane treated with anything other than disinterest or outright contempt. It was Mia Wilson, and even that relationship was mercurial at best. At times they could be seen walking down the hall with their arms linked. At other times, a teacher would show up with the pair of them in the front office, reporting that they'd been shoving one another around in the girls' bathroom.

Sloane spotted Natalie in the corner, waved, and walked over.

"Hi, Sloane. How are you?" Natalie said loudly over the noise from the drill, placing her free weights down on the ground.

"Fine, thanks. You haven't seen Coach Nick or the trainer, have you? Coach Carmen?"

"No, sorry. I haven't seen either of them."

Thankfully, Harry took another break from his work, and they could hear one another without shouting.

"That's okay." Sloane seemed to be staring at Natalie's chest. After a second she said, "I like your shirt."

It seemed like Sloane's compliment was an attempt to deflect a hint of scorn. Natalie looked down at the tie-dye and laughed. "Oh, this? It's old. I made it myself."

"What? You did?"

"Yeah. I mean, I did the design."

"Wow." Sloane nodded appreciatively. "So, what are you doing up here?" Her tone indicated that she was bored and filling the time. "I only ever see you in the office."

"Oh, I just started using the school gym a little bit ago. Whole Life Fitness raised my membership by twenty dollars, and I was told it was okay if I just work out here instead."

Sloane mulled this over while regarding Natalie with curiosity. Natalie realized that this was the sort of problem the girl could simply not comprehend. Twenty dollars? A quarter? These were meaningless amounts of money.

"Cool. What time is it, anyway?" Sloane asked. She readjusted the hairband around the ponytail starting high on the crown of her head. "The trainer is supposed to be here. I have to get a shot."

"A shot? What kind of shot?"

"An anti-inflammatory for my knee. I damaged my meniscus, and my mom's worried I'm not playing my best, so now I have to do private sessions *and* see the trainer. My mom's all worried about which school I'm going to get into. So."

"You're only a freshman, right?"

"Yeah, but Coach Nick is going to get me scouted and signed next year. At least, that's what my mom thinks. He told her he's going to do 'everything within his power.' He's got connections."

After a brief break, Harry started drilling again, and Sloane covered her ears. "Ugh. Who is he?"

"That's Mr. Doyle," Natalie answered, slightly baffled. Harry was around the school all day every day, whistling and cleaning. "You don't know Mr. Doyle?"

"No. What's he doing?"

"He's —" Natalie stopped and looked over at Harry. "So, what are you up to there, Harry?"

"Just putting a lock on the door. Coach Carmen keeps medication in here."

Sloane shrugged her shoulders and turned

to look back at the entrance of the mezzanine just as Coach Carmen walked in, carrying a first-aid kit.

Natalie waved to the trainer, who she knew only in passing. She was a muscular lady who had nearly made it to the 2012 Olympics in shot put. Coach Carmen waved back at Natalie, but she was focused on Sloane. "I'm a little late. Sorry. Training room, please."

Natalie watched Sloane trudge childishly behind Coach Carmen, behaving as if she'd been sent to bed early. The two of them continued into the training room, passing Harry, who seemed to have finished his work and was packing up his toolbox.

A few minutes later, when Sloane and Coach Carmen appeared back out on the fitness floor for stretching, Natalie slipped in her earbuds and searched for some good running music on her phone. As she started on the treadmill at a walking pace, she wondered what it would be like to be Sloane. So wealthy and talented that the world was your oyster. So special that Coach Nick would do "everything in his power" to make you happy.

Behind Natalie's back, whatever Coach Carmen was doing to Sloane was causing the girl to make a loud noise that was somewhere between a whine and a scream.

Natalie bumped up her speed from walking to jogging and focused on the machine beneath her feet.

The cries from across the room might as well have been coming from a television show. Natalie felt little to no sympathy. She seriously doubted Sloane had ever known any real pain at all.

Police Video Excerpt,
Falcon Academy Conference Room
Interview: Bellman, Natalie Marie
(Continued)

Natalie's eyes dart back and forth between Detective Bradley to her right, and Detective Larson, who is asking a question from behind the camera.

"Did you have a problem with Sloane Elliman-Holt?" Detective Larson asks, flipping through Natalie's private planner.

"A problem? No."

"But you wrote, 'I have to say, she's not a particularly likable girl. Full of herself, mean to others and worst of all, flirtatious with boys, teachers, coaches, even school dads. Just like her mom. She embodies everything that's wrong with this school and the entitled kids that go here.' "

"So, you didn't like Sloane," Detective

Bradley says. "And it sounds like you didn't much like the mom either. Is that correct?"

"No," Natalie says, turning in her chair towards Detective Bradley. "No. I mean yes, it's true. I didn't much care for either of them. But you have to understand, Mrs. Elliman and her daughter had issues with *everybody.*"

"Could you give me an example?" he asks.

"Okay," Natalie said. "They had issues with one another. Mother-daughter problems that were severe. They fought. All the time. Sloane was always getting in trouble with her boyfriend, Reade, and Mrs. Elliman was always furious with her."

"Did *you* ever have any altercations with Mrs. Elliman?" Detective Larson asks.

Natalie doesn't answer.

"Hmm?" Detective Larson prompts.

Again, no answer from Natalie.

"In your own words . . ." Detective Larson begins to read. " 'Friday the sixteenth. Twenty-mile bike ride plus thirty minutes of abdominals. Ate well. Grilled chicken and steamed spinach. The hungrier I get the angrier I get. Mrs. Elliman talked down to me again. I'm afraid one of these days one of these parents is going to say the wrong thing to me and I'm going to just snap.' "

6

Late spring was Asha's favorite time of year. The air smelled of evergreen and a variety of mountain flowers, dominated by lilac. It was still cool enough that ceiling fans provided just the right breeze. She knew that several couples were driving in from out of town to see the Leopold estate, and she was on her way there to get the house ready.

Speaking to her sister, Kareena, on her headset as she drove up the mountain, she passed turnouts for trailheads, shuttle stops to local resorts, ski and bike racks, and carports sheltering snowmobiles and other all-terrain vehicles. Upset, Asha was driving slowly around the sharp switchbacks. Cars were starting to accumulate behind her, waiting for a passing lane. She was oblivious. "I'm going to tell him, Kareena," she said. "My appointment with the doctor is this week. It makes sense to wait until after

I get the official confirmation, right? Rather than jumping the gun?" Asha kept weaving over onto the shoulder of the road. She took a deep breath and tried to focus. "No. I don't think he's going to be over the moon. I've got to go. I'm here."

The Leopold house was the most expensive in one of the older, less flashy suburbs on the outskirts of Falcon Valley, which, for a number of reasons, made it a tough sell. It had been on the market for nine months, and the Leopolds had only recently acquiesced and approved the idea of an open house.

Asha parked her car and attached some balloons to the wrought iron fence at the driveway entrance with twine and tape.

Inside, everything looked perfect. The ivory jute-fiber area rug had been the right choice after all. The texture and neutral color set off the luscious view of Mount Trinity, its green-and fawn-colored fields highlighted in the picture window. Asha placed an opulent bouquet of white Asian lilies in the sea-glass-green vase on the entrance table before going into the kitchen and preheating the oven. After pulling a square package of Pillsbury ready-to-bake oatmeal raisin cookie dough from her purse, she broke the dough apart, spread it out on a cookie tray, and slipped it into the oven. While she waited, she walked slowly around the house, pretending that she was a buyer, looking for imperfections.

After scrubbing away a strange, damp stain on the staircase wall leading down to the basement, she checked her phone. Almost noon. People would be arriving any minute. The oven timer went off, and she took out the cookies and transferred them to a cooling tray. She always went to great lengths to make sure her homes smelled like cookies or citrus, comfort and tranquility.

As she walked down the hall, she caught a whiff of something skunky. She covered her nose with the sleeve of her Kenzo floral-print blazer and entered the library that had served as Mr. Leopold's office. It was a spectacular, utterly unique room: round and two stories, with an old-fashioned library ladder for the upper floor. On one side was a window looking out over the valley toward the mountains, and the bookcases were filled with antique hardcovers and exotic knickknacks from around the world. Built into the curved wooden wall was a brick fireplace, a fluffy fur rug stretched out in front of it.

Next to the fireplace, on the floor, touching the rug, was a pillow, one a person would use for sleeping. Plump and plain, in a faded flowery cotton shell. It didn't belong in this marvelous, perfect room, and it had not been there two days earlier.

Asha patted her hand against her chest in a useless gesture to quiet her heart, which had begun to beat faster. Kneeling, she ran her hand across the carpet. She flinched and jerked back with a cry. A bead of blood pulsed out from the tip of her finger and Asha stopped it with the inside of her jacket sleeve. On closer inspection, there was a foot-wide area in which tiny shards of green glass were scattered and mostly invisible in the long fibers of the rug. With little time to spare and no idea if the Leopolds owned a hand vacuum, she got on all fours, rolled up the rug, and pushed it behind the sofa. Then, her pulse racing, she turned back to face the room.

It was obvious. Someone had been there. Something had happened.

The flowers on the pillowcase were light coral in color. Asha was almost sure that the pattern matched the paint in one of the upstairs bedrooms. She brought the pillow to her face and sniffed. Marijuana? Those e-cigarettes, perhaps? The Leopolds did have grandchildren. College-aged, she thought. It was possible they'd been in the house.

There was no reason to be worried. Or frightened.

But she was. There seemed to be no safe places in her life anymore. Her marriage, which had never been perfect but always good enough, had become a source of constant anxiety. Her happy, good-smelling, well-staged home for sale seemed suddenly haunted, and she had the urge to leave.

She tucked the pillow underneath her arm and walked out of the library, down the hall, up the stairs, and to the room she thought the pillow had been in the last time she'd visited. It really was a pleasing guest room. Bright and sunny, containing a big bed, neatly made except for a missing pillow.

Asha heard a noise from inside the walk-in closet. With a barely audible gasp, she whipped around to see the sliding door was partially open.

She backed away as quietly as she could, but she was wearing heels. When she stepped off the area rug, they suddenly sounded loud against the hardwood floor. How stupid she'd been not to just run and call the police! Asha felt her knees go weak as the sliding closet door opened.

Natalie poked her head out. "Oh, hi, Asha."

Asha thought maybe she was hyperventilating. She couldn't speak. Taking short, quick breaths, Asha finally managed, "Thank God it's just you." Asha didn't bother crossing the room to the chair. She put her back against the wall and slid down into a cross-legged position.

"I'm so sorry I scared you. Who did you think it was?"

Asha shook her head. "I don't know. A bad person who wants to hurt me, maybe."

"What? Who would want to hurt you?" Natalie asked, slipping down the wall to have a seat next to her.

"I'm just a hormonal, pregnant, paranoid lady who doesn't know what's up from down right now. I'm sorry, Natalie."

Natalie looked a little shocked. "Are you pregnant?"

Asha let out a weak laugh. "I guess that cat's out of the bag. You and I have only talked a handful of times, and yet you now know more about what's going on with me than my own family. That's not a very great state of affairs, is it? I can't believe I blurted that out. Please don't say anything."

"Who would I say something to? Of course not. But seriously, should I call someone? A doctor? Your husband?"

"I'm fine."

"You're not fine. You're really shaking. Give me your hand. Do you mind?"

Asha placed her hand in Natalie's.

"Breathe," Natalie said, using her thumb to rub Asha's palm. "You're okay. Breathe in through your nose and out through your mouth."

They sat like that for a minute.

"Feel a little better?" Natalie asked.

"Getting there." A second later, Asha asked, "You didn't break a vase downstairs, did you? Or move anything from one room to another?"

Natalie looked confused and shook her head. "No."

With her other hand over her heart, as if to calm it, Asha asked, "What about a bracelet?"

"What about a bracelet?"

"I lost one. Do you know anything about it?"

"I'm not following, Asha. Are you sure you're okay? Are you sure I shouldn't call your husband?"

"Yes. I'm sure. What were you doing in there?" Asha asked, gesturing towards the closet.

"I got here ten minutes ago, and the front

door was open. I looked around for a little bit, and then I ended up in here and saw the paintings stacked in the back of the closet."

"I never looked through those," Asha said, appearing to relax even more.

"There are some really nice ones. The family should have an estate sale. Are you ready to get up?"

"Yes."

Natalie hauled herself to her feet and then leaned down to take both of Asha's hands in hers. Asha stood for a second, took two faltering steps, and had to sit on the bed. "This is embarrassing. I'm okay, though, really. I'm just going through a lot right now."

"What can I do to help?"

"Nothing, thank you. It's just the normal stuff. Some problems at home."

Natalie leaned against the bed next to her. "I'm familiar with that sort of situation. Anything you want to talk about?"

It felt far too personal to tell Natalie that she was afraid her husband had grown tired of her. "It's nothing more than family nonsense. Mia, my daughter. Teenage drama."

"I know Mia."

"Yes, of course you do."

"She a great kid." Natalie paused. "Isn't she?"

"Oh gosh, yes. She is. It's just. I don't know. I feel like I'm losing the connection that I've always had with her. In the last year she's started hanging out in these chat groups with artists and musicians and wants to be a photographer or filmmaker in Los Angeles, and she thinks I'm a boring Midwestern real estate hack." Asha pulled a tissue from her pocket and blew her nose. "She wants to move out of the state, far away. The only thing I know how to do is to help her with what she wants, because maybe then she'll see how much I love her and not dismiss me the way that she does."

"Honestly," Natalie said. "Having kids seems so hard. I don't know how anyone does it." She caught herself. "Wait. Shit, I'm sorry. I forgot you're having another one."

"How dumb am I? And with a man who might be leaving me," Asha said without thinking. Suddenly she leaned away from Natalie. "I don't know what's wrong with me. I shouldn't be sharing such personal things. I apologize. It's not appropriate at all, and I ordinarily wouldn't behave like this, but —"

"It's okay," Natalie said. "It's fine. I wish —"

Before she could say anything further, the

voice of an elderly woman came singing out from down the hall. "Hello? Anybody here?"

Asha took a deep, steadying breath. "Here we go. How do I look? Can you tell I've been crying?"

"No, you have that trendy smoky-eye thing going. You look great."

"Really? Okay. Thank you." Asha stood up and called, "Be right there!" She turned back to Natalie and said, "I'm really sorry that I have to run like this."

"No worries," Natalie said. "I have to go anyway. If you need to talk, you know where to find me. I'm pretty much always at my desk."

"Thanks, Natalie." Asha waved goodbye before straightening her jacket and walking to the door of the bedroom, singing, "Here I am!"

Natalie breathed a sigh of relief. From her jeans pocket, she pulled the four pills she'd found in the sequined party purse, which had been stuffed along with some high-heeled shoes in a compartment of the hanging organizer in the closet. She'd become pretty good at identifying pills, and unfortunately these were just aspirin. Not every house was a winner.

After leaving the Leopold estate, Natalie

headed to Jay's house on the other side of the valley, ten miles away. Upon arriving at his wooden A-frame cabin with the adjacent carport sheltering all the bikes, motorcycles, snowboards, skis, sleds, and four-wheelers that he couldn't currently use, she let herself in the side door to the kitchen. She grabbed a Two Souls IPA from the fridge for Jay and carried it out to the patio coffee table that sat on a concrete slab at the edge of his overgrown yard. "Hello there," she said, putting the beer down in front of her brother. His dragon-head cane leaned against his chair.

"Much obliged," he said, grabbing the beer and raising it. He had hair the color of Natalie's before she'd dyed it a darker, burnt auburn. Jay's was a gentle ginger red. It was leonine and too long, a bright, wavy halo around his head. On his jaw he had growth that was more than stubble but not quite a beard, and his eyes were like hers — hazel and striking, with just a hint of here-comes-trouble.

"No problem," Natalie said, taking a seat across from him and then leaning to one side so she could pet Rocky.

"I meant to ask. Did you get some money a couple of weeks back?" Jay asked, extending his bad leg out to rest on one of the patio chairs.

"You mean from Dad? Yeah," she answered, pulling Rocky up onto her lap. It was easier than letting him claw her bare legs. "I only just got it, though. It had been returned to sender, and then he forwarded it to Mom, and then she forwarded it to me. It smelled like he fished it out of a pitcher of tips that had been marinating on a beer-soaked bar. Which is good, really, right? It means he's got a bartending job right now."

They sat quietly for a few minutes while Natalie ran her hand down the back of Rocky's neck.

Jay suddenly laughed. "Do you remember the J.J.?"

"The what?"

"The J.J. It was a drink he named after me. Remember how much I liked Dr. Pepper?"

"Yeah."

"You were there, but maybe you were too young to remember. He called me to come into the kitchen and said, 'I invented a new drink.' It was . . ." Jay started laughing again, but this time so hard he ended up coughing. He thumped his chest with his fist and went on. "It was Dr. Pepper, vanilla vodka, and a splash of grenadine. The worst part was, he wanted me to try it."

"Shut up. No, he didn't."

"And I was about to, when Mom came in and smacked that drink right out of his hand."

Natalie pushed back her chair. "Okay," she said. "Come on, Rocky dog. Let's put on your leash and go lose ourselves in the woods for a while."

"You know what?" Jay said, sliding Rocky's leash across the table to her. "Sometimes I make myself a J.J."

Natalie hunkered down beside his chair to attach the dog's leash to his collar. "Is that a good idea? I don't know. I try not to think about him too much."

"Dr. Pepper with vanilla vodka is really good. But it makes me miss him. When he was fun."

"Here," Natalie said, handing Jay Rocky's leash. "Take this for a sec. I'm just going to use the bathroom quick."

By the end of the forty-five-minute walk with Rocky, the Vicodin she'd taken from the bathroom medicine cabinet was kicking in. She stopped on the trail up the hill from Jay's street and called her mom. "Hey, Nat," Betty answered.

"Hi, Mom. Just wanted to check in and make sure everything's going well there."

"It is. No problems. You and your brother okay?"

"Yeah. Great."

There was a slight pause, and Betty said, "How are you feeling?"

"Really well."

"Oh good." Betty sounded relieved. "I worry."

"I know you do. But I'm a lot better now, I swear." After a short chat, Natalie said, "I need to run, okay? Love you."

After hanging up, Natalie let Rocky sniff the underbrush to his heart's content while she took a couple of minutes. Then they continued on down the path that led to the woods behind Jay's backyard. Before opening the patio door, she used the sleeve of her coat to wipe away some dirt on the glass so she could lean in and inspect her reflection.

It was fine.

Jay wouldn't be able to tell that she'd been crying.

7

Aside from her kickboxing classes, there were few things that helped Brooke relax as much as grooming her horses. The morning had been wonderful, spent entirely at the stable and then having a euphoric ride through the fields on her favorite mare, Apple. She was in a good mood when she arrived home. That was about to change.

After showering, Brooke traversed the mammoth home to search Sloane's bathroom. Her skin caviar luxe cream had gone missing, and though Sloane had her own jar, she was always running out and borrowing without asking.

The cleaners weren't due for another two days, and Sloane's bathroom was a wreck. Tubes of body sparkle oozed like toothpaste next to the sink, and Sloane's hair was everywhere. In the sink drain, in the shower drain, on the floor, in a gnarled ball on her hairbrush. The Swiss skin caviar cream would have been easy to spot. The jar was bright blue. The only blue item in Sloane's top drawer was a small medicinal-looking spray that resembled the travel-sized antibiotic Brooke had long ago carried around in her purse to disinfect Sloane's scrapes on the playground.

Brooke was curious. She picked it up and turned it this way and that. When she was at home, Brooke wore her reading glasses on a cord around her neck. She raised them to her eyes and squinted at the tiny print to read, "Phat Richard's Deep Head Oral Anesthetic Spray."

Brooke gasped and dropped it onto the counter. She wondered if she was losing her mind. Was it just candy-flavored medicine for sore throats? This was not true, and she knew it.

Using her phone, she searched Phat Richard's Deep Head Oral Anesthetic Spray and found that the product had several reviews, most of which recommended it for "deep throating without gagging."

On top of everything else, Sloane was having sex.

She was several months away from turning sixteen.

Moreover, it appeared it wasn't just your average old groping, "what-are-we-doing" horny teenager humping, but a variety of creative, mature-audiences-only acts that were somehow harder for Brooke to accept.

Brooke had first had intercourse with a boy named William, one of her Castle Peak Camp archery counselors. He'd been twenty and she'd been seventeen, so this development with Sloane wasn't entirely unexpected.

But this was different.

Brooke tore Sloane's room to pieces in a methodical rage. It was lunchtime, Sloane was at school, and Brooke swore under her breath while she searched the mattress and box spring, ransacked drawers, and rifled through every bag in Sloane's closet. An hour later, she'd discovered just three more controversial items: a tube of mint-chocolate-chip-flavored lube, a box of condoms, and a felt pouch containing the "Let's Do It Dice Game" still in its plastic packaging, which read, "An awesome fucking game!"

Brooke took photos of each item and texted them to Sloane along with a message that said, Stay classy.

She actually went as far as grabbing her car keys and purse with the intention of heading down to the school to drag Sloane out yet again, but she had second thoughts.

In the past few months, she'd barged into the office to summon her daughter from class several times: once when she'd found a joint in a makeshift Tupperware ashtray on the Juliet balcony off Sloane's bedroom, and then again when she'd found a stash of Dexedrine and Ritalin pills in a plastic Ziploc in her soccer team bag.

Instead of getting in her car and driving down to the school, Brooke did something arguably more stupid.

She texted Reade's mom, Linda Leland.

I'm letting you know first. Sloane and Reade will no longer be seeing one another. I'm forbidding it.

A second later Linda texted back.

Thank you. You beat me to it. I wish you luck with her. You have all my sympathy. Girls are just harder.

A fog filled Brooke's head. A small drink might help, so she went to the garage and grabbed the limoncello from the big freezer. She had two shots and then checked the time. Sloane would be busy with school and private training for the next four hours. Gabe would be working from home at the new apartment, overseeing the team of millennials he employed to run his "PSYCHE" active outdoor men's fashion line. It was a hobby job that Gabe took very seriously and one that Brooke had financed initially to make him feel happy and productive. She continued to finance it in the hopes that their separation wasn't permanent.

It took her twenty minutes to drive to the other side of the valley. She parked in the lot outside the Koi Creek Apartments and wondered if she should call him first. "Fuck it," she said out loud.

She used her card key to access the elevator, which opened directly into the entrance area of a single residence, like a fancy Manhattan loft. Brooke had been expecting to hear Gabe's music. Maybe some Nirvana or Pearl Jam. He should have been seated, working at the desk in the living room by the sliding glass doors that looked out over the golf course.

It seemed like no one was home.

"Gabe?" she called, unwrapping herself from her multilayered shawl. She tossed it onto the arm of the couch. "Gabe?"

Years earlier, just after they'd gotten married and before Sloane had been conceived, Gabe had caught her making out with another man. They'd been at a house party in Telluride, and he'd banged on the door of the bathroom door until Brooke had emerged alongside the drunken host. "We were just doing a line," Brooke had said. Gabe had replied, "Great, no problem, give me one too." There was no cocaine for Gabe, and it was obvious to everyone that there had been none in the first place. He'd forgiven her. After all, they were young, wild, and rich, and fearlessly played outside the rules.

Four years after Sloane was born, Brooke joined a morning playdate group that included a couple of dads. After grabbing a coffee in town, Gabe had stopped by Pilgrim's Park to surprise his wife and daughter, only to find that Sloane was being looked after by the other parents. After an investigation of the playground, pond, and picnic area, he found Brooke sitting in a car with a man, engaged in deep discussion. She rolled down the window and said, "Hey, honey! What are you doing here? This is my gay friend, Doug."

Gabe had replied, "If you're gay, why do you have an enormous boner for my wife right now?"

Those were just two of the times Brooke had disappointed him. Six years, eight years, ten years, twelve. Incident, incident, incident, incident. No proof of anything more than casual dalliances. No admissions. No breakdowns, no physical fights, accusations, or begging. Just less trust, comfort, and love.

Gabe had tolerated her need for attention until a cold night the previous December, outside the Soccer Barn. Christmas lights had been strung through the trees, making the parking lot of the indoor soccer arena strangely festive and romantic. She'd been wearing her favorite hand-knitted stocking cap, and her icy skin was pink and glowing. Coach Nick had made a controversial decision to replace the team's midfielder with Sloane because the opposition team's best offender was incredibly fast. Sloane had risen to the occasion and run up and down the field, showcasing her defensive skills while never slowing down on offense. She shut down the other team handily while at the same time scoring three goals to win the game. Dozens of spectators gathered to give her high fives as she left the field. While Gabe waited inside by the locker room for Sloane to get changed, Brooke had walked outside to enjoy the feeling of cool air and victory. Coach Nick exited on his own, and she called him over to where she was standing under a tree on the snowy edge of the parking lot. He gave her a quick hug.

Brooke placed one hand on his neck and

pulled him in for a kiss. Her tongue went searching and found his. Her groin pushed forward and he was aroused. "Oh," she said, against his skin. "That's nice."

"Brooke," he said, his voice hoarse.

"Yes?"

Coach Nick was looking over her shoulder. He ran his hand over his face. "Jesus."

Gabe was standing behind them.

Two days later, Gabe left for a hotel, and five days after that, Brooke bought an apartment on the opposite side of the river where he could live while they saw a therapist and worked things out. Gabe had said, "Don't buy it. I may not stay."

Brooke had more money than she could possibly spend in several lifetimes and didn't mind the cost. She said, "It's an investment. I can rent it. And it's someplace Sloane can come and spend time with you while we sort this out." It had never occurred to Brooke until recently that Gabe might not forgive her and eventually come home.

The apartment was a beautiful three-bedroom penthouse with a spacious, modern kitchen and a huge open-space living area with a home theater. The balcony looked out over the golf course, tennis courts, picnic tables, and firepits. At the far end of the property was a trailhead sign. After a few twists and turns on the map, you could hike or bike anywhere you wanted in the valley after walking out the door.

There was a bowl of moldy limes on the kitchen counter. The refrigerator was empty, and in the freezer there was only a bottle of Stolichnaya that was almost empty.

He was gone.

She dialed his cell phone. No answer.

Looking around, she saw the landline, a metal and black plastic contraption. Strange, really, given that they were antiquated and mostly useless. She picked it up and called him again.

He answered with a weary resignation. "You're in the apartment, I see."

"Hi, Gabe."

"What's going on?"

"I wanted to talk to you about Sloane," she said. It was the one thing that he couldn't refuse.

"Is something wrong?"

"Yes. A lot is wrong."

"How can I help?"

You can help by parenting. You can help by forgiving me and coming home, Brooke wanted to say. *You can help by being part of our family again.*

She was about to tell him what she'd

found in Sloane's bathroom and then had second thoughts. What if he blamed her, and her parenting? Brooke took a deep breath and looked out the window. In the distance, two tiny golf carts were zipping along a concrete path. "You know she wants to go to UCLA, of course."

"I know *you* want her to go to UCLA."

"She wants to. Just ask her!"

"Fine. What's the problem?"

"Well, now her friend Mia wants to go there, too."

"I don't understand. That's great. It's good to have friends with you wherever you go."

"No. No, no, no. You're missing the point. Coach Nick has a thing with one of the recruiters for UCLA. They played together or hung out together, I don't know. But if this contact is going to take one of Coach Nick's girls, it's only going to be one, do you understand? One."

"Mia isn't as good a player as Sloane. She's talented, obviously, but she's not nearly as aggressive, and I don't think her ball handling skills are on par with Sloane's."

"The rules are all over the place now, Gabe. It's not just who's the best player. They care about diversity and adversity.

That's what they call it. You can look it up. It's part of how the universities choose who they're going to allow in. It's part of the admissions process."

"Adversity and diversity?"

"Yes. Exactly. Mia is brown, Gabe. She's brown. Her mom is Indian. If Coach Nick recommends them both and Mia is almost as good as Sloane, they'll take Mia because she's brown."

"Brooke, you sound like a racist nutjob. Which I know you're not. But seriously, stop. There are plenty of spots at plenty of colleges —"

"How are you going to feel if Mia gets accepted to UCLA and Sloane has to go live and play in some armpit part of the country?" Gabe sighed loudly, and Brooke was perturbed. "Seriously, Gabe. How will you feel?"

"More importantly, Brooke, how will *you* feel?"

"What are you now, my therapist? I will feel shitty, Gabe. I will lose sleep. I will feel like I'm a bad mom, and I should have done more and tried harder and been better —"

"This sounds a bit like the speech you gave me when I was moving out."

"It's all true! I should have tried harder. I should have been better. For you and

Sloane. Help me here, Gabe."

"I'll do whatever I can for Sloane. As for us? Come on, Brooke. What's done is done."

Brooke sank down onto the plush couch. "Please don't say that. I love you. I'm going crazy without you. Please don't say, 'What's done is done.' We have a history. We took a ferry to Ibiza together. We wrecked a motorcycle together." Brooke started to cry. "We lost a baby together and we made another one and we raised her together. We belong together. You're the only one who makes me laugh. Please, Gabe. I'm sorry. I won't do it again. I won't. I promise."

"Brooke, I'm not even angry anymore. I loved you, and I will always be there for Sloane. But you aren't losing your mind because you lost me. You're losing your mind because you've never lost. Period. You've always gotten everything you wanted, and you need to win. I wish I could give you the win you need, but I can't. I'm sorry."

"Your stuff is gone, Gabe. Without even telling me."

"Can you blame me? I didn't want to live there. In an apartment you bought me, to try to keep me close, to keep tabs on me? God. I felt like a kept man."

"Where are you?"

"I decided I was more comfortable staying with Tabitha for the time being."

"You're living with the underage Spin instructor?"

"Twenty-three. She's twenty-three, and she was a double major in kinesiology and nutrition at —"

"Please, Gabe, stop. I don't want to know what she studied in high school. Could you put her on the phone, please?"

"Stop with the crazy demands. Why do you think you can yell at someone to do something and they'll automatically do it?"

"Put her on the phone!"

"I can't put her on the phone. I'm not with her. She's at work. She works. Like a normal person."

Brooke understood then that her uniqueness, her money, her beauty and privilege, had suddenly gone rotten. She was no longer as desirable as normalcy. Boring was better. Young and dumb was better. Poor and needy, low-maintenance and thankful. That was what was attractive. The world had turned upside down.

She hung up. With the back of her right hand, she smacked the Italian salad bowl on the counter. It flew down the length of the bar and off the edge, shattering when it hit the floor.

Brooke clutched her hand and opened her mouth in silent agony. She'd hit a vein, and a purple bruise was spreading rapidly, already the size of a quarter. This had happened to her mom when she was diagnosed with a blood disorder at the age of seventy. Brooke was getting old.

After a few minutes, the pain subsided.

Brooke picked up the multicolored shards from the bowl, put them in an old Walgreens plastic bag along with the moldy limes, and dumped it all in the trash.

She poured herself a shot from the vodka bottle that was in the freezer. After she finished it, she called Coach Nick.

He didn't pick up, so she dialed him again. And again.

With each unanswered call, she grew more resentful. She poured herself the last of the delicious freezing vodka. Her tongue and throat went cold. Eventually she left a voice mail message.

She said, "Just so you know, I don't like to be ignored."

Police Video Excerpt,
Falcon Academy Conference Room
Interview: Bellman, Natalie Marie
(Continued)

Detective Larson walks into the frame and deposits a mug of tea in front of Natalie. She then disappears. Natalie tries to take a sip and finds the tea too hot. She touches her lip and makes a face before pushing the mug away.

Detective Bradley is reading his notes silently. After a minute he looks up. "You said a little while ago that Sloane's biggest problem was with her mom. Was it just your typical, 'I'm mad that you don't approve of my boyfriend' type of problem? Or more than that?"

"I don't think Sloane liked the fact that her mom was also, I don't know. On the prowl."

Detective Bradley raises an eyebrow. "On the *prowl*?"

"Yes," Natalie confirms. "I heard through the school grapevine that Sloane was upset that her mom had cheated on her dad, and that he left the family afterwards."

Detective Larson pipes up from behind the camera. "Who did Brooke cheat with? Do you know?"

After a long pause, Natalie shakes her head.

"Are you sure?" Detective Larson goes on. "Are you sure it wasn't with Asha Wilson's husband, Phil?"

Natalie leans back in her chair, looks up at the ceiling, and lets out a long breath. "Did I write that in the planner? I don't remember writing that."

"You did," Detective Larson says, and then there's a long stretch of silence. "Did Asha Wilson know what was going on?"

"She did," Natalie answers.

"And how did she find out?"

Natalie reaches over to pull the tea towards her and tries again to take a sip. It's still hot. "Oww," she says.

Detective Larson ignores this and repeats the question. "Natalie. How did Asha Wilson find out about her husband's infidelity with Brooke Elliman?"

"She found out when I told her."

8

The apartment complex where Natalie lived was inexpensive and mostly empty during the off-season. Though Falcon Valley was twenty minutes from the closest ski resort, it still had its fair share of identical chalet-style apartment complexes lining the hills, ideal for people who weren't able to afford ski-in and ski-out accommodations. Natalie had gotten a very good deal on her little place. While she'd enjoyed the winter hustle and bustle of families coming and going, making a racket with all their skis and boards, boots and poles, the spring had been relaxing and quiet.

She had plans with Yvonne later that evening to grab sushi, and she figured she had plenty of time to get in a workout first. It was a sunny, crisp, and breezy Saturday. Perfect running weather. Natalie left her apartment and drove to the school, parking her car out in the back of the sports pavilion before walking up the hill behind the foot-ball field to the start of the cross-country course. She was surprised to see someone standing near the stone bench that marked the entrance of the running trail that went into the woods.

As Natalie approached, she saw that it was a tall woman in a skirt, jacket, and heels. Not exactly the right outfit for the cross-country course.

It wasn't until Natalie got even closer that she realized the woman was crying.

For a second, Natalie considered asking if she could help, but then the woman sank to her knees and began scratching at the ground below the bench in a frenzied way. Natalie wasn't comfortable witnessing this display of either instability or profound grief.

She gave the bench a wide berth and darted into the woods, sprinting far and fast, away from all that sadness.

When she finished her run, the woman was gone. Natalie walked over to the bench. She'd sat there many times recovering, but she'd never noticed the engraved plaque underneath. It had always been hidden by grass, leaves, snow, or dirt. Now it was uncovered.

The woman had cleared away the winter's

accumulation of brush to reveal a shiny square of marble bearing the following inscription:

In loving memory of Jill Ruiz. Your wings were ready, but my heart was not.

Walking down the hill and across the football field, Natalie felt heavy-hearted, picturing the sobbing woman clawing at the ground. It must have been the girl's mother. Imagine, she thought, to lose your child that young. It brought to mind a saying her own mom had repeated to her often when she was younger; *Be kind. Everyone you meet is fighting a battle you know nothing about.*

Natalie was still thinking of Jill Ruiz's mother five minutes later, when she rounded the corner leading to the mezzanine, completely in her own world, and collided with Coach Carmen, who was barreling down the stairs. "Oof!" Natalie exclaimed, falling backwards onto her butt.

Coach Carmen was sturdier. "Sorry," she said, sounding unashamedly insincere. She didn't stop to offer a hand. If anything, she continued hurtling down the corridor looking even less in control.

For a split second, Natalie was ready to say, *You should watch where you're going,* but the words were right there: *Be kind.*

Instead, she called, "Hey, are you okay?"

No answer from the disappearing woman. Natalie shook it off, climbed the stairs and walked onto the mezzanine.

Coach Nick was there.

He was alone. Natalie suddenly remembered that it was a three-day weekend. Lots of families would have left town. The music was much louder than when the students were around being trained. She recognized the band. He was listening to Mumford & Sons and singing passionately about living his life as it was meant to be.

He was facing the mirror with his back to her. She watched him quietly. For a second, she thought he was talking to himself, but then she glanced down at the ground. A big, shaggy, gold-colored dog was lying off to the side, chewing on some sort of toy. All of a sudden he exclaimed, "Yes, you know it, you know it, you are a good boy," and leaned over to give the dog a scratch around his floppy ears.

Turning his attention back to his weights, he took a second to get his grip right on the barbell below. With a strained exhalation that she could barely hear over the music, he raised it to waist level. Letting out another similar grunt, he brought the barbell up to shoulder level. He held it there, his whole body trembling. Sinewy lines of definition cut through his arms, and yet he wasn't bulky. Just healthy and perfectly made. Finally he raised the bar over his head, and the sleeves of his T-shirt slipped down around his arms, revealing the rounded swells of his shoulders.

Natalie was staring. As her mind wandered, so did her eyes, slipping down to the several inches of strapping back visible beneath the bottom of his shirt. In the mirror, she could also see his stomach: two grooves on either side of his abdominals, forming a V-shape narrowing as they disappeared under the waistband of his shorts.

The dog barked and stood, looking in her direction.

Coach Nick lowered the barbell and dropped it to the floor. She felt the vibration under her feet.

Sweat was running down his cheeks and neck, and his tousled hair was damp. His blue eyes were locked on hers in the mirror. "Hey, you," he said, in a familiar way that suggested they knew each other better than they did.

"Hey," she said back, forcing herself to walk forward rather than back away. Her heart was racing, and her cheeks felt like they were on fire.

Coach Nick put one hand on his dog's

head and said, "This is Jackson. He's friendly. But maybe too friendly, if you know what I mean." Upon being introduced, Jackson promptly crossed the mezzanine and greeted Natalie with a curious and vigorous investigation of all her personal scents.

"Yes. You're not kidding," she said with a laugh. She did an awkward dance trying to extricate herself from Jackson's probing nose.

"Good thing you're a dog person," Coach Nick said. Jackson seemed satisfied with his investigation and sat, panting with his tongue out, wide eyes begging Natalie to reciprocate the attention.

"How'd you know?" Natalie asked, patting Jackson's head.

"You have a little painting of your dog on your desk, don't you?"

"Oh," she said. "You noticed that? Wow. Yes, I do. That would be Rocky, my brother's dog."

"You have a painting of your *brother's* dog on your desk?"

"Well, yeah. I painted it."

"Oh!" he exclaimed. "That's cool. I remember thinking it was really good."

"Thank you." Natalie realized that she wanted Coach Nick to think she was clever and funny. She wanted it suddenly and very badly. They stood there, smiling and quiet. He wiped away some sweat from his forehead, and she coughed. "So, Coach Carmen just nearly knocked me down a second ago on the stairs. I thought maybe a bomb went off up here."

"Oh, did she?" he asked, shaking his head. "Sorry."

"Everything okay?"

"Sure." Nick nodded for a beat too long and then seemed to change his mind. "No. Actually, I'm lying. It wasn't okay. We had a disagreement about how to discipline a student who made a really terrible mistake. Carmen was upset. I don't blame her. It's hard when kids you like mess up and you have to . . . you know . . ."

"I get it."

"So, artist," he said. "Is it okay to ask why you're doing office work instead of being a painter?"

"It's called money."

He smiled. "Money. It's always money, isn't it?"

"It is," she answered. "I was going to be an art teacher once upon a time, but I had to drop out of school a little early. Family stuff."

"It's nice to finally talk to you. Why

haven't we done this before?"

"We've exchanged a few words."

"That's true. And I think I did try to flirt with you once."

"And I think I might have flirted back."

"When I was dillydallying in front of your desk?" Nick reached out and tucked a loose lock of her hair behind her ear, sending an unexpected warm tingle up Natalie's neck.

"Or was it when I came over and gave Mia Wilson my water bottle on the basketball court, and I caught you looking down my tie-dye tank top?"

He shook his head. "I did not. I don't even remember the tank top in question. It wasn't blue, orange, and white with little knots at the shoulders, and you weren't wearing a neon-green sports bra underneath it."

"Hmm, that's too bad. I was hoping you'd remember me."

"I apologize for the fact that you made no impression on me whatsoever."

"Forgiven," she answered.

"Can I interest you in a game of Horse? Let's play something."

"Horse?" she asked. "Basketball is not my thing."

Nick leaned away and assessed her. "You could have been a point guard. What are you? About five-four?"

"Precisely," she said. "And a lousy shot."

"So, you don't want to play Horse. Okay." Nick rubbed his chin while he pretended to think. "There's other things we could do. I could buy you a drink?"

"I'm sorry. I don't drink."

"What?" Nick didn't look disappointed, just surprised. "Don't take this the wrong way, but you look like a drinker. You've got that party girl look about you."

Natalie snorted. "I hope I don't have that look about me when I'm sitting in the Falcon front office."

"No, you don't. And why don't you drink?" he asked. "If you don't mind me asking."

"I was a bit of loose cannon back in the day. I've got some other vices, but alcohol wasn't working for me."

"All right. Fair enough. No drink for us then."

"A Powerade Mountain Berry Blast would be pretty great right about now, though. And maybe some tater tots or cheddar bites? If you still wanted to take me out."

"Let me get this straight. Are you inviting me to the Sonic drive-in down the road?"

"That's exactly what I'm doing."

Nick grinned. "You're my new favorite

person. That's Jackson's number one restaurant." Nick turned and snapped his fingers, and the golden retriever trotted over. "Isn't that right, Jackson? Do you want to go to Sonic?" Jackson barked and began to wag his tail. "His favorite is the popcorn chicken."

"What a lucky boy," Natalie said, already wondering where this could possibly be going. She hadn't been so nervous, excited, and hopeful about someone in a long time. The fact that she had a date with Yvonne in a couple of hours was the farthest thing from her mind.

Yvonne had glued fake eyelashes to her lids and was wearing green-colored contacts. She was dressed up in black bell-bottoms, platform boots, and a see-through shirt over a silver bra, all because Natalie had said, "I'll tell my brother to meet us. I don't know if he'll come, but I can ask. Is that okay with you?"

Yvonne was humming along with the music in the lounge of Sakura while she picked at edamame, drank sake, and scrolled through her Snapchat. She had no idea that Jay was ashamed of his cane and his limp, and that he'd chosen not to join. Also, she had no idea that for the first time in years,

Natalie was in the presence of someone she enjoyed so much that she completely, one hundred percent, forgot about her other plans until it was too late to appropriately cancel.

At a quarter to eight, when she was already fifteen minutes overdue to arrive, Natalie texted Yvonne. So sorry stomach bug please forgive me rain check for next weekend? I will treat to apologize!

You okay?

Yvonne closed her tab and got a takeout box of seared ahi and a kamikaze roll.

I'm barfing, Natalie shot back. Yvonne had no idea Natalie was lying naked in bed while Nick was using the bathroom.

Just so you know when it's your treat I'm getting the lobster caviar roll and my own bottle of Veuve

As you should gurl huge hug and thanks for understanding

No biggie feel better

The rest of the bottle of sake went down smoothly. As Yvonne was walking out, she spotted Brooke Elliman, a Falcon mom she didn't like, sitting at a bar table not far from the entrance, sipping something green in a martini glass.

"Hi there, Mrs. Elliman," Yvonne said, because there was no way to walk past without an acknowledgment.

"Oh. Hi. Miss —"

"Chun."

"Chun." Brooke seemed distracted.

"Everything okay?" Yvonne asked, feeling a little loose and neighborly after having an entire sake bottle all to herself.

"Fine. Everything is fine. My friend's late, that's all. And not answering my texts. Annoying."

"If it makes you feel any better, I got dressed up — and stood up," Yvonne said, gesturing down at her fancy pants and platform shoes.

"I didn't get stood up," Brooke responded flatly. And it was true. Coach Nick had never promised to meet her. She'd told him that she would be at Sakura that night "with friends" and that he should swing by. When he said, "That sounds like fun," she'd taken it as a yes. She'd been wrong. It seemed like not a single day went by that Brooke didn't feel more belittled and unappreciated.

Yvonne immediately raised both hands and said, "Oh no, of course you didn't get

uh . . . stood up. My bad. See you at school."
Brooke went back to her phone. *Are you coming or not?*

9

Sloane Elliman-Holt, wearing Gucci silk twill track pants and a hoodie, trotted up the stairs leading from the driveway to Greg Woodson's front door. She'd been dating Greg's close friend, Reade, for several months and had been spending a lot of time at the Woodson house. The porch was an enormous stained concrete slab bordered by urns potted with a variety of ferns and flowers. At opposite edges were slanting pillars of red rock inspired by the surreal beauty of the local canyons.

She rang the doorbell, and Mr. Woodson opened the door. He waved her in distractedly as he continued to converse on his headset about something that involved the words *methane, biodiesel,* and *landfill.*

Sloane slipped off her shoes and left them by the door. As she walked past the kitchen, she glanced in and saw Greg's mom sitting at the breakfast bar with her laptop open and a glass of wine. Her name was Suzy, and on previous visits, Sloane had found her to be unexpectedly nice, considering she was reputedly a cutthroat businesswoman.

"Hiya," Sloane said, zipping by with a little wave in an attempt to get past without stopping to talk.

Suzy looked up and appeared to be delighted. "Hi there, Sloane. Nice to see you! Did your mom just drop you off?"

"Uh-huh," Sloane lied. She'd begged a ride off an older girl from her soccer team.

"Darn. If I'd known, I would have gone out to say hi. Is Mia coming over tonight, too?"

"Probably not," Sloane answered, reluctantly doubling back to stand in the door frame.

"Oh. Too bad. How are you?"

"Good. And you?"

"Great, thanks. I do love it when you come over," Suzy said. "I'm always the only girl in the house."

Suzy had to be pushing fifty, Sloane thought, but if she wanted to call herself a girl, fine.

"How are your mom and dad?"

Sloane hesitated. "Okay."

"What are they up to these days? I haven't

seen your mom in ages."

"She stays busy with her board meetings, charities, and horses."

"And your dad?"

"You know, it's weird," Sloane said, very little inflection in her voice. She might as well have still been talking about her mom's charities and horses. "He left."

"What?" Suzy lowered her wineglass to the marble countertop with a crack and then had to steady it to keep it from toppling.

"Yeah. They had a fight, and he left and hasn't been back for, like, months."

"Sloane, I had no idea. I'm so sorry."

Shit, Soane thought. Suzy was starting to inch her little bony butt off the bar stool. She actually was going to get up, come over, and go in for that hug. "It's fine," Sloane said urgently, backing up. "I'm going downstairs now. Please. Is that okay?" The deer-in-the-headlights look in Sloane's eyes was not lost on Suzy.

"Of course, it's okay." Suzy sat back down and reached for her wineglass. "I really do hope everything works out for the best."

"Thanks, Mrs. Woodson."

In the basement, Reade was doing lines off the coffee table, and Greg was holding a gray metal canister and a full balloon. He'd gotten ahold of his favorite, nitrous oxide.

Reade saw Sloane emerge at the bottom of the stairs and stood up, arms out. She never got tired of being wrapped up against his powerful chest. "What took you so long?"

"My mom made mani-pedi appointments for us earlier. Then I had to wait until she was on the couch watching her show so I could leave without her looking out the window. Sorry."

Reade said, "That's so cute," followed by his best boy-band smile.

He regularly posted photos of himself on Rich Kids of Instagram, and he fit the bill. Thanks to his parents' wealth, he'd benefited from expensive acne medications, human growth hormone injections, the best orthodontists, three years of personal training sessions with Coach Nick, bleached teeth, electrolysis on spots of unwanted hair, highlights and lowlights, nutritious food, and a personal masseuse to relieve stress. In his photos, he often posed sitting on the hood of his white Mercedes-Benz G-Class SUV Wagon, sticking his tongue out while throwing gang signs with both hands.

Sloane and Reade had been dating on and off for a few months even though they had little in common except for wealth and sports. And cocaine.

"Can I get a bump?" Sloane asked.

With a gentlemanly, "Allow me," Reade took a vial from his jacket pocket and tapped some out on the glass tabletop. He used his Falcon student ID card to cut it up and then form two thin lines.

Reade's phone rattled on the coffee table.

Greg said, "Oh, see if that's Jeremiah. He's with Alistair and Kasper. They're supposed to be coming over to do a death dab challenge for Kasper's YouTube channel."

Reade looked at his phone. "It's Coach Nick. What time is it? Greg, turn the music down, will you?"

"What does he want?" Greg asked.

"How should I know?" Reade answered, and said brightly as if he'd not been drinking and doing cocaine for hours, "Hi, Coach. Yes, I got your message. Tomorrow two to four instead of one to three. It's not a problem at all." Greg and Sloane were watching Reade. "Just hanging out with Greg and Sloane. What about you? Oh really? Nice. Lasagna's the best. Okay. Cool." Reade's expression changed from toleration to exasperation, and he said, "Sloane, Coach Nick would like to FaceTime with you for a second."

Sloane mouthed, "No," but Reade had

already hit the FaceTime button and turned the phone towards her.

She pulled it together. "Hey, Coach Nick," she said, waving.

The image was Nick in his own kitchen, walking around while cooking. He had his phone in one hand. With his other, he tasted a red sauce from a wooden spoon. "Hi, Sloane. How's it going? Everything good?"

"Yes, thank you."

"Okay," he said. "I'm happy to hear that. Your mom told me that you and Reade were taking some time apart. Did I get that wrong?"

"Shit," Reade said softly.

"Oh, it's fine," Sloane said. "I just swung by Greg's house to pick up my jacket. I left it here the other night so, anyway, that's all I'm doing. I'll be leaving in a sec. I'm not banned from seeing Reade or anything. Whatever you heard from my mom —"

Reade gestured for her to stop talking by drawing his hand across his neck.

"So, um, I'm leaving in a minute. Less than a minute." Sloane sniffed.

"Well, okay. You know, if you need anything, just don't hesitate to reach out. We're all here for you. Your mom and I are working together. Great things to come."

"I know that. I totally know that. Thank

you. Again."

"Use good judgment, Sloane."

"I will, Coach Nick."

Reade turned the FaceTime back on himself. "Well. It was nice of you to . . ." he paused ". . . check in with us. Tonight. We appreciate it."

"You kids behave yourselves, all right?"

"Don't worry, sir, we will." Reade hung up and said to Sloane, "What is wrong with that guy?"

"He's just looking out for me. My mom asked him to. That's all."

Greg came over and sat down, his pupils huge. "What an intrusive dick. I could ask my dad to get him fired."

"Fuck getting someone to fire him," Reade said, tossing the phone onto the couch. "It would be easier just to get rid of him ourselves. And more fun too."

10

On one side of the football field, the crew from Premiere Party Rental was busy setting up the enormous inflatable movie screen in front of the goalposts. Asha was on the opposite end by the parking lot, having a look through several plastic tubs filled with granola bars, Fruit Roll-Ups, and baggies of popcorn. It was "Outdoor Movie Night" at Falcon Academy, and even though the sun wouldn't set behind the mountains for another hour, families were already spreading out their blankets, unpacking picnic baskets, and discreetly sipping cocktails out of plastic tumblers. The younger students ran amok around the field while the older ones had spread out across the upper portion of the bleachers in small clusters.

"I'm here, I'm here," Brooke called breathlessly, running across the field gingerly in boots with heels.

Asha, who had just begun to transfer organic Gatorades into a cooler filled with ice, looked up and smiled. "Hi! Judy and Dave are late too. Don't worry."

"Sorry," Brooke said, reaching Asha's side and taking in the festival atmosphere of the fundraiser appreciatively. "To be honest, I totally forgot that I let myself get roped into this the last time I was up at the school. Sloane reminded me."

"Well, I'm glad you remembered. Can you help me with the folding table?"

"Here," Brooke said, picking it up off the ground and starting to release the legs. "Let me just do it myself. You know, your condition and all, little mama. I take it Phil and the kids are in on the secret by now?"

Asha glanced at Brooke and hesitated.

"What? No? Asha. You've got to tell them. How far along are you?"

"It's early days. I think it's too soon to be making a big deal about it. Especially when Phil is acting a little off. I'm just being cautious."

Brooke did not look at all convinced. "Okay. Well. Phil has a lot going on. Give him some time, then, you know, to sort things out."

"Sort what out?" Asha asked, stopping what she was doing.

"You know —"

"No, I don't know." She put her hands on her hips and blew a piece of hair off her face. "Sort what out? What exactly are you talking about?"

Brooke appeared to be suddenly flustered and at a loss for words. Very unlike her. "I just meant, you know, life, kids, work. We all have a lot on our plates, and I assume he's no different. I shouldn't have said anything. I don't know anything." She paused. "I obviously pushed a button. I'm sorry."

Asha's hands were still on her hips defiantly as she mulled over this answer. After a second, it was as if the wind left her sails. She sighed. "No, no. That was my fault. I'm not myself these days." She grabbed a Gatorade and wrestled with the cap. "Mia and all this college stuff. Ugh."

"The college stuff," Brooke said, bristling. "Well, maybe if Mia hadn't decided suddenly that she wanted to go to UCLA, the school her best friend has been dreaming about for her whole life, it wouldn't be so complicated."

"Well." Asha threw up her hands and laughed as if she'd messed up again. "I guess I pushed a button too."

Brooke rubbed her forehead as if she had a headache. "Yes. It's true. I never used to be this on edge. Doesn't it seem like everyone's on edge lately?"

"Mia certainly is. What's happening between our girls, anyway?" Asha shook her head sadly. "Why aren't they friends anymore, the way they used to be? Is it just this stupid issue that they both want into the same college? I mean, does anyone stop to think they might both get in? That would be wonderful."

"I think that's unlikely, Asha." *Impossible.* "And anyway, they're still friends. It's just more competitive than it was when they were little. At least they had that sleepover at your house last weekend."

"The girls haven't had a sleepover at our house in months," Asha said, looking alarmed. "I hope Sloane didn't —"

"No, no. You're right," Brooke said. "I'm confused. Time flies when you're busy, and I have been very, very busy. My dad's retiring as chairman, and I've had to go to tons of board meetings in Denver that drag on all evening. Gabe was in charge of Sloane, and I just didn't check in because I was so busy and — you know what, speaking of which, oh my God, I have to run."

"Oh? What? You're leaving now? Already?" The slightly frantic look on Brooke's face stopped Asha from saying more.

"I completely forgot about a conflicting commitment. Asha, I'm so sorry."

"Of course, that's fine. Thank you for helping me with —" Asha looked around at all the snacks and drinks left to be arranged and sold throughout the evening. "With opening the table."

"You're welcome," Brooke said, backing away and scrounging in her oversized purse for her phone. She turned and race-walked towards her car, fingers flying over the screen.

You have been lying to me

You were not at Mia's house when you said you were

No response.

You know that you ARE NOT ALLOWED TO SEE READE LELAND much less spend the night with him!!!!!!!!!!!!!!!!

No response.

Where are you right now?

No response.

Tell me where you are I don't want you

seeing that boy I mean it where are you I am considering calling the police

what don't freak out n dont call the police mom ffs pls u dont want them involved in this

In what? Involved in what?

someone from the school is probably going to be calling u I got into some trouble do me a favor and try not to lose your shit like always

It wasn't until Asha had handed out organic Gatorades to several dozen Falcon athletes that the words hit her like a punch to the stomach.

My dad's retiring as chairman and I've had to go to tons of board meetings in Denver.

Asha took the key card she had found in Phil's trash can out of the zippered compartment in her purse where she was keeping it and double checked the hotel. Le Méridien.

She texted Brooke.

I've got some overnight business in Denver myself. What hotel do you like?

Brooke never responded.

Police Video Excerpt,
Falcon Academy Conference Room
Interview: Bellman, Natalie Marie
(Continued)

The tea has cooled down, and Natalie is holding the mug up to her lips while she looks at the table. Most of her face is in shadow. At the moment, no one's talking.

Detective Bradley is checking messages on his phone, but the camera is still recording. Natalie sets her tea down and stares longingly out the window. It's snowing.

After a second, Detective Bradley puts his phone on the table. Natalie senses his gaze and turns away from the window to face him. "Do you know the difference between manslaughter, murder one, and murder two?" he asks.

Natalie nods.

"Okay. I just wanted to make sure. Because if *someone,* who has been a good person their whole life, gets really upset and makes a mistake in the heat of the moment, a mistake that ends tragically, in a way that they regret . . . if that person comes forward and confesses, things are not nearly so bad for them in terms of consequences. Do you understand?"

"How am I supposed to understand any of this? Two people? Was it murder? Suicide? An accident? How am I possibly supposed to understand?"

"*Someone* was slowly dying while you were in the sports pavilion, Natalie. *Someone* was bleeding out that afternoon and evening, while you were walking in and out as if you hadn't a care in the world."

Detective Larson appears from out of frame, and her hand drops onto Natalie's shoulder. "What do you think happened in the gym that afternoon, Natalie?"

"I think," Natalie says, after pulling her shoulder away from Detective Larson's touch, "that *someone* did something that was very, very bad."

11

Natalie was bent over her computer, typing up a flyer inviting all parents to consider signing their children up for summer camp at the Wilderness Science Center. *A unique experience especially suited for students with an interest in animals and the outdoors, with registration beginning —*

She looked up to see Nick standing there. "Hi, Miss Bellman. How are you?"

"I'm fine," she said, her face lighting up. "How are you, Mr. Maguire?"

"Good." He stood there looking at her, and she sat there looking at him, both wearing goofy smiles. Yvonne cleared her throat.

"How can I help you?" Natalie asked him.

"Are we hanging out this afternoon?" he whispered, glancing over his shoulder at Rex, the security guard, whose head was slightly turned in their direction as if to hear better.

Natalie nodded vigorously.

"Awesome," he said softly. "I can't wait." He resumed talking in a normal voice. "I'm over here because I've got an issue that I need to discuss with Mark."

Yvonne looked up from behind her computer screen. "He's free. If you want to see him now, I'll let him know."

"Thank you, Yvonne," Nick said. "That would be great."

After leading Nick back to the study, Yvonne returned and said, "Is it me or was Mr. Maguire just now acting like he'd undergone, like, a lobotomy? Jesus, drool much?"

Natalie felt a pleasant warmth bloom like a flower in her chest.

After the meeting with Nick, Mr. Dilly came out to see Natalie and Yvonne. "Girls," he said, putting his hands on his hips and looking up at the ceiling as if the sky was about to fall. He seemed at a loss for words. "How can I put this? We have a situation, and it's going to require a very sensitive approach. I think the best thing to do would be to call the boys in first. Determine the collateral damage. Let's do that before I speak with the . . ."

He paused. "The other party."

"I'm sorry, Mr. Dilly," Yvonne said. "Can you be a bit more —"

"I have to use the bathroom," he declared, making a face. "I'll be right back."

When he was gone, Yvonne leaned over and said to Natalie, "Do you know what this is all about?"

"I have no idea," Natalie answered. "It's weird, right?"

"I wonder what kind of situation we're in for?"

"A delicate situation? A dangerous situation?" Natalie used her chin to gesture in the direction of the office bathroom. "Or are we at stage three — a diarrhea situation?"

Yvonne, who had little self-control when it came to laughing, had to cover her mouth. When she was able to speak, she said, "Stage four. Dead body situation. Somebody must have kicked the bucket!"

Five minutes later, Mr. Dilly reappeared, a little grayer, with some sweat on his upper lip, and said, "Now, listen. This all has to remain private. I can't have either of you talking about this. Understand?"

They both nodded.

"All right then," Mr. Dilly said. "This is what we'll do."

Mr. Dilly asked Natalie to contact the parents of five boys, a group who had been hanging out together for years. They were an odd ensemble comprised of two athletes, a theater geek, a drummer in the marching band, and a good-looking video gamer with his own YouTube channel.

The message she was asked to convey to the parents was clear: a meeting was mandatory, and time was of the essence. Natalie managed to schedule a sit-down in the study for the next day just after lunch for representatives of three out of the five families involved.

Reade Leland's mom, Linda, stayed at home and the word around the school was that she literally "stayed at home." No one had seen much of her in the past few years. Rumor had it she liked her benzos, so Natalie wasn't surprised when the woman volunteered her husband for the meeting. Reade's father, Howard, called Natalie back right away. She suspected he ran his cybersecurity company remotely, so it wasn't a problem for him to take some time off for a school meeting.

Even at Falcon, where many of the families had some ties to fame or fortune, the Solomons were somewhat unapproachable. Natalie left a message on Jeremiah Solomon's mother's work phone. She was an advertising executive.

It was Jeremiah's dad, Derrick, a retired

NFL player, who called back an hour later in response to her measured invitation to visit the school the following day. "I want to know what this is all about right this second," he said. Natalie reiterated several times that she had been explicitly instructed to keep the issue extremely confidential, which Mr. Solomon eventually came to appreciate.

Suzy Woodson was very protective of her son, Greg, so she agreed to the meeting without much in the way of information, despite the fact that she spent half of every week in Denver as the busy CEO of a large cable television company.

Neither of Alistair Reynolds' parents returned Natalie's calls. Two hours later, she walked down to the theater, where Alistair was having debate class, and asked if he could perhaps get in touch with one of them for her. He responded that they were at a yoga retreat in Costa Rica. His aunt was house-sitting with him and his sister. When Natalie asked when his parents would be returning, his answer was, "Three weeks. Or five. Sometime this summer."

Kasper Nowak and his family had abruptly left the country just the previous day, and though it was their habit to summer in Poland, this was the first time they'd begun their vacation before the end of the school year.

The following afternoon was a circus in the front office, with the parents coming and going with their heads hanging low as if they were celebrities who didn't want to be photographed by the paparazzi. The boys were less effacing. At one point, Reade Leland slouched against the wall next to Natalie's desk with his arms crossed over his formidable chest for thirty minutes. His long bangs hung down below his well-tended brows, but she could still see his eyes. Green and cold, they were both gorgeous and unsettling. Reade was an undeniably handsome seventeen-year-old. He played lacrosse in the spring, wrestled in the winter, and was the captain of the soccer team in the fall. To Natalie, he looked like the sort of boy who would go on to pledge a good fraternity, major in economics with a minor in sexual assault, and eventually become a businessman like his dad. Had his circumstances been less affluent, she assumed he would have been just fine because of his looks alone. There was always Chippendales, reality television, and porn.

Eventually Natalie said, "The headmaster is ready for you now, Reade."

He gave her a slight up-jerk of his chin in acknowledgment. She felt, intuitively and somehow hopefully, that he was in massive trouble.

Jeremiah Solomon was the last to leave the study. Natalie noticed that Greg Woodson was pacing in the hallway. As soon as he saw Jeremiah, he grabbed him by the arm and started dragging him down the hall.

Judging by appearance alone, they were unlikely friends. Jeremiah was not only a good football player like his dad, but he was considered a cool kid, with short, dyed-blond dreadlocks, dual diamond stud earrings, and full male-model lips. Greg, on the other hand, had a gaunt face covered in acne and knock-kneed bird legs that had required braces until the eighth grade.

His mom, Suzy, loved her geeky son very much. She'd been actively courting the friendship of "the best boys" in the Falcon Valley area since Greg was in elementary school by inviting them on irresistible play-dates. Reade Leland had accompanied Greg by private jet to the Rose Bowl in Pasadena to see Eminem perform when they were eleven. Jeremiah had accompanied Greg and his parents on their family spring break holiday to their waterfront villa in the

Florida Keys for five years running. Other Falcon boys had been similarly romanced over the years. Suzy had accomplished her mission to keep her son from being ostracized, but she couldn't make him handsome. She had succeeded in creating a teenage boy who was ridiculously entitled, as well as furious at the world. In time, this close group of privileged friends had whittled down to a party of five: Greg, Reade, Jeremiah, Alistair, and Kasper. At after-school happy hour gatherings, many of the teachers secretly referred to the pack of wild boys as "the dingoes."

Today, Greg was wearing faded and ripped jeans that were belted about halfway up his rear end, high-top sneakers that weren't laced, and a baggy gray sweatshirt. He didn't need to dress like a billionaire. Everyone knew who he was and what he was.

As Natalie watched the two boys head down the hall away from her, she saw Greg Woodson shove Jeremiah so hard that the bigger boy almost fell.

Natalie jumped to her feet. "Yvonne, I'll be right back."

The boys turned left, going through the double doors that opened onto the covered walkway leading to the sports pavilion.

Natalie was about to go through the doors too when she realized they had stopped on the other side. Greg was shouting, and it was easy for her to listen to their conversation.

"Can you believe this? 'What did the photos look like? How many were there? Who shared them with me? Who did I show them to?' On and on and on, oh my God I have a headache!"

Jeremiah's voice was as deep as if he were a grown man, and he always sounded serious. "That sucked. My mom is going to cry when my dad tells her. I don't know what I'm going to say. This is terrible."

Greg, on the other hand, sounded like a squeaky hysterical boy in the middle of a voice change. "What kind of stuff did they ask you?"

"Same shit as you."

"Humor me with a recap."

"You know. Like did you look at and share the photos, who with, whether I posted them anywhere."

Satisfied that Greg Woodson and Jeremiah Solomon were not about to get into a fistfight, Natalie pushed the heavy door open and acted surprised to see them. She smiled brightly. "Hi, boys," she said. "Are you headed over for sports?"

Jeremiah nodded and looked away. "Yeah."

Greg stared at Natalie coldly. "Did you want a word with us, Miss Bellman?"

Natalie felt the little hairs on the back of her neck stand on end, and she answered, "No," before letting the door fall closed.

At the end of the day, Nick was again alone in the study with Mr. Dilly when Mrs. Elliman appeared outside on the sidewalk. She was pressing the entrance buzzer to be let in repeatedly, as was her habit. At first, Natalie didn't suspect any connection between Mrs. Elliman's arrival and the earlier parade of parents and students, as she had never been asked to place a call to Sloane's mom.

Rex went through his usual rigmarole to let her into the building. Mrs. Elliman appeared agitated and even slightly disheveled, if it was possible to be disheveled in a gray-and-black designer ensemble of cashmere and leather. Natalie had never seen her looking anything less than flawless. "Mrs. Elliman, are you looking for Sloane? Can I call her for you?"

"No," she answered. "Leave her out of this debacle for now. Is he in there?"

"Who?" Natalie asked, and then realized how ridiculous it sounded. "I'm sorry. Are you here to see the headmaster or Mr. Maguire?"

"Both," she answered, wiping one eye in a despondent way.

"Okay, let me just —"

"No, no." Mrs. Elliman crossed behind the desk to the hallway. Natalie and Yvonne looked on in astonishment as the woman proceeded to enter the study where Mr. Dilly was oblivious to her arrival, without so much as a perfunctory knock.

Forty-five minutes later, it was nearing the end of the school day, and Yvonne and Natalie were finishing up their administrative work.

Mr. Dilly poked his head out of the study and said, "I'd like you to go ahead and pack up, ladies. I know technically you're on the clock for another thirty minutes, but let's just make it an early day."

Without waiting for an answer, he went back into his office to continue his conversation with Mrs. Elliman.

"Sweet," Yvonne said. "Let's go to happy hour at Tequila Harry's. I'll buy you a Coke."

"Sounds good," Natalie answered.

"Don't dillydally now, little miss, or I might have to, I don't know, get out my whistle," Yvonne said with a wink.

"What?" Natalie smiled, reaching under her desk for her bags.

"You know what I'm talking about. Mr. Maguire. Always flirting with you."

"Nah. That's crazy talk," Natalie answered, grabbing her jacket. She wasn't ready to tell Yvonne; too new.

"He's such an old dog," Yvonne said. "He's after everybody."

"Is he?" Natalie asked, suddenly frozen in the process of packing up her things to go.

"Totally. Me, Denise, Berta, Mrs. Leland, Mrs. Elliman. All the moms, really, even the lunch lady."

"Rosie is like, seventy," Natalie said.

"Yeah, but he makes her laugh like she's being tickled."

"You know what, Yvonne," Natalie said, "I forgot. I need to go walk Jay's dog. I'm so sorry. My bad. I can't do happy hour."

"Let's pick up a six-pack and surprise Jay. I'll come with you."

"I'm sorry. I really can't."

Yvonne put her hands on her hips and said, "Fine. Another time then. I'd like to remind you, however, that I still haven't collected my caviar lobster roll and bottle of Veuve owed me from the last time you made plans with me and then canceled."

But all Natalie could think about was how

many women Nick was sleeping with.

At home that night, Natalie social-media-stalked Nick, and his long-distance, long-time "friend" named Amelie Bernard, as well as Brooke Elliman and Linda Leland, the two Falcon moms Yvonne had said he was known to flirt with on occasion. Amelie, more often referred to as Millie, was the most threatening. She was an actress, albeit an out-of-work actress. Young, petite, and with a little edge to her. She wore a pink streak in her white-blond hair and frequently glared at photographers with pure hatred that was somehow very sexy.

Brooke and Linda were surgically improved good-looking cougars whose Instagram pages showed them attending charity events in designer clothes. Natalie felt slightly better. They seemed a little too manufactured for what she felt was Nick's taste.

Eventually Natalie took a Vicodin and worked on her most recent pet portrait request through Etsy, in this case a bit of a challenge, as she'd never before been asked to paint a ferret wearing a striped sweater. She finished at eleven and stood back, thinking that it might be up there with her favorites. Her phone beeped and she had a text from Nick.

I just wanted to say good night, sleep tight and I miss you

An explosive surge of happiness made her feel almost dizzy, and Natalie wanted to celebrate. She played a love song by Ellie Goulding on her laptop and spun around the studio as if it were a dance floor bathed in pulsing, colored party lights.

She was so thankful she'd come to Falcon Valley. For the very first time in her life, she was the lucky one, thinking, *It's almost too good to be true.*

12

Asha's feet were freezing. She wished she hadn't taken off her socks. The nurse hadn't said anything about socks. It was just, "Get undressed and here's your gown." She could have kept her socks on. Her feet had nothing to do with a pelvic exam. Someone knocked on the door of the examination room.

"I'm ready," Asha called from her prone position on the table. The door opened. Asha tilted her head to the side and saw her gynecologist, Dr. Ruiz, enter the room. "Hi, Elena," she said.

Elena responded warmly while sanitizing her hands in the corner. "Hi, Asha. This is such an amazing and wonderful surprise!"

"So, this is happening?" Asha asked. "It's real?"

"The lab test says it's real. Are you excited?"

"I'm scared."

"Of course you are. That's completely normal, to be nervous."

"I don't know how I can do this."

"You can do this, Asha. And you've got Phil. Where is he, by the way? I would have thought he'd want to be here for this."

Asha closed her eyes and took a deep breath. "He's got other stuff going on."

"Other stuff besides a new baby? Must be important."

"I'm afraid so. Yes. Very important."

Elena began to examine Asha's breasts. "Well, you're going to be good. You're strong. You're healthy." She moved on to probing her abdomen. "I'm very confident that we can get you through this pregnancy without any major problems and that you're going to be the mom of a wonderful little girl who you will love so, so much."

"A little girl?" Asha asked. "It's too soon to tell, isn't it?"

"Oh," Elena said, reaching for her speculum. "It's far too soon, I would imagine. Can you put your feet in the stirrups, please?"

"But you did say little girl. Is it something about the way I'm carrying the baby?"

"No," Elena said, her voice a little off. She cleared her throat.

Asha lifted herself up a little to look her

doctor in the eye. "Is everything okay?"

"Fine. I'm fine. I apologize." Elena began the pelvic examination, and Asha went quiet, gritting her teeth. "I guess," Elena said, as she opened Asha up, "I might have been projecting a little. Hoping for a girl for you. My time I had with my daughter was the best, most beautiful, happiest part of my life."

Then Asha remembered. The doctor's daughter had died a few years ago.

Driving home from her appointment, Asha felt unusually hopeful. Elena had said she had every reason to expect a normal pregnancy despite her age. She was a healthy, strong woman, and she'd already given birth to two children who were "thriving."

Thriving.

Asha loved the sound of the word. She said it out loud. "Thriving." Despite the fact that it was closing in on dinnertime and they usually had pizza on Thursdays, Asha pulled into McDonald's for the first time in several years. Baby wanted french fries. She'd just get a small. Maybe a medium. When the voice came over the loudspeaker to ask her for her order, she said, "A Quarter Pounder with cheese, large fries, and an apple pie."

After pulling into the garage at her house, she considered wolfing her "snack" down right there in the car. Her kids were rarely allowed fast food, she never bought it for Phil even though he liked it, and she didn't want to get caught. On the other hand, it sounded far more fun to take it to her office and enjoy it slowly while she perused social media.

With her bag of food in her hand, Asha quietly opened the door from the garage into the house. From upstairs she could hear the sound of Oliver practicing his trombone in his bedroom. The bathroom door off the kitchen was closed, and she could hear some sort of newscast. Phil was in there, scrolling through Twitter, no doubt.

She kicked off her shoes and trotted barefoot down the hall. Just as she was about to turn into her office, she stopped. Mia was in there on her phone. Asha was about to go in anyway when Mia's voice stopped her cold. Her daughter was upset. Angry. Scary.

"Screw you," Mia said. "Screw all of you!"

Asha took a step back and covered her mouth with her free hand. Mia never spoke like that. Mia never went in her office. In fact, Mia rarely raised her voice or even left her own room for any reason other than to join the family at the dinner table.

"No," Mia said, and Asha heard a drawer slam closed. "No. I said no."

Why not go on in, say hello, and act like everything was normal? It was her office, after all. But that wasn't going to happen. This wasn't a conversation Asha felt comfortable interrupting. In fact, she felt like she needed to hear the whole thing.

"I told you, I don't want anything to do with it. Not only do I not want to be a part of it, I don't even want to talk about it. Do what you want to do, but do it without me. I don't care." There was a long pause and then Mia screamed like a crazy person, "I don't care I don't care I don't care! You know what, Sloane, tell Reade I said to fuck off and leave me alone."

It sounded like the conversation was over. Asha didn't want Mia to catch her eavesdropping on such a personal exchange. And, she thought, really, what more could a mom want than a daughter who felt comfortable saying no to something she didn't want to do? "This is good," Asha whispered, trying to comfort herself as she tiptoed back the opposite way down the hall.

Phil surprised her just as she was about to turn the corner into the kitchen, and she let out a quick, sharp scream.

"Whoa!" he said. "Sorry. Are you okay?"

She was not okay. She thrust the McDonald's towards him and said, "I brought you a snack as a surprise. I've got to go to our room for a second."

"Thanks," he called after her, opening the bag.

Upstairs, she ran down the corridor, realizing she was going to be sick. It was no use. She wasn't going to make it to her own. She veered into Mia's room and then her bathroom, and after throwing up several times, she fell back and wiped her mouth with toilet paper. Mia was standing in the doorway.

"Hey, honey," she said. "I'm sorry. I must have eaten something bad and couldn't make it to —"

Mia cut her off. "I'd prefer it if you didn't come in my room anymore without my permission."

"What?"

"You heard me," Mia said, crossing her arms across her chest. "Am I allowed some privacy in this family, or is it only Dad that gets to do whatever he wants without telling the rest of us where he goes or who he sees?"

"Mia! What are you talking about?"

"I'm talking about personal autonomy. Okay? Can you please just leave my room so I can have my own space to my own self?"

Asha pulled herself up and left, staggering into the hallway, feeling sicker than before. She had followed the rules and tried to be the best she could be for all of them. And yet. *What has become of the family that was supposed to love me?*

13

Brooke stood on her deck, which was high above the road that ran alongside the river and main street. Down below, the cars coming and going looked like toys.

The clock tower at the Falcon campus stuck up in the center of it all like the middle finger. Like it was saying, *Good job, Brooke Elliman, your daughter's a whore.*

She'd said things she regretted. Shouted things. While Sloane sat at the kitchen table, picking at a hangnail until it bled, Brooke had asked her, "Did you want those boys to think you have no self-respect? That your body is theirs for pleasure without your consent? That you don't love yourself enough to choose who gets to enjoy your beauty? My God!" Brooke hadn't been prepared for this, so her words fell out of her mouth like she was quoting some self-help manual from the discount table at the bookstore. It sounded cliché and puritanical, and she doubted she was reaching her daughter. "Why? Sloane. Answer me. Why?"

"Those photos were just for Reade. It was bad timing that I sent them to him while he was at Alistair's birthday party and some guys were looking over his shoulder. I never meant for anyone else to see them, and neither did Reade. It was between me and my boyfriend, and it got out of control. I do have self-respect, and it was a mistake. I made a mistake."

"Did he ask you to do it, or did you do it on your own?"

"He asked me. But I said yes. Please, Mom. Drop it. I don't want anyone else to know or anyone to get into any more trouble."

That conversation had taken place two days earlier, after the meeting at the school. Brooke had forced herself to take some time to think, process, and cool down before she allowed herself to react. Time was up. She couldn't wait any longer. She wouldn't go to the police, per her daughter's request. But she wasn't going to pretend it hadn't happened.

In the distance, there were fields dotted with small objects. Cows, horses, haystacks. Light green grass gave way to red boulders and gray peaks. There was still snow. There would always be snow. Brooke could see, though it was just a speck on the mountain opposite, the apartment building where Gabe no longer lived. There was also a paved road leading away from town, up, up into the adjacent hills, towards the Lelands' ranch and many of the other high-priced homes where families were raising boys that liked to look at and share photos of her daughter's naked body.

Brooke raised her phone and took a deep breath. "Hello, Mrs. Solomon. This is Brooke Elliman calling in regard to — well, I'm sure you know why I'm calling. If you could get back to me at this number, I would very much appreciate it."

She returned to her laptop and scrolled through her PTA directory until she came across the number for the Woodsons. Before dialing, she took a swig of her Cakebread cabernet. "Yes, hello, Mrs. Woodson. This is Brooke Elliman calling. If you would give me a call back at this number, I would very much appreciate it."

She repeated this procedure two more times, leaving the exact same message for the parents of Kasper Nowak and Alistair Reynolds.

There was just one call left to make. Reade's mother, Linda. Before dialing,

Brooke poured another glass of wine and sat there, staring at it for a full minute. Then she upended it into her mouth and drank the entire thing.

"Hello, Linda. This is Brooke Elliman calling. If you would give me a call back at this number, I would very much —"

She paused, feeling the wine pushing back up her throat. Phat Richard's' Deep Head Oral Anesthetic Spray. The Let's Do It Dice Game. (An awesome fucking game!) Mint-chocolate-chip-flavored lube. The future. Sloane's future, possibly ruined. The family, embarrassed. In the eyes of the world, the Elliman cake billionaire humiliated and humbled. "I would very much like to speak to you about what your son has done to my daughter —"

"Brooke?" Linda Leland suddenly picked up, and Brooke was absolutely astonished.

"Y-Yes. It's me."

"Hiiiiiii. I feel so bad about everything. I'm glad you called. It's so important that we talk about this for the sake of the kids."

"You're aware of what your son did?"

"I'm aware of what our kids did together, yes. Oh my gosh. It's so very upsetting."

"What they did *together*?"

"Together, yes," Linda said. "I'm extremely disappointed with Reade and his friends. But Sloane can be very convincing. She's remarkably . . . mature, isn't she?"

"She's fifteen, Linda."

Linda's voice was a little dreamy, like a stoned poet with a guitar on her lap. "Please, Brooke. It just means, you know, that some girls are ready for things before we, as parents, are ready for them to be ready."

"That's bullshit. That makes no sense. Are you high?"

"I'm sure it's very hard for you to hear this, Brooke. But the whole thing was Sloane's idea."

"Linda. Come on. We were both teenagers once. I know you don't have a daughter, but you have to understand that these girls, they don't plot their own abuse."

"Well, it's a *little* more nuanced than that I think, Brooke," Linda answered in a singsong way. "Reade was only the recipient of a gift from your daughter. My husband and I believe taking those photos for him was an honest, loving gesture on her part, no matter how poor her judgment may have been. But trust me, Brooke, I do realize my son isn't completely innocent."

Brooke resisted the urge to throw the phone against the wall. "I want a formal apology. In writing. A confession, if you will."

"Reade would be happy to apologize. That's a great idea. They can exchange apologies, and that will really help the healing process —"

"No! You don't understand what I'm saying. I want to see real consequences."

Linda was quiet for a second and then said, "Is that how we're going to talk to each other, then?"

"Yes. Reade should be punished. I would like to see your son dressed in a jumpsuit, picking up trash with his bare hands on the side of the highway."

"Fine. How about this? Reade no longer picks up trash. I've told him to stay away from your daughter." Linda was clearly awake now, and her soothing tone had been replaced by steel.

"You *bitch,*" Brooke said. "How dare you —"

"Mom!" Sloane yelled, coming up behind her and grabbing the cell phone out of her hand. "Mom? Stop. What are you doing?" Sloane ended the call.

Brooke stood up, found that she was shaking, and all she could think to do was grab her daughter. She pulled Sloane in for a desperate hug.

"What's wrong with you?" Sloane asked.

"I don't know," Brooke whispered. "I

don't know. I swear to God, I'm ready to murder someone."

Police Video Excerpt,
Falcon Academy Conference Room
Interview: Bellman, Natalie Marie
(Continued)

"Do you want to tell us any more about this tie?" Detective Bradley asks.

"I don't have anything more to tell you about the tie other than what I've already told you," Natalie answers.

"Do you want to tell me anything more about anything? This is getting exasperating. If you're innocent, you should be talking more."

"I'm just tired."

"Well, guess what, young lady. We're tired too. We're all tired. Work is tiring. Investigations are tiring."

Natalie nodded in agreement.

"You know I'm gonna keep doubling back on you."

Natalie spoke so softly that it was almost not an answer. "Okay. Whatever that means."

"We went over this. The people from the surveillance video that were in the gym yesterday are, in the following order, Assistant Athletic Director Nicholas Maguire. Linda Leland and her seventeen-year-old son, Reade. Reade's fifteen-year-old girlfriend, Sloane Elliman-Holt, and Sloane's mother, Brooke Elliman. And a woman by the name of Asha Wilson. And then there was you. In and out twice."

"And I said fine, I don't know, but if that's what you say, I believe you."

"Out of those people, who had problems with who?"

"Who had problems with who?" Natalie laughed. "Everyone had problems with everyone. The whole bunch. Every single last one of them had a reason to hate the other. Sometimes it felt like I was trying to do my job in a shark tank."

14

On the last day of school, it was all Natalie could do to stop herself from joining the students as they ran and wrestled in the halls, honked their horns, and blared music in the parking lot. It was summer vacation, and she would have Nick all to herself without the frustration of the Falcon moms flirting with him at every opportunity. She and Nick both had summer work responsibilities at the school, though far less than during the academic year. Her plan was to spend as much time as possible with Nick, and to move the evolving relationship forward from where it seemed stuck in the "casual fun" zone.

Two weeks — two wonderful weeks — of summer vacation passed by in a heartbeat. During that time, when they saw each other at school, Natalie's eyes would meet Nick's, and all it took was a small conspiratorial smile to make them sneak off to a storage closet or an empty classroom. They had been on several walks in the woods, a couple of visits to Sonic to get Jackson his popcorn chicken, and an evening drive in Nick's truck up to a scenic overlook, where they'd held hands and watched the sunset. They'd never been out for a "real date." Jay had pointed out that this was strange. But Natalie was willing to wait.

It seemed like perhaps her patience was about to be rewarded.

Nick had asked her to meet him in the athletic office that afternoon, and she'd had a nervous but hopeful feeling that they were about to take some sort of meaningful next step.

The school was mostly silent, and the halls without windows were gloomy. In the courtyard, the fountain continued to recycle its water and spit it into arcs over a beady-eyed, predatory falcon, but there was no one around throwing coins.

When Natalie arrived at the office to meet Nick, it was empty. Planning to look for him up on the mezzanine, she returned down the hall, which was lined with photo after photo of Falcon teams dating back decades. A picture hanging opposite the doors to the basketball courts caught her eye. She'd never taken much interest in the endless row of photos, but today the corridor was quiet and eerie, and something about this one had captured her attention for the first time. It was a portrait. Just one girl, kneeling with a soccer ball. All the team photos had the same plain wooden frame, but this one was special. It was shiny and silver.

Natalie leaned in to read the small print and realized the photo was of Jill Ruiz, the daughter — she assumed — of the woman Natalie had seen kneeling by the memorial stone bench on the ridge overlooking the valley and the school.

"Natalie!"

She spun around. There was Nick, silhouetted in the sunlight streaming in through the window behind him. She ran, and when she reached him, threw her arms around his neck. "Hey," she said, burying her nose in his chest. "Are you all done with work?"

"I am," he said. "Listen. I kind of went out on a limb and bought some stuff to make you dinner. Would that be fun? Are you hungry?" He seemed nervous, and she found it incredibly cute and sexy. "I mean, I don't know. Do you *want* to have dinner and hang out after? We could maybe get in the hot tub later?"

"Yes," Natalie. "Yes, to it all."

It wasn't just a hookup. It was a real date.

An hour later, Nick was cooking in loose athletic shorts and a T-shirt. The sliding doors leading off the kitchen were open. Jackson was happily gnawing on a dried pig ear while sunning himself on the balcony. Natalie was barefoot, and Nick was in a talkative mood. He opened a bottle of sauvignon blanc and poured himself a glass. "I know you don't drink," he said, "but it goes against my upbringing to not at least offer. Is that wrong? Am I being bad?"

"Not at all," Natalie said. "I'll have a little bit."

It felt nice, after several years, to have a small amount of quality wine in a long-stemmed glass. She swirled it around, smelled it, and tasted it.

"You look like a wine snob," he said, laughing.

"Oh, you know it," she answered. "Only the best. This barely meets my minimum criteria. The bouquet is off."

"You're kidding, right?"

"Of course I am. I don't know much about wine. My brother and I used to sometimes drink Gallo. I think it was like, four dollars for a jug that was bigger than my head."

Nick ripped open the bag of penne and dumped it into the boiling water. While stirring it with a wooden spoon, he said, "You're very easy to be with."

"Thank you," she said, raising her glass. "So are you."

"Makes me wish I had never —" He stopped stirring, looked back at her, and said, "Never mind."

"Never what?" she asked, taking a sip of her wine.

"It's complicated," he said.

"Come on, Nick. It's okay. What?"

"Never wasted so much of my life on a certain type of person. You know about Millie, right? It seems like everyone does."

"Millie is Amelie Bernard? The actress?"

"Yes."

"I only know what I've heard around the school." This was a lie. "Are you still . . ." Natalie hesitated ". . . involved with her?"

Nick peered down into the pasta water, and it was clear that he was buying time. "It's been a difficult relationship. She and I have broken up and gotten back together many times. At this point, we haven't seen one another in four months."

"That's not exactly an answer to my question."

Nick nodded. "I know. I'm sorry. I don't want to lie to you."

Natalie tried not to let the devastation

show. "I see. I feel like maybe that's my cue to go?"

"No. Please don't go. I'm going to tell you the truth."

Her stomach was in knots as she waited. "I can handle it." She wasn't sure if she could or not.

"Millie and I had — have — an agreement. We called it the 'dignity pact.' The idea was that if we fooled around with someone, it was best to spare one another the pain of going over the details. But if we moved on into a real relationship, we promised we would tell each other so that no one was humiliated or, you know, had the rug pulled out from under them."

"And?"

"And I've been waiting to see where this thing between us is going. I haven't told her about you yet. Maybe I should have. I was being cautious. I don't even know if you would take this seriously, given that you're so young compared to me. It's a scary feeling. That's the truth."

Natalie took another sip of her wine.

"You're not going to leave?" he asked.

"No, I'm not going to leave."

He pulled over one of the kitchen chairs so that he was sitting and facing her. He took her hands in his. "So?"

"So?" she repeated.

"So, I think I just kind of asked you if you're serious about me."

Natalie leaned forward and kissed him gently. "I am."

The penne was overcooked into a rubbery mess when they came back from the bedroom a half hour later, so Nick had to throw it out and start over. They drank more wine. It was delicious and made Natalie feel warm, fuzzy, and funny, and she wanted more, more, more. That was the problem and why she'd stopped drinking in the first place.

After they ate and Jackson had his dinner, they all three went into the living room. The big dog required half the couch, so Nick and Natalie sat practically on top of one another on the other side.

"Do you want to watch something?" Nick asked. "Maybe listen to some music?"

"Sure," she said, a glimmer of mean tease in her eye. "I'm okay with, like, Frank Sinatra, or whatever old vinyl records you have around."

"Oh," he said, pretending to be offended. "I see how it is. Very funny. I think you might have me confused with my dad? I'm forty-eight, not seventy-eight."

She held the couch pillow up against her

face to stifle her laughter.

"And guess what? I do have some Frank Sinatra. So now you're going to pay for age-shaming me, because we're going to listen to Frank. All. Night. Long. On repeat. While you try to sleep. Like you're a prisoner of war."

"You know what we should do?"

"Not listen to Frank Sinatra?"

"We should go outside and sit on the patio. It's such a pretty night. I've got something nice from my brother we could smoke."

"I don't smoke," Nick answered quickly.

"Oh, that's okay," Natalie said, faking a contrite look. "I don't very often."

"I don't like to do too much of anything that messes with the temple, if you know what I mean."

"I can see that," she said, reaching out to put her hand on his six-pack stomach. "And a very nice temple it is."

"Thank you. But just because I don't want smoke in my lungs, what with all the training I do, doesn't mean I don't like to relax," he said. "I think I might still have a couple of pot brownies from the dispensary in the pantry, but I definitely know I have a bag of gummies."

"That's even better. You scared me there

for a second. I was afraid you thought I was some sort of drug addict."

"Nah," he said. "I'm one of the cool kids. Which would you prefer, if it turns out I do have them both?"

"A gummy, I think."

"I'll be right back."

The wine and the sex and the delicious dinner and the fluffy dog . . . Natalie had not been so relaxed and carefree in a long time.

He came back into the room a minute later with two candies on a napkin. She plucked one up and looked at it. "How potent are they, do you know?"

"They're ten milligrams."

"Oh. Perfect. I haven't had one of these in a long time, but I'm pretty sure the last time I did, it was shaped like an actual Haribo gummy bear."

"Not anymore," he said. "They changed it so kids don't accidentally eat them. Even though some kids these days do stuff that's way crazier than edibles."

"I'm sure," she said, putting the candy in her mouth. "I've heard about our students and all the trouble they get into at their parties."

"It's probably worse than you think.

Honestly, I've seen some pretty shocking stuff."

Natalie resituated herself so that she could look straight at him. "Now I'm intrigued."

"Can you keep a secret? Seriously, if this were to get out, I would probably lose my job."

"I won't say a word."

"Well," he said. "Okay. I've been dying to tell someone. It has to do with all that hullabaloo in the office a few weeks back. You must have been wondering what was going on."

"Of course. The dingoes and their parents. Sudden mysterious suspensions?"

"Yes. So, you know Alistair Reynolds, right? His mom asked me and a couple of others from the sports office, Coach Carmen and Coach Andy, to chaperone an overnight birthday party for him on their ranch in Basalt."

"The mom wanted a woman to help chaperone a boy's sleepover birthday party?"

Nick laughed. "Yes. I think a lot of the moms like it when Coach Carmen is there too. Kind of like the woman is the chaperone for the chaperones."

"Really? Okay."

"Anyway. The Reynolds' barn has bunk

beds and can comfortably sleep twenty-four."

"Just a nice little guest house for their *second* home."

"Exactly. Carmen and Andy were going to ride out with me in the van with the boys. Ten of them, leaving on a Friday after school. And Alistair's little brother, Edmund, was there with two friends. And it wasn't a van that showed up. It was a Hummer limo for twenty stocked with snacks. They weren't drinking outright in front of us, but it was clear a few of them had brought some little bottles and were sneaking it into their Cokes."

"You're kidding. What did you do?"

"I kept an eye on the situation, but in a way, my hands were tied. When the parents are paying you gazillions of dollars an hour to do these events, it's kind of agreed that you're going to look the other way when it comes to a little bit of 'boys being boys.' "

"Hmm."

"But then it got worse. There was a feast when we arrived. Two caterers serving bison filet. Wild duck. Local salmon. But no one was eating because they were all in the bathrooms. I decided I was going to go bust them for whatever they were snorting, but when I went in, I found a group of ten boys looking at some images on a phone that they obviously found very shocking and funny. They didn't even know I was there, they were so glued to the screen. I leaned over and had a look. It was upsetting."

"What was it?"

"Photos of a Falcon girl. Inappropriate photos."

He didn't say the girl's name, but Natalie knew. She'd been there when Mrs. Elliman had showed up at the school looking like the world had ended.

"I confiscated the phone with the images, but they'd already been shared. I called Alastair's mom, who was up at the main house, and told her the party was over and why. She was furious with me. The shit hit the fan. I literally considered going to the police. I had a very serious disagreement about how to handle it with another one of the coaches, of which you're aware."

"I am?" Natalie asked, and then remembered the afternoon when Coach Carmen had nearly knocked her over in the stairwell, she was so angry and out of control, running away from a conversation with Nick. "Oh, right," she said. "I know what you're talking about."

"In the end, I took the matter to the headmaster. Bringing that to the attention of Mr. Dilly and having to deal with the parents' reactions was one of the hardest things I've ever had to do. And the poor girl. She's definitely been damaged by the experience."

"What a nightmare."

"It's infuriating," Nick said, closing his eyes and shaking his head. "Right before I stopped the party, Carmen said to me, 'Are you sure you want to do this? Look around. I bet you we're looking at the sons of the wealthiest, most powerful families in the whole damn state. Maybe the country.' And I thought to myself, I know stuff about these kids that could ruin their lives. I mean, literally, ruin their lives. I know the crimes. I know the drugs. I know the lies and the cover-ups. I was just sick of it. I didn't want to look the other way this time. Even now, I feel like I should have done more. But would I have lost my job? I don't know. They were punished, yes, but to the extent that they should been? They missed some school, got slapped on the wrist. I'm so angry. Do you know what I mean?"

"I do, Nick," she said. "I understand exactly how you feel."

"It's nice," he said, putting his arm around her and pulling her in close. "To be with someone who not only understands but is the complete opposite of all of that." He kissed Natalie's jaw, and she felt the urge to pull him down on top of her again. "Anyway, there was a lot of resentment. Against me for reporting it, among the boys' parents blaming one another, and even against the girl who was the victim. I've never seen civilized people acting so crazy. I honestly thought they were going to kill each other."

15

With Phil out of town again negotiating a "big deal," Asha was on her own to accompany Mia to the meeting with Mr. Maguire to get her signed up for summer private training.

A gray rubber wedge held open the front door of the sports pavilion. Asha and Mia went inside. There was a small lobby, a short flight of stairs that went up to the gym, and a long hall that led back to the locker rooms, the pool, and the stairs to the mezzanine. In front of them was a brick wall with a window. On the other side of the glass, Coach Carmen stood up and waved them around to the door. The sports office was a large room lined with desks and computers. Coach Carmen gestured towards two chairs. "Welcome to my cubicle," she said. "Please, have a seat."

"I was under the impression we were meeting with Mr. Maguire this evening,"

Asha responded, sitting.

"Yes, that's right. And I'm Carmen Sorella. The kids know me as Coach Carmen. Coach Nick got stuck in some traffic, and he'll be about fifteen minutes late. We can get started without him. I'm the licensed physical therapist, so I would be the one helping Mia deal with the issue of her shin splints. A great deal of her therapy would be under my supervision."

Carmen began to detail at length the different ways she planned to help Mia with her injury. Pain reduction, gait analysis, muscle stretches and strengthening, range of motion work, custom orthotics for arch support and on and on . . .

Asha tried to focus. Carmen was saying, "With an emphasis on activity modification over the summer, we can really reduce —"

"I'm sorry," Asha interrupted. "What activity modification are we talking about?"

"Replacing high-impact with swimming and cycling, primarily. Keeping the pressure off the shins."

So far, the meeting was not going the way Asha wanted. She was there to get extra-special help and attention from Mr. Maguire, not activity modification from Coach Carmen. "You know," Asha said, "we're not really here for this small problem with Mia's shin splints. It's not too big of a concern, really —"

"Oh, I'm afraid I would have to disagree," Carmen said. "Are you in pain when you're playing, Mia?"

"A little," she answered. After glancing at her mom, she said, "Like, sometimes. Not all the time."

Asha was not interested in paying one hundred twenty dollars an hour to Coach Carmen for instructing Mia on the proper way to do toe-raises for calf strengthening. This was about Mia being recruited for a Division I college team of her liking. "Mia has played soccer since she was five, and her shin splints have only been a nuisance, which we've treated with ibuprofen. They haven't stopped her from being one of the most promising players that Falcon has seen in many years. I was given the impression that these private training sessions were designed to advance —"

"Mrs. Wilson! Mia!" Nick said, rushing through the door of the sports office like he'd just sprinted across town. "So sorry I'm a few minutes late."

Mia mumbled, "Thank God," at the same time that her mom stood up to reach for his hand.

"I'm so glad you're here," Asha said. "It

seems like maybe there was some confusion about the reason we set up this meeting."

"Really?" Nick asked. "What's the problem?"

"We're more interested in a proactive approach to preparing Mia for the recruitment process than we are in her undergoing lengthy physical therapy for a minor injury."

Coach Carmen didn't say anything, but she was obviously annoyed.

"Okay, I see," Nick said, grabbing a chair and rolling it over. "Don't worry. I'll be working closely with Mia on all aspects of her preparation for college sports. She's going to get a lot of individual attention from me and Coach Carmen. That's the way we run the program. We share all the hats. Coach Carmen was probably discussing her plan of action to address Mia's injury, which is crucial if you want to have Mia playing at her optimal level next fall. I'll be stepping in on a regular basis to work with Mia on strategies for achieving her highest level of fitness and nutrition, as well as balancing the stress of homework and academic performance with the pressure that comes along with her unusual athletic talent."

Asha was finally pleased. "And what about preparing 'the package'? I heard from Brooke Elliman that there are a number of things we can do to promote Mia in the eyes of the top schools. That there is something like a package with videos, letters, essays, etcetera?"

"Yes," Nick said. "I'll spearhead that for Mia. Everything you mentioned and then some, and I will be personally reaching out to my own network on Mia's behalf. My goal is to get Mia at some tournaments and camps next fall where she can be noticed by the scouts representing her favorite schools."

"That sounds amazing," Asha responded. "Mia, doesn't that sound amazing?"

"*Totally* amazing," Mia said. Asha darted a look to see if that was sarcasm and embarrassment in her daughter's voice. It was. Asha wondered if Mia would prefer if she never spoke at all.

Nick pulled a piece of paper from a folder on the desk and looked it over briefly. Then he turned to Mia and said, "I made these notes the last time you and I sat down to do an evaluation of your experience here at Falcon. Please correct me if I'm wrong, but this is what I came away with from our discussion. Mia's dream college would be strong in liberal arts, ideally offering a film undergraduate degree."

Asha was nodding along as he talked up to this point, but then, little by little, she began to feel uncomfortable.

"Mia is looking for a change, an environment that is inclusive as well as diverse. She sometimes feels lonely in Falcon Valley, lacking in positive interactions with others of her ethnicity and without positive role models who . . ."

Asha's eyes slid to the side to see how Mia was reacting to this bullshit. No positive role models? What? *I'm sitting right here.*

But Mia wasn't rolling her eyes. She was watching him intently, and he kept glancing up at her as he talked. "One thing Mia knows for sure is that she wants to be able to travel. Both domestically and internationally, with a view to one day living and working overseas, possibly in Southeast Asia with a particular interest in Thailand. So, a school with a variety of foreign study opportunities abroad would be ideal."

Asha coughed and tried to smile, but she was absolutely sick. A semester overseas was one thing, but moving abroad? Did Mia want to get as far away from her as possible?

"I think a UC school rather than a private institution. No fake utopias. Real people, multicultural, progressive values. More adventure. A place where she can reinvent herself a little bit."

Reinvent as who? Asha thought angrily.

"Did I get that right, Mia?" he asked.

"You did," Mia said. "Just right."

"In the meantime," he said, turning to address Asha, "the best thing we can do is to make sure the university Mia wants will want her in return. Coach Carmen and I are pretty sure we can make that happen."

Coach Carmen, who'd been silent all this time, gave everyone a thin smile and a somewhat insincere nod of agreement.

Asha turned again to look at Mia, who was glowing. Pleased. Validated. Enjoying the spectacle of her mother realizing how little she understood about her plans to be reborn as someone totally different and then escape from her tedious family.

"Of course," he went on, "we need to be realistic. There's a lot of competition for those coveted spots. Even right here at our rather small school, there are contenders. It's going to be fierce."

Asha took a deep breath, choked down her ire, and said, "Whatever you think is best. I'll defer to your judgment." She reached into her bag and produced her checkbook. "Mia, you know I support your choices. What do you want to do? Start the privates next week?"

■ ■ ■ ■

At home an hour later, Asha said to the black cylinder sitting on the counter next to the sixty-jar wooden rotating spice rack, "Alexa, set timer for five minutes."

The sleek electronic device lit up briefly with a blue glow and responded in a polished feminine voice, "Five minutes, starting now."

Asha flipped each of the four chicken breasts sizzling in the pan and went back to her kitchen laptop. The page she had open said, "YOUR DUE DATE IS:"

She typed in, "December 16."

CONGRATULATIONS! YOU ARE ELEVEN WEEKS AND ONE DAY PREGNANT! Your baby is the size of a fig. Your baby will be a Sagittarius whose birthstone will be turquoise.

Following the initial rush of euphoria was a sour surge of anxiety. Asha had waited far too long to tell Phil. It had to be tonight. She couldn't keep it to herself any longer, and if he was unhappy about it, that was just tough.

The Alexa alarm went off, and Asha was, for one unsettling second, reminded of the oven timer beeping in the Leopold house a few weeks earlier, just before she'd found the pillow that stank of marijuana.

Asha turned off the heat underneath the chicken, covered the pan, and walked up the stairs and down the hall to give Oliver a dinner warning. He got upset if he was in the middle of a game and was forced to leave without plenty of advance notice. She paused outside his room. Oliver was seated at his desk in front of his computer, wearing the headset that Phil had gotten him for his birthday, playing *Fortnite.* When she knocked, he gave her a quick wave that was not a greeting but rather a dismissal. *Go away.*

Asha poked her nose in. "Hi, Oliver," she said, glancing around. It smelled like rotten fruit. "Dinner in thirty."

Oliver cast a confused look in her direction, then back at the screen. He yanked his headset off. "What? I was in the middle of a round, and now I'm dead."

"I'm sorry. Dinner in thirty," Asha said, retreating. "That's all."

Oliver put his headphones back on and went back to pounding the keys.

Phil was still not home. Mia was in her room studying. The burner underneath the chicken was off, and the rice was on simmer. There was no reason she couldn't lie down for ten minutes. The idea of closing her eyes, even for a brief amount of time, was intoxicating. She went into her room, closed the blinds, and stretched out on the bed. From down the hall, she could hear Oliver shouting at the top of his lungs, "Over there! He's over there! Hit one, hit one. One down, one down!"

Asha pulled a blanket over her face. It didn't help. She said to her bedroom Alexa, "Alexa, play babbling brook."

The sound of water rushing over stones in the wilderness filled the room and drowned out Oliver's voice. Asha closed her eyes.

That's how Phil found her forty-five minutes later.

"There you are," he said, standing in the double doorway. "I didn't even know you were in the house."

Asha tried to sit up. "I fell asleep."

"I can see that. You left the stove on and came up to take a *nap*?"

Asha was suddenly very awake. "Why are you talking to me like that?"

"What? In an irritated tone? Maybe because I'm irritated with you."

"Why?"

"Because irresponsible behavior irritates

me, and you've been acting irresponsibly lately."

"Jesus," Asha said, rolling off the bed. "What have I done?"

"You don't know where your keys are, have you seen my phone, what day is it again? Napping, leaving the stove on, and . . ." He paused dramatically. "Mia says you signed a form for her, saying she's allowed to get medical injections from the trainer. No one said anything to me. Did you do that?"

"The medicine for Mia is just an anti-inflammatory shot every once in a while when she needs it. It's no stronger than Advil."

"Then why not just give her Advil?"

"I don't know! I'm not the trainer, am I? This is what college athletes do, okay? It's supposed to cure her shin splints so that she'll be competitive next fall when the recruiters are all scouting her. It's very common. Just a little prick." This made her laugh. " 'Little prick.' Kind of like the way you're acting right now."

"Oh. So, this is funny to you?"

"Kind of. Yeah. It is. Two can play this stupid game, you know. I can ask you what the hell is wrong with you lately."

"I'm trying to close a big deal, and on top

of that, I'm worried. I'm worried about work, I'm worried about the kids, and I'm worried about you!"

Asha thought of what Brooke had said to her at the school movie night weeks earlier. "Phil has a lot going on. Give him some time, you know, to sort things out." So, Brooke had been right. Phil did have worries, lots of worries. When had he confided in Brooke about these concerns? What the hell was going on? A high school soccer coach knew her own daughter better than she did, and now Brooke had the inside scoop on her husband's mental fitness to deal with family matters? Even though they hadn't seen each other in ages? Asha was livid.

"Oh my God," she said, straightening her clothes. "Cut me some slack. So, I took a nap. You're overreacting."

"If I have to go out of town on business, I need to know that you're manning the ship." He filled the doorway, stopping her from going past.

"I'm manning the ship, Phillip. Get out of my way. You're being a ridiculous asshole."

He stepped aside and said, "Am I?"

"Yes, you are," she said, heading down the hallway to the top of the stairs.

"I'm not the ridiculous asshole who signed

my teenage daughter up for private training sessions with David Beckham. I believe the ridiculous asshole who did that without talking to me first was you, Asha."

"We *did* talk about it."

"I never said yes. I would *not* have said yes. Have you seen the handout the trainer sent home with her? Pills containing eggshell membranes? Hot stone therapy and foot arch massages? Training logs and a special diet?"

"She wanted to."

"Mia wants to swim with sea turtles in Micronesia and dig latrines for orphans in Guatemala, but we're not signing her up for that tomorrow."

"I think it will be good for her."

"You think it's going to be good for her to do these shady-ass private sessions with Rob fucking Lowe?"

"Do you have any other reason for not liking Mr. Maguire aside from the fact that he's an attractive man?"

Phil ran a hand through his hair. He was sweating. "What if she decides she, you know, likes him?"

Asha laughed out loud. "That is crazy, Phil! That is the craziest thing I've ever heard. He's got to be what, forty-five?"

"I've seen how women around here act

when he walks up. Every single one of you reaches for your lipstick at the exact same second."

"Not me. Don't lump me in with them."

"I'm right though, aren't I?"

"Mia's not going to develop a crush on Mr. Maguire, Phil."

"How can you be so sure?"

"What was the name of her last boyfriend?" Asha demanded. "No, better yet, name one boy she's ever been interested in." Phil frowned. "You can't, because it hasn't happened, even though she's fifteen and drop-dead stunning and her best friend has a boyfriend."

"What are you implying?" Phil asked, following Asha. "You can't just walk away after making a claim like that. Do you know something I don't know?"

"Shh, she'll hear you," Asha said, navigating the stairs with one hand on the banister.

"Does that mean what I think it means?"

"I don't know what it means! It could mean anything. But what if it does?" Asha asked. "Are you going to call up my uncles in Mumbai and get the wheels turning on an arranged marriage? You're acting like a Neanderthal. Leave her alone! And you know what? Leave me alone, too!"

Phil followed her down the stairs and

grabbed her arm. "This is serious. Don't play with me."

"No, Phil. Don't play with *me.* I'm eleven weeks pregnant, and our baby is the size of a fig, and I am tired and forgetful and also extremely hormonal. I am not having this conversation with you right now."

"You're pregnant?" he asked, his face turning quickly from flushed to a milky white.

"Yes. I am. Now take your hand off my arm and walk away right now before I yell for the kids and tell them Daddy is hurting me and I need help. Do you understand?"

Apparently, he did.

16

It was proving very difficult for Brooke to keep close tabs on Sloane during the breezy, sunny, empty, lazy days of the seemingly endless summer break. She'd suggested that Sloane might get a job. At a clothing store, a tourist trap, maybe even a fun restaurant, to which Sloane had responded, "Sure. I can do that. What kind of job did you like when you were my age? Or *any* age? Oh sorry, my bad. You've never had a job, have you?"

Brooke decided that was not a conversation she wanted to pursue.

At the moment, Brooke was alone in the waiting room at the dermatologist, enveloped in a cocoon of cool jazz, the overwhelming scent of essential oils, and the glow of a lavender vanilla candle. It was awful.

"Brooke Elliman?" a woman in a white jacket called, swinging open a door.

"That's me," Brooke said, throwing aside one of the magazines on offer in the room that was too dark to read in.

The recommended window between Botox injections was four to six months. Brooke had only gotten her last treatment three months earlier, but Gabe was shacked up with a girl twenty years younger, and the other man she found attractive was a coach who was constantly surrounded by teenagers who hadn't yet experienced their first wrinkle. Brooke was determined to stay relevant and competitive.

She was escorted to an examination room with a comfortable recliner. A few minutes later she was joined by a woman with flawless skin, carrying a tray with an array of small needles. After using an alcohol wipe to sterilize Brooke's face, the aesthetician said, "I'm going to start just above your eyebrows. Then we'll move up to your hairline, and then at the end, we'll do the fine lines around your eyes. And here we go."

"Um," Brooke said, feeling the first sting and trying to remain relaxed. "Ow. *Ow.*"

"Very good. I've just completed the area above your right eyebrow."

"Thank you for the blow-by-blow, but seriously, I'm not nearly as interested in what you're doing every single second as I am in us just being done."

The aesthetician laughed. "I understand, Mrs. Elliman."

Brooke glanced down into her lap where her phone was resting. Gabe had taken Sloane out to lunch, but it appeared he'd already dropped her off. The little red dot that was Sloane was now back in the house.

After the uproar about the photos of Sloane, Brooke had forced her daughter to log into her Facebook, Instagram, TikTok, and Snapchat accounts so Brooke could change the passwords. This was simply a punishment. There was not much Brooke could do if Sloane allowed Reade to take more photos of her on his own phone, and so Sloane was grounded.

"Should I take it away entirely?" she'd called Gabe to ask.

"I don't think so," he'd replied. "To leave a teenage girl without a phone is to leave her helpless in the event of an emergency. Also," he pointed out, "if you want to be able to track Sloane's activity, her phone is the only way to do so outside of having her microchipped."

"Can I do that?" Brooke had asked in follow-up, and Gabe had responded, "Actually, no. I looked into it, and the battery pack required is too big to be implanted under her skin."

"So, if she gets to keep her phone, is there any way I can stop her from texting this boy, Reade?"

"I don't know, Brooke," Gabe answered. "There's probably an app for that. I'll look into it and get back to you."

That had been several days earlier.

The aesthetician completed the last six pokes into Brooke's temples to soften the hint of crow's feet in the corners. "All done."

Brooke stood up and looked in the mirror. "I'm bleeding."

"Yes, you are." The aesthetician handed her a cotton ball. "Why don't you have a seat in the tranquility lounge and wait for it to stop? I'll bring you a green tea or a glass of chardonnay."

Brooke checked her phone again. Sloane's two-hour private training session was in an hour. "I've got to get home." She pulled half a dozen twenty-dollar bills out of her wallet to tip the aesthetician twenty percent on the six-hundred-dollar treatment.

"Thank you, Mrs. Elliman. I look forward to seeing you again very soon."

Brooke exited the Med Spa, located in a suburban shopping mall, into the bright sunlight of an early July morning. She lowered her sunglasses over her eyes and pulled her keys out of her Birkin bag.

"Look who it is," a sugary voice called. A woman was walking down the sidewalk, straight towards Brooke. She had wavy white-blond hair. Beach tousled, some would say, and a willowy, reed-blowing-in-the wind body that looked like it was no stranger to yoga and Pilates. She wore a gauzy sundress with a big leather belt, cowboy boots, and a long denim jacket, and was clinking as she walked, laden with indigenous jewelry.

"Crap," Brooke whispered. "Linda." She was about to remove her sunglasses for a standoff when she remembered that she might be bleeding in several places. She stopped and waited for Linda to approach.

"What a surprise," Linda said sweetly.

Brooke was instantly suspicious that this was an ambush. She told herself to behave. They were in public. "Good morning, Linda."

"Are you coming from the . . ." Linda looked around.

"From the Med Spa?" Brooke prompted. "Yes. I am. I was in desperate need of a massage. Are you headed there yourself?"

"Oh no," Linda said, pointing to the other

side of the parking lot, past the Hobby Lobby. "I'm headed to the Bullet Hole."

"What?" Brooke leaned in questioningly. She thought Linda had said the Bullet Hole.

"The Bullet Hole," Linda confirmed, shifting her weight so that her denim blazer swung slightly to the side. She was wearing a gun holster on that big, pretty, bedazzled leather belt.

"Oh," Brooke said, frowning. "The Bullet Hole is the firing range, right?"

"Yep."

"I always took you for kind of a . . ." Brooke searched for a term other than *tree hugger*. "A pacifist type."

"Oh yeah, I am, for sure," Linda answered, tossing her hair. "But I mean, come on, this is Colorado, right? You know. Howard and I are responsible gun owners. You need to be able to look after yourself here." Linda paused. "If you're a mama bear like me, you've got to be able to protect your kids. Know what I mean?"

Brooke was thankful for the sunglasses, because she could feel her eyes widening in disbelief and complete fury. "Sure do," she managed to reply casually.

"You have a gun, right?" Linda asked.

"Absolutely," Brooke lied. She had no idea what had happened to the pistol Gabe had once stored in a gun safe in the basement. He might have taken it with him when he left. She had never touched it nor asked about it.

"Well, I gotta go," Linda said. "Have a nice day."

"And you have fun at the Bullet Hole."

"Thanks!" Linda waggled her fingers and walked on down the sidewalk.

Once she was in her car, Brooke googled the Bullet Hole. It was closed on Mondays. Linda had to have been following her. She had been in that parking lot for only one reason.

On the way home, Brooke kept an eye out for the sight of Reade's giant white G Wagon. If it came tooling down the mountain from the direction of her house, Brooke would know that he'd been to visit Sloane. The girl had only been alone for an hour, but that was enough time. It wasn't likely, especially since Brooke had made it clear that she'd had a camera installed to record the front door. On the other hand, she didn't put it past that boy to bring over his rock-climbing equipment so he could scale the side of her mansion just to get into Sloane's pants.

There was no G Wagon in the driveway.

The house seemed quiet. Brooke put her purse down in the kitchen and then pushed the button on the intercom. "I'm home."

Sloane's voice responded a second later. "Hi."

"What are you doing?"

"Reading."

"Get dressed for your private, will you? We'll leave in fifteen."

"Okay."

Sloane sounded depressed, and it made Brooke sad. What else was she supposed to do, though? How else could she keep Sloane from self-annihilation?

Ten minutes later, Sloane showed up in the kitchen with her backpack, dressed in leggings, a T-shirt, and her tennis shoes.

Brooke filled up Sloane's water bottle from the filtered tap on the fridge and then pushed a piece of paper along the counter towards her. "Don't forget to give Coach Carmen this. Put it in your backpack."

"What is it?" Sloane asked, knotting her hair with a band.

"It's the waiver about your Ketorolac injections. You have to sign it."

Sloane took the pen Brooke handed to her. "How much longer do I have to do those?"

"Every few weeks until your knee gets better and you're able to impress the scout from UCLA and get your letter of intent."

"I don't like them," she said, signing the paper.

"It's one teeny tiny little needle."

"I don't like needles," Sloane said, giving Brooke a wide-eyed glare. "Unlike some people I know. Spectacular bruise, by the way."

"I'm going to remind you of this conversation when you're getting Botox at forty-four," Brooke said breezily. She wasn't going to let Soane get to her.

"Please. You probably won't even still be alive when I'm forty-four."

And, there it was. Sloane had gotten to her. "What a cruel thing to say! You should be grateful I haven't shipped you off to Italy to commit you to some isolated Catholic monastery in the mountains where the nuns throw potatoes at you if you even think about letting boys take naked photos of you when you're fifteen!"

"Nice."

"Get in the car."

"You might want to grab a tissue. The blood is about to drip down into your eye."

"Get in the car *now.*"

They arrived early for the private. Sloane

went upstairs to the mezzanine to get started with Coach Carmen, but Brooke was hoping to have a conversation with Nick.

She pushed open the sports office door and was shocked by what she saw.

Miss Bellman from the front office was sitting on his lap.

Actually, that wasn't an adequate description of what was happening. Miss Bellman was straddling him in his office chair. Her legs — clad in running shorts, athletic socks, and tennis shoes — hung to either side of his body. Her hair was pulled back into a tiny ponytail. She looked at Brooke and said, "Shit, Nick."

"Christ!" Nick blurted. He attempted to stand then and there, which caused Natalie to fall backwards off his lap, catching herself with one hand on the desk.

"Excuse me, I'm sorry," Brooke said. She didn't leave.

"Natalie — Miss Bellman was just about to go, weren't you?" Nick said.

"Yes," Natalie answered, looking around for her things.

"Thank you, Miss Bellman," he said, fumbling to untuck his shirt and pull it out over his shorts before standing. "For — um — your help with that. I will see you in a few days."

"Yes, you will." Natalie grabbed her workout bag and a bottle of water from the desk.

Brooke glared at Natalie in a way that was unnerving. It was more than just the fact that Nick had rejected her and gone for this pale, spotty, ginger-haired office assistant. It was Gabe too, and his twentysomething fling. The only thing these girls offered was plain, simple, boring youth, and yet the men were eating it up like it was an extravagant Michelin five-star feast.

Natalie left, brushing past Brooke without a word.

Once Natalie was gone, Nick said, "I'm so sorry. I do have a personal life. I try to keep it under wraps," he said, gesturing helplessly with an uncomfortable laugh. "To no avail, obviously. That was awkward."

"I thought you were still with Millie. That's what you told me."

"That wasn't a lie, exactly. Millie and I haven't 'officially' ended our relationship."

Brooke flipped her hair back behind her shoulder, and for a second, she looked like a hurt teenaged girl. "It stings a bit, seeing that. When we had our 'moment' and then didn't have any more, I thought you were just being faithful to Millie."

"What happened between you and me,

Brooke —"

"I understand. It was just a kiss."

"But it wasn't just a kiss, was it? Because a week later, your husband moved out. You two are separated now. Don't you think I feel some sort of guilt and responsibility?"

"It's not your fault. It isn't. It's all on me."

"Please don't be so hard on yourself. This is a gray area for me too. I train your daughter. I'm her coach. I could be accused of showing favoritism to her if you and I were to get involved, and we don't want that, right? Because we both want me to do my absolute best for her and for her to shine on her own. I don't want even one person out there to say I put her forward because of any reason other than the fact that she's remarkable. And I hate to say this, because it sounds, I don't know. Kind of overly sensitive. But there have been times when I've felt like —" He cut himself off uncomfortably.

"Like what?"

"That your interest in me is somehow transactional. For lack of a less politicized term, I occasionally get the feeling that you're offering me something in return for my loyalty, and that makes me uncomfortable."

"I can't *believe* you just said that," Brooke

snapped.

"Why? If you were me, you wouldn't be wondering if your interest in me and your interest in what I can do for your daughter were somehow related? Am I supposed to just ignore it?"

"It's not transactional. It's just —" Brooke struggled to find the right word. "It's real. I like you. I like talking to you. I like how you care about my daughter."

"But Brooke, don't you see? I don't feel like it's appropriate for us to go there, no matter how attractive I find you, given that I am inextricably involved in the future of all Falcon students, not just Sloane."

Brooke mulled this over before crossing her arms defensively. "I see what you're saying. You're going to recommend Mia to the UCLA scout, aren't you?"

"No," Nick said. "I'm going to represent both girls and let Janet decide who's right for their team."

"You're going to choose Mia. Even though I've been paying for the privates for over a year."

Nick threw up his hands. "You're proving my point. I don't make the choices, Brooke. I help and I advise, and I do what I think is best. That's what I've been doing for Sloane all this time."

Brooke studied him with a curled lip. "Interesting," she said.

"What's interesting?"

"You do make choices. You chose her. I wouldn't have thought she was your type."

"Mia?" he asked, at a loss for where the conversation was going.

"No," she said, sighing in a way that made her seem depleted somehow. Done with it all. "Miss Bellman."

Nick tented his fingers together and leaned back in his chair. "Brooke. I care about your daughter's future. And honestly, I care about you too. But I don't understand why you seem to think that you know me so well. I really don't think you know me at all."

Police Video Excerpt,
Falcon Academy Conference Room
Interview: Bellman, Natalie Marie
(Continued)

Detective Larson has taken over Detective Bradley's chair and Natalie's planner is out on the table in front of them both. She keeps tapping at passages like an after-school tutor.

"I'm looking at mid-July," Detective Larson says.

Natalie has located a loose string at her wrist and is busy twirling it around a cuff button. Coiled. Uncoiled. Coiled. Every few minutes she uses one foot to scratch at the other. Her eye has begun to twitch.

"I used to be a college athlete," Detective Larson says. "This workout entry for the end of the week in late July says, 'Biceps, triceps, overhead press. Twenty minutes of core, six miles, squats and lunges, two thousand calories.' "

"Yes."

"You did all that and allowed yourself two thousand calories?"

"I don't really remember exactly, but that sounds correct."

"And then it says, 'Down to one hundred and five. Yay!' To me that seems like you lost twenty pounds pretty fast."

"I guess so."

"This regimen doesn't seem sustainable," Detective Larson goes on. "And the weight loss seems impossible." She pauses. "But then again, maybe not that surprising. Not considering all the drugs that were involved."

17

The summer break was passing by far too quickly. Natalie had meant to drive back to Denver and stay a week with her mom. She and Yvonne had tossed around the idea of a girls' getaway weekend at the Cheyenne Spa. Also, she'd intended to accept and complete half a dozen pet portrait requests she'd received from Etsy customers.

Instead, she'd been tired. Very tired, yet strangely happy and content. Nick loved nothing more than to hike, bike, run, and lift weights on their free summer break days, and she had been joining him with a smile on her face even when her legs felt like lead. He simply had more stamina, and she didn't want him to think she couldn't keep up. She was young, after all. And so she did keep up: pretending a twisted ankle was painless, taking more of Jay's painkillers to help with a pulled muscle in her lower back, saying she was fine when actually she was suffering from seasonal allergies. At night she crashed, completely wiped out, her body aching. In her free time, she dreamily reflected on her last get-together with Nick and looked forward to the next. It was a feverish chapter, a first love, a first understanding of real lust and longing. She felt like she was under a spell, a wonderful spell, and that her routine life had been transformed into something far more meaningful and hopeful.

Jay disagreed. "To me, this whole story about his famous on-again, off-again Canadian girlfriend is like, a loser band camp lie. Do you know what I mean? Guys go to summer band camp and there's this one guy who says he has a girlfriend, but she lives in Canada so no one can ever meet her. It's weird."

Natalie was unpacking some groceries for him. "No need to be so judgy," she said. "It's still early days." It wasn't, really. It had been almost three months, but Natalie was trying not to think about that. "I brought you Ben and Jerry's, by the way."

"Awesome," he said, taking the white plastic shopping bag from her. "Ooh. Urban Bourbon. Thanks for not getting me Chunky Monkey." He grabbed a roll of fat and said, "I hobbled into the bathroom this morning and had a good long look in the mirror. My Tom Hanks *Cast Away* beard is, like, the envy of every hipster, but my once athletic bod has gone to pot. Literally to pot. Weed."

"Don't worry. You've still got that a-dork-able thing going on. We need to get you out more, though. Even if it's just for a walk."

Rocky was lying down in the corner with his head resting on his front paws. Both eyes were fixed on Natalie, and he cocked one ear to the side at the word *walk*.

"Don't look at me that way," she said in response to Rocky's moody, expectant stare. "You need to just hold your horses while we have ice cream. If you're good, you might even get a treat."

Rocky's tail started thumping back and forth against the wall.

Natalie got two small bowls out of the kitchen cabinet and grabbed a scoop from the drawer. She scooped up their ice cream, and they immediately took their seats at the kitchen table. They had done this countless times.

"You sound like you're maybe getting serious about the coach," Jay said unhappily.

"Please don't call him the coach. His name is Nick."

"Natalie, don't take this the wrong way, but I'm not quite ready to accept that my sister, who has a ton of daddy issues because ours left, is going to end up with some sort of father figure as the love of her life. You deserve so much more than that."

"I like what I've got right now, Jay. It would be nice if you would stop making me feel bad for being happy."

They ate the rest of their ice cream in silence, and when Natalie was down to her last bite, she offered it to Rocky, who was very excited to lick the spoon.

"Come on, boy," she said. "Walk? Who wants to go for a walk?"

Rocky did, and danced gleefully at her feet, making it nearly impossible to clip on his collar.

"I'm sorry," Jay called, looking down into his empty ice cream bowl as she left the kitchen.

"I don't care," she answered.

It wasn't true. She did care. If anything, she cared too much.

As usual, she grabbed a Vicodin from her brother's bathroom before setting out into the hills with Rocky for his walk. It had become one of her favorite routines: the beauty of the woods, the joy of a happy, healthy, curious dog, the comfort of a relaxing pill, the anticipation of seeing Nick, who she adored, and who made her feel valuable.

An hour and a half later, after freshening up at her apartment, she pulled up outside Nick's townhome, ready for a hike. She'd mostly been able to forget the strained conversation with her brother. Not important. Other people weren't supposed to understand. She wasn't naive. She knew she was infatuated, and she was enjoying every second.

She and Nick loaded Jackson up in the truck, and drove through town and another thirty minutes to the opposite side of the valley. They stopped in a wide spot in the road, not far from a trailhead with a wooden sign for Tuttle Lake Trail.

They started walking, and Jackson had an enthusiastic pee on just about everything he could find. Natalie had to stop and sit twice, feeling dizzy, but she told Nick it was nothing. It took three quarters of an hour to thread their way through the forest and clamber up and over boulders before emerging at the lakeside, surrounded by cliffs and tall trees.

As she turned in a circle, admiring the natural amphitheater created by the surrounding rocks, Nick took a steel stake from his backpack and drove it into the ground with his boot. He looped Jackson's leash around it and put out a collapsible rubber bowl. After pouring some water for the dog, he opened his backpack and produced a giant plaid picnic blanket. Natalie helped him spread it out over the grass on a ledge overlooking the lake.

He began to pull out some sandwiches. "I got tuna salad, egg salad, and chicken salad. I figured we could share depending on which one is your favorite. Or, if you're not that hungry, it can be one for me, one for you, and one for Jackson."

Upon hearing his name, Jackson began to wag his tail.

"That's sweet," Natalie said, leaning towards Nick to give him a peck on the cheek, while putting her hand on his leg.

He took hold of her wrist and turned it over to the inside, to see her tattoo better. It looked like a bar code that you might find on something at the supermarket, it was so small, rectangular and dense. It said,

SELF
LOVE

Nick held her arm and looked in her eyes with some concern. "How have I never noticed that before?"

"Well, it's only tiny," she answered.
"And you usually wear that big old black leather bracelet over it. Right?"
"Right. I do." She laughed. "I bought that big old black bracelet specifically for the purpose of covering it up when I don't feel like talking about it."
"Do you feel like talking about it now?"
"I don't know." Natalie never wanted to discuss it, but here he was, genuinely curious, caring about what she might say. "Something bad happened that I struggled with, and when I got a little older, I got this tattoo to remind me that I loved myself no matter what."
"I'm sorry that something bad happened to you," he said.
"It's okay."
"Did someone hurt you?"
Natalie nodded. "But I don't want you to think that I'm some wounded and broken person. I'm not. I'm good. I've got a little baggage, maybe —"
"Shh. That's not what I was thinking at all. In fact, the actual thought that was going through my mind was, 'She's perfect.' "
"Really?"
"Yeah. And I know I'm probably about a decade late, but maybe I can kiss it better?"
She nodded again.

"It's okay?" he asked, touching her bottom lip.

"It's okay."

His mouth was about to cover hers when his phone rang. The moment was over. He pulled it out of his pocket, looked crossly at the screen, and pressed a button to ignore the call.

"Is something wrong?"

"Brooke Elliman keeps calling and texting me, saying it's important."

"Oh." Natalie was frustrated but thought it best not to say more.

"I don't need to talk to her now. I'll call her later." He turned his phone facedown on the blanket and smiled at Natalie. "Between you and me, she's a little . . ." He spun one finger next to his ear. "Cuckoo."

"Really? In what way?"

"Just in a hyper-intense, emotional, melodramatic kind of way. She's very needy, and she's used to getting all of her needs met as soon as she snaps her fingers. She has a temper."

"What sort of needs are we talking about?"

"Oh no," he answered. "Ha. Come on. Don't go there."

"Is she trying to *go there*? With you?" Natalie's tone was teasing, but it was clear she wanted to know.

Nick looked slightly uncomfortable.

"I thought she acted really weird when she walked in on us the other day in the sports office. Way more shocked than she should have been. I mean, we're all adults."

"Well," Nick said. "That's true. I mean —"

"What?"

"I do kind of have a history with her."

"Did you sleep with her?"

"No."

"Are you sure?"

Nick burst out laughing. "Yes, Natalie, I'm sure. I know who I've slept with. I can write that down and give you the whole list if you'd like."

"That sounds like it would be some fun reading for me, but I'm going to pass."

She'd expected a sarcastic, funny comment in return, but for the first time since they'd started dating, Nick seemed unamused by her humor. "Good," he said. "It would be nice if it didn't come up again."

As they drove home, Natalie said, "We're about to pass the turn-in for my apartment. Do you want to see it?"

"Do you want me to?"

"Sure," she said, nodding. "We could order some pizza."

Natalie had been thinking that having him

over to her place was some sort of rite of passage that would mean they were getting more serious, but she regretted her invitation the second they walked in the door. She'd tried to make the small space cozy. Shabby and furnished mostly with repurposed and brightly painted antiques from yard sales, the studio had a determined cheeriness to it. It was artsy in a mainstream Urban Outfitters way with throw pillows on the floor and wine bottles plugged with dried flowers or melted candles. What was unique about the somewhat squalid place was the menagerie of watercolor paintings everywhere, as if it were a tiny low-rent art gallery without enough wall space. Jack Russell terriers and pugs hung next to a potbellied pig and an aloof, exotic bird.

"Your paintings are really something," he said, strolling around to look at each in turn, his hands clasped behind his back. It took about thirty seconds to make his way around the entire room.

"Those are the ones I did back when I was an instructor at Pinot's Palette in Denver. I don't have many new ones because I sell them."

He nodded and said, "Mmm. Very impressive." Natalie had hoped that Nick would find her apartment kind of youthful and charming, but she could tell, as he sat on her Goodwill couch, that he wasn't comfortable. Suddenly it was as if her creative space came across as a cheap, embarrassing artist's squat. "I do like it," he said, crossing his legs. "It's got so much personality."

She felt that she needed to reverse course, so she gave him a playful smile. "And now that you've seen my place, should we go back to yours and get in the hot tub?"

"Great minds think alike," he said, standing. Natalie tried to ignore the relief on his face.

The next morning, Natalie was in Nick's bed. Jackson was also there, down by the bottom, snoring and twitching in his sleep. She woke up to the sound of a phone ringing. "Nick," she said, nudging him.

"Hmm, baby?"

"Your phone."

He grabbed it and peered at it. After a second, he typed in the passcode to retrieve a message. He didn't cover the keypad with his hand, and she recognized the number. It was the address of Falcon Academy. 2258.

"Shit," he said, sitting up.

"What?"

"I'm going to have to deal with this."

"Is everything okay?"

"Brooke Elliman. She's saying she *has* to see me. It's *urgent.*" He rolled his eyes and pushed the comforter down to his waist. "I've got to get up."

"Wait. You're actually going? Really? Where?"

"She's got an apartment just up the road at Koi Creek. It's only a five-minute drive. I'll be back soon. We can have lunch before I go to the gym for my privates."

Natalie turned away, but he caught her expression. He raised himself up on his elbow and looked down at her with a funny smile. "You don't like that, do you?"

"Like what?"

"It bothers you. I've noticed. It's not just the Brooke thing, but it's the training sessions too. Am I right?"

"No," Natalie said. "Who is it today, anyway?"

"Reade, Mia, Jeremiah, and Sloane."

"Good money, I guess," she said, disliking the tone of her own voice. She was being horrible, and they both knew it.

"Someone is jealous," Nick sang, grinning. "And I don't mean Jackson."

"Okay, okay. Maybe slightly," Natalie admitted. "I'm human. I wish it was us, going for a run or a bike ride instead."

"Well, let's do that, then."

"Do what?"

"I'll train you."

"No," Natalie said, shaking her head. "Come on. I was just joking."

"We should do it, though," Nick said, starting to get excited. "It would be fun. Do you like to swim?"

"Not really."

"Okay, so a triathlon is out, but we could prep for my Muddy Funster duathlon together. I bet we could get you down from a body mass index of twenty-five to eighteen and you'd look and feel great."

Natalie stared at him. "What's wrong with my body mass index?"

"Nothing's wrong with it," he answered. "You're lovely. But didn't you used to be an athlete?"

"An athlete? Not really. I played rec softball. I rode bikes with my brother and snowboarded with my friends a few times a year. I work out to stay in shape, but I was never any fitness freak."

"Well, would you like to be? I can show you what I do with my 'trainees.' We can come up with a program and set some goals. It's more time together. I'll have someone to run and ride with. Come on."

Natalie looked sleepy and doubtful. "I don't know."

"I haven't even told you the best part."

"What's that?"

"I'm going to give you my friends and family discount. Only ninety dollars an hour. That's twenty-five percent off."

Natalie hit him with her pillow, and he grabbed it and hit her right back. She was already wondering what Jay would say if she told him that she had decided to let Nick tell her what to eat and how many push-ups to do. "I'll think about it," she said.

"Fair enough," he said. "And now I have to go. The cake empire queen doesn't like to be kept waiting."

Natalie went back to sleep while he got ready to leave. Two hours later she woke to the sound of Nick running the sink in the attached bathroom. "Nick?" she called. "You're home?"

"Hey, Sleeping Beauty," he called back.

"So, how did it go with Mrs. Elliman?"

"Fine," he answered. "Annoying, but fine. She's obsessed with getting her daughter into the right school and thinks I can help. That's really all it is."

Natalie had been hoping for a little more detail.

"That was some nap. I must be wearing you out," he said playfully, standing in the bathroom door and looking gorgeous.

"I know," she said. "Lately it's like I'm always tired."

"The great thing about us starting to train together is that you'll have more energy in no time."

"I hope so, because right now, honestly? I feel like crap."

"Really, babe?" Nick asked. He scrounged around underneath the sink for a second and stood up. "Do you want something to help you wake up?"

"If it's a Red Bull or a shot of espresso, then yes."

He laughed. "It's not. It's Adderall. Millie left it here the last time she visited. That was probably six months ago, but I'm sure it's fine."

"Millie has ADHD?" Natalie asked, one finger rubbing at the corner of her eye. It was practically stuck shut.

"No. I mean, I don't think so. She probably pretended she did to get some psychiatrist to give her this prescription. She's a good actress, I'll give her that. But I know she just used them when she needed more energy for work and stuff. And, you know, the obvious. Weight control."

"I haven't had an Adderall since the day I had to take my SATs. How many are there?"

Nick shook the prescription bottle. "It's

full. Well, almost. I took a couple myself."

"You did?" Natalie began to get dressed, looking amused.

"Sometimes you just need to clean the inside of the refrigerator with a toothbrush, alphabetize your books, organize your closet according to color, and match all the loose socks."

"Sometimes you do," Natalie answered, laughing. "I'll take one."

He handed her the whole bottle and said, "Keep it." As she popped a pill into her mouth, he said, "Oh, and I got you something while I was out."

He left the room and returned with an A5 notebook. The spiral binding was red, the cover was a metallic gray, and in the center was a shiny silhouette of Winnie the Pooh looking at a honeybee buzzing above his head. Underneath his feet along the bottom of the notebook were the words, "Winnie the Pooh: My Sweetest Adventures Always Include You."

"What's this?" she asked.

"A planner for our workouts. To log your progress."

On the first page it read, "You are braver than you believe, stronger than you seem, and smarter than you think."

"Christopher Robin said that to Pooh,"

Nick said, pointing to the quote.

The rest of the pages in the notebook were lined, with a tiny, playful gray stamp of Pooh hanging from three helium balloons in the bottom right corner.

"It's cute," Natalie said, thinking that it was actually a little bit weird.

"Cute like you," he responded. "You can keep track of your training. Diet, goals, a summary of thoughts and achievements." He kissed her on the top of her head and said, "You'll see. This planner is going to change your life."

18

Sixteen weeks and six days, thought Asha, as she pulled up to the Hertzels' house. Her baby was the size of an avocado. Lately she'd found herself constantly googling bad news about later-in-life pregnancies and wondering if her family was going to be intact to give the new child a safe and happy home.

Asha was on the porch, flipping the numbers on the combination padlock securing the front door, when she realized she was going to throw up. She lurched towards the flowery shrubs that bordered the sidewalk next to the drive. Up came the chicken soup and the slice of sourdough toast that she'd eaten earlier at home.

As she bent over with her hands on her knees, she spotted something that caused a second round of uncontrollable vomiting. There was a used condom hanging from one of the low branches of the bush with the white blossoms.

Asha kicked the bush vigorously several times, hoping no one would drive by and see her attacking the shrubs like a lunatic asylum escapee. Finally, the condom dropped onto the ground, landing in the pool of puke. She then used her foot to scoop mulch over it all until neither was visible.

She pulled herself together, entered the house, and brushed her teeth at the kitchen sink with her finger and some baking soda she found in the side door of the fridge. Showing this house was the last thing she wanted to be doing. Someone had had sex in the bushes. Who did that? It seemed suddenly like a crime scene.

People came and went, and Asha barely noticed. Thirty minutes before the open house was due to close, Asha sank into a chair at the kitchen table. She didn't have any more energy left, and to be honest, she wasn't expecting any offers. Most of the visitors had been summer tourists. She allowed her eyes to drift shut just for a moment.

"Hi," Natalie said, placing a hand on Asha's shoulder.

Without thinking, Asha covered it with her own hand. "Hi, Natalie. I didn't know you were here."

"I just walked in a second ago. I'm kind of seeing someone new, and I was driving home from his place and saw the sign, so I thought I'd stop by. I've been thinking about you."

Asha sat up straighter and said, "Really? Sit down for a minute. Who's the lucky guy?"

"I don't want to jinx it yet."

"Oh, sure. I get it."

Natalie took the chair on the other side of the kitchen table and leaned in with her chin in her hand. "How's —" with one finger she made a clandestine gesture towards Asha's belly "— the little one?" she whispered.

"The baby seems to be doing great," Asha answered. "I wish I could say the same."

"I'm sorry to hear that. What's going on?"

Asha's eyes went to the window for a long moment, and she realized that what she wanted more than anything was to just tell someone. Maybe Natalie would be a voice of reason. Maybe she would say it sounded like nothing. She didn't look like the sort of person who would be judgmental.

Natalie was waiting quietly, a concerned dimple between her brows. "Does this . . ." She appeared to be choosing her words carefully. "Does this have to do with the other week when you said you're having a baby with a man who might want to leave you?"

Asha was shocked. "Did I say that?"

"Yes, when we were talking about Mia."

"Oh Lord, Natalie," Asha said. "It must have slipped out. But it's true. I'm so sorry. I feel like I shouldn't be bothering you with this."

"I don't mind at all. My parents had a lot of problems when I was growing up. It's nothing new to me. What is it? Is he unhappy about the baby?"

"If he is," Asha said, "he won't admit it. He says he loves me and is excited for the new chapter in our lives and that he just has a lot on his mind."

"That doesn't sound so bad."

"If it was only that, I'd be fine. But I really think it's possible he might have met someone else."

"What's he done to make you worry?"

"I found a key card to the Le Méridien hotel in Denver in his office trash the week after he was supposed to be away on business in Phoenix."

"Shit," Natalie said, wincing. She thought about mentioning that she used to cocktail there, but decided it wasn't the right time to tell Asha about the swinging singles scene that went on up at the Le Méridien rooftop bar.

"I know," Asha said. "It doesn't look good."

"How did he explain the key?"

"When I finally got up the courage to show it to him, he said it was old, from last year. That it was stuck in between some business cards in his wallet."

"That's believable, right?"

"I don't know, Natalie. He just seems very different these last few months, and I'm worried. We've been through a lot together, and I still love him, but I don't like feeling so suspicious and insecure. Scared, even."

"Scared?" Natalie's expression changed. "Did he do something to scare you?"

"A little bit." Asha seemed ashamed. "But I'm not perfect either. Obviously."

Natalie leaned in to meet her eyes. "Whatever's going on is not your fault."

"I know." Asha flicked away a tear. "Thank you. I'm so sorry, Natalie."

"You have no reason to be sorry."

"I haven't always been the nicest, have I? To you? I admit I might have thought —"

"You don't have to explain anything. That's in the past, okay? You need to focus on what you can do to feel better."

"Lately I just feel scared all the time. Not

just of him, but in general. In my open houses. On my own. Vulnerable. You know?"

"Sure. We all feel vulnerable sometimes."

"Do you think I would feel better if I got some . . ." Asha paused. "Some protection?"

"Like what? Like a gun?"

"That's what I was thinking."

"Do you know how to shoot one?"

"No."

"Then probably not. You're more likely to end up hurting yourself. But you could do what I do."

"Which is what?"

Natalie opened her purse and pulled out a little can of mace attached to a red piece of plastic, about two inches across, roughly the shape of a cat's face and ears.

"I have mace already," Asha said.

"This is a kitty knuckle," Natalie said, pointing to the cat. "It's cool. Looks cute, right? A lot of women use them as key chains, but it works like a brass knuckle. The eyes are just the right size to slip your fingers in. Your pointer and your middle. See?" She demonstrated. "And then once you've got your fingers hooked through there, look at the ears. Nice and sharp." Natalie smiled. "Deadly. You lock your fingers in and swipe at someone's neck with this, and you're going to take out their jugular super quick and bam, blood everywhere. No more worries."

"Ugh," Asha said. "I'm not sure I'm ready to rip someone's throat out."

"Really? Okay." Natalie put the kitty knuckle away. "That's understandable. You know, you can get a cute pink Taser from Amazon for less than thirty bucks."

Asha had forgotten about the used condom for a brief period while talking to Natalie. She remembered it after she closed up the house and passed the bushes where she'd buried it under the mulch. Once she was in her car, she decided to call Phil and see if he would answer. Again, he was supposed to be in Phoenix.

"It could have been there for a year, Asha," he said when she told him about the condom. "Someone had sex. It happens. You know that. You're pregnant. You're even culpable yourself."

"You're just brushing this off?"

"No, I'm listening. Even though I'm supposed to be in a meeting with Rucks and Nielson advising them about a property in Vail, I'm listening to my wife rant about finding a rubber."

"But in the bushes? Who does that? Nobody just has sex in the bushes, Phil. And nobody does it in one location and then carries their used prophylactic to another location and disposes of it there."

"I disagree. Just because you're too uptight to do something like that doesn't mean other people don't. I think it's quite likely that more people than you realize probably do sometimes get down and dirty wherever and whenever they want."

Asha felt a great red wave of fury sweep through her body. *Uptight?* He'd just basically called her a prude. She muted the phone and yelled, "Asshole!"

"Are you still there?" he asked. "Hello?"

She chose to ignore his hurtful jab. "Or did someone have sex in the house and wait until they were leaving to toss it off to the side? Why do that? They have trash cans in the house. The Hertzels are in St. Barts."

"I understand what you're saying, but I think you're overreacting. People do crazy things, Asha. Anyone can have sex in their car in someone's driveway and toss a rubber out the window."

People do crazy things, Asha. Maybe she should ask him if he had done any *crazy things* in the past few months. Anything at the Le Méridien hotel in Denver?

"This house is off the beaten path, Phil."

"You need to try to keep your blood pressure down."

"That's true," she answered. Dr. Ruiz had put her on medication. "I'm going home and getting in the tub."

"Okay. I've got to run anyway. The Barson guys are waiting."

"I thought you said you were meeting with Rucks and Neilson."

"That's right," he said. "Enjoy your bath."

Twenty minutes later, Asha pulled up outside of her own house. A white Mercedes G Wagon was parked at the end of the driveway, and Mia, Sloane, Reade Leland, and Greg Woodson were all standing on the front lawn. Asha knew what Mia looked like when she was angry, and she immediately knew that her daughter was fuming over something. Sloane grabbed her arm, and Mia yanked it away. This happened again. Mia kept turning toward the house as if she was trying to get away from them. Asha stopped short of opening the garage. She parked her car and got out. "What's all this?"

"What's all what?" Sloane said amicably, smiling at Asha. "We're just dropping Mia off."

Asha wasn't buying it. "Mia, what's wrong?"

"Nothing, Mom."

"We were just leaving, Mrs. Wilson," Reade said.

"Good," she said. "Go."

The teenagers didn't waste any time. The G Wagon was roaring down the street thirty seconds later. Mia walked away and went inside. Asha followed close behind. Oliver was standing in the foyer at the bottom of the stairs. "They were being horrible to her," he whispered to Asha. "I saw."

"Mia?" Asha called. "Mia?" No answer. She was already at the top of the stairs and on her way down the hallway towards her bedroom.

Asha followed and knocked on the door.

"Come in," Mia said in a sulky tone that indicated she wanted to be alone.

Asha stood in the doorway. "Whatever just happened out there frightened your brother."

Mia was sitting on the edge of her bed. "He's a little wuss."

"Don't talk about him like that, and don't talk to me like that. I don't know what's wrong with you lately, but frankly, I've had just about enough."

"Sorry."

"What's going on? What was that all about? I thought you were supposed to be having a private with Mr. Maguire this afternoon, and he was going to drop you off after."

Mia rolled her eyes and collapsed backwards against her pillows. "One, nothing's going on. Two, that was all about a very boring disagreement with Sloane. Three, I did have a private training session, and four, I didn't need a ride from Coach Nick because Sloane and Reade were there working out on the mezzanine, and Reade drove me home. Satisfied?"

"No, Mia, I'm not satisfied. I'm sad. I miss you. You're so angry lately. I don't know what I've done to —"

"Mom, stop." Mia sat up and looked in Asha's eyes. "I'm not mad at you, okay? I'm sorry. I didn't mean to take it out on you. I'm just frustrated."

"What is it? What was the disagreement with Sloane?"

Mia sighed.

"Does this have anything to do with the fact that you've started doing the private training sessions this summer? That Mr. Maguire is helping you in the same way he's been helping Sloane?"

"That's one of many reasons why she's being a bitch."

"Language."

"Sorry, but it's true."

"I was afraid of this," Asha said, starting to pace. "I could tell that Brooke didn't like it when I started advocating for you to get the same special treatment as Sloane. I don't know what she's thinking, but —"

"I do," Mia cut in. "She thinks we're selfish."

"What? Selfish?"

"Yeah. Sloane told me her mom said it was selfish of me to suddenly decide I'm interested in a school that Sloane has been wanting to go to her entire life."

Asha had already assumed that this was the case, but hearing it out loud enraged her. "Brooke Elliman called *us* selfish! Because she went to a certain school twenty-five years ago, you're supposed to step aside and make sure her daughter goes to her alma mater? And who cares about *your* hopes and dreams, right?"

"It's okay, Mom."

"No! It's not okay. Not with me." There was a massive rushing sensation through Asha's veins. Her arms felt tingly and electric. "I need to watch my blood pressure," she said, a little breathless. "I was going to have a bath."

"You should do that. Relax. Please, Mom."

"I will. But I'm not letting this go."

Mia nodded. "Okay. Whatever."

Leaving the room, Asha felt her blood continuing to boil as she walked down the hall. She ripped her blouse off over her head. Once in the bathroom, she turned on the water in the tub and then used the blouse to fan her face, which felt like it was baking in the oven. In the mirror, she saw all the lines on her forehead, the tension in her jaw, the shininess of her irate eyes.

It was not "whatever." It was Brooke, having opinions about everything: about Asha's initial reluctance to announce her pregnancy to her family, about poor, busy Phil and his heavy workload, about high-definition cameras, which colleges were good and which were not, who had the best ball-handling skills on the soccer team when she'd never even played the sport, about which parents were letting their kids run wild and who had gained weight and who had gotten some work done, and which athletes deserved preferential treatment from Mr. Maguire.

Asha didn't know her own daughter anymore, and it came down to one thing. Her messed-up friendship with messed-up Sloane. Mia had been having issues with the other girl for some time, and Asha thought back to when she'd overheard the two arguing on the phone. *"I told you, I don't want anything to do with it. Not only do I not want to be a part of it, I don't even want to talk about it. Do what you want to do, but do it without me. I don't care. I don't care I don't care I don't care! You know what, Sloane, tell Reade I said to fuck off and leave me alone."*

Wearing just her bra and her elasticized mom-to-be jeans, Asha abandoned the filling tub to head downstairs and fetch her phone. A couple of clicks later, she'd ordered what Natalie had described as *a cute pink Taser.* It was arriving in two days from Amazon Prime. Though it solved nothing, really, it made Asha feel better. Like she was finally taking control.

19

Resigned to the single life, Brooke had decided to try online dating. The only site she was willing to consider was Elite Singles, and even there, she'd found very few men she wanted to meet.

Arnold Aven, an arctic engineer from Russia, had seemed like a decent prospect. Brooke had agreed to meet him for what he called a "casual caviar and vodka date" at Pravda in Blackswift. In his midforties, he was fit and classically handsome. Brooke had liked his accent and found his anecdotes about his childhood in a dank suburb of Moscow interesting, but not fascinating enough to take her mind off her daughter. Sloane was having dinner with Gabe, and because she wasn't ready to spend the night at Tabitha's, was being dropped off afterwards.

Brooke checked her phone. Sloane was back at the house, and it was only ten o'clock. She pictured Reade speeding through town to see Sloane while Brooke was out on a meaningless date that was not going to lead anywhere. Even though Arnold had just ordered her a very nice glass of expensive champagne, Brooke faked an emergency text. "Oh no," she exclaimed, standing. "My daughter is at a party where all the kids are drinking and is begging me to come get her right away. I'm sorry."

Nothing could have been further from the truth, but Brooke liked the way it sounded. She excused herself with a curt goodbye. A miffed Arnold Aven was left staring at her empty barstool while he opened Tinder and searched for a last-minute backup.

Brooke summoned an Uber, climbed in, and texted Sloane: He wasn't my type. Early finish. You up for a few episodes of the Bachelor?

sorry mom already in bed

Okay. No problem. Should I bring you a hot chocolate up when I get home or just let you sleep?

sounds nice yeah thanks do that pls

In their kitchen, Brooke heated up some

milk and fished the tin of Cadbury drinking chocolate down from the top shelf of the pantry. She made one for herself as well and poured a generous amount of whiskey into it. While she waited for the drinks to cool down, she scrolled through her phone and looked at a dozen photos the Russian engineer had taken of her at her own request, using the excuse that she'd gotten a new phone and was curious to see if the upgraded camera was really as good as the salesman had claimed.

In one she looked exceptionally beautiful, and she especially liked the way her cleavage was on prominent display in her low-cut blouse. After she changed the filter to Midnight, the photo could have been taken in a Parisian bistro. She might as well have been a thirty-year-old socialite hanging out with actors and models. Brooke posted it to Instagram with the caption, Another Friday, another fun date! #neverbetter #allthesingleladies #timeofmylife.

She picked up the mugs and took them to Sloane's bedroom. The lights were off. Brooke didn't have a hand to knock so she called, "Sloane, I've got your cocoa. Honey, are you awake?" The door was just barely cracked. Brooke used her forehead to nudge it open so she could peer inside.

Sloane fumbled with the light next to her bed. After a second, she managed to turn it on. Brooke swung the door in a little farther using her foot. "Sorry, Mom," Sloane said. "I fell asleep after you called."

"It's okay," Brooke said, setting the drinks on the dresser. She couldn't help herself. She picked up a pink hoodie off the floor and flung it onto Sloane's chaise lounge. Then she moved the tennis shoes from the middle of the room to a spot by the door.

Sloane watched silently as Brooke tidied away a few other items. "Do you want me to get up and clean my room?" she asked.

Brooke chose not to react to the sarcasm. "No, I don't," she said, bringing the mug over and setting it on Sloane's bedside table. "I'll just leave this here and see you in the morning. I'm sorry for waking you."

"It's okay," Sloane mumbled, turning the light off again. Brooke heard a muffled groan escape her daughter's mouth as she collapsed into the pillows.

Back in the kitchen, Brooke sipped her whiskey-laden hot chocolate, fighting back an overwhelming sense of helplessness. She wanted to reach out to someone so badly. *Hi Nick,* she texted. *Can you talk for a few minutes?*

She deleted it.

Hi Nick. I wanted to apologize to you about the other day. Are you awake?

Deleted.

Brooke cried into her hand for a few minutes and then poured some more whiskey into her empty mug. She was just about to go to her medicine cabinet for an Ambien when she had an idea to do something she normally didn't do. What if she went up and had a heart-to-heart with her daughter? Woke her up and told her that she loved her, supported her, believed in her future, and would do anything for her. Anything.

Brooke knocked softly on the door. "Sloane?"

When there was no answer, she slipped into her daughter's dark bedroom. "Sloane?" she said. "Sloane? Sweetheart?" She switched on the overhead light.

Sloane's comforter was thrown down, and the bed was empty. "Sloane?" she called in the direction of the bathroom.

Again, no answer. The mug of hot chocolate was still full.

Brooke glanced down. The tennis shoes were no longer sitting side by side at the edge of her daughter's door.

"Sloane!" she shouted again, already well aware that it was futile. After racing back down to the kitchen, she grabbed her phone from where she'd left it on the breakfast bar.

It took one tap to start tracking her because she'd left with her phone, probably assuming that Brooke was passed out in an Ambien haze. After staring at it for thirty seconds, Brooke could see that Sloane's little red dot was moving down the mountain in the direction of the town center. Reade had come to get her, and she'd clearly slipped out one of the dozens of doors in the massive mansion.

"You've got to be kidding me," Brooke said, watching the dot. Was Sloane headed towards Gabe's empty apartment? She'd discovered Sloane using it on several occasions. Once, she'd been there with Mia, and Brooke was fairly sure the girls had been smoking marijuana even though they said they were just making a TikTok video. Another time, she'd found Sloane with a small group of kids watching a slasher-style horror movie and eating burnt popcorn out of paper bags.

Brooke flew around the kitchen. Purse, keys, shoes, jacket.

She nearly fell down the stairs that led into the six-car garage. After catching herself by grabbing the handrail, she took a deep breath.

Usually she was careful. She used a car service any time she liked. But now, a car service was not convenient for the task at hand.

Two glasses of wine and some whiskey. Brooke hesitated and tried to take inventory of her faculties. The room wasn't spinning. If anything, it was crystal clear and extra-sharp with the intensity of her fury. She climbed into her car, raised the garage door, and backed out into the night.

After turning right down Morning Star Road, she checked her phone again. The little blip on the screen had come to a stop, and it was not on the far side of town where Gabe's apartment was located after all. "Where are you going, then?" Brooke asked, picturing Sloane climbing out of the back of Reade Leland's car to attend some scummy middle-of-the-night pot party at a college student's apartment down in the village.

It was a two-lane road with a number of switchbacks, and Brooke drove it nearly every day. She glanced down at her phone propped up in the center console. The blip was once again on the move. So, Sloane wasn't staying at a scummy middle-of-the-night party after all. Maybe it wasn't even a party. Maybe it was a drug dealer's house. Brooke's foot pressed harder on the gas. The blip seemed to be heading back up on the same route Brooke was driving. Was Sloane coming home?

No, she wasn't.

The blip had stopped again. This time the location was more confusing. It looked like Sloane was stopped somewhere along the road leading from the town back up to Big Elk Estates. There were hardly any cars out, and it was a night with no moon. Brooke actually passed Reade's Mercedes G Wagon before she glanced in her rearview mirror and came to a screeching stop.

One last look at her phone confirmed her suspicions. Yes, she'd just passed the red blip that was her daughter. She threw one arm over the back of the passenger seat and started reversing. Reade had parked up at one of the many scenic outlook turnouts in the area. What were they doing in the back seat? Taking more photos? Enjoying a few rounds of the Let's Do It Dice Game?

Brooke's thoughts turned darkly to Linda, who believed she was such a tough mama bear with her rinky-dink little lady gun and her bullshit about girls *just being harder.* Yes, girls were harder, mostly because they had to put up with being stalked by boys like

Reade. Brooke was actually looking forward to seeing the look on Reade's smarmy, spoiled, predatory teenaged face when she caught them. Then, lo and behold, she could see him in her rearview mirror. There he was, looking stunned in her taillights. He'd stepped out from behind his SUV to see who was pulling up next to him. Probably drunk, since he hadn't bothered to zip up his pants yet. Brooke shook her head, wondering what Sloane saw in a kid who would pull over on a dangerous mountain road, stand on a cliff in the middle of the night, dick in hand, having a piss.

I'll just scare him, she thought.

She hit the gas.

20

After the accident on the side of the road with Reade Leland, Brooke had thought perhaps she was having a nervous breakdown. What had possessed her to press down on the accelerator? Pure fury, she supposed. To her credit, she'd hit the brake a split second later, but the damage was done. Her bumper knocked Reade down into the gravel, his cargo pants around his ankles. She jumped out of her car. It was not a pretty sight, him struggling to stand up. "Are you crazy?" he yelled.

"Are you hurt?" she countered, in the same angry tone.

"A little," he said. "What's wrong with you?"

Quite a lot at this point, she'd thought, but the main thing was that she'd been drinking. Brooke had needed to get away. She'd dragged Sloane out of Reade's back seat, driven her home, and stayed up the rest of the night making plans to leave town.

At three in the morning, she'd managed to reserve a suite at Shutters on the Beach in Santa Monica. Even though it was a last-minute escape, and neither of them had slept much the night before, Brooke resolved to approach the trip as if it were a wildly fun and spontaneous mother-daughter getaway.

One hastily booked private flight later and they were sitting at the hotel's outdoor bar, drinking San Pellegrino sparkling waters. The patio overlooked the Pacific Ocean, and the scent of fresh-baked bread wafted in from the restaurant. Brooke was starting to feel slightly better.

Sloane, not so much. She'd been sick and sad ever since getting busted. She hauled herself up out of the chair and started walking unsteadily away.

"Where are you going?" Brooke asked.

"Bathroom."

"Fine," Brooke said, confident that Reade Leland was not hiding in a stall, waiting to trap her daughter in the public facilities of Shutters on the Beach in Southern California. She began googling the best restaurants in Santa Monica on her phone.

They would stay at Shutters for the first few days while Brooke made all the appropriate calls to set up meetings with people in power during this unannounced and unofficial visit to the UCLA campus. They would have lovely meals at outdoor cafés in Venice on Abbot Kinney, shop in Beverly Hills and on Melrose, and take after-dinner strolls on the beach boardwalk or along the Third Street Promenade.

When Sloane returned from the bathroom, Brooke asked, "How are you feeling?"

"Miserable."

"At some point you're going to have to give me some answers."

"Look. You caught me sneaking out. Ground me. Take more shit away. Call me names. I don't care. I just want to go to our suite and lie down."

"Where did Reade take you? Where did the two of you go?"

"How many times do I have to answer the same question, Mom? Jesus. It was just some condominium in town where Reade knew some guy who would sell him alcohol." Sloane had given Brooke the same answer several times over the course of the previous twelve hours — that is, when she wasn't either sleeping or pretending to be asleep. "Can you please see if the room is ready?"

Brooke spoke to the man at the front desk

and collected their keys. Then she went to the restaurant and asked the bartender to recommend a nice red blend from Napa. He suggested the 2016 Dominus Estate and she said, "Wonderful." He opened the bottle and reminded her to let it breathe.

Up in the room, Sloane flopped facedown on her bed, and Brooke began to drink her wine in the Jacuzzi-sized tub with a view of the beach.

Twenty minutes later, Sloane opened the bathroom door and held Brooke's phone out. "It's her again. I'm giving you this. Turn it off if you don't want to answer."

"Just put it on a towel next to the tub." Brooke leaned her head back and waited. When it rang again, she dried her hand on a washcloth and picked it up. "Hello?"

"Finally!"

"Hi, Linda," Brooke said, as if everything was normal.

"Where are you?"

"I'm in Los Angeles."

"What are you doing in Los Angeles?"

"Sloane and I had planned a trip to look at schools."

Linda made an exasperated noise and said, "What exactly happened last night?"

"Did you ask your son?"

"Yes, and he says you backed into him,

told Sloane to get out of his car and into yours, and then drove off. That's the definition of a hit-and-run."

Brooke sat up in the tub and held the phone directly in front of her mouth. "Your son came and coerced my daughter out of her bedroom in the middle of the night. Your son took my daughter to do some sort of shady purchase in town and then pulled over on the side of the road to do whatever else it was that he had in mind. I was trying to rescue her —"

Linda began giggling in her high-pitched, girlish way.

"What's so funny?" Brooke demanded.

"It's just how you said 'rescue.' I'm trying to picture Sloane as a damsel in distress and I can't. I mean . . ." Linda had slipped into her soothing voice. "She's got a lot of powerful feminine energy, that one."

Brooke ignored this. "Look. When I pulled in next to Reade's car, he was standing there with his *penis* in his hand."

"He's a boy, Brooke. He was peeing on the side of the road. I bet you've even done it."

"Well, whatever. I barely touched him with my bumper."

"Come on. You know very well that you knocked him down."

"He was fine. He might have needed a Band-Aid."

"Reade told me that he thought you were drunk. When are you coming home? Reade is very upset, and I think we need to all get together and talk about what happened."

"Linda, if you want to make a big deal about this, I can make a big deal out of the photos your son shared with his friends of my daughter. I'll take it to the police, which I probably should have done in the first place."

Linda exited the call without further comment.

The wine and the bath had revitalized Brooke somewhat. She was proud of the fact that she was still brave enough to get on a plane in the middle of the night and run off to Los Angeles, brave enough to stand up for herself and her daughter. There was a little something she'd been saving for Linda, and it seemed like the perfect time to share it. Brooke tapped around on her phone until she located the article she'd managed to dig up a few days earlier: "HIGH SCHOOL ATHLETE FACES TEN YEARS IN PRISON FOR SEXTING WITH UNDERAGE FEMALE CLASSMATE."

The subtitle was, "Even for those under

the age of 18, disseminating pictures of someone also under that age is still sexual exploitation of a minor."

Brooke attached the article in a text to Linda, and as she pressed Send, she thought, *Here's some powerful feminine energy for you. Enjoy.*

Brooke dried off and entered the bedroom feeling much better than she had before. "Sloane, come on, honey, get up. I'd really like to take you out. We both need to cheer up. It will be fun. A mom-daughter night, West Coast style."

Sloane picked her head up and said groggily, "Did you speak with Reade's mom?"

"Yes, I did. Reade is fine. Linda and I have come to an understanding. It's all okay."

"I really don't feel so great."

"It's a beautiful evening, Sloane. We're in LA. There's a swanky Spanish restaurant I want to take you to on Main Street. Come on, doll."

"That sounds nice, but . . . I don't know."

"Carpe diem, Sloane. Please?"

The restaurant was called La Bodega. Located down a back flight of stairs in a brick cellar, it was rustic and beautiful with wine bottle chandeliers and exquisite crystal glasses arranged on all the tables. Brooke said, "You could live here and go to places like this on dates, you know? This could be your life if you get in."

"It's nice." Sloane had showered, blown out her hair, and put on some makeup. A couple of young busboys kept gawking at her every time they walked by the table. They nearly collided into one other, and Sloane laughed out loud. Brooke thought she looked almost happy.

"I was hoping you would like it." Brooke beamed at Sloane. "Tomorrow I'll show you the villa across from the cemetery where I lived with my four sorority sisters."

"Across from a cemetery? Yuck."

Their server placed some small dishes on the table: olives, grilled shrimp with garlic, and two pieces of toast layered with thin slices of Manchego cheese and jámon serrano.

"It was the veterans' cemetery, and we didn't think it was creepy at all. It was majestic. Yes, that's a good word for it. *Majestic.* And our place was so well-located. Westwood, Santa Monica, and Beverly Hills are great places to go out and enjoy yourself. You could learn to surf, and you could Rollerblade up and down the boardwalk from Will Rogers Beach all the way down to the marina, and I'll come to visit you all the time."

"Okay, Mom, calm down. You're getting all excited."

"Tomorrow we'll walk around the UCLA campus, and we'll get yummy cookies at the coffee house and eat them in the sculpture garden."

"I'm not supposed to be eating cookies," Sloane said, selecting a big green olive out of one of the ramekins.

"Oh, screw your diet. You're on vacation. And if you want, I can see if I can't arrange an informal introduction for you the following day at USC."

Sloane looked up, chewing on the olive. She swallowed and said, "What? I thought you *hated* USC."

"*Hate* is too strong of a word. I'm a Bruin, and the Trojans were our rivals, but that doesn't mean I hate the school. I'm trying to keep an open mind. If you didn't get into my college, USC would be a good second choice, and you'd still get to live here in Los Angeles. I think we need to be practical at this point. Mia seems to have her heart set on UCLA as well, so. That's the unfortunate reality."

"Do you think Mia would get into UCLA and not me?"

Brooke almost said, "Of course not," but it didn't seem like the time to lie. "Maybe. Anything is possible, but we'll make sure you're happy wherever you decide to go. In fact, I was thinking, while we're here, we can rent a convertible and drive up the coast. See Pepperdine and UC Santa Barbara. Those are good schools. I love Santa Barbara. You will too. It's so amazing. There's a Ritz-Carlton that is almost as gorgeous as being in the south of France, and I want us to have lunch there together."

That was when Brooke noticed Sloane was crying. Quietly, no theatrics.

"What's wrong?" Brooke asked, looking around to see if anyone had noticed that she'd made her daughter cry.

"Why are you still being so nice to me?"

The truth was, part of the answer to her daughter's question was selfish. Brooke had recently realized that she had failed at marriage. The hope of Gabe coming back was long gone. She didn't want to fail at motherhood, too. "I just love you. So much."

"But I've been horrible."

"You've been human. I have regrets about things I've done. How could I not understand when you do too?"

"Are you talking about Dad?"

"Yeah, I am. But also, you know, just

recently, I feel like maybe I failed you. You asked me not to go the police about the pictures and I said okay, because I know you were scared for it to get bigger and bigger. But I feel like now, in retrospect, we should have pushed back against Coach Carmen, who wanted it all kept quiet, and just done what Nick recommended, you know? Because —"

Sloane cleared her throat. "That's not how it happened. You've got it wrong."

"How have I got it wrong?"

"It was Coach Carmen who wanted to go to the police, and it was Coach Nick who wanted to protect me and Reade. He didn't even want to tell Mr. Dilly, but Coach Carmen insisted. She was the one who confiscated Reade's phone. We wouldn't have gotten in trouble at all if it had been up to Coach Nick. Nobody would have known. He had our backs the whole time."

"Oh," Brooke said. "I guess I misunderstood. Or maybe I wasn't listening well enough. I was just so furious with that boy for what he did. I couldn't see straight."

"That boy," Sloane mimicked. "Reade isn't what you think."

"Maybe that's a subject on which we can agree to disagree," Brooke responded, spearing a shrimp with her fork.

"He's more sensitive that you realize."

"I'm sure he is."

"He's a wounded person who lost someone he cared about. When you get to know him, really get to know him, there's a lot of spirituality there. A lot of guilt and sadness."

"Oh, honey," Brooke said, placing her elbows on the table and lacing her hands together. "I'm sure he has a lot of good qualities, or you wouldn't have fallen for him, but —"

"Anyway," Sloane interrupted. "We don't have to talk about Reade. I know I've messed up a bunch, and I'm sorry."

Brooke reached out her hand across the table, and Sloane took it. "Everybody makes mistakes."

This was abundantly clear to Brooke several hours later back at the hotel, when Sloane had been fast asleep for an hour.

She'd made a big mistake and underestimated the other mama bear. Brooke was sitting on the balcony overlooking the beach when she received an email from SexySokkerStarz@yahoo.com. It had been sent to her directly, and had been CC'd to a number of addresses ending in athletics .ucla.org. Attached was a large photo file, and as it began to download, Brooke felt hysteria starting to crawl from her stomach up her throat. The image was Sloane, posing with her hair loose, looking incredibly pretty. Also looking incredibly underdressed, in barely there shorts, a sports bra that didn't quite cover the bottom swell of her breasts, knee-high socks and black cleats. She was holding a soccer ball against one cocked hip. The subject line read, "Sloane Elliman-Holt Sizzles On and Off the Field!"

Brooke had been assured that such photos of her daughter had been deleted, but why on earth had she trusted the Lelands?

She entered the dark hotel room, grabbed the card key off the nightstand and left, walking stiffly down the hallway to the elevator and then through the lobby. Out on the patio, she took the wooden staircase to the sand. There were a couple of people still hanging out at the beach who watched with interest as the angry lady leaned her head back and screamed at the sky.

21

The first time Nick's phone rang that night, Natalie ignored it. He'd gotten up and out of bed and spent close to an hour in the living room. She could hear him pacing and talking, tapping on his computer, and then pacing and talking some more.

When he finally came back to bed, she said nothing. In fact, she pretended to be lightly snoring so he wouldn't know that she'd been listening to his every movement.

And then, an hour later, Nick's phone again woke her from a deep sleep. Natalie groaned and sat up. "It's like you're a firefighter or something. What's with all the middle of the night calls?"

Nick grabbed his phone and got out of bed, flashing her a quick look of disapproval. "It could very well be a real emergency," he said, and then left the room.

"I'm sorry," she called after him, but he was already pulling the bedroom door shut.

She sat there in the dark, looking at the sliver of light under the door, listening to the murmur of his voice. Jackson was awake too, and had begun panting at the foot of the bed. Natalie crossed her arms over her tank top and scowled. After a second, she walked silently over to the door and listened. Nick was telling someone to calm down. Then he said, "Send it to me. Send it to me right now." Then there was a long pause and he said, "I can't understand what you're saying, Brooke. Please, stop crying."

"You've got to be kidding," Natalie whispered, and went back to the bed. Again. Again, this crazy woman was bothering her boyfriend in the middle of the night. Then, it occurred to Natalie that he wasn't, in fact, her boyfriend, and very few women would call a man in the middle of the night, crying and needing some sort of help, if they weren't sleeping with him. Natalie was suddenly very sure that Nick had misrepresented his relationship with Mrs. Elliman. It had to be intimate for her to behave this way. It had to be. She sat there, leaning back against the pillow, fuming and feeling stupid for not seeing it sooner. Obviously, she was not his priority. Time ticked by, and his voice got louder and then softer, then loud again. Natalie honestly couldn't believe how much attention he was giving to Mrs. Elliman at three in the morning.

When he finally returned, Natalie was prepared to initiate their first real argument. She hadn't expected him to come into the bedroom, flip on the lights, and say, "I am so sorry. That was absolutely bonkers, that call."

"What happened?" Natalie asked, her curiosity edging out her anger.

Nick sat down in the chair in the corner. Jackson jumped down from the bed and went to him. Nick patted the dog for a second before responding. "Well. Somebody played a prank on Mrs. Elliman."

"What?" Natalie was both shocked and tickled to death. It seemed impossible.

"Yeah," he said, and then started laughing. "I mean, I shouldn't laugh. It's wrong to laugh. It's not really funny, but —"

"But what?"

"Somebody sent her an email. Let's just say it was an unflattering email, that painted Sloane in a bad light, and they made it look like they'd copied it to practically the entire UCLA athletic department."

"Oh my God."

"Yeah. I know. But it was fake. I mean, the sender address didn't originate in the USA, and I'm in touch with these college coaches pretty often, and all their emails end in .edu, not .org, so the email went nowhere and didn't do anything except give Mrs. Elliman a panic attack. It was just a prank."

"A cruel one, though," Natalie said, feeling slightly bad about finding it funny. "Who would do that?"

"I don't know," Nick answered. "I mean, she's so sweet and kindhearted." Nick smiled at Natalie, and she grinned back.

"You have a point there." And just like that, Natalie had forgotten that she had been eager to argue. "I guess if we're both wide awake . . ." She threw back the comforter and patted his spot.

He said, "You read my mind," before climbing in and pulling her top off over her head.

After they'd finished, Natalie waited twenty minutes with her eyes closed, to be sure that Nick had fallen back asleep. When his breath was even and slow, she eased out from under the covers, watching him for any signs of waking. There were none. She tip-toed quietly around the bed. Jackson looked up at her, and she leaned down and patted him for close to a minute. Then she slipped Nick's phone off his bedside table and carried it with her into the bathroom.

She opened it using his code, the school's street address, 2258, and looked at his call history. It was, in fact, Brooke who had phoned last. But the call before that had come from Linda Leland.

On their way to the school in the morning, where Nick had to do his training sessions and where Natalie had left her car, they stopped at Casey's General to get gas.

"I'm just going to run in for a drink," he said, pulling into a parking space. "Do you want anything?"

"Peach Snapple, please," Natalie said, pulling her phone out to scroll though headlines in the news. She'd taken an Adderall, and it was making her feel fidgety.

Ten minutes later, Nick hadn't returned. Natalie turned off the ignition, pocketed the keys, and grabbed her purse. She went in the side door and saw him immediately.

There was another woman in Nick's arms. His hand was moving up and down her back, robotically performing the socially accepted affection that went along with grief and consolation. After a moment of quiet surveillance, Natalie concluded that the woman was of the handsome variety, with sharp features, a tight bun at the back of her head, a long neck, and statuesque posture. Close to Nick's age, if not a bit older. She was crying in that quiet way that some people do, when their entire body is motionless, as if they are paralyzed by grief.

Natalie knew she'd seen her somewhere before.

Nick was talking in her ear, and after a moment, the woman began nodding. She pulled away from him, and Natalie watched as she placed a long-fingered hand against his cheek.

Natalie spun on her heel and left the shop, returning to Nick's truck with the searing sensation that a knife had been thrust into her stomach.

A few minutes later, Nick returned with a kombucha for himself and the Snapple that Natalie had requested. He slid into the driver's side and reached for the ignition. "Where are the keys?"

"Oh," Natalie said, scrounging through her purse. "I took them. I went inside to see what was taking so long."

Irritation flickered across his face as she handed the keys over. "Sorry about that. I ran into someone I know."

"I could see that. It appeared that you know her very well."

He closed his eyes for a second, and then placed the keys on the console. He sighed and faced Natalie. "Please don't be that way. You know how much I care about you. Let's not spoil something that's so easy and wonderful with a lot of unnecessary drama."

Natalie nodded, but she was clearly upset.

"Hey." He reached over and touched her chin lightly, turning it to make her meet his eyes. "I told Millie about you. She and I aren't going to be seeing each other anymore."

Natalie felt the pleasure of hearing those words roll through her whole body. She took a deep breath and commanded herself not to clamber onto his lap.

"And," he went on, "there's nothing going on between me and that woman inside. You shouldn't be jealous of her. She's one of the unhappiest women I know. Not that she doesn't have a good reason to be."

"Why?" Natalie asked, pretending that her head wasn't about to explode. *I am the only one. I've won. Millie has been banished.* "What's wrong with her?"

Nick started the car and backed out of the parking spot. "She lost her daughter in a car accident."

"How do you know her?"

"From school. She's a Falcon mom. Or was, I should say. Her daughter's name was Jill."

Natalie knew then where she'd seen the woman before. She'd been the distant figure on the hill by the memorial bench. Up by the cross-country course.

Nick went on. "Her daughter died two years ago now. She was sixteen. A good athlete. Soccer, track, and basketball. I trained her briefly. I really thought she had a bright future."

"I take it they have no younger children, or I would have seen the mom around the school?"

"No. Jill was Elena's only child."

"That's so sad." Natalie curled her hands together and looked out the window. "What kind of accident was it?"

Nick proceeded down the switchbacks that led to the school. "She was alone. Driving in her car."

"And what? Was it icy?"

"No. It wasn't even winter."

"So what happened?"

"She'd started dating a boy who was a year younger than her. Rich, athletic, popular, but who ran with a crowd of boys that were into all sorts of bad stuff."

The dingoes, Natalie thought. "Was it Reade Leland?" she asked, and then said, "Sorry, that's none of my business."

"I'd have to say 'no comment' anyway,"

Nick responded. Natalie felt that his body language confirmed her suspicion. "Anyway, I overhear all kinds of things from the kids. According to them, Jill was doing drugs, drinking, sneaking out at night. She started skipping school and was talking about dropping out of sports. It was difficult for her mom and dad. They were meeting with Mr. Dilly once, sometimes twice a week."

Nick's description didn't square with the photo Natalie had seen of Jill in the hallway outside the sports office. She'd looked happy, very young and innocent with bright eyes and beautiful skin. Her hair had been pulled back in a headband, and Natalie thought she remembered that she'd been wearing braces. "So, what happened? I mean, what kind of accident was it?"

"Driving under the influence of something or other. You know how it is. We never found out. It was a single-car crash. She was speeding and drove off the road into a tree. She died then and there. At least she didn't suffer."

"The bench up on the hill, with the engraved stone plaque underneath. That's for her, right?"

"Yes. There's a nice message on it. 'Your wings were ready, but my heart was not.' "

Natalie was touched that he knew. "What

a tragedy."

"I know," Nick said, shaking his head and pulling up to Natalie's car in the sports pavilion parking lot. "And the worst part is how common this sort of thing is these days. I mean, I grew up an hour north of Los Angeles, and I saw some wild behavior in my day. But now, just wow. I always thought I'd get married and have kids. There've been times when I've had regrets that I never did, but on the other hand, I'm not sure how good of a dad I would be with everything that's going on in the world. You've got all these students using Tinder. And at Falcon, they have so much money that they live in a fairy-tale world where there are no consequences and no limits on what's possible."

As he spoke, Natalie remained fixated on one sentence. *I always thought I'd get married and have kids.*

Never too late, she thought.

Natalie decided then and there in the school parking lot that she was in love with him.

Later that night, Natalie was still hyper from the Adderall. She spent a bit of time adding some details to a pet portrait commissioned by a cat lover in Utah, cleaned her bathroom, folded her laundry, looked at Facebook, showered, drank a beer that had been left in her fridge by Jay several months earlier, and rummaged through her cabinets, wondering if she would be able to eat. Nothing was appealing. Finally, she googled the deceased teenager named Jill Ruiz until she found her obituary.

Falcon Valley, Colorado: Services Scheduled for Teenager Killed in Single Vehicle Crash

Services have been scheduled for Falcon Academy sophomore Jill Ruiz, 16, who died in a weekend crash. Visitation is from 9 a.m. to noon Wednesday, October 18, at the Everett Family Funeral Home. The funeral service will follow at 2 p.m.

Jill was a talented athlete and violinist. She loved horses, hiking, skiing, and especially summer camp in Estes Park.

"Our hearts and prayers go out to the Ruiz family today. She was an intelligent, kind, beautiful girl who brightened the hallways of Falcon with her smile every day," said Falcon Academy Headmaster Mark Dilly.

The accident happened last Sunday at the intersection of Camp Creek Road and Maple Boulevard. Jill died at the scene.

Jill's parents are Louis Ruiz, an attorney at Klein & Carrol, and obstetric physician Elena Ruiz, M.D.

The family has asked that, in lieu of flowers at the service, to please contribute to SADD, Students Against Destructive Decisions.

"Please keep Jill in your hearts," said Mr. Ruiz. "My wife and I will never get over this sudden, tragic loss of our best friend and the greatest gift of our lives, our amazing daughter. Hug your children and tell them they are loved. We did that the last time we saw Jill, and we will forever be thankful for that one small blessing."

Natalie clicked on a photo of Jill's mother, Elena, and stared at it. Despite the sad story Nick had told her, she still couldn't shake a vindictive feeling against the attractive woman who'd been stroking his cheek.

Eventually she brushed her teeth and climbed into bed. She rubbed her jaw, trying unsuccessfully to stop grinding her teeth. It was impossible to keep her eyes shut. As the time ticked by slowly and sleeplessly, she accepted that she was not likely to drift off naturally. She took a Vicodin.

An hour later, when she was still awake,

she texted Nick. Missing you badly tonight xoxoxo.

He didn't text back and he didn't text back and he didn't text back. What was he doing? Who was he with? Maybe he was on the phone with Linda or Brooke. Maybe one of them had insisted on seeing him in the middle of the night. Why was she so jealous and paranoid? The Adderall. Of course.

She took another Vicodin. Two hours later, still obsessing about the unanswered affectionate text, she took a third. She placed an Adderall on her bedside table with a bottle of water, knowing it was the only way she would be able to wake up. "This is dumb," she said out loud in the dark, empty room. She tossed and turned, changing the pillow to the cool side and kicking at her sheets. "Pull it together. Before things spiral out of control like last time."

Police Video Excerpt,
Falcon Academy Conference Room
Interview: Bellman, Natalie Marie
(Continued)

"The man's tie you claim you took out of the school's lost and found," Detective Bradley says. "Let's talk about that for a second."

Natalie uses two fingers from each hand to massage her temples. "It's just a tie. Like I said. It looked like one my ex used to have, and so I thought maybe I'd return it."

"But you kept it," Detective Larson responds from behind the camera. "Hid it. In the back of your desk drawer with your stolen drugs."

Natalie looks up sharply. "It was an impulsive decision to take it. I barely thought about it. I saw it in the lost and found and figured it might be a good excuse to talk to him. Every day, every second, I wanted to find some reason to talk to him, some legitimate conversation that would mean I could just be near him for a little bit. Okay? I know it's pathetic, but that's what it was. Just me being pathetic."

"And yet you never did give it to him, did you?" Detective Bradley asks. "Never took it down there to say, 'Is this yours?' and be nice and ask him how he was doing?"

"No. I never did."

"Why not?"

"At some point it became clear to me that he had begun to hate me, and nothing I could do or say was going to change that."

22

Thrilled to have finally closed the deal on the Hertzel house, Asha came home with two big bags of takeout. She placed them on the counter in the kitchen and then dropped her purse and briefcase inside the door to her office. "Kids! Phil!" she called. "I've got steak and shrimp fajitas from Mi Ranchito."

She was feeling a little bit better about things. Of course, the big commission on the Hertzel house was nice, but what made her even happier was that she'd decided to take some time off work once the baby arrived. Soon, she'd no longer be spending so much time alone in the open houses, which she'd started to find unsettling. In the meantime, her Vipertek stun gun had arrived in the mail, and she felt safer. Mia had brought the package in from the porch the previous day, and they'd inspected it together. It had an LED flashlight, an emergency siren, and a pink rubber nonslip case. "It's cool, Mom," Mia had said. "Good for you." If only Phil would stop being so moody, she might actually feel like her previous, more confident self.

Asha heard the toilet flush just off the kitchen. "Hi there," she said as Phil emerged. "Can you get the kids?"

"Sure." Instead of going upstairs, he said, "Alexa, announce."

"What's the announcement?" the gadget asked.

"Oliver, Mia. Kitchen. Dinner."

Oliver answered from his own Alexa and his voice filled the room. "I'm just finishing a match with Kameron. We've almost won. I'll be down in five."

Phil began rifling through the bags and pulling out the chips and salsa.

"Mia didn't answer," Asha pointed out. "She's home, isn't she?"

"I think so."

"You don't know?"

"I said I think so."

"Did you pick her up from her private?"

"No."

"Phil!" Asha glared at him.

Phil checked his phone and said, "I've got a message saying she had a ride home. Also, I heard the door slam."

"Father of the year award," she muttered, marching off towards the stairs.

"What was that?" he called.

She didn't answer.

Asha knocked on Mia's bedroom door. "Honey?"

"Yeah?"

She entered to find Mia curled up in bed with her phone very close to her face. "Hey. Are you okay?"

"I'm fine. Just tired."

"You're tired a lot lately," Asha said, lowering her increasingly awkward body carefully down to sit next to her daughter.

"I know."

"I should take you to see your doctor."

Mia shook her head. "I'm not that kind of sick. I'm just sick of people. Sick of all the demands and warnings and advice, and sick of soccer —"

"Sick of soccer?" Asha asked, stunned. "I didn't expect you to say that."

"I thought I would like doing the privates, but Coach Nick is just always talking about the future and my potential and the 'competition we're facing.' Every second is about trying harder and being my best self and all the stuff we have to do next to keep things moving in the right direction. It's tiring and stressful, to be honest. I just don't even care about getting into a Division I school. I just want to be happy again."

"Oh no, Mia. This makes me very sad. I want to help. What can I do? How can we fix this?"

"I don't want to fix anything," Mia replied gloomily. "I want to quit."

Phil had appeared in the door. "Quit what?" he asked.

"The private training sessions," Mia answered.

Phil turned to Asha. "See?"

"You don't have to make this an 'I told you so' situation," Asha responded testily. "You don't understand the problem we're facing with these scouts, and —"

"I do understand the problem," he said. "The problem is you."

Asha was speechless.

"I'm done talking about it. I'm done, Asha. I don't want them making her wear a heart monitor while she runs miles and miles in the heat. I don't want them recommending collagen peptides for her joints. I don't want the anti-inflammation injections or the 'mindful meditation for athletes.' I don't want her going to the privates anymore. Period!"

Asha knew then that she was going to back down.

Mia propped herself up against her pillow, and Asha put a hand on her leg under the comforter. "The whole idea was that by doing the privates you'd get the 'special treatment.' If we stop, the special treatment stops. Are you okay with that?"

Mia nodded. "Why don't we just do it ourselves? You bought that same camera that Sloane's mom has. I can edit my highlight reel myself. Dad can help with my essays. Let's just see what happens if I try to get in on my own without doing the privates. They're so expensive anyway."

Phil nodded in agreement. "In my opinion, people make way too big a deal out of the name of the university. You can get a good education lots of places. You might even have more fun at a shitty school."

Mia laughed and wiped her nose. "All I really want is to go somewhere and meet some nice, interesting people. Different would be good. It would be cool to get to know more of like, other kids who aren't descended from six generations of white Colorado ranchers. I mean, the last time you took me to India I was what? Eight years old? I can barely remember it."

"I'm sorry, Mia," Asha said. "I didn't know you felt that way. Phil? Can we start planning a family vacation? I'll call my aunt.

Get some recommendations for a nice rental on the beach south of Mumbai. Can we do that?"

Phil nodded. "Yes. We certainly can."

"Anyway," Mia said. "I'd like to go to a college that's not mostly rich, white kids. Been there, done that. Time to try something else. Plus, lots of schools have film programs now. I mean, I could even go somewhere in the Midwest. Like Chicago. St. Louis maybe. Kansas City. As long as it's not right here in Falcon Valley where everyone is so mean and messed up. Anywhere else but here would be fine."

"Well," Phil said. "I'm done shouting, then. That's great news and a big relief. Let's eat."

Asha nodded, feeling slightly ashamed for the way she'd pushed her daughter, but also relieved. They were all in agreement now. "I'm just going to get out of my work clothes and into my comfy stuff. You and the kids can go ahead and start without me."

"Sounds good." Phil smiled at Asha in a way that he hadn't in a long time. Asha wondered if maybe they'd turned a corner. Maybe everything was going to be all right.

In front of the bedroom mirror, she hummed as she took out her earrings. She went to place them in her jewelry box and there, pushed to the back but clearly visible, was her favorite gold cuff bracelet with the two iridescent opal stones on either end that she'd believed had been lost or stolen. She'd been so upset about it that she'd nearly accused Natalie Bellman of being a thief. But there it was. She must have never taken it off in the Leopolds' house after all.

Well, she thought, *Phil was right.* She was the problem. Forgetful and irresponsible. Always misplacing her keys, losing jewelry, imagining things. And look, instead of bringing her phone up and charging it next to the bed, she'd left it downstairs in her purse in the office. After pulling on her drawstring pajamas and a long shirt, she walked down the stairs. She could hear Oliver talking loudly in the kitchen, and then Phil laughed. She smiled at the sound of her happy family as she continued down the hall.

Turning into her office, she gasped. Mia was bent over her purse, which was still where she'd dumped it, along with her briefcase. It wasn't clear which of the two of them was more shocked. "You frightened the life out of me!" Asha said.

"Same here," Mia answered. "You snuck up on me."

"I didn't mean to. I thought you were in

the kitchen."

Mia shrugged. "I was just on my way there."

Asha glanced down at her purse and waited for an explanation. She cleared her throat. Finally, she said, "Were you looking for something in there?"

It took Mia forever to answer.

"Did you need some money, maybe?" Asha was clutching at straws here. Mia had her own bank card and access to whatever she needed.

"No," Mia said. "I just —"

"What?"

"I wanted to see your Taser gun again."

"Oh?" Asha said, her eyes popping open. "Oh, of course. I can see why that would interest you. You can't carry one until you're eighteen, but I'll get the instruction manual out, and we can look it over together after dinner. Does that sound good?"

"Great," Mia said, and walked out the door and towards the kitchen.

With her fake smile still plastered across her face, Asha stood there for a moment, staring down at her open purse. Mia had ransacked it. Something was going on. Asha was sure of it now. Too much strange behavior, too much anger and sadness. And now Mia was suddenly looking to get her hands on that stun gun? Asha thought of the look on Mia's face when she'd been trying to get away from Sloane and Reade in their front yard and how Oliver had said, "They were being horrible to her."

And just five minutes earlier, Mia had said that she'd be happy to go to college in Colorado as long as it wasn't in Falcon Valley, *where everyone is so mean and messed up.*

That was it, then. That was what was going on. Sloane and Brooke were infuriated that Mia had showed an interest in "their school" and coerced her into quitting the privates and giving up on her dream. Could Brooke be crazy enough to retaliate against Asha by seducing Phil? Maybe. Was Mia being bullied by the girl who was supposed to be her best friend? Likely.

Asha was worried. People did crazy things when they were mad and scared, and she wasn't just thinking about her daughter.

23

The idyllic, sunny, sleepy summer was soon coming to an end. A rainstorm had blown through Falcon Valley the night before, and Natalie had stayed up until midnight painting with her window open so she could listen to the drum of the water hitting the roof of her apartment along with the periodic claps of thunder.

The morning was perfect. Everything washed clean, dew on the leaves and lawns, a smell like camping and childhood. Natalie took Starbucks to Jay's. She wanted to walk Rocky before lunchtime so she could spend the whole afternoon with Nick.

After she and Jay had been sitting on the back patio drinking their coffee for a while, he lit a joint that had been resting in his ashtray. He took a small drag and offered it to Natalie. "No thanks," she said. "I'd probably end up taking a nap on your couch."

"Is that a bad thing?"

"I don't want to feel tired," she answered, rubbing her eyes. "I hate being tired during the day, and I've been tired a lot lately."

Jay was looking at her funny.

"What?"

"You've lost a lot of weight."

Natalie answered, "Why, thank you."

He looked concerned.

"Why are you looking at me that way?"

"I don't know. I don't want to piss you off, but I thought you looked fine before."

"At least you didn't say 'better.' "

Jay laughed. "But I see you caught my meaning."

She didn't care what her brother thought. Nick had said to her just the day before that her body mass was perfect, he was incredibly proud of her, and they should do the Tuttle Lake hike again before it got too cold so he could admire her in her swimming gear. "I'm just working out a lot more. Training for that Muddy Funster duathlon that I'm hoping to do with Nick."

"Okay. Well, try not to lose any more or I really am going to worry. To be totally honest, you look like you could use a vacation. Or a doctor's appointment. Or maybe a box of Krispy Kremes."

Natalie gave Jay the middle finger with a smile, and he gave her one back with an equal amount of sarcasm. Then Natalie left to go meet Nick for their bike ride.

They did an advanced trail that ran between a field filled with yellow flowers and Big Blue Creek. It ended with a challenging climb up a dusty zigzag through lodgepole pines, and the blast down on the other side had Natalie's forearms stinging from hitting the brakes before every rock and tree root, afraid she was about to go over the edge.

Afterwards, they each had a beer on Nick's balcony. Then they showered together and spent some time in his bed. Natalie felt a little dizzy and sick, and they decided that she'd overdone the workouts for the week. Nick told her to rest. "Stay here if you want," he said, kissing her shoulder. "I've got some emails I need to send."

"School stuff?" she asked, and then hated herself for being clingy and demanding, acting like a snooping middle-aged wife. She could hardly help it. It seemed like every time she walked into a room where he was working, he closed down whatever file or email he had open.

Nick looked at her oddly and said, "Yeah. Back-to-school is a really busy time for me."

"Do what you need to do," she said, trying to sound carefree. "I'll be here." It was four thirty in the afternoon on a weekday, and it felt wonderfully decadent to have the opportunity to curl up in cool sheets that smelled like Nick's body wash. She loved these lazy naps in his room, the shutters closed, the fan whirring above. Soon school would start, and life would have to go back to normal.

She woke up to find Jackson next to her, circling and pawing to make himself a comfy spot in the bedding. It seemed like it might be late. Natalie started to get up, and her hip felt sore. She groaned. Jackson looked worried.

"Natalie?" Nick was in the living room. He walked to the bedroom door and said, "Was that you? Are you okay?"

"Yes," she answered, pressing two fingers into the painful area. "I think I pulled a muscle on our bike ride." She glanced at Jackson, who had finally created his perfect place to lie down. He rolled onto his back for a belly rub, and Natalie obliged. "Don't worry, I'm fine."

Nick walked in, bare-chested, with a cup of tea in his hand. "I think it might rain again tonight." He went to the window and opened the shutters. "Storm clouds rolling in."

She swung her legs out of bed and joined

him. His bedroom window faced the town, but beyond that were pastures, which gradually gave way to a stretch of rolling, forested foothills. Behind those were giant mountains. The moon was already rising, and even the stores in the strip mall, with their tourist-town alpine touches, seemed picturesque and romantic to Natalie. She slipped her arm around Nick's waist.

"My birthday is next week," she said, her lips against his upper arm.

"Really?" He sounded delighted.

"Umm-hmm." She nodded, feeling slightly shy for having mentioned it.

"Twenty-five?" he asked.

She nodded again.

"I loved being twenty-five. It's a fantastic time in life."

"I'm going to treat myself to a nice dinner," she said, as casually as if she were commenting on the weather. "I was thinking of a steak at the Golden Ox. Would you like to come with me?" She looked up at him, and the hope in her eyes gave away the fact that asking this question was hard for her.

Nick closed the shutters on the amazing moon and set his tea down by the bed. He walked over to his closet and began rifling through T-shirts on a shelf. For a while he didn't say anything, and she felt awkward and nervous. With his back turned to her, he said, "Let's have dinner here. Anything you want. I can buy Wagyu from the Farmer's Collection. It will be way better than the Golden Ox."

The fact that she was talking to his back emboldened her for a moment, and she said, "You still don't want us to be seen together, then?"

"I just offered to make you a special dinner for your birthday. What's wrong with that? Why do you have to turn it into something else?" he asked, pulling a shirt over his head and turning around.

Natalie wasn't sure how to respond. She raised a finger to her mouth and started to chew a nail, then quickly stopped. "I mean, you don't want to go dinner at the Golden Ox with me. Because it's a place where we might bump into someone from the school."

"Okay," he said, walking out of the room abruptly. "Guilty as charged."

Natalie grabbed his robe from the back of the bathroom door and belted it around her waist. Then she followed him. He was standing in the kitchen, staring into the open refrigerator. Jackson had followed him and was hoping for a treat. Spots of drool dotted the tiles.

"Has Jackson eaten?" she asked, hoping to change the subject.

"I feed my dog, Natalie," Nick answered in a clipped tone.

"I'm not trying to annoy you," she said.

"Well, try harder." He pulled out a plastic container of turkey and set it on the counter.

"It's just that —"

He turned to face her. "It's just that it seems you're not willing to take my feelings into consideration when it comes to this issue of making a public display of our relationship."

"Yes, I am."

"I've been getting by just fine in the isolated affluence of Falcon Valley for a while now. People know me and hire me to work with their kids. They think I'm in a long-distance relationship, and that's easy for them to understand and accept. I'm not sure what the parents around here would think if they found out that I'm actually seeing a woman who could easily be my daughter. People will not understand. I have no idea how that will then translate when it comes to my job."

Natalie raised her arms in an exaggerated stretch and then adjusted the robe around her neck. "I think," she said, walking over and sitting on one of the barstools, "that people would be far more accepting than you realize. Families aren't all *Leave It to Beaver* Cleavers anymore."

He looked up quickly. There was an unusual intensity to his eyes that made her feel uncomfortable.

"I mean," she said, forging ahead. "Just that men your age get married and have children with younger women all the time."

Nick cleared his throat and said, "Is that what you want, Natalie?"

"What?"

His hand dropped to Jackson's head, and he seemed deep in thought. "A family? Children?"

"No," she answered brusquely. "Of course not. Not now. Someday. But not now."

Nick looked up from Jackson into her eyes. "It only just now occurred to me that this —" He gestured to her and then at himself. "This thing we have going is preventing you from meeting someone who shares your hopes and dreams for the future. Someone closer to your own age who wants what you want."

She sucked in her breath, realizing her blunder. She jumped down from the barstool and wrapped her arms around him. "I know what I want. I want you. That's all."

He pulled away and said, "You're right.

Men my age do get married and start families. I know that. But I have to be honest with you. That's not me. I'm set in my ways. I like my little townhouse. I like my job and my dog and my weekends the way they are. And yes, I like what we have. I love it. It's been a really happy time for me, but . . ."

"But nothing," she said, sounding slightly frantic. "Just forget I said anything. Forget the stupid Golden Ox. That was — that was — that was just me being weird, okay? We'll have my birthday here and play music and sit on the balcony and watch the sunset with Jackson, and it will be great. Just forget that I said anything."

He put his hand on the back of her head and pulled her towards him. She stood on her tiptoes to reach his mouth, but his lips went to her forehead. "I wish it worked that way," he said against her skin. "But it doesn't."

"I'm sorry."

"I am too, Natalie. I really am. I owe you an apology, and I need to think about what it is that I've done. I've been irresponsible with your feelings. With your life. With your future."

"No, Nick —"

He was getting emotional, and he held up

a hand. "I need some time."

"I'll take a walk and come back. I can take Jackson with me."

"No. I need some time to figure out if I can do this with you or not. If I can give you what you want. I care so much about you, Natalie. That's why I don't want to hurt you anymore. Let's take a break, okay? Just for a little while. I've got so much to do with school starting. Let me take some time for myself. Please?"

Natalie was trying her hardest not to cry. "And then, after a break, we can try again?" she asked.

Nick didn't answer.

"Did you decide you wanted to go back with Millie?"

"No."

"Are you ending this because you've gotten involved with someone else?"

"No. I'm not. But to be clear, just because I told you things were over with Millie, that didn't mean I was making a commitment to being only with you."

"But I thought that. And you knew I did, and you let me go on thinking that was what was happening."

"And now I'm correcting that mistake."

She slapped him. "You could have just told me the truth rather than make a fool out of me."

Nick touched his cheek and shook his head. "I don't think it was me that made a fool out of you," he said quietly but firmly. There was a coldness to his face Natalie had never seen before. "I'd like you to leave."

"No. I'm not going. You're going to have to deal with me."

"You want me to deal with you?"

"Yes."

"How about this? I call the police and tell them you just assaulted me. You hit me. Right?"

"Wow. I slapped you, big deal. Are you scared of me?"

Nick looked up at the ceiling and exhaled, his hands on his hips. "I'm not scared of you. But are you scary? Yes. Just get the fuck out of my house."

"I'm not going anywhere."

"Yes, you are." Then he grabbed her arm and showed her the door. A few minutes later, her things were tossed out too, without another word. Shivering, she changed back into her clothes on the porch, and left his bathrobe behind, hanging over the arm of a wooden chair.

24

The elementary school kids were playing tag on the playground, and the teenagers were camped out at the cluster of picnic tables, scrolling through their phones. A couple of parents were helplessly trying to get the little ones to behave before someone got hurt. A silver aluminum foil balloon escaped from where it had been tied to a canopy and drifted into the blue sky. From the parking lot, a migration of families carried over their camp chairs and picnic blankets. There was the sound of laughter and conversation. It was the fourteenth of September. The Parent Teacher Association was holding their traditional picnic in Pilgrim's Park to celebrate a successful first two weeks of school.

For Natalie, it had been hell without Nick. There had been nothing more than brief, work-related interactions, and he seemed to be avoiding the mezzanine whenever she was there working out. Her calls to Nick went unanswered, while her texts received cryptic replies, like, Let's give it a little more time.

On one side of the grassy square, there was a long table covered with catering platters from Mona's; grilled chicken and a spinach salad topped with pine nuts, sun-dried tomatoes, and crumbled feta. Mona's may as well have set up a sign that read, "Grown-up food." On the other side of the park, JF's "Junk Food" truck was distributing street tacos, chips, and guacamole.

Asha was behind the wine bar, which she'd set up in the shade of a large cottonwood tree. Phil arrived from the parking lot with a case of Shiraz.

"Thank you," she said. Sweat was trickling down her back. It wasn't all that warm, but she was at the start of her third trimester, and she was uncomfortable. She'd chosen this particular spot for the wine bar because she thought it would be cool, but as the sun moved, it kept peeking through the tree branches and landing on her neck and arms. Asha desperately wanted to go sit down in a lawn chair and dump a bottle of water over her head the way Mia sometimes did at the end of a difficult game.

There was a line just starting to form for

the drinks when Natalie popped up suddenly at Asha's side and said, "Hi."

"Hi, Natalie," Asha responded. "Nice to see you." She found herself doing a double take. Natalie looked different. Tired. "Red or white?"

"White, please." Taking her wine, Natalie leaned in and said, "Do you think you might have a minute to sneak away and talk in private?"

"Of course. When it slows down, I'll come find you."

"Thank you."

As Natalie walked away, Asha watched with concern. Tired wasn't really the right description for how Natalie looked. Maybe sick.

Brooke walked up and took a position at the very end of the wine line. Under different circumstances in the past, she might have gone straight up to Asha and cut in front of the others, but she wasn't feeling as ballsy as usual. For one thing, Howard Leland, Reade's dad, was several people in front of her. Brooke was almost sure that Linda would not be attending the picnic because she shunned most school functions, but at this point, Brooke didn't want to have anything to do with the husband either.

Howard was the CEO of a cybersecurity

company with international tentacles. Brooke was certain that he'd helped Linda create the untraceable email containing Sloane's image that had caused Brooke to derail for an entire night in Los Angeles. Nick had calmed her down by pointing out that the message hadn't actually been sent to anyone in the UCLA athletic department. Still, it was proof that the photos were *out there.*

Nick had called it a prank. Brooke perceived it as a warning. A second warning, after having been treated to the flash of Linda's gun on her hip. And this time, Brooke was paying attention. Yes, she had lots of money to throw at her problems, but she didn't have the guts to risk Sloane's future.

Brooke had been on her best behavior ever since.

Once Howard Leland had his glass of red and walked away, Brooke waved over the head of the people in line in front of her. "Hey, Wilsons!"

Asha didn't respond enthusiastically. She nodded and held up a finger, indicating she was busy.

Phil said, "Red?" and Asha looked at him over her shoulder. He was already pouring Brooke's cup. So, he knew without asking which type of wine she preferred.

"Thanks," Brooke said, taking it and moving to one side so she could chat in Asha's ear while Asha served. "This is so nice, isn't it? Such a pretty night."

"Lovely," Asha said.

"Looking forward to the games starting soon?" Brooke asked.

"We sure are."

"Something smells good."

"It's the street tacos," Asha said. "They're amazing."

"Thanks. I think I'll stick to food that wasn't cooked in the back of a Winnebago. I'm having dinner later in Denver anyway. I have an early board meeting, so Gabe's going to stay with Sloane, and I'm driving down tonight."

"Ow!" Phil made a face and grabbed a napkin. He'd cut his thumb with the corkscrew. Asha gave him a long stare. "Are you okay?"

"I'm fine," he said, but he was glancing in Brooke's direction.

Brooke seemed suddenly uncomfortable too and said, "Well, I'll just be —"

"Where do you stay when you go to Denver?" Asha asked suddenly.

"Where do I —" Brooke looked confused. "Where do I stay?"

"Yes," Asha said sharply. "I asked you once before. I texted you. You never texted me back. I might have business in Denver myself someday and I'd like to know where you stay."

All of the parents in the wine line were quietly observing, and Phil began to suck on his bloody finger while taking in the odd scene out of the corner of his eye.

Laughing breezily, Brooke said, "I stay at the Four Seasons. I just love it. They have that rooftop pool, and it's just around the corner from —"

"So, you don't stay at the Le Méridien?" That was the moment that Asha suspected she was being lied to, as Brooke's eyes immediately leaped towards Phil. Asha swiveled and caught her husband returning Brooke's expression of alarm.

"No," Brooke said, newly subdued. "I don't. I prefer the Four Seasons. Excuse me. I have a few people I need to talk to before I get on the road. Have a nice night."

Natalie spent some time talking with Yvonne and a couple of teachers, and then excused herself to walk around the park with an eye out for Nick. She spotted him with some kids by the picnic tables and was about to pass by to give him an informal, friendly wave, when she caught his look of warning. She steered clear, her heart sinking.

While Natalie started back towards Yvonne, she was flagged down halfway by Asha. "Hey," she said. "I needed to get away from that table for a few minutes. I've been looking for you. You wanted to talk to me, right?"

"I did," Natalie said. "It's nothing big." Seeing Nick had left her feeling drained. "I only wanted to check in, see how you are. See how things with Phil are going. If you're feeling better."

Asha's lower lip trembled slightly, and she took Natalie's elbow. "Just walk this way with me for one second," she said, leading Natalie toward the edge of the pond. "It's not better. It's worse. I don't want to say too much, but I think the card key I told you about? The one from the hotel in Denver? I'm pretty sure he's lying about it. I don't think it's from last year at all."

"The Le Méridien, right?" When Asha nodded, Natalie hesitated for a heartbeat, then said, "I used to work there. At the bar. I still have friends. Do you want me to see if I can find out anything?"

Asha's grip on Natalie's arm got tighter. "You used to work there?"

"Cocktailing."

"Who do you know?"

"My ex-boyfriend is a concierge. He's nice. He might be able to help."

"Oh gosh," Asha said, finally releasing her death grip on Natalie's arm. "Then it all becomes real, doesn't it? I become the suspicious wife with a baby on the way and he becomes the cheating husband. I don't know. I don't know."

Natalie looked up, and there, across the park, Brooke was sitting down next to Nick at the picnic table.

"Can I have some time to think about it?" Asha asked. "I want to be sure I'm comfortable with whatever the outcome is before I ask such a big favor of you."

Natalie could barely concentrate. There was static in her head. She looked at Asha. Her words sounded like a badly rehearsed speech. "Yes. You can get back to me. I'm so sorry, but I have to run. Let's talk more later."

Natalie left Asha by herself at the edge of the pond.

By the time Natalie had walked over to the bench, Brooke had moved closer to Nick. Her head was tilted towards his, her glossy hair hanging down her back. Natalie imagined how nice it would feel to grab a handful of that shiny mane and give it a good hard yank.

"Excuse me."

Brooke paused and looked over her shoulder. "Miss Bellman," she said, sounding exasperated. "What?"

Natalie was standing there, fiery explosions of red making each cheek look as if she'd been smacked. "I'm sorry to interrupt."

Nick turned around to glance at Natalie. He was expressionless, except for a certain glint in his eyes. She'd seen it before. He was quiet, but he was furious.

"Go on," Brooke said.

"The headmaster is looking for Mr. Maguire. He needs him for something."

Brooke frowned. Natalie was kneading one hand with the other, chewing on her lower lip in a way that looked painful. "Okay then." She leaned in to give Nick's shoulder a friendly bump with her own and said, "We'll finish talking about it some other time."

Nick nodded and stood. "I'll go find Mark."

"Thank you," Natalie said. She turned her back on both of them and started walking away.

Brooke cleared her throat, tossed her long hair like one of her prize mares, and followed. "Miss Bellman," she called.

Natalie stopped walking and turned to face Brooke. The bright spots were still there on her cheeks, and her jaw was rigid, as if she were trying to hold in her words. After a slight pause, Natalie said, in a polite tone, "Yes?"

Curling one long tendril of her hair around her pointer finger, Brooke said, "I feel like maybe I've upset you in some way."

Deadpan, Natalie replied, "What gave you that impression?"

"You seem angry. With me."

"I'm not feeling well today," Natalie answered. "That's all."

"Okay," Brooke said, making a sad face. "I'm sorry about that. But listen —"

"What?"

"I don't really know you personally. And I would never jump to conclusions about what you might be thinking, but please understand that I am not after your boyfriend. If that's what he is."

Natalie didn't say a word.

"It's not like I would ever actually date my daughter's soccer coach, you know, a glorified gym teacher. I think he's a great catch for you, though. I just thought you should know my position, so you don't have to worry."

■ ■ ■ ■

Thirty minutes later, Nick found Natalie by the bar. It had been abandoned by any servers and was just a bunch of half-empty open bottles and cups up for grabs. "Mark wasn't looking for me, Natalie," he said, doing his best to keep his voice even.

She was drinking a large cup of wine. "I know."

"I think I should take you home," he said quietly.

"What? And have people see the two of us walk away from the picnic together?" Natalie asked. "That would be a scandal, right?"

"I'm afraid maybe you might be on the verge of making some sort of scene."

"If I was going to make a scene, Nick, it would have been a short while ago while Mrs. Elliman so graciously handed me the reins to you as if she were offering me one of her horses."

Natalie took another sip of wine, and Nick touched her arm. "Could you please stop drinking? It's a bad mix."

"A bad mix with what? The Adderall that you gave me?"

"Okay." Nick put a hand on her lower back and said, "Please, Natalie. Come with me. You don't want to do this."

She looked around at all the parents packing up their gear and spooning food into Tupperware tubs. Chuckling, chatting, their arms draped around their kids as they said goodbye to Mr. Dilly and the teachers. She liked her job and didn't want to lose it by throwing a temper tantrum in public. It wasn't worth it. "You're right," she said. "I don't. Let's go."

Nick walked with her out of the park and steered her toward his truck. "Please tell me you weren't going to try to drive."

"No," she answered. "Yvonne was going to take me."

As they walked, he spoke softly, under his breath. "I'm really surprised that you would do this, considering how we were nearly there."

Natalie stopped. "Nearly where?"

"To being ready for a second chance."

She actually lost her balance when he said this. "What? Seriously?" She raised her voice. "You are playing with me!" she yelled, drawing the attention of at least one family heading to their car.

With a disgusted shake of the head, Nick opened the door to his truck for her. "Go ahead and get in."

Once they were inside, he asked, "Can you

please calm down? Can you stop putting on a show while all the families from the school are about to walk by and see us?"

Natalie tucked her hair back behind her ears, and nodded, pulling herself together. "Yes. I can."

He started the engine and began to back out of the parking spot. She looked up. "Did you mean what you said?"

"Which part?"

"About us being close to giving it another shot."

"Yes and no. I said that because —"

"Yes and no?" she asked, throwing up her hands. "Yes and no? Really? What about a straight answer? I just want some honesty, because I obviously don't understand what's going on. You know what? Never mind. I'm leaving."

He locked the door from his arm rest. "Don't do this, Natalie. There are people everywhere. They're walking by and looking at us."

"Let me out. I'm going to bang on the window."

Nick rubbed his face and took a deep breath. "What if we go back to my place and talk things over?"

The next morning, when Natalie woke,

there was a white plastic trash can next to the bed. She was naked. Before she could scream, she reminded herself that her best chance to get away was to make no noise at all. A feeling of profound panic swept over her, and she rolled onto her side to look around the room to see if the walls were papered in race car and heavy metal posters. It was too dark to tell. There were no voices from the next room, no music coming from down the hall. She couldn't see her clothes on the chair or the floor or anywhere. *I'll need to steal a sweatshirt,* she thought, just before knocking over a lamp.

The door opened. Nick appeared there, silhouetted against the light from the living room.

I'm at Nick's. I'm at Nick's. It's okay. I know where I am.

"You're up," he said.

"Yes, just now. Sorry about the lamp."

Nick laughed. "About the lamp?"

"Yes," Natalie said, dropping to her knees to look for her bra and underpants. "I mean, I'm sorry about the whole night. Do you know where my clothes are?"

"In the dryer. They'll be ready in ten minutes."

"What?" Natalie asked. "Why are they in the dryer?"

Nick leaned against the doorjamb. "You don't remember?"

"No," she answered. There was no way to read his face. He was just a dark shape in the doorway, arms crossed over his chest. She covered her eyes. "What did I do?"

"You had an accident."

"I don't know what you mean." The shame was making her light-headed. She couldn't find her normal voice.

"Just the kind of accident that kids have in bed sometimes. It's fine. I'm not upset with you about that."

A bad taste swelled up in her throat and she swallowed it down. "I'm so sorry. I don't know what to say."

"Accidents happen."

"I need to go home as soon as my clothes are ready."

"That's a good idea. Listen, there's something I want to tell you."

Oh God, how could it get worse? "What?"

"I went through your purse last night and found the Adderall. I thought we initially agreed it was just for occasional use. The way Millie used it. But I feel responsible, and I can see that you've developed a dependence on it. You've lost too much weight. Your goal was one hundred and eight and you must be what? Ninety-five?

That's not healthy."

"I'll be more careful."

The dryer in the laundry room beeped, and Natalie was tempted to dash in, grab her clothes, and make a break for the door naked just to get away from the disappointment on his face.

"I've taken the pills away," he said. "So, if you go looking for them and they're not there, you know why. What else can I do? It's affecting you in a really negative way. I care about you, and I don't want to see you like this. You scared me last night. You blacked out. You may even have been having some delusions. Hallucinations. It was very sad for me to watch. I want you to get healthy. Who knows? If you can get better, maybe we can even work this out."

Once she was dressed, Natalie left his townhouse and sat down on a curb by the main road, even though she knew she looked like a hitchhiker or a junkie. She ordered an Uber to take her back to her car and prayed for the nausea to pass before she puked in the back of some poor driver's car.

You had an accident, he had said, enjoying her humiliation.

Natalie slipped off her leather bracelet, dropped it in her bag, and rubbed the tattoo on her wrist with her thumb; the tattoo that disguised the inch-long scar underneath, something called a "hesitation wound."

I hate him, she thought. And yes.

Accidents happen.

Police Video Excerpt,
Falcon Academy Conference Room
Interview: Bellman, Natalie Marie
(Continued)

Detective Larson is in the seat adjacent to Natalie. Something has changed in the room. Natalie looks defeated, and Detective Larson is leaning towards her without her previous aggression. In fact, she appears sympathetic.

Natalie is slouched in her chair, hair hanging forward to hide her eyes, one hand over her mouth.

Reading out loud from the planner, Detective Larson says, " 'I don't know what to do. I've had thoughts about hurting myself. I've had thoughts about hurting other people. I need help.' "

Detective Larson looks up and waits for a reaction. There is none from Natalie. She turns a page. "Later, you go on to write, 'Today I stole. A new low. I hate myself.' "

Natalie makes a disturbing, hurt noise behind her hand, and Detective Bradley says, "I think maybe we should all take a little break."

25

Asha knocked politely on the side of the door to the sports office. It was humming with activity. The school's athletic director, Lars Jaeger, who was also the football coach, was reclining with one long leg up on a free office chair, holding court like a movie star. Seated around him were half a dozen coaches.

"And so," he said loudly to the room, seeming to be on the verge of concluding a story, "I finally pulled James out and sat him down. 'James,' I said, 'what's going on out there? Should I call you Cinderella today?' And he said, 'I don't understand, Coach Jaeger. What do you mean?' And I said, 'All you've been doing this game is running away from the ball!' "

The coaches all exploded with laughter. Lars had a good fifteen years on even the oldest of the other coaches, and he was their boss.

"Hello!" Asha sang. She knocked lightly again.

"Mrs. Wilson, hi," Nick said, standing up. "Come in."

"Okay," she said. "But it's kind of crowded in here, and I don't know if you've noticed, but I've gained some weight!"

Again, all the coaches erupted into laughter. If there was anyone they laughed louder for than the boss, it was a parent.

"You're looking very radiant, Mrs. Wilson," Lars said in a gallant way.

"Thank you. I feel a bit less than radiant, but I appreciate the compliment."

"Lars," Nick said. "Would it be okay if Mrs. Wilson and I used your office for twenty minutes?"

"Fine," Lars said, standing up. "I'm headed out to set up for practice anyway."

"Come on back with me," Nick said, motioning to Asha. She followed him into the only private office in the sports pavilion, and he grabbed a chair for her. "How much longer?" he asked, indicating her belly with his chin.

"About nine weeks."

"Boy or girl?"

"It's a surprise."

"Oh?" he asked, looking impressed. "That takes a lot of self-control, doesn't it? To hold off on knowing?"

"I found out with Mia and Oliver. I wanted to get their rooms just right, that sort of thing. Third time around, I'm trying to be a little more relaxed." She rolled her eyes, laughing, and said, "Key word is *trying.* I'm not really succeeding. I'm as neurotic as ever."

"You're just a concerned parent. Your kids are very lucky."

"That's nice of you to say."

"Which brings me to the reason I asked you to meet with me."

"Yes. I think I know why. It's because we've canceled Mia's private sessions."

Nick nodded. "That's right. I was starting to get really worried. Almost a month into the school soccer season and yet she's a no-show for her therapy and recruitment consultations. What's going on?"

Asha folded her hands over her stomach. "I'm sorry. I should have spoken to you about this sooner. Mia — well, and her father — they came to the decision that the privates weren't really helping. She has so much going on at this point, it just seemed like too much."

"So," he said, "help me understand. Are we pausing, or are we canceling?"

"Canceling," Asha said uncomfortably.

"Like I said, I should have told you."

Nick shook his head in disbelief. "Even though you have another prepaid month of individual attention?"

Asha waved her hands. 'We don't want a refund. It's our fault. We thought we needed it, but we don't."

"I disagree."

"Well . . ." Asha didn't know how to respond to this.

"It's just — her performance this fall hasn't been quite what I'd hoped." Nick looked very disappointed and concerned. "And I don't know if it's her injury going untreated, or if it's that 'fear of success' that some great athletes experience, or even academic stress." He paused. "But I'm afraid it might be something more serious."

"Like what?" Asha asked, and to her own dismay, she was whispering in a shaky voice. She'd been afraid of this.

"I've noticed some things. And I hear things —"

The baby was squirming inside. Asha felt slightly light-headed. She wished she could use the bathroom. "Please just tell me."

Nick reached out and grabbed a pen from Lars's desk and twirled it between his fingers. "It's hard to talk about."

"Is she being bullied?"

Nick nodded and said, "Possibly."

"By Sloane?"

"What?" Nick asked. "No. I mean, at least I don't think so. Those two girls have always had an on-again, off-again friendship, what with the constant comparisons to one another that they have to deal with, but —"

Asha interrupted. "Then what? Who?"

"There are a few boys —"

"Mia's not even interested in boys," Asha said, and Nick raised an eyebrow.

"That may be the case, but she's been spending a lot of time with a certain group. A certain dangerous group."

Reade. "And these boys are bullying my daughter?" Asha asked.

"There are different kinds of bullying. Dragging them into drinking. Parties. Peer pressure. That sort of thing." Nick put his hand up. "Now, don't get me wrong. Some of that is just being a teenager. Figuring out who you are. Having fun. Rebelling against your parents. But, you know, Mia reminds me of this really wonderful girl that used to go here. Her name was Jill, and she was like Mia — extremely gifted. But then this girl started running with a kind of wild crowd. And her schoolwork suffered. And she started thinking about dropping out of soccer, and the next thing you know —"

"Yes, yes. I'm aware. That's my doctor's daughter you're talking about. She died in a car crash. She'd been drinking and hit a tree, I think."

"That's right. That's what happened."

"What makes you think Mia is getting into that kind of trouble?"

"The kids talk. I listen."

"But —" Asha didn't know how to respond. "Mia's fifteen. I keep tabs on her. I know where she is all the time."

"I'm sure you do your best. And yet, she's struggling. Wanting to quit the things she loves? That's never a good sign."

"It's true that I've been worried about her. And she does seem different. And we're not as close as we used to be, so maybe I wouldn't even know. Do you think she's depressed?"

Nick nodded.

"So, it's not Sloane. Mia's not just having problems with her best friend?"

Nick leaned forward on his elbows and said, "I think Sloane might be having the same sort of problems that Mia is having. And I wouldn't be so quick to blame the girls. I know a lot of people like to say that teenage girls are cruel and fickle and all that, but in this case, I think the problem is probably the boys."

"Okay," Asha said, wondering how on earth she was supposed to handle this. "Okay."

Nick reached out and put his hand over hers, which was shaking. "You still have several pre-paid privates. I'm happy to refund them, of course. But why don't you use at least one? Have Mia come in again whenever it works for you, and I'll spend some time talking to her about how bright her future is and how important it is to stay focused right now. I'll give her my best pep talk and try to get her excited about life, sports, and school again. Can we agree on that?"

"Yes, of course," Asha said. "I'll get back to you with a couple of days and times that work and I'll bring her in." *Phil doesn't even need to know.*

"Great," Nick said. "And in the meantime, please be careful. There are some things I can't really talk about, but there's no law against me telling you that the girl who died — your doctor's daughter? The boy she'd gotten involved with . . . it was Reade Leland."

"Oh my God," Asha said. It suddenly felt like the world was tilting, and Mia was already in a speeding car, a bottle of something fiery tipped up to her mouth, heading straight for a tree. "I'm sorry. Could you point me in the direction of the closest bathroom?"

26

As if in slow motion, or maybe more like an old, flickering, low-quality home movie, life went on, frame after boring frame. Natalie watched, listlessly and fish-eyed, from behind her desk.

The leaves on the deciduous trees started turning yellow, orange, and red. Mr. Dilly got the flu, and then he gave it to Rex, and they were both out for a week. Reade Leland was voted homecoming king. Sloane was not selected as the homecoming court Sophomore Royal Representative, and Mrs. Elliman called to inquire about whether a recount might be in order. Asha came and went from the school once or twice a week to volunteer for this or that, as she usually did. Her baby belly got bigger while Natalie waited for her ex-boyfriend in Denver to finish lurking through private computer records and get back to her about whether Phil had stayed at the Le Méridien recently without his pregnant wife, or not. Asha had never asked her to do this. Natalie had made the decision on her own. Most upsetting was that day after day, Nick did not look at her. Did not talk to her. Did not call her extension. Avoided the front office. She had not been going to the mezzanine. She was not in the mood to lift weights.

While Yvonne was grabbing lunch in the cafeteria on a pristine, perfect October day, Natalie slipped away from her desk and went into the empty conference room with the intention of closing her eyes briefly.

Yvonne woke her up just before Mr. Dilly caught her dozing with her head on folded arms, and then, ten minutes later, brought her a strong coffee. "I'm worried about you."

"I'm tired," Natalie answered. "Thank you for the coffee. I've been staying up late at night painting. I've got a lot of orders from Etsy."

This was a lie. Natalie had indeed been staying up late, but even though she'd received several requests for paintings, she hadn't replied to the potential clients. She'd been suffering from headaches and had been spending time driving around town to see if Nick's car was at his townhome. Sometimes it actually was in its parking space. Sometimes it was at the grocery store. Once, she had nearly been spotted driving past him while he was fueling up at Casey's General, where she'd walked in on him embracing the doctor.

The office was so quiet that Natalie thought she was going to fall asleep yet again. Yvonne called her mom and started chatting about an upcoming wedding. Rex had his phone balanced on his big thigh under the desk, surreptitiously playing *FarmVille,* and Mr. Dilly had gone to the library to give a joint presentation along with Becca, the school nurse, on the school's updated Snack Safely allergy guidelines.

Natalie felt jittery and weak. Even though Nick had taken the prescription bottle from her purse a while back, she'd still had a small stash of Adderall at home. She'd been rationing them and alternating with the Vicodin as if she were adjusting the temperature in a bathtub: too hot? Add some cold. Too cold? Add some hot. Good, bad, great, terrible, worse, worst. It had been three days since she'd had anything to help her stay alert and warm. It was all cold now. The Adderall was gone.

Pulling up Google on her computer, she typed in, "What happens when you stop taking Adderall?"

The top article was titled, "The Adderall Crash."

> Adderall is a stimulant, so when it wears off, it can leave you feeling sluggish and disconnected. When you suddenly stop taking it, you may have symptoms of withdrawal. Some people have an intense craving for more Adderall. You might be unable to feel normal without it.
>
> Other symptoms include: insomnia, intense hunger or conversely intense nausea, anxiety and irritability, aggressive thoughts and urges, panic attacks, fatigue, unhappiness, depression, and suicidal thoughts.

After reading the entire article, Natalie reached underneath her desk and pulled out her Winnie the Pooh planner. With her head down and the notebook in her lap, she scribbled, "I don't know what to do. I've had thoughts about hurting myself. I've had thoughts about hurting other people."

Natalie came to a decision. She stood up and told Yvonne, who was still on the phone with her mom, "Back in five."

She closed the nurse's door behind her and began to feel wobbly with the fear of being discovered. Becca's keys were in her desk, easy to find. Natalie opened the locked cabinet. There were so many Falcon students taking Adderall, Ritalin, and Vyvanse that Natalie was able to quickly dump out two handfuls of pills, throw them into her bra between her breasts, and replace the bottles on the shelf within a minute.

Back at her desk, she put them away in her purse and washed one down with a sip of warm Diet Coke. She leaned back and raised her arms in a huge stretch and waited. It wouldn't take too long for the day to turn around.

"How's Jay?" Yvonne asked.

"The same," Natalie answered. "I'm going over after work. Do you want to come?"

Yvonne looked absolutely elated. "Yes. Yes, I do."

Natalie arrived at Jay's first because Yvonne had wanted to go home after work and "get cute."

It was a nice evening, and they were seated outside eating Chex Mix and listening to music. Rocky scouted the perimeter, sniffing for any signs of rodent interlopers. Her phone vibrated. Yvonne was on her way. Natalie texted back that she and Jay were sitting on the patio in the yard behind the house. Natalie said, "Yvonne's going to come over for a little."

Jay looked down at his unimpressive stay-at-home outfit and said, "When?"

"Now."

"Do you think I should go change my shirt?"

"No. She likes you. She likes rumpled stoners in Pixies T-shirts from the eighties that belonged to their dads. You're fine."

"Wow. She must be nuts." He was obviously ecstatic.

Yvonne showed up with a six-pack of beer, which seemed to impress Jay. "You didn't have to do that!" he said, using his cane to try to stand when she appeared at the back gate.

"Don't get up!" Yvonne said, hooking her arm over the fence to undo the latch. "I'm good." Rocky met her as she walked in and jumped up on her with his muddy paws.

"Rocky, get down!" Jay said.

"He's fine," Yvonne said. "Don't worry." She gave Natalie a hug and put the beer on the table. "What's going on, kids? I see you're enjoying some Chex Mix. This looks like one of my mom's Go-Stop card parties."

Jay's face brightened. "Do you like to play cards?"

"Are you kidding me?" Yvonne asked,

handing him a beer. "Love cards. What's your game? Gin rummy? Poker?"

Natalie said, "I'll go get the bottle opener. It's in the kitchen in the drawer underneath the calendar, right, Jay?"

"Yeah," he answered, gazing in a stoned, smitten way at Yvonne. She looked very appealing in her baggy cargo pants, boots, teeny tiny tank top, and giant hoop earrings. Natalie realized that they might actually hit it off.

The headache that had been plaguing her for days on end had not gone away. Instead of turning towards the kitchen, Natalie went straight back to Jay's bathroom cabinet to pilfer some pills.

After she delivered the beer opener out to the two of them on the patio, she said, "I just can't seem to get rid of this headache, guys. I'm so sorry. If neither of you minds, I really think I better go home and try to nap it out."

"I'm sorry, sis," Jay said, giving her arm a pat. "Feel better."

By the time Natalie reached the backyard gate, Yvonne was giggling at something Jay had said. Natalie glanced back at them, hoping it would happen.

Someone should be happy.

At six o'clock, Natalie was back at her

apartment. She stretched out on the couch and waited for the Vicodin to help her relax and make the headache go away.

She slept for five hours, woke up, and looked at the clock. *Almost midnight on a Friday. Party time. I wonder where he is.*

Natalie made a cup of herbal tea. She snooped through the Facebook and Instagram feeds of the other Falcon Academy coaches to see if anyone had gone for drinks with Nick and posted a photo. No luck. Finally, she got in her car, resigned to driving over to his place. Maybe once she saw his truck parked in the dark lot, she'd be able to sleep.

His truck was not outside the townhouse.

Great, she thought. Now she had a stomachache *and* a headache. She was on a mission. First, she drove past the Old Mill. That's where he liked to go sometimes with the other coaches and his teacher buddies for beers after work. She really didn't think he would still be there, but there was a chance. No luck. His car was not parked down the road from Brooke Elliman's house, and neither was he at the twenty-four-hour diner where she knew he sometimes liked to go for a late-night second supper of steak and eggs after his biggest workout days. She had no idea where Linda

Leland lived, so that was a nonstarter.

Natalie realized she was back close to where she'd started: his apartment. She remembered him mentioning that Brooke Elliman had an apartment just five minutes from his, over at Koi Creek. *Why not swing by?*

There was a familiar car in the luxury apartment parking lot, but it wasn't Nick's. It was a light gray Audi, and she recognized it from seeing it outside the front office for pickups a number of times. It belonged to Phil Wilson.

27

The fall feast took place the third week in October. It was an elegant affair held in the massive clubhouse of Big Elk Estates, a top choice for weddings and anniversaries, situated in the heart of the neighborhood that surrounded the private school.

Asha had long ago signed up to help plan the Fall Feast, and Brooke had been guilted into it by Tina, the Falcon mom who owned the stable where she kept her horses.

Gift baskets had already been prepared for coaches and teachers, but each year they got something special for Mr. Dilly. The committee had decided to meet at the Tuscan Grill for happy hour to discuss the headmaster's Fall Feast goody basket, as the event was just two weeks away. Tina had taken the liberty of ordering the antipasto platter and Italian lemonades for the table.

Brooke would have preferred wine.

"And something I just thought of," Tina

said, rubbing a baguette around in a dish of olive tapenade, "is the new dog salon, Collar and Comb. We should definitely get him a gift certificate for that place. He loves to spoil his corgis."

"Which gives me a good idea," Ethan Hayes said. "How about we pair that with an afternoon at Scotch and Scissors? That's hilarious, right? Daddy and doggies both get groomed? We could call it a pamper package!"

"Sounds like a basket of diapers," Brooke said.

Ethan laughed uproariously. "It does!"

Asha said, "I like it. It's unique. I think that's a definite yes."

"I'll get some gift cards and a bottle of Macallan," Brooke said. "That was easy." Suddenly consulting her phone, she said, "And on that note, I'm out. Sloane's texting me. I have to go."

Tina pursed her lips and said, "Aww. Poor thing. How is she?"

"Excuse me?" Brooke said, placing her wallet on the table.

Ethan looked like he was about to choke on his bite of bread and glanced in horror over at Tina, who appeared to be startled by her own words. "Well," she sputtered. "I mean, I just —"

"You just what?" Brooke demanded. "What does that mean, *poor thing*?"

"Only that Candace said that Linda said that Reade had invited Heather to go with him to the Silvermans' Halloween party, and that it's always hard for young people when they split up. I remember having my heart broken by —"

"Nobody broke Sloane's heart."

Asha began to fan herself with her cocktail napkin.

"Of course not," Tina said. "That's not what I meant."

"You said it, and you called my daughter a poor thing. Nobody broke up with Sloane. I told her she couldn't see Reade Leland anymore, and if his mom is telling anyone anything different, she's a big fucking liar."

Asha raised her hand to wave at the server and called pleasantly, "Check, please?"

Finally managing to swallow, Ethan said, "You have every right to feel that way. After what happened, if it was my daughter, I would have done the exact same thing."

"After what happened, huh? Great," Brooke said. "So, you know about that too? Fantastic." Brooke stood and headed for the door. Out on the sidewalk, she turned towards Sakura Sushi, where she planned to down two glasses of wine at the bar.

Behind her, Asha was calling her name.

Brooke spun around and said, "Did I forget something?"

"No, no," Asha said, embarrassed to find herself short of breath. She was wearing tennis shoes, her only shoes that didn't hurt her feet, and a flowery maternity dress. As she speed-walked after Brooke, she held her stomach with one hand. She felt ridiculous. "I'm sorry," she said, finally catching up. "I know you said you have somewhere to be, but —"

"I lied. I don't have anywhere to be," Brooke said. "I just didn't want to be *there* any longer."

"Right," Asha said nervously. "Listen. I totally understand. I know things between us have been a little bit tense."

"A little," Brooke said, and Asha couldn't tell if she was being sarcastic or not.

"I was just wondering if sometime, preferably soon, if you and I could get together for coffee and talk."

"Asha, I'm not sure it's a good idea for us to sit down and discuss the whole UCLA thing. Honestly, I just feel that —"

"Mia doesn't want to go to UCLA anymore. That was just a temporary lark, I suppose. She's all over the place. I can't keep up. She's on to the next idea, and she's literally doing her very last private training session with Mr. Maguire at the school as we speak. She wants to quit them."

Brooke cocked her head to one side, interested. "Well, then, what about now? I was just heading down to Sakura to sit at the bar for a little bit."

Asha checked her phone. "I don't have any messages from work. Are you sure?"

"Absolutely," Brooke said, continuing to walk. "How's your work going? I see a lot of For Sale signs around Big Elk. Are people coming as well as going?"

"It's been a little slow," Asha answered. They reached the big red double doors of Sakura, and Brooke held one open for Asha, who went on to say, "I'm looking forward to taking a break for a while. I've just got a single house left, and I only took that one on because the seller is the doctor delivering my baby."

"Can't say no to him," Brooke commented.

"Her," Asha answered. "But yes, you're very right. I would never say no to her. She needs to get out of that house. She and her husband have some very sad memories there."

"That's a shame," Brooke responded, not really listening. "On second thought, let's get a table. You wouldn't be comfortable at the bar, would you?"

"No, not really. Thank you. That's very thoughtful."

After they'd been seated, Asha ordered a miso soup, and Brooke requested the wine list. Brooke laced her fingers together and leaned forward. "So. What do you want to talk about?"

My husband, and the weird way the two of you act like you know each other better than you should.

She couldn't say that, and the truth was, she suspected that she was imagining things. What she really needed to talk about was the girls. Asha unrolled her black cloth napkin and began folding it into triangles. "I've been really worried about Mia. She's been moody and distant lately, and I just don't know what to do."

"Sloane's moody and distant too. That kind of goes along with the age, don't you think?"

"She's just so sad. And now, Mr. Maguire has told me that he thinks Mia is involved with the wrong crowd. Partying, drinking, all the bad stuff."

Brooke glanced to their right. "Excuse me," she called to the server. "Forget the wine list, if you don't mind. Could you please just bring me a nice chardonnay?"

"I think Mia's getting into trouble," Asha said.

"I'm sorry to hear that."

"Do you think Sloane is doing the same?" Asha asked. "From what I understand, Mia and Sloane have been hanging out with someone who's a bad influence."

The server arrived with Brooke's glass of chardonnay. She took a large swallow, then said, "Reade Leland. I suppose he's the bad influence you're talking about?"

"Yes. I heard he's dangerous, even."

"Asha," Brooke said, running a hand through her hair. "Okay. Yes, Sloane has been getting in trouble. With Reade Leland. That's what Ethan was talking about just now back there at our meeting. The *horrible thing* that happened."

"What was it?"

"Sloane took some sexy selfies and texted them to Reade and they got leaked, and at this point, I think pretty much everyone knows."

Asha sighed sympathetically. "I didn't know."

"Well, you're not the big school gossip, are you? Thank God. You don't stick your nose in other people's business constantly. We need to work together to figure out how to get Reade out of our lives and away from our daughters. We need to make sure Mia and Sloane are safe. We might have to make some big changes, but we can handle it. We have to."

Asha exhaled loudly and looked relieved. "Knowing you're in this with me makes me feel so much more hopeful." Impulsively, Asha got up and went around the side of the table to give Brooke a hug. Her belly got in the way, sending the chardonnay over on its side, soaking the table and then running directly for Brooke's lap.

"Oh, for heaven's sake," Asha said. "I'm like a clumsy elephant. God, Brooke. I'm so sorry."

Instead of standing up, Brooke pulled Asha in closer and patted her back while she allowed the wine to soak into her Escada blond suede pants. She couldn't believe how good it felt, after being snubbed by so many women after the fallout of her flirtations during her marriage, to have an ally again. At the same time, she was thinking of Phil, and how handsome and forlorn he'd looked as she walked up to him at the Ocean Prime raw bar in Denver, halfway through his bottle of muscadet, hunched over the last few in a tray of Shoal Bay Olympia oysters.

"It's fine, Asha," Brooke said. "It's totally fine. I swear. I'm the one who's sorry."

An hour later, just down the street from her house, Asha pulled to a stop next to Mr. Maguire's pickup truck, where he was parked at the side of the road. "Hello, you," she shouted while waving, after rolling down her window.

Nick rolled his own window down and looked up. He appeared to be unhappy. "Mrs. Wilson," he said, in a tone that indicated he wasn't inviting a casual conversation.

"I take it you just dropped Mia off?"

"Yes."

"How was the last private? Was she receptive to your advice?"

"It was fine."

"What's wrong?" Asha asked. "You seem upset."

"When I dropped her off just now, your husband was home."

"What? He was? Shit."

Nick nodded. "I'm sorry. I realize that the two of you weren't in agreement about this final session."

"I've got to go," Asha answered, already driving away.

Phil was drinking a glass of water in the

kitchen when she burst through the garage door into the house. "What are you doing home?" she asked.

He tossed the glass into the sink and said, "What was she doing with him after we agreed it was over?"

"What are you doing home?" she repeated.

"I forgot some things I needed."

"Like what?" Asha shouted incredulously. "Like what did you forget that you don't have backed up on your computer or phone? You're supposed to be in Phoenix right now. Phoenix," she repeated. "Did I miss something? *Phoenix?*"

"Yeah," he answered, angrily approaching her. "Except I'm not in Phoenix. I'm here because I forgot my —" The area between his eyebrows creased.

"Forgot what?"

"My wallet."

Asha stared him down and then leaned in to fish his wallet out of his back pocket. She held it up and then tossed it on the bar. "Liar. Not even a good liar. A stupid liar."

"Fine," he said. "I missed my flight because I fell asleep, if you want to know the truth. But you lied too. You said she was done with the privates and then he shows up here to drop her off after two hours of brainwashing."

"He wasn't brainwashing her. Please."

"No, just injecting her with witch doctor potion cures and telling her that we're bad parents who don't know what's best for her."

"Why aren't you in Phoenix? Have you ever even been in Phoenix this past year? What the hell is going on?"

"You tell me what the hell is going on. When he dropped her off just now, she was so exhausted and out of it, she could barely walk. Is that what you want for our daughter? Honestly, Asha, I'm so —"

Oliver, trombone in hand, appeared at the bottom of the stairs and said, "I heard shouting. Is everything okay?"

"Yeah, honey, yeah," Asha responded, putting her arm around Phil's waist. "Everything is . . ."

"Great." Phil gave his son a thumbs-up. "Everything is awesome."

Feeling worried, wronged, and sickened by all the drama, Asha pulled her arm away from Phil's waist and walked off. She left the kitchen, hauled herself up the stairs, and knocked lightly on Mia's door. There was no answer. She cracked the door open. It was dark. The blinds had been drawn, and Mia was in bed, under the covers. "Mia," Asha called softly. "Mia?"

"Yeah, Mom?"

"Are you feeling all right?"

"Not the best."

"What can I do? Can I get you anything?"

"Maybe later. I'm just sore and tired. I'm gonna sleep it off."

"Are you sure?"

"Yes. I'm fine," she mumbled, turning to face the wall and pulling a big pillow over to hide her face. "Okay?"

"Okay, honey. Okay." Asha closed the door, feeling a sense of impending dread and confusion. Mia needed help. Things were *not* fine. Something was very, very wrong.

28

The air had a wintery bite, even though it was only late October, the cusp of autumn. An early mountain snow was on its way. The night was clear, though. Cloudless and starry. Beautiful, crisp, sweet, scented with pine. A perfect night for the Fall Feast.

As the cars showed up in the turnaround in front of the Big Elk Estates clubhouse to be valeted to spots around the neighborhood, some of the men didn't bother with anything warmer than their suit coats. It was a formal affair — not black tie because some of the employees wouldn't have been able to attend — but many people looked like they were showing up for the Academy Awards. Families walked in small herds. Little girls in lace and tiny heels. Boys scratching at their special-occasion starched collars. Moms with sparkly earrings. Dads with belts that were pulled a notch too tight.

The entrance to the clubhouse was lined

with tables and parents.

Asha was seated next to a sign that said, "THREE-COURSE DINNER FOR TWELVE AT FROMAGGIOS INCLUDING TWO ROUNDS OF TOP-SHELF COCKTAILS." She saw Natalie walk in and stood up. "Natalie, hi! You look so nice."

"Thanks, Asha," Natalie said. "I got cleaned up." She'd been feeling better after her trip to the nurse's prescription cabinet and had tried to look her best. "You look nice too."

"Natalie, don't even." Asha ran a hand over her volcanic mountain of a body, which she'd covered in a parrot-themed kimono. "I'm ready, and it's not even time. I can't walk properly. My ankles are so swollen, and I've got the varicose veins and everything."

"It's going to be so worth it. Just a little longer."

"It is. You're right. So —" Asha pointed down the hallway "— this is all a blind auction. You write down a bid on a piece of paper, and if you win, you get the prize. I didn't have anything to offer myself. I mean, who wants a free house-staging tutorial?"

"Me," Natalie said. She was serious.

"I'll give you one whenever you want. But no one thought that was going to be popular, so I'm sitting at the Fromaggios table. Are you interested in bidding on a three-course dinner for twelve at a fancy restaurant?" When Natalie made a face, Asha cupped a hand to the side of her mouth and said, "Me neither! I don't know more than a few people I want to have dinner with, do you? But we've had a lot of offers. If you walk on down, it gets crazier and crazier. Lift passes, jeep excursions, a week at Club Med in Greece. Golf and tennis lessons. Cool sculpting and personal training. There's so much. Go check it out."

While they were talking, Brooke and Sloane walked in, looking impossibly similar and glamorous in short black cocktail dresses. Brooke's had a lacy top layer while Sloane's was flashy and sequined. Both wore over-the-knee black boots that invited the question of whether either of them might also have a cat-o'-nine-tails whip in their matching leather purses. They turned directly into the dining room and didn't see Asha and Natalie.

As she watched the staggeringly beautiful Brooke walk away, every nuance of her perfect hips on display in the clingy dress, Natalie felt a surge of fury. "Is Phil here?" she asked quietly.

"No. He wanted to be, but he had a work

trip that he had to reschedule because of a missed flight."

"Really? Umm-hmm."

"Why do you ask?" Asha said, looking slightly alarmed.

"I called my friend. My ex who still works at Le Méridien. I know you didn't ask me to, but I did."

Asha froze in the middle of organizing her table. "And?"

"Phil stayed there. He had dinner in his room. Dinner for two with wine. Last March. He's stayed there since. Three times. More of the same. Room service and wine."

"That's just —" Asha winced and clutched her stomach. "Impossible. I was worried, but I didn't really think . . ."

"I'm sorry."

Asha felt like her whole life was slipping away. "There could be a mistake. Phil Wilson is a very common name."

"A few nights ago, Asha, I drove by Brooke Elliman's apartment building —"

"You mean her house up on the hill?"

"No, an apartment complex. The new one called Koi Creek. She either leased a unit or bought it for her husband when he left. I drove by it because I thought maybe she had something going on with the man I'd been seeing for a while, and I just wanted to know."

"And?"

"It was one in the morning. My ex's car wasn't there, but Phil's was."

"Oh God. Oh God, oh God, oh God." Asha looked ready to collapse. "How could he? I didn't think he would. And her! She and I just had a heart-to-heart the other day. I was mad at myself for suspecting them of doing that to me. I thought I was wrong and paranoid and crazy. I thought we were good. Jesus. I've got to go home. I don't want to ruin Mia's party. Can you drive her home when it's over?"

"I took an Uber, but I can certainly bring her home in one. Is Oliver here?"

"He's at a sleepover, thank God. Please just let Mia know I was tired. She's used to it. She'll understand." Asha grabbed her purse from underneath the table.

"Should you be driving?" Natalie asked.

"Heartache doesn't stop me from driving. I can cry while I drive." Asha threw her purse strap over her shoulder and headed for the door.

Escaping her boring table for the clubhouse bathroom, Brooke sat on the toilet and scrolled through Twitter. After a second, she wrinkled her nose. It was a fancy facility with wooden walls. Brooke knocked. "Hello? Whoever you are, I can smell you smoking. The smoke alarm will go off, and you'll be busted and embarrassed and in a load of trouble. Put it out, please."

From the next stall, Linda said, "Brooke?"

"Linda?"

It was quiet except for the sound of two toilets flushing and then they exited simultaneously. Aside from them, the bathroom was empty. Brooke glared at Linda, who went straight to the sinks to wash her hands. "You carry a gun and you smoke?" Brooke asked, wearing an expression that was a mixture of amusement and contempt.

"I'm complex," Linda answered, holding her hands out towards the paper towel dispenser and waiting.

"I don't appreciate your sarcasm."

"Brooke," Linda said. "Your voice is hurting my ears."

"How dare you. How dare you speak to me that way? How dare your son treat my daughter the way he has, and how dare you tell people that he broke up with her? I'm absolutely sick to death —"

"Oh my God. Be quiet. Please."

Brooke inhaled, and said, "I will not."

"Fine then," Linda said, drying her hands and crumpling the towel up into a little ball.

"Don't be quiet. Mouth off to everyone here about how unfair life is for you and your daughter. Find someone to argue with and belittle and threaten. Enjoy yourself. I know that's what you like to do. Everyone here hates you to death, so it should be easy for you to go start a fight with literally anybody else. Not me. Not tonight. I don't go out all that often and I came to have fun."

Linda left the bathroom, and the heavy door swung shut behind her. Brooke stood there motionless for a second, replaying the conversation in her head. She gave the middle finger to the closed door and said, "Bitch, bitch, bitch," before turning towards the mirror and fishing around in her purse for her lipstick.

Natalie walked around miserably looking for Mia, but with no success.

At seven thirty, Mr. Dilly stood at the front of the ballroom and used a spoon to ding ding ding against his scotch glass. There was a small stage, a podium, and a microphone. "If you could all make your way to the tables, that would be excellent. Thank you!"

The 118 upperclassmen were seated together at tables of twelve in the back. The families and faculty were at the front.

Natalie, Yvonne, and Rex had been seated with Harry Doyle, the boss of the custodial crew, the three lunch ladies, two volunteer crossing guards, and the groundskeepers. No one at Natalie's table was paying attention to the speakers on the stage. They were engrossed in their platters of sirloin steak with mushroom duxelles cream sauce.

Instead of eating, Natalie was staring across the room at Nick, who looked very handsome in his suit and whimsical tie, a Vineyard Vines with a soccer ball pattern against a light blue background the exact color of his eyes. Natalie hated that tie because he'd told her once that it had been a gift from Millie.

Doggedly, Natalie followed his every move throughout the dinner. Linda Leland didn't show up to many school events, but when she did, was a dead ringer for Gwyneth Paltrow dressed in a Stevie Nicks costume of scarves, tunic, and beret. She came up behind Nick's chair and put both of her hands on his shoulders. Leaning down so that her hair made a curtain around his head, she appeared to whisper something in his ear. Natalie couldn't help herself. She shot up out of her seat.

"Where are you going?" Yvonne asked

through a mouthful of roasted rosemary potato.

"To the bar."

"Grab me a vodka tonic, will you? Thanks, girl."

Natalie asked for two. "Make them doubles," she said. While she waited, Brooke Elliman appeared beside her. It was all Natalie could do not to audibly groan.

"Good evening, Miss Bellman," Brooke said, turning her back to the bar and leaning against it, elbows on top.

"Hello, Mrs. Elliman," Natalie said, willing the barman to move more quickly.

"I've been wanting to have a word with you," Brooke said. "I'm happy that we've run into each other."

"Are you really? I guess you enjoyed our last conversation more than I did."

Brooke leaned her head back and laughed. "Touché."

Natalie couldn't take much more, knowing that Brooke was sleeping with Asha's husband. "Why can't you just behave like a normal middle-aged woman? Leave people in relationships alone. Join that site eHarmony, or OurTime, and date some nice single old men?"

This grabbed Brooke's attention, and she gave Natalie the evil side-eye for a second before saying, "People don't usually speak to me like that."

"And now you're going to have me fired, right?"

"No. What you said was bitchy. But I've said a lot of bitchy things myself. To you and to a lot of other people. I am middle-aged, and if I'm going to make a change, now's the time. And right now, for starters, I feel like apologizing to you more than I feel like getting you fired."

"Thank you for the apology." Natalie picked up her drinks. "But I'm not the one you should be apologizing to."

"What do you mean?" Brooke asked, finally standing up straight.

"I've got to go," Natalie said, walking away.

This time, Brooke didn't follow.

On the way back to her table with the drinks, Natalie stopped to ask one of Mia's friends, Jeremiah Solomon, if he knew where she was.

"Bathroom," he answered.

Natalie dropped Yvonne's drink off, saying, "Be right back."

"Where are you off to now?" Yvonne asked. "Sit down and hang out."

"In a sec," Natalie said.

Just then, Nick was called up to the stage.

He joyfully jogged through the sea of parents and students to the sound of applause, waving to everyone and treating them to his devastating ear-to-ear boyish smile. Natalie downed her drink in several swallows and plunked it on the table.

"Damn, girl," Yvonne said. "Slow and steady wins the race. Take it easy."

"I'm fine," Natalie answered, wiping her mouth with her sleeve.

In the clubhouse, there were four meeting rooms, a kitchen, a men's bathroom, a women's bathroom, and a family bathroom. Natalie checked the women's bathroom first and didn't find Mia. She walked down to the family bathroom, tried the handle, and it was locked.

Inside, several people were arguing.

She heard Sloane's voice. The girl, loudly, said, "Reade, *stop.*"

Someone else was crying, loud messy gasps between brief periods of silence and then more sobbing.

Natalie banged on the door. "Hey! Hey! Open up." She stopped and stood back, waiting. Everything went quiet. "Open up," Natalie said, again, knocking. "I'm not leaving."

The door flung open so suddenly that Natalie jumped. Her clutch purse, which she'd been carrying underneath her armpit, dropped to the floor. The clasp sprang open, and the contents scattered. Natalie was face-to-face with Reade. "I'm sorry," he said politely, wearing an expression of profound concern. "I didn't realize it was you, Miss Bellman. Is something wrong?"

"Who's in there with you?"

He opened the door wider until Natalie could see both girls in the corner by the toilet. Sloane had one arm wrapped protectively around Mia's shoulder. "It's just Mia and Sloane," he answered. "We were having a private conversation. What can we do for you?"

Natalie gave Reade a long up-and-down inspection and then looked back at the girls. "I want them to come with me, please."

"Come on," Sloane said to Mia. The girls walked out submissively, their heads bowed and their arms hanging by their sides, but Natalie detected an undercurrent of tension. Reade remained inside, one hip against the sink. "Let me help you, Miss Bellman." He crouched down, picked up Natalie's clutch purse, and started collecting the scattered items: a lipstick from under the toilet, a hair band that had landed in a dirty corner and which she knew she would never use again. After tucking her things inside the purse, he handed it to back to her as if he were the world's most chivalrous gentleman.

Natalie didn't thank him. She just grabbed it out of his hand. To the girls, Natalie said, "Is there anything you want to tell me? I might be able to help."

Sloane shrugged and said, "Like what?"

Mia shook her head.

"Fine then," Natalie said. "Sloane, maybe you should go find your mom."

"Okay," she said, walking away without a word to either Reade or Mia. After a second, Reade followed.

"I'll go find mine too," Mia said, looking this way and that as if wondering where she might be able to hide.

"Your mom had to go home and said to tell you she suddenly got very tired."

"Fine. I'll get a ride. No big deal."

"Your mom asked me to take you."

"Really? And we have to do that? I mean, I'm fine. You don't need to."

"I think I better do what your mom asked me to. Just come find me when the party's over. I'll be waiting."

"You know, I really don't want to stay," Mia said, eyes on the floor.

"There's going to be music afterwards, and your mom was hoping —"

"They play terrible music, Miss Bellman.

It sucks. Can we just go?"

"But —"

"Please?"

"Of course," Natalie said, opening her purse and looking for her phone. "I'll just order us an Uber — Damn."

"What?"

"My phone isn't in here. It must have fallen out when I dropped my purse."

"It will be on the floor in the bathroom," Mia said. "Let's look."

They went back inside, but it wasn't there. Mia pulled out her own phone. "I'll ring it," she said. "What's your number?" Mia dialed it and they waited. There was no sound whatsoever.

"I suppose there's a chance I left it at my table," Natalie said.

They weaved back through the dining room while Nick continued to pace the stage, spouting compliments to the students, parents, and faculty. As they passed his table, Natalie saw his phone was next to his plate, mostly covered by a white cloth napkin.

Nick had been seated at the rear of the table, and everyone had angled their chairs to face the stage. They were all raptly listening to him as he strode back and forth, waving his muscular arms around in the air, espousing confidence in the greatness of the year to come.

The temptation was there. Right there. Easy. Calling her name. She decided she didn't care. Natalie leaned over and fished the phone out from underneath the napkin. It would only require a second to look and see who he'd been texting and calling while he was taking his endless break from spending time with her.

"What are you doing?" Mia asked, giving Natalie an odd look. "I'm not sure that's a good —"

"It's fine. Coach Nick won't mind if I use his phone to call us an Uber."

There was a sudden lull in the presentation. Nick had stopped speaking midsentence, and Natalie looked up, the phone in her hand. She nearly dropped it. He was staring right at her from the stage with shocked indignation. Without hesitation, she typed in his passcode, the school's address, 2258. Suddenly the phone was wrenched out of her hand. Lars Jaeger, who was usually the friendliest man on earth, said in his loud and accented voice, "What do you think you're doing? That's Nick's phone."

There was the clattering sound of forks being lowered to plates and heavy glass goblets thunking down onto cloth-covered tables. Then a hush fell over the room. All eyes were on Natalie and Lars, including Nick's.

"Oh, I know it is," Natalie said, followed by a quick nervous laugh. "I just need to call an Uber to take Mia Wilson home. Her mom had to leave sick. It's a bit of an emergency, and I don't have my phone on me, so I thought I'd borrow Mr. Maguire's."

Lars looked at Natalie while rubbing his long, cleft chin. His bushy white brows knitted for a second, and then he appeared to relax. "Of course. I see. I'll order you one."

After a few taps on his own phone, he said, "There's one just around the corner."

Up on the stage, Nick had apparently decided he was done talking and was having some trouble replacing the microphone on the stand. His hands were shaking. Natalie was suddenly terrified. "Let's go, Mia. Thank you, Mr. Jaeger."

"No problem, Miss Bellman."

Natalie actually pulled on Mia's arm to make her move faster, out into the hall and towards the front doors. "I had a coat," Mia said, trotting alongside Natalie but looking back towards the dining room.

"It's okay," Natalie answered. "They'll have it for you at the school on Monday. Come on, come on."

When they burst out into the cold evening and saw headlights coming down the road, Natalie took a deep breath, thinking, *I beat him. We're out.*

She was wrong.

"What was that about in there, Miss Bellman?" Nick asked, appearing on the sidewalk. Natalie wondered if he'd actually leaped off the stage and sprinted after them. "What were you doing with my phone?" That moment of fury she'd seen up on the stage had been replaced by a paternal expression of concern and confusion.

"I needed to call a car to take us home."

"It appears you knew my passcode."

Natalie didn't respond.

"Why didn't you use your own phone?" Nick asked.

"I can't find it. I lost it. I dropped my purse."

"Okay," he said. "That's what's going on, then. I see."

"Nothing's going on," Natalie answered. "Except that Mia's mom was sick and had to go home, and she didn't want to make Mia leave the party early, so she asked me to bring her home."

"The party's not over for another few hours."

"I know," Natalie said. "But some of the

kids had an argument, and —"

"I wanted to go," Mia interrupted. "I asked Miss Bellman to take me now."

"Where's your coat, Mia?" Nick asked. "You must be freezing."

"I left it at my table."

Nick immediately removed his sports jacket and draped it around Mia's shoulders. "Right. Well, listen, Mia. I can't let you leave with Miss Bellman. That would be a big failure on my part."

"I'm fine," Natalie said.

"You're not fine," Nick answered, exasperated. "Anyone can see you're not fine."

"I wasn't going to drive," Natalie said, just as the Uber pulled up next to them at the curb.

Nick stepped forward and opened the back door. "Natalie," he said softly. "Please just go."

"But —"

"I'll make sure Mia gets home safely. I take her home from her privates occasionally, don't I, Mia?"

"Yes."

"Her parents are fine with it."

"Mia, is that okay?" Natalie asked, dubious.

"Sure," Mia answered with a one-shouldered shrug. She seemed utterly unconcerned with which one of the school employees was going to chauffeur her back to her house.

"You should leave now, Natalie," Nick said. "I'll call you on your home phone later to check and make sure you made it safe."

Feeling exhausted and embarrassed, Natalie did as he asked. She got into the Uber and went back to her apartment. After pouring herself a big glass of water and taking her landline receiver over to the bed with her, she lay down fully clothed and stared at the ceiling. Even though she didn't really believe him, there was still a smidgeon of hope. Unable to sleep, she waited for hours.

Eventually she took two Vicodins and drifted off. When Nick did finally call, early in the morning, his message went to voice mail.

Police Video Excerpt,
Falcon Academy Conference Room
Interview: Bellman, Natalie Marie
(Continued)

"Can I get up and walk around a little bit?" Natalie asks.

"I don't see why not," Detective Larson answers.

The camera shakes for a second while Detective Larson removes it from the tripod, and then it follows Natalie as she stretches and circles the conference table. Detective Bradley has picked up her planner and is reading in the corner of the room.

"It's unusual for October," Natalie says, gesturing out the window. "So much snow this early."

Detective Larson's voice from behind the camera says, "Crazy, isn't it?"

"Natalie," Detective Bradley says, and

Detective Larson turns the camera on him. He points to the planner. "You seem to have been pretty convinced that Mr. Maguire was carrying on some sort of torrid love affair behind your back while you were dating. What made you so sure?"

"It was just a feeling I had," Natalie answers. "A feeling that he was one way with me and a different way with others. At first, I thought he was just a private person, and I tried to be understanding about that. Eventually, though, I started to think that he was hiding something from me."

"Did you ever figure it out?" Detective Bradley asks. "If he had a secret or not?"

Natalie hesitates, then says, "No."

29

After Natalie had been driven away from the Big Elk Estates clubhouse, Nick shook his head and said with a laugh, "Well, that was awkward!"

Mia gave him a half smile and redid her ponytail. "It's no big deal."

"I'm sorry you had to see that. Miss Bellman is a very nice woman, and she's good at her job, but you know, sometimes people overindulge. She used some pretty poor judgment tonight."

"Yeah," Mia said. "I understand."

"Okay," he said, giving her a light tap on the top of her head. "Come on, kiddo. Let's go."

Nick led Mia across the parking lot towards his truck. He looked back at the clubhouse before opening the passenger side door for her. The lights from the front door spilled out onto the sidewalk, warm and inviting. All the guests were gathered closely inside, enjoying the tail end of the meal, looking forward to dessert, more rousing speeches about the fantastic future of all the students, and after that, disco favorites played by a popular local cover band. There wasn't even an errant smoker standing outside.

Once they were seated in the truck, Nick put the heat on full blast. They drove out of the parking lot and turned right up the main road, which led towards the Wilsons' neighborhood. For the first minute, they rode in silence, but Nick kept glancing over at Mia. Finally, he said, "Miss Bellman said some kids had an argument?"

"Just the same old," she said placidly, staring out the window. "Not worth mentioning."

"You don't want to tell me?"

"It was about soccer."

"I don't believe you." Nick took a left turn up Canyon Drive. Mia frowned but didn't say anything. He wasn't taking the most direct route to her house. "Did it have anything to do with what you and Sloane and some of the boys were planning to do later on tonight?"

Mia's head spun around, and she looked directly at him, evaluating.

Nick made another turn, this time onto a

side street lined with enormous houses, all with big, shiny floor-to-ceiling windows and flanked by lodgepole pines, red boulders, and rows of sculpted bushes.

"You took a wrong turn," Mia informed him.

"I know where I'm going."

She stared at him. There was a long and uncomfortable silence.

"What was the argument about?" he asked, the wheel sliding through his hands as he turned yet again.

She crossed her arms across her chest, defiant and silent even though she was being driven to an unknown destination.

"I think," he said, his eyes fixed outside at the night, "that it was about you not wanting to let your friends party in the empty houses your mom is selling anymore. I think in the past couple of months you've gotten a conscience about the crimes you've committed."

"Crimes!" she echoed, unimpressed. "Whatever. I'm not sure what you're talking about. And you're totally going the wrong way."

"No, I'm not."

As they ascended the mountain, the houses had larger plots, with great dark patches of well-tended lawns stretching for acres in between. They reached a driveway bordered on either side by stone towers. Nick turned in, and Mia's demeanor changed abruptly.

"Tell me what's going on. Why are we here?" Mia demanded, her veneer of insolence crumbling. She was looking around, panicked.

They reached the top of the driveway, where there was a large parking area outside the four-car garage of a sprawling Spanish-style villa. "I'm doing an intervention," he said.

"What's that supposed to mean?"

There was a weeping willow drooping over the drive, casting a large shadow on the pavement, which was partially illuminated by landscaping lights. Nick parked underneath the willow, turned off the ignition and said, "You were supposed to meet up with your friends here tonight at one in the morning. You were going to let them in using the key codes your mom keeps in a notebook that she carries in her purse. You were going to drink and smoke pot and who knows what else."

As pretty and innocent as Mia often managed to appear, she had a savage side. She seethed with irritation that she'd been caught. "No," she said. "What makes you think that?"

"It doesn't matter." Nick sighed and tapped his hand against the dash a couple of times. "What does matter is that, in my estimation, you're about six months away from ruining your life. Being arrested for trespassing in one of your mom's houses. Jumping in a car with a drunk teenage boy who takes a mountain turn too fast and you end up dying at the side of the road or at the bottom of some ravine."

Mia blew some air out of her mouth in a way that conveyed disdain.

"You think I'm full of it?"

"I think you're overreacting. No one's died."

"Really?" Nick asked. "Want to bet? Let's go in the house. You'll see."

"Take me home, please," Mia said, primly folding her hands in her lap. "I don't like this. I've had enough."

"I don't like this either," Nick said. "I don't like having to teach you a lesson. You're one of my favorite students, but let's get real. I could turn you in to the police myself if I wanted to."

She closed her big brown eyes, and her chin dropped to her chest. It wasn't clear if he had actually gotten through to her or if she was playing a part. "I'm sorry. Please don't tell anyone. Please don't tell my mom."

"Mia, I'm trying to keep you out of trouble. That's why I'm doing this."

"I said I'm sorry. What more do you want?"

"I want you to take me inside."

"What? No. I can't do that."

"Sure you can. You have the code. You've been inside this house before with your friends. I know you have. I know all the stuff you've done."

Mia's face was scrunched up now, and scared, a little bit sick. "Why do you want to go in there?"

"So I can show you the bedroom of the girl who was your age, who reminded me of you, who died two years ago because she started to do the same stupid stuff you're doing."

Mia didn't respond right away. In fact, her expression contained a hint of morbid curiosity. "Are you serious?"

"Deadly serious. All you have to do is unlock the house and come inside with me, and then you'll understand. I'll show you."

A minute later, Mia opened the front door to Elena and Louis Ruiz's house and allowed Nick to enter. "Don't turn on the overhead."

"I won't," he answered, pulling out his phone and turning on the flashlight.

"Which one's her bedroom?" Mia asked.

"I'll know it when I find it," he answered, heading for the stairs.

"What was her name?" Mia asked, following him.

"Jill."

"I've heard about her. She used to hang out with Reade."

"True," Nick said. "Briefly."

"If she died two years ago," Mia said, a step behind him on the stairs, "they probably cleaned out her room."

"They didn't," he answered. "It was too hard for the mom. She left it alone."

"How do you know?"

"She told me." Nick turned his flashlight down a long, dark hall.

"I've never been up here," Mia said, sounding freaked out.

"You kids like the basements, don't you?" Nick answered. "That's what I heard, anyway."

He shone the light into two open bedrooms before arriving at a third, which had a closed door. "This one. This must be it."

He reached out, turned the doorknob, and pushed.

The bedroom had a large window, and the

moon was three quarters full. The light from the sky outside played over part of the four-poster bed, a sliver of a desk, and a zebra-print chair with a hot-pink blanket folded and draped over the back. He touched the blanket. His hand lingered there, and after a moment, he brought his hand to his nose and made a noise.

It sounded like he was either choking or crying. "You okay?" Mia asked.

"Yes," he answered, sounding anything but okay. "I just wasn't ready for how this would feel."

Mia shifted her weight uncomfortably.

Nick walked over to the desk and played his phone flashlight across it. It was the sort that had a glass top over the wood. "Look at that," he said. "Some of her photos are still here."

"Let me see," Mia said, coming to stand beside him. There were a dozen or so, slipped underneath the desk's glass, and more than half were of the Falcon Academy girls' soccer team. The girls wore their hair back in a variety of unique, colorful headbands. Many of them were oily-faced with acne, and a few had big smiles that revealed glinting silver tracks across their teeth. They did cartwheels in the rain, made peace signs while gathered around a table covered with cups of frozen yogurt, and posed in a pyramid on the school soccer field.

"Is that her?" Mia asked, pointing to a girl who seemed to be present in all of the photos.

Nick didn't answer.

"Is that her?" she asked again.

"Yes," he managed in a hoarse voice. "That's her."

"She was pretty."

"She was." He turned to Mia and stared at her, drinking her in for an unpleasant amount of time. Then he touched the glass over Jill's photos once more. "She was a very pretty girl." He took a deep breath and said, "Okay."

"Thank God. This is creepy. Let's go."

"One more minute," Nick said. "I just want to make sure you understand the significance of this. Of why I brought you here."

"I've learned my lesson," Mia answered, aiming for sincerity but falling short.

"I don't think you have," he said, taking a seat in Jill's chair. He loosened his tie and breathed a sigh of relief as he pulled it away from his neck. "I need a show of faith. I want you to tell your mom and dad you want to start the privates again. You need my supervision. That's obvious."

"Done. I'll do it. All of it. I swear. Back with the privates. No more houses, no more drinking, no more middle-of-the-night parties. Okay? I didn't even like them. I wanted to stop. That was what the argument back at the clubhouse was really about."

"And no more of this either," he said, holding out his phone.

"What?"

"Come here."

She approached warily.

"When you go to parties with boys and you pass out, dangerous, awful, irreversible things happen. I don't want you to feel ashamed of yourself, like Sloane. I don't want you to die, like Jill. I don't want you to get in any more trouble. I don't want this to happen to you ever again."

Mia took the phone out of his hand. Nick wore an inscrutable but intense expression as she began to scroll through a series of photos that were clearly her, but none of which she had any recollection whatsoever of taking.

30

At first, for a moment, Natalie felt a contented, Sunday-morning calm. It wasn't a workday, and she didn't have to get up. She'd woken without an alarm, and after peeking at her bedside clock, she'd burrowed back in for more sleep. As she cuddled into her pillow, however, her eyes popped open.

Bad things had happened last night.

Terrible, shameful things. Telling the truth to Asha. The cruel way she'd spoken to Mrs. Elliman. The completely irrational and rash decision to grab Nick's phone. The humiliation of hearing the words, *Go home and go to bed, Natalie.*

She jumped up and went to her kitchen counter, where her clutch purse was lying open next to a glass of water. No phone. She'd hoped against hope. Inside was only her driver's license, a debit card, a red lipstick, and hollow ChapStick containing a couple of Vicodin and one Adderall.

There were amends to be made. Of course she would have to apologize to Nick. She knew they would never get back together now, but it was something she needed to do for her own peace of mind. First, however, Natalie had to talk to Asha and make sure she was all right after hearing the truth about Phil. Also, Natalie wanted to make sure that Mia had gotten home all right. Asha was supposed to be having an open house. Maybe she would cancel it, but Natalie didn't think so.

She walked into the kitchen, opened up her laptop, and typed in, "Open houses near me." The screen filled with results, and Natalie scanned them. Asha was having a showing at noon.

Natalie wasn't sure what she needed more: a Vicodin to help her feel better about how she'd behaved the previous night, or an Adderall so she could get up, get out, and do what she needed to do. She decided on both at the same time and got into the shower.

The house was situated on several acres, surrounded by a beautifully landscaped garden. It was Mediterranean in style, with a lush weeping willow billowing over the top of the driveway, a rust-colored, tiled roof, stone walls, and wrought iron accents. As Natalie walked through the foyer, she stopped at a curved table by the door. On it was a blown glass vase filled with a classic arrangement of lilies, green-and-white hydrangeas, and tulips. Asha must be doing all right. This was a signature touch of hers, these flowers, and she must surely have brought them from the florist that morning. She wasn't at home, grieving beneath her blankets.

On the shelf below the bouquet was an ornate, carved wooden picture frame. Usually there were very few personal items left in these houses, but this glimpse into the owners' lives remained. The photo was of a beautiful dark-haired family: a smiling man with a moustache, an elegant, kind-eyed woman, and a girl with an infectious and enormous smile.

It was Jill, and the woman in the photos was her mom, Elena Ruiz. This was where they had lived together before the car accident that took the teenager's life. Natalie suddenly wanted to leave, but not without having a word with Asha.

After a quick search, Natalie located Asha in the master bedroom, surrounded by a small crowd of clients. She was wearing an embroidered maternity dress with an asymmetrical hem and a long matching scarf. Though Asha looked tired and not nearly as radiant as usual, Natalie was relieved to see her at work. Asha usually spoke so poetically, but today her presentation to her captive crowd sounded robotic and monotonous. She was going through the motions. Natalie wandered out of the room to wait until Asha was done. It was necessary to speak with her alone to find out for sure if she was okay.

Two doors down, there was a bedroom that looked like it belonged to a teenager. Natalie knew immediately that it must have been Jill's. No one had turned it into a generic study or a workout room. Natalie hesitated before going in, feeling like an intruder, but in the end she couldn't resist. It was colorful and cozy, a room for a modern-day princess who was very loved. Jill had been incredibly lucky once upon a time. Natalie trailed her fingers over the top of the desk, looking at photos of Jill with her friends and teammates during happier times. She sat in the black-and-white chair in the corner with the pink throw blanket over the arm, and stared at the four-poster bed, wondering what it would have been like to grow up with such luxury.

Her eyes dropped down to the floor. In the corner, beside the chair leg, was a coiled ball of silky fabric. Familiar somehow. Light blue. She reached down. It was a Vineyard Vines men's necktie, and the pattern on it was tiny soccer balls. It felt as if she'd had the wind knocked out of her. She took a great big breath as if she'd just popped up to the surface after a long underwater swim.

She picked it up, stretched it taut between her hands, and imagined strangling Nick with it.

As Asha was saying goodbye to a couple by the front door, Natalie came hurtling down the stairs two at a time. "You're not going, are you?" Asha asked. "I'm almost done. I was hoping we could talk."

"I'm sorry, Asha. I actually can't stay."

"You look upset," Asha said, motioning her over to one side of the room. "Don't be. Listen. It's for the best. Thank you for telling me. I needed to know. For my sake, and for the baby's sake, and for Oliver and Mia, too."

"Did Mia get home safe last night?" Natalie asked, hoping Nick had at least gotten the girl home safely before coming to this house to meet Elena for some secret midnight tryst.

"She did. Thank you."

"I didn't bring her. Nick — Mr. Maguire — insisted he would do it. He wouldn't take no for an answer, and Mia said it would be all right with you."

"Oh, that's okay," Asha said. "She didn't tell me, but it's fine. I was just drained and depressed. I had to lie down. She came into my room to say she was home, but that was all."

"All right. Well, good," Natalie said, realizing that she still had the tie in her hand. She scrunched it up and held it against her thigh to hide it, but it only served to make Asha look down. "Just wanted to make sure. I really need to go."

Asha pointed to the tie. "What have you got there?"

"Nothing." Natalie felt as childish as she sounded.

Asha looked up into Natalie's eyes and then down at the man's tie crumpled in her fist. "May I see that?"

"It's just a tie."

"Is it from this house?" Asha asked, baffled.

"I'm not stealing it," Natalie said. "I know who it belongs to. I'm going to give it back."

"What do you mean? That makes no sense, Natalie. Please. Let me see it."

"I can't. I just can't." Natalie lunged for her shoes over by the door on the floor and ran.

Asha stood by the door and watched as Natalie, barefoot, leaped over a rock and then hightailed it through the grass to reach her car.

"What is wrong with you, Natalie?" she said out loud. It all seemed surreal. What was going on? It was as if some collective madness had suddenly taken over the town and erased rational behavior. She'd never *really* thought Phil would stray, she'd never thought Mia would become so withdrawn and furtive, she'd never thought she'd be scared to do her own job or to have another child. Many thoughts and memories and inklings started coming together. Asha had an unsettling feeling that something important was trying to make itself known. It was there. She just needed to stop and think and let it come to her.

Though the house still had a few visitors, Asha walked down the stairs to the basement in-law suite, went inside the bedroom, and locked the door. Selling Elena's house was suddenly the last thing on her mind. The bed was a very tall antique, so it took some effort to get her bulging body up there, but once she made it, it was unexpectedly comfortable. Asha lay back and breathed. In. Out. In. Out. So, was Natalie a thief after all?

Asha didn't think so. The mystery of the missing bracelet had been solved. It had never been missing at all. Or had it? Mia had been very sneaky lately. Speaking on her phone in Asha's office, telling Sloane she "didn't want anything to do with it." To do with what? And why had she been in there in the first place? Then, Asha remembered finding Mia practically with her hand in her own purse, claiming to have been interested in the new Taser gun. Was she stealing? Was she on drugs? Was it true that she was doing all of the things Mr. Maguire had accused her of, and Asha just hadn't wanted to believe it was really that bad? But maybe, she thought, it was even worse. Slowly, it started to fall into place. The pillow that was in the wrong room and smelled of marijuana. Shards of broken glass in the carpet. The used condom. "Oh God," she said out loud.

Exactly as Mr. Maguire had suspected.

Phil's car outside Brooke Elliman's apartment? Not him after all. There was a more likely explanation. Asha pictured her own bedroom: Alexa playing the soothing sound of a babbling brook all night long, the trickle of water in the humidifier, and the gentle hum of the aromatherapy diffuser. Asha would never have heard the garage door opening. Phil often used his Bose noise-canceling headphones, and they made him a very deep sleeper. Lately he was out of town a lot, and when he was home, he spent many nights in the basement because of Asha's "pregnancy snoring." It would have been easy for Mia to sneak his car out for a couple of hours.

Mia.

It had been Mia all along. She had been the one in the houses.

What about the significance of the tie? Why would Natalie steal one of Mr. Ruiz's ties? And one like that, such a silly one, with soccer balls all over it? Asha was sure the tie didn't belong to Mr. Ruiz. He was an impeccable dresser, more of an Italian silk cravat kind of guy. So, if the tie had looked familiar, then where had she seen it, if not in Mr. Ruiz's closet?

And then she knew. She could see it plain as day: Mr. Maguire walking into the Fall Feast looking dapper and excited. He'd stopped by her little table, given her a peck on the cheek, and thanked her for her help with the fundraising auction. He'd been wearing the turquoise silken Vineyard Vines tie with the soccer ball pattern. Later that night, he'd given Mia a ride home, and for some absolutely unfathomable and possibly horrifying reason, they had stopped here and been in Elena's daughter's room.

It might still be a mystery, but it was no longer a secret. Asha was about to get to the bottom of exactly what the hell had been going on behind her back. She pulled herself to her feet and waddled up the staircase into the open-plan two-story great room. She stood in the middle, by the stand-alone fireplace, cupped her hands around her mouth, and yelled, "The pregnant lady is not feeling well! I'm terribly sorry! Please be thoughtful and get your things. The open house is over. Now!"

"Hi, Mom," Oliver said when Asha practically collapsed into their house, out of breath. He was sitting at the breakfast bar, eating a bowl of cereal and watching YouTube on his iPad.

"Where's your sister?"

"In her room."

"Thanks," Asha said, giving him a distracted pat on the arm as she passed.

Asha knocked on Mia's door. No answer. Asha went ahead and entered. "Mia?"

"I'm taking a bath, Mom," Mia called

from the bathroom. "I'll be out in twenty."

"I need to talk to you now. Can I come in?"

There was a notably long stretch of time before Mia answered, and Asha had to remind herself that at eight months pregnant, it wasn't probably a good time to ram a wooden door down with her whole body.

"I guess," Mia responded eventually. "If you want to. It's not locked or anything."

Asha opened the door. Mia was hunched over, her arms around her knees. The water was still gushing out of the faucet into the tub. Her hair was wet and tangled, hanging down her back. She looked up at Asha and said, "What's wrong, Mom?"

Asha realized she was shaking. "I'm on to you."

"Okay, what?" Mia stared at her. "You're acting really weird."

"You have to tell me what's been happening. All of it," Asha said. She lowered the seat to the toilet and sat, cradling her belly. "I love you, and I'll forgive you, but the most important thing now is that I help you. You have to tell me. What exactly has been going on? What have you been keeping from me?"

"I don't know what you're talking about." Mia took the washcloth and began to wipe her eyes.

"I may be old, pregnant, and naive, but Mia, so help me God, I am not stupid, and I realize now that you've been lying to me." Asha reached over and turned the water off.

"About what?"

"Don't do this!"

"Do what? You have to tell me."

Asha hit the marble tiled wall with her hand and said, "Just stop it! I know you! I love you! Stop doing this to me! Please!"

The washcloth dropped into the tub and floated there, over Mia's stomach. She stared downwards. "Okay. Fine. I'm done. I don't want to feel like shit about myself anymore. What do you want to know? I'll tell you."

Asha wasn't even sure where to start. "Have you been sneaking out at night?"

"Sometimes. Never on a school night."

"And how did you get out?"

"Through the side door in the piano room."

This was unexpected. That particular door was rarely used, and in fact had a large, heavy leather chair positioned in front of it. "Do you have a key for that door?" Asha asked.

"No."

"So, you left the house unlocked while

your whole family was in here asleep? When anyone could have come in, robbed us blind, or hurt us?"

"I'm sorry!"

"Have you . . ." Asha closed her eyes and took a deep breath. The question she was about to ask was more meaningful than Mia could imagine. "Have you ever taken your dad's car?"

"Only a few times. And only after I got my learner's permit. Usually someone comes to get me, and I walk down to the street."

"Those times you took it, where did you go?"

"Once I drove to the Leopolds' house, and another time it was the Hertzels'. I also drove to Sloane's."

"The house or the apartment?" Asha followed up quickly.

"The apartment in town."

"Okay," Asha said, exhaling. "Okay." So, Natalie had seen Phil's car outside the apartment, but it wasn't him. Now Asha just had to find out who he had dinner with in his room at the Le Méridien. "And when you say," Asha continued, "that you drove to the Leopolds' and the Hertzels' — I take it that means you've been letting your friends into the houses I'm selling? For what, parties?"

"Small get-togethers only. But yes. I always cleaned up afterwards."

Asha thought about pointing out that she'd done a pretty poor job of it, considering the broken glass and used prophylactic, but she stopped herself. "What about my bracelet? The one I thought I lost at an open house last spring and magically reappeared months later?"

"One of the boys took it. Kasper or Alistair, I think. I had to fight with Sloane to get it back for me. It took forever."

"Mia," Asha said, one hand going to her forehead. Her expression was a mixture of disgust, disbelief, and fury. "I've done everything I can possibly think of to be the best mom to you, and you repay me in this way? Why?"

"I didn't want to, okay?" Mia pulled her knees in closer to her body. "We always used to hang out in Greg's basement, but his parents started being stricter last spring. It was Reade's idea to sneak into one of your houses. I knew you kept the codes in the little notebook in your purse, so that's how I got us in. Everyone thought it was so fun. I mean, except me. I didn't think they would want to keep doing it, like, every other weekend. I tried to get it all stopped."

So that explained Mia rummaging around in her purse for the codes and shouting over the phone to Sloane that she didn't want to "have anything to do with it" anymore. Asha leaned forward towards the bath. "One last question. Did you go to the Ruiz house last night?"

Terror flashed quickly through Mia's eyes. This clearly upset her more than all the other questions combined. She folded the washcloth carefully into a blindfold. Leaning back, she placed it over her eyes. "No," she said, with finality.

"But you did."

"No," she said again, sounding much like she had when she was just a little girl, denying a crayon mark on the wall. "I didn't."

"I know you did, and I want to know what happened in that house."

Mia was paler than usual, her lips more purple than pink. She removed the washcloth blindfold from her eyes and sat up to turn the hot water back on. Asha immediately reached out and shut it off again. "What happened in that house?" she demanded.

"There were no kids there. There was no party."

"Was Mr. Maguire there?"

Mia didn't answer. She kept twisting the

washcloth in her hands.

"Jesus Christ, Mia, come on! We're not talking about kid stuff. This isn't teenagers sneaking out. We're talking about a grown man who —"

"Mom —"

"Just tell me! I have to know!"

"He took me there to do an intervention. Okay?"

"Wh-what?" Asha stammered. "An intervention?"

"Yes. He wanted to talk to me about getting in trouble. To warn me about what happened to your doctor's daughter after she started drinking and going to parties and stuff like that. Basically, it was just like, 'Cut it out,' and I told him I would. He said that if I kept my promise, the whole thing would be our secret, and he wouldn't tell anyone what I'd done. That's it. That's what happened. That's all."

Asha shook her head in disbelief. "That's all? Oh, Mia, you have no idea —"

"I do! I get it!" Mia hugged herself, still trembling, and Asha didn't know if the water really had gone freezing cold or if she was on the brink of a panic attack. "I'm done with all that," she managed to say through chattering teeth. "I almost messed up my entire life. I won't lie to you anymore.

Coach Nick taught me a lesson. Please, please, please don't tell him I told you. He might turn me into the police for trespassing. Or worse."

"Worse? How? What could possibly be worse?"

"Can you p-p-please pass me a towel? I want to get out."

"What else have you done?" Asha repeated loudly.

"Nothing!" Mia exploded. "Nothing, okay? Can you just ground me or send me to boarding school or juvenile detention or anything at all except talk about this anymore! Can't we please just forget it ever happened?"

"I will never forget this. Any of this," Asha said, heaving herself to her feet and throwing a towel toward the tub. "When your dad gets home from his business trip tonight, we're going to all sit down and figure out how long you're going to be grounded and what other restrictions are necessary. I'm incredibly disappointed, Mia. You have no idea. I feel like I don't even know you." Asha slammed the bathroom door behind her when she left.

Five minutes later, Asha was on the phone with Brooke. "Mia said it was an 'intervention.' She said he 'taught her a lesson.'

Those are her words. That's what she thinks. That he wanted to warn her about what had happened to this girl, Jill Ruiz, who died in a car accident."

"That is completely messed up," Brooke responded. "It's inappropriate beyond belief no matter what sort of trouble the girls might have been getting into."

"I'm so pissed off I can't think straight."

"Take deep breaths."

"My pulse is pounding in my ears."

"I'm sure it is," Brooke said.

"What should I do?"

"He's training Sloane right now. I think we should go to the school and confront him. Tell him that we know what he did and that we think it's unacceptable and possibly a crime. I'll meet you at the school."

"Are you leaving now?"

"I'm out the door."

"I'll meet you there," Asha said, grabbing her keys and checking to make sure her stun gun was still in the zippered compartment of her purse.

31

It was starting to snow when Natalie pulled into the parking lot at the rear of the sports pavilion. Nick's truck was there, but that was it. Maybe he was alone. The tie, which she was planning to confront him with, was wadded up in a ball inside the right pocket of her coat.

Natalie closed her eyes for a second. Her first stop after the open house had been Jay's, where she'd downed two beers, swiped a Vicodin, and ranted at length to her brother that Nick had been cheating on her with a rich, older doctor all along. Jay had said, "I really wish you'd just punch that guy right in the face for me. I hate him."

She'd left an hour later to go straight to the school. The mixture of the uppers and the downers had her in a fog. Angry then sleepy. Agitated then calm. Sad, thinking she should just go home. Go home and paint something crazy. Go home to her warm bed.

It was the tattoo that convinced her to stay. "Self love," she said, giving herself a pep talk while looking in the rearview mirror. "Your words matter. Say what you need to say. He should have had enough respect for you to at least tell you the truth."

Eventually she got out of her car. She slipped and collapsed sideways onto the ground. It took a long time to get to her feet. After brushing the snow off her face and out of her hair, she managed to walk the rest of the way to the back door without falling again. The door was propped open.

Natalie stood at the bottom of the stairs leading up to the mezzanine and listened. Music was playing, and there was a murmur of voices. Nick's, she was sure. And a female. Conversational but loud, trying to hear one another over the music. The clanging of weights. The girl yelled, "Come on, dude, you can do better than that! That was weak!"

Sloane. Flirting. Sure, Sloane could talk to Nick like that. She could talk to anyone any way she wanted.

Everything was spinning.

Natalie slumped against the wall. She grabbed onto the railing with both hands and fell to a sitting position on the bottom step. The beige bricks were undulating like a curtain blowing in the breeze. She closed her eyes.

Just for a second, she told herself. *I'll just rest for a second and then I'll go home. I'll drive very slowly, taking only surface streets, and I'll go into my nice, safe apartment and get into bed and forget him forever.*

Above, where the staircase opened onto the mezzanine, she could hear Sloane's laughter. Nick was singing along to the music as if he hadn't a care in the world. As if he hadn't recently been in a relationship that mattered, and was fulfilling and special, and that he'd ended by simply stepping away and going on with his life.

The last thing Natalie could recall before waking up later in her car was thinking how much she hated them both.

32

Brooke swung her beige Mercedes into the sports pavilion back lot just after Asha. She parked and opened her car door. "Asha, wait," she called. "I'm here. Hold up!"

They entered the back door of the sports pavilion together. Grunge rock from the nineties was blasting. "Come on," Asha said. Brooke noticed she was wheezing and flushed.

"Take it easy," Brooke said, as they started up the stairs. "Slow down."

"I'm fine."

They looked around the upper level. The cardio machines were on one end, the weight lifting apparatus was in the center, and there was a mirror along the wall that faced the balcony looking out over the basketball courts. At the far end was the door to the trainer's room. It was closed.

"Where is he?" Asha asked, panicked eyes darting back and forth.

"Good question," Brooke answered, taking a deep breath and trying to stay calm. She put a steadying hand on Asha's arm and said, "We'll find them."

After a momentary hesitation, Asha headed towards the other side of the mezzanine. Brooke followed. Asha knocked on the training room door. "Hello? Anybody in there?"

Inside the room, something dropped and hit the floor, but no one responded.

Brooke tried to open the door and realized it was locked. She rattled the knob, yelling, "Who's in there? Sloane? Are you in there?"

There was a noise from the other side of the door, but it was faint. No voices, only a hint of movement.

"Oh, for fuck's sake, who's in there? Open the door!"

With that, the door immediately opened. Nick slid out gingerly, one finger to his lips, as if he'd just successfully put an infant down for a nap. "Shh." He quietly pulled the door closed behind him, taking the women in with an expression of dismay and disapproval, as if they were the problem. "What's the ruckus?"

They both stared at him. "Ruckus?" Asha asked. "You want to know what's 'the ruckus'?"

"Is Sloane in there?" Brooke demanded.

"Can you lower your voice please?" he asked calmly, slipping his phone into his shorts pocket.

"Why?" Brooke asked. "The music is ear-splitting. Just answer me. Is Sloane in there?"

"The music is just white noise. And yes, she's in there. We were doing her ten-minute guided meditation, and she fell asleep. I decided to let her rest. There are so many demands on her coming from so many different directions right now. Sometimes they just need a safe space to relax."

"Move," Brooke said.

He put his back against the door. "Just be patient. She was already waking up. I'm sure she'll be out in a minute."

Asha was staring at Nick. Unblinking, oval-eyed, jaw clenched. "Mia told me about your *intervention.*"

"Oh, did she?" Nick smiled in a way that indicated he was fine with that.

"Yes," Asha answered, undeterred. "She begged me not to talk to you about it. Said it was a secret. That you'd threatened to turn her in to the police. Do you want to explain?"

"It's called mentoring," he said. "That's

what you hired me for, isn't it? You both wanted a personal trainer and a mentor for your daughters, and that's all I've tried to do. Help them. Sometimes I use slightly unconventional methods, but that's how I get results. That's how you create strong competitors who can succeed in the real world. Your daughters needed guidance, and I provided it."

Brooke banged again on the door. "Sloane? Answer me! Are you in there?"

"Mom?" Sloane's voice was slurred.

Brooke gave Nick an unexpected shove, grabbed the doorknob, and pushed the door open. Sloane was sitting in a plastic chair by the back of the room behind the training table. She was bent over, attempting to tie one of her shoelaces. It wasn't going very well. Her body was swaying from side to side, as if she was about to face-plant off the chair.

Brooke wheeled around towards Nick. "What the hell is going on here?" she asked, her voice quiet yet ferocious.

"What do you mean?" he asked, crossing his arms on his chest and appearing to be totally puzzled.

"Brooke," Asha said, appalled. "Oh my God. He did something."

Nick said, "Okay, come on now. Don't be

ridiculous." He shook his head and laughed. "Sloane's fine. She fell asleep. Mrs. Wilson, I think you need to sit down. The bench press is just over here, and given your condition you should relax and —"

"Stop that!" Asha said. "Stop acting like we don't understand what is right in front of our eyes! We're not stupid! We'll see what the police make of you taking my daughter into an empty house with you last night when you were supposed to be bringing her home! We'll see what they make of this. You, behind a locked door with a fifteen-year-old girl who is clearly under the influence of something!"

"You're out of your mind," he responded.

"Oh, shut up, Nick," Brooke said, reaching out to pull the door to the training room shut again.

"What are you doing, Brooke?" Asha asked.

"I don't want Sloane to hear what I'm about to say."

Nick raised his eyebrows. "All right. Ladies. Let's just back this up a little. I can see you're both very upset —"

"Did you touch her?" Brooke asked.

Nick held up his hands incredulously. "What?"

Brooke repeated herself. "Did you touch her?"

"No. Of course I didn't."

"You're lying. You're going to go to jail for this," Brooke said.

Nick laughed, and he looked boyish somehow. Like a kid who'd been caught. "No. You don't understand."

"I think we do understand," Asha said. "And I think the police will understand as well."

"Hmm." Nick clapped his hands together as if he were standing in front of a class. "Okay. Let's run with this, then. I have two girls who've been entrusted to me by their parents to help get them into a good college. And both of these girls are drinking, doing drugs, sneaking out at night, trespassing and throwing parties in other people's homes, and sending X-rated photos of themselves to all the boys in the school, and yet —" He rolled his eyes towards the ceiling. "And yet the moms are mad at *me,* for stepping in and trying to help?"

"Not Mia," Asha said. "She didn't send around photos. I don't believe you. Mia didn't do that."

"They all do that," Nick said, pulling his phone out of his pocket and clicking on his camera roll. He extended it so Asha could see. "Here's a nice one. There's that cute silver dragonfly ring Mia always wears. I've got more if you want —"

"Give it to me," Asha said.

"My phone? No, that's okay. I'll hold on to it. But if you want to have a look, there it is."

Asha's hand dropped into her purse, and she pulled her stun gun out of it. She dipped her shoulder and dropped the purse to the ground so she could more easily hold the Taser like a pistol. It was pointed at Nick's chest. "Give it to me."

"Mrs. Wilson," he said. "Do you even know how to use —"

"Give it to me," she shouted, lunging forward. Her baby bump made her ungainly and she tripped. As Nick jumped backwards, she fired the electrode wires downwards, just missing his thigh. Still, she managed to cause him to drop the phone. Brooke dove in, scooped it up, and looked at the screen. She swiped a couple of times, her face turning red and enraged.

"You're both out of control," he said. "This is going to end badly. I'd like my phone back, please."

Brooke turned the screen of the phone towards Nick and said, "These photos weren't taken at a party. These aren't sexy selfies," she spit. "You took these!" Brooke pointed at the training room. "In there! And that's the back of your hairy hand pulling Sloane's shirt to the side just now while she was passed out."

Nick darted forward and grabbed his phone back. "Wrong," he said. "You are way, way off base. How dare you insinuate such a disgusting thing when all I've done is try to help —"

"Shut up," Brooke said, and used the right hook she'd perfected in her TITLE boxing workouts to smash the left side of his face with her fist. He staggered backwards into the squat rack, and the back of his head smacked into one of the upper hooks. He let out a pained, "Ahhh," and looked surprised when he touched the spot and brought his hand away. His middle three fingers were red with bright, shiny blood. For a second it looked like maybe his knees were going to give, but then he staggered a few steps to the side so he could lean against the balcony. "Huh. Well. I think that seals the deal, doesn't it? I guess now we know who's really going to jail," he said nonchalantly. "I'm done with you two. Goodbye, ladies."

"No," Asha said, sounding almost conversational. She had moved to a place beyond hysteria. All she felt was resolve. "You're not going to just walk away."

Nick wiped the blood from his fingers off on his T-shirt and gave her a skeptical smile. "Come on. Really? The parents here love me. They respect me. I've been doing this job all over the country for two decades without a single complaint. Sloane and Mia are delinquents. Drinkers. Promiscuous potheads. The last thing you want is for those photos of your daughters to suddenly find their way into the inboxes of every Falcon family. Am I right? So, watch me. Watch me walk away."

Asha dropped the Taser, which only had one charge in it to begin with, in order to attack him with both hands. They went for him at the same time, and with the combination of Brooke's strength and Asha's one hundred seventy pounds of baby weight, he went over the balcony fairly easily.

Brooke leaned out and looked down at his body, which was as horribly contorted as if it had been thrown from a terrible car accident: a crash dummy smashed up on the court. "Let's see you walk away from that, motherfucker."

33

An hour later, after Natalie had woken in her snow-covered car and discovered her own footprints, she stood in the hallway outside the basketball courts. It hurt her brain, trying to piece together what had happened earlier, when she'd come into the sports pavilion. She remembered hearing Nick's voice. He'd been training Sloane and shouting encouragement in that fatherly way of his. Sloane was laughing, all tinkly and light and girlish. Natalie had felt queasy with envy and regret. She'd known then, suddenly, that she would never be the one to laugh with him again like that. Their time was finished. And after that? What? Natalie struggled to find the memory. Nothing was there except . . .

She'd been very, very angry.

The sports pavilion felt empty. No sounds. No movement. There was no sign of Nick, but his truck was still in the parking lot. He had to be there somewhere, even if she couldn't smell his Icy Hot or cologne. She took a few steps towards the darkened gym, her pulse quickening as she began to suspect that something was wrong, and she was totally alone. Some sixth sense was drawing her towards the doors.

Natalie curled her hand, leaned in, and made a cup for her eyes against one of the rectangular windows.

It took a second to see anything at all. The court was dim, aglow only from the small green emergency lights situated over the doors and in the corners of the room. Her eyes were adjusting. Something was there.

She jumped away from the door as if the glass had burned her skin. Her hands flew up to cover her mouth. A scream almost escaped, but she stopped it in her throat with a choking noise. Not far from the door was what looked like a crumpled pile of clothes and broken body parts, motionless in the middle of what appeared to be a spreading pool of blood.

What the hell did I do?

After a second, Natalie crept back to the window, forcing herself to look again, trying not to cry. Whatever it was, it remained motionless.

Until it didn't.

She could see then that it was a body, and one arm was reaching out slowly.

Vertigo hit her hard, and she grabbed onto the big metal push bar to hold herself upright. After a second, she gathered her courage and opened the door. There was a smell. Sweat, copper, and something fetid.

She started inching closer, approaching as if the dark heap on the floor might be a bomb that could go off at any second. There was a dark mess. Her first impression had been right. Blood.

One step closer and she knew, with gut-wrenching certainty.

It was Nick, splayed at the edge of the basketball court. He wore a blue shirt, sports shorts, socks, and trainers. He was on his stomach, and the hair on the back of his head was all matted and sticky.

"Nick?" she whispered.

He didn't answer.

"Oh Christ, oh Christ," she whispered. Her own footprints in the snow leading from her car to the door and then back were suddenly all she could see, dark spots at the edges of her vision.

The crevices in the hardwood maple floor had become thin black streams, slowly spreading out in straight lines and right angles.

"No, no, no," she said, feeling more helpless and hopeless than she ever had before in her life.

He turned his head. One eye was swollen almost completely shut, but she could see a sliver of white. His mouth, those once perfectly shaped lips, moved slightly. "Natalie," he managed. "Call," he said, his words sounding like mud in his mouth. "Nine. One —" His fingers fluttered.

She didn't even have a purse with her, and her phone was gone. Her hands were empty. Useless.

He made a weak gesture.

Natalie looked over and saw his cell. She hadn't noticed it because the phone was black, and it was screen-down in his blood, only six inches away from his hand. "I've got it," she said, picking it up. It was all she could do to hold on to it, she was trembling so violently. She wiped the blood off on her skirt so that she could see the screen.

It was spider-webbed with cracks, but the phone seemed to be functioning. She typed in his passcode, 2258, but she messed it up and it didn't work. Her hands weren't doing what she wanted them to do. She tried again. Still nothing. Was she in shock? Nick managed to whisper, "Natalie?"

"I'm here," she said, her voice ragged. "It's okay."

She wasn't looking at him, but she heard him breathing in a labored way, as if there were something stuck in his throat. He sounded like he was in terrible pain. "Help me," he managed, though it barely sounded like words. "Please."

"I'm trying to. I will. I promise. I'm trying." Her frustration was mounting, making it hard to concentrate. There was a clamor in her head, and she could hear herself repeating the words, "Come on, come on, come on." The third time she typed in the code 2258, the phone opened back up to the camera, which must have been in use at the time of Nick's fall. Natalie was about to close the camera and bring up the number pad to call for help, when the icon in the lower left corner caught her eye. It was a miniature image of the last photo taken in the roll, and it was a flesh-colored close-up. Even with it being that small, Natalie had a feeling she knew what it was. She touched it, bringing it up on the screen.

Everything came to a stop. She was looking at Sloane. There was very little background, but Natalie recognized the taupe-colored cushion on the cot in the training room. The girl appeared to be asleep, and it was a photo that should never have been taken. At first, Natalie didn't understand what she was seeing. After that, disbelief. Then outrage. She swiped again to be sure. And again. There were probably a dozen, and then there were more after that, of Mia with the same blurry background, also asleep. Natalie stopped scrolling. She'd seen enough.

Rather than calling for an ambulance, Natalie put the phone back down where she'd found it. "You're sick," she said, nearly falling backwards in her haste to get away.

"I'll be okay," he said in a hoarse voice, out the side of his mouth. "If — you help."

"I'm not helping you."

Nick's shattered body moved slightly, and he cried out in agony. He was able to crawl a couple of inches, moaning with each miniscule movement. She waited to see if he was going to be able to get to it, and when the phone was almost within his grasp, she used the tip of her boot to nudge it away from his outstretched hand.

Nick didn't give up. He flung his arm out ahead like a swimmer, placed his palm against the shiny surface, and tried to drag himself forward yet again. A tortured roar came out of his mouth at an impressive volume for a man in his condition. He reached for the phone and this time he came very close.

Natalie made a decision.

She kicked it away a second time and then brought the heel of her boot down on it with enormous force.

Nick looked like he wanted to say something else, but he gave up. He put his head back down on the floor and closed his eyes.

Natalie stood there, waiting for something to happen. Nothing did.

Where was the chaos? Not in her head, as she might have expected. She felt sleepy and sated, as if she'd just finished a rich and delicious snack.

34

Natalie didn't try to sleep that night, not even for a few minutes. What was the point? Inside the bathroom, she'd curled up on the floor of the shower with the water running, hoping to keep the neighbors from hearing her crying.

At seven in the morning, she ordered herself to go through the motions. Get showered. Brush teeth.

She gagged on the toothbrush and dry-heaved over the toilet.

Put on clothes. She chose a high-collared dress and ankle boots. No lipstick. Not a day for drawing attention.

After extracting the bloodstained skirt from her laundry basket, she carried it with two fingers, like she had a dead rodent by the tail, into the kitchen. She rinsed it, placed it in a Target bag from under the sink, tied it up in a knot, and left it down there behind the dishwasher pods, bleach, and sponges. Out of sight, out of mind.

Coffee. Toast. As it turned out, toast was not a good idea. *Don't fall over. Don't get back in bed.*

Natalie had one last look in the bathroom mirror. There was nothing more she could do. She took a pill to help her stay on her feet after the restless night and washed it down with some water from the sink.

As she passed the garbage dumpster in the parking lot on the way to her car, she was reminded of the corporeal smell of fresh human blood leaking, pooling, and congealing. She covered her mouth with her hand, swallowed down the foul taste of total desperation, and hoped for the best.

A dozen or so teachers had gathered in front of the academic building. As if focused on a theatrical performance, they were all quiet, with their eyes looking in the exact same direction.

The lawn outside the sports pavilion was a hornet's nest of frenetic activity. There were blue uniforms, orange coveralls, and several people in identical outfits of khaki pants and black jackets. All of them were frowning, serious, and busy. Men and women marched authoritatively back and forth between patrol cars and the front entrance to the pavilion, and all of them seemed to be mumbling into their shoulders where their radios were clipped.

Two officers were stationed on either side of the front doors. One lifted and lowered the yellow tape across the entrance to the sports pavilion so people could come and go. It was like a bizarre game of limbo, with police contorting to duck underneath. The second officer stood there with a pad and paper, keeping some sort log.

Yvonne raised her arm up over the heads of the teachers and motioned Natalie over. She was standing between the flagpole and the bronze statue of the school mascot, a falcon with giant wings and a lethal beak.

"Hi," Natalie said, instinctively slipping her arm through Yvonne's. "What's all this?" she asked, wondering if her friend would detect the hint of fear in her voice.

"The story is, as of yet," Yvonne whispered, "still unfolding."

"That's a lot of police officers," Natalie whispered back.

"I know." A white wisp escaped from the corner of Yvonne's mouth. She'd been sneaking a quick vape.

"Do they — I mean, do you — know what happened?"

"No," Yvonne said, her voice breathy with

drama. "Police showed up. There'd been a 911 call. The cops arrived, and Rex walked them to the sports pavilion. I wasn't here yet, but Rex said two ambulances showed up, and two stretchers came out the front door."

"Two!" Natalie exclaimed, her eyes popping open in alarm. She looked away self-consciously and told herself to *shut up, shut up, shut up, shut up.*

"Two." Yvonne took one last puff and put the JUUL back in her pocket. After exhaling, she cupped one hand to the side of her mouth and said quietly, "I heard the phrase 'puddle of blood' from one of the teachers."

Some of Natalie's coffee shot up her throat and filled her mouth. She cringed visibly and plunged her ice-cold fingers deep into her fluffy pockets. They slid across silk.

"Oh dear God," she said out loud. She'd completely forgotten. The necktie was still right there where she'd shoved it the previous evening. A flood of emotion caused tears to spring to her eyes. It was wadded into a little silken ball in her pocket, like crumpled tissue.

"Are you okay?" Yvonne asked.

"I'm just cold," Natalie answered, her teeth beginning to clack uncontrollably in her mouth.

"I think they'll let us go inside soon," Yvonne said. She took off her own scarf and draped it around Natalie's shoulders. "Let's go see what they say."

"Thank you," Natalie said, twining it twice around her neck and over her chin, concealing almost all of her face. She lowered her head and followed Yvonne, hoping no one would look at her, home in on her eyes, and realize that she was terrified.

"Get ready," Jay said, pointing out the window. "Here comes another. How many is that now?" He looked at his dog, who was perched on the thick arm of the big old recliner at full alert, trembling with the excitement and horror of the morning.

They watched another police car go racing by. Rocky growled, low and steady, his hackles rising between his shoulders.

Jay sat in that spot looking down at the valley often, out of boredom and a nosy curiosity about the vacationers who rented out the condominiums across the way. Today he was glued to the window, simultaneously patting Rocky and smoking a joint. For the last hour, the police had been zipping back and forth on the main road just down the mountain from where Jay's rental house was located.

The epicenter of activity was definitely in the vicinity of Falcon Academy, where Natalie worked.

Rocky whined as a new siren wailed in the distance. "It's okay, Rocky dog," Jay said, but he was almost one hundred percent sure that wasn't actually true. He hoped to God there wasn't a shooter at the school, and he kept scrolling the news on his phone. Nothing.

He started texting Natalie.

Worried about u

R u in a safe place?

Jay took a drag from his joint and relistened to the voice mail his sister had left him the previous night. She'd called from her landline, which was strange, and said, "Jay? Are you awake? Can you talk? I did something I shouldn't have done. Oh man. I'm screwed. Call me at home."

And now this.

Looking out the window, he half expected a helicopter to arrive and hover over the village while soldiers rappelled to the ground.

There was a chance, he supposed, that Natalie had done what he'd suggested and just punched "that guy" right in the face. He hoped not. As difficult as it was for him to imagine how a break-up argument, even one that included a flying fist from his little sister, could wind up shutting down an entire school, he thought it was possible. He didn't know how much she'd had to drink the previous day, but he did know that she'd been out of control and enraged, and for that reason he was worried. If it came to a showdown between a legendary Falcon Academy coach and the unsophisticated young office assistant he'd been sleeping with on the sly, it would be no question who people would believe.

35

Mr. Dilly suspended school for the day. For the next couple of hours, Yvonne and Natalie ran about between the office, the school lobby, and the entrance foyer, ferrying students out to their nannies, drivers, and parents. By the time there was a lull in the traffic, Natalie was perspiring enough to worry about stains seeping through the fabric of her light blue dress. She went to the bathroom and splashed water on her face. The whites around her eyes were spider-webbed with thin red threads. The sight made her think of the blood that had been slowly seeping its way down the thin cracks between the boards of the basketball court.

Back at her computer, her intercom buzzed.

"Natalie?"

"Yes, Mr. Dilly?" she answered.

"Could you ask Rex to come into

the study?"

"Of course. Right away."

"I heard him," Rex said, standing up in a way that suggested he resented being asked to do so. He shuffled past Natalie and into the back of the office, towards the study.

Headmaster Dilly's playlist of classical favorites was piped at a soothing volume throughout the office, and Natalie, who had never found it irritating before, wanted to rip the speakers off the walls. She considered the possibility that this might be the onset of a migraine. Searing, ripping, horrendous pain throbbed in the back of her head, in the same spot where she'd seen that golf-ball-sized hole peeking out through Nick's hair.

She glanced over at her winter coat hanging on the rack in the corner next to Mr. Dilly's charcoal herringbone wool trench. Her eyes dropped to the pocket. She stood, walked over, and retrieved the necktie. She crammed it under the plastic tray towards the back of her desk drawer, hiding it with the other things she didn't want anyone to find. Yvonne, busy scrolling through Instagram posts at her own computer, didn't even look up.

Natalie had just sat back down at her desk when Rex returned from the study and left through the side door, trudging down the hallway towards the classrooms. Natalie glanced at Yvonne, who shrugged and mouthed, "I don't know."

"Girls?" Natalie nearly jumped out of her skin when Mr. Dilly appeared behind her.

"I'm sorry," he said. "I didn't mean to startle you." He was accompanied by a tall woman and a wide man, both nicely dressed in suit jackets and dark pants. "Natalie, Yvonne, this is Beth Larson and Ken Bradley. They are detectives from the Major Crimes Division in Denver."

Both detectives extended their hands, first to Yvonne and then to Natalie. The woman was middle-aged, with grayish-blond hair in a low-maintenance pixie cut and icy-blue, piercing Nordic eyes. "Call me Beth," she said.

"Okay," Natalie said, glancing at Mr. Dilly, who she had been calling *Mr. Dilly* for a year, and who had never once asked her to call him Mark. "Beth."

Ken was Black and bald, with a charismatic smile and cheerful round cheeks. "I hear you ladies are sort of the eyes and the ears of the school," Ken said.

Before Natalie and Yvonne could answer, they were interrupted by the arrival of the Athletic Director Lars Jaeger, who was waving a piece of paper. "I've got it," he said. "The register of the weekend privates, as requested. You know where to find me if you need anything else?"

"Yes, thanks," Ken answered, passing the paper to his partner.

As Lars left, Rex returned to the front office after a notable absence. He walked in and stood there silently, his arms hanging motionless at the sides of his meaty hips. The expression on his face was hostile, and his eyes seemed to be boring into Natalie. He cleared his throat, and as simple as that was, it sounded like an accusation.

Natalie couldn't help herself. "Rex? Is everything . . ."

"Rex's taking us down to the Health and Safety Chamber to look at the CCTV footage from yesterday," Mr. Dilly cut in. Everything at the school had a fancy name. The student cafeteria was referred to as the Falcon's Roost Café. The Health and Safety Chamber, which sounded like it was part of NASA, was a walk-in closet filled with computers. "We'll be . . . what, about an hour, Rex?"

Rex said, "Sure," still staring at Natalie.

After they walked away, it was all she could do not to verbally command the room to stop spinning. It felt like she was about to swallow her tongue. She nodded and reached out with one hand to steady herself on her desk. The CCTV footage would show her going in and out of the sports pavilion twice the previous evening. It would likely confirm that she was the last person to leave the school. At least, the last who wasn't brought out on a stretcher.

At the desk adjacent to Natalie's, Yvonne's mobile kept vibrating. She was receiving all sorts of texts from teachers speculating about what had happened in the gym.

"Rohan thinks there was an accident with a student, and the school is trying to keep it on the down low," Yvonne whispered to Natalie, who didn't answer. "But Gail thinks there was a fight, not an accident."

"Does anyone know who died?" Natalie asked. "Has anyone said who the . . ." She swallowed. "Who the two people were? Two, right? It seems like there were definitely two?"

"Two," Yvonne confirmed. "Probably two people who got in an argument, don't you think?"

"Yes, probably." Natalie closed her eyes very tight and just let her fingers rest on the computer keyboard, where she was supposed to be typing up a flyer about donations of canned food for Thanksgiving. Who else had been in the building when she saw him lying there bleeding from his head? Who had been there, watching, hiding in the dark? Or worse, who else had been hurt? Who else had been suffering, possibly dying, in some other part of the gym?

It was as if she were back in the sports pavilion. Natalie could taste it in her sour mouth, like two dirty fingers down her throat. There had been the usual lingering funk of sweaty teenagers. Their adolescent pheromonal stench sank into the mats and the practice jerseys, but in her nose now was the porta potty smell of sewage. Blood and piss, shit, fear and death. Natalie considered pulling the office trash can over and putting her head in it. Yvonne was oblivious.

What were they looking at right now? Right down the hall. What were they seeing on that surveillance footage? God, she was perspiring. How wide was the scope of the security camera? Was it a close shot on the back door, so just her going in and out? Or was it a wide frame, featuring her staggering pell-mell, wasted, across the parking lot like a zombie screaming for brains? Was it something worse that she couldn't possibly even imagine?

It seemed the time had come to consider

all her options.

1) There was the truth.

2) There was the possibility of standing up and walking out the front door, dashing to her car, and escaping to some seedy motel, where she would have to ask her brother to bring cash and a burner phone and hide forever.

3) And finally, there was lying. Lie like her life depended on it.

Natalie looked up and saw Oliver Wilson running down the hall, a panicked look in his eyes, followed by Mia, who came rushing into the office.

"Something wrong, kids?" Yvonne asked, standing.

"My dad ordered us an Uber," Mia answered. "We have to leave. Something bad has happened and we have to go, and we have to go now." Outside in the car park, a handful of children were being dismissed into a line of cars by their teachers. A black sedan cut to the front and pulled to a stop. Mia glanced at her phone. "That's him," she said to Oliver, who looked like he was putting all his effort into not crapping his pants.

"This isn't how we do it," Yvonne said. "This isn't school policy."

"I'm sorry," Mia said, pushing Oliver

towards the door. "We have to get to the hospital right away. It's my mom."

"It's your mom? What?" The blood drained from Natalie's face. "What happened to your mom?"

"I don't know yet," Mia answered. "I didn't see her this morning."

"But . . . but . . ." Yvonne pointed to the parental sign-out sheet. "Are we just supposed to let you walk out?"

Mia didn't bother to respond, and seconds later, she had steered Oliver out of the school and down the sidewalk to the awaiting sedan. She opened the back door, threw her brother's things inside, and gave him a shove. She climbed in behind him, and the sedan pulled away from the curb at a high speed, going the wrong way through the entrance. Natalie and Yvonne stood there in stunned silence.

Eventually Yvonne said, "Oh my God, oh my God!" She turned to Natalie and patted her own cheeks like the kid from *Home Alone*. "What was that?"

"I have no idea."

"Aren't you friendly with their mom?"

"Sort of," Natalie answered. "I was. I mean, I am."

"Do you think something happened to Asha Wilson?"

"Yes." The answer had slipped out, but it was true. Natalie turned to look down the hall, expecting to see them coming for her.

It was just Mr. Dilly on his own. When he threw open the front office door, he said, "Natalie, the detectives want to speak with you in the Health and Safety Chamber."

Some sort of strange instinct for self-preservation took over in the form of a massive adrenaline rush, and she decided to go with choice number three. *Lie like you believe it, like you are the best liar ever.*

"Okay," she said, surprised to find that she sounded more or less normal. As she walked away from her desk, she glanced over at Rex. He made a point of looking away out the window.

The hallway leading to the large closet that contained the surveillance equipment seemed endless. She rubbed her tattoo with her fingers and took short, shallow breaths as she went over some things to remember. *Eye contact. Don't fidget. Don't fold your arms over your chest. Don't protest too much. Keep it simple.*

The door to the room was closed. She knocked.

"Come in," Beth called.

Natalie opened the door and stepped inside. Ken was seated at a small desk in front of six monitors mounted on the wall, looking at his phone. He ignored her. To Beth he said, "The crime scene technician just arrived. He's over in the gym now."

"Is it Pete?" Beth asked.

"It is."

"Good," Beth answered. She was also seated, facing Natalie. There was no other chair in the room. To be fair, there really wasn't room for one. Beth pointed and said, "Close the door behind you, please."

After a second, Ken put his phone away, looked up, and folded his hands in his lap.

There was a keyboard, hard drive, and laptop on the desk. Ken pressed a button and then pointed at one of the many monitors. "Who's that?" he asked, pointing to a woman wearing a coat with fluffy white fur at the collar and wrists. The woman walked into frame from the parking lot behind the sports pavilion and entered the back door of the building.

Not only was the coat unusual, but it was currently hanging on a rack by her desk. There was nothing else Natalie could say except, "That's me."

"You go in at 4:08, and then ten minutes later, you go back out. At 6:12 pm you go in again. At 6:32 you leave for the second time. Can you tell me what you were doing and who you saw?"

"I was looking for my earbuds. I didn't see anyone."

Ken raised an eyebrow. "Looking for your earbuds? Okay. Twice?"

"Yes," Natalie said nodding. "That's right."

"Did you find them?"

"Not the first time, but the second time I did. I thought I'd left them in the little cup holder on the treadmill on the mezzanine, but they weren't there. I couldn't find them anywhere else, so I went back later to look again and realized they'd fallen behind the machine."

Beth opened a small notebook and jotted something down. She passed the notebook to Ken.

"Do you have your phone with you?" he asked. "I'd like to have a quick look at it, if you don't mind."

"I lost my phone Saturday night at the Fall Feast."

"At the what?" Ken asked.

"At the Fall Feast. It's a school thing. A fancy dinner for upperclassmen and faculty."

Ken and Beth shared a look.

Natalie felt as if she were facing a firing squad.

Beth passed Ken another note. He read it and said, "What were you going to do with your earbuds if you'd lost your phone?"

"Nothing. I just wanted to find them."

"But you spent all that time and effort coming to the school twice, when you could have just looked for them this morning when you came to work."

"They were expensive."

"All right," Ken said, readjusting his large body in the small chair. His new posture was tilted towards Natalie. "So, let me tell you something about me."

"What's that?" she asked politely, though the absolute last thing in the world she wanted was to get to know him better.

"I spent four years as a polygraph examiner in Memphis. I've probably heard more confessions than a priest." Ken rubbed his chin thoughtfully. "I've given tons of polygraph exams. You know how they work?"

"A little line goes squiggly if you lie," Natalie answered. "That's what I know. From those true crime shows."

"Yeah, well, there's lots more to it. The bands around your chest tell me how fast your heart is beating. The chair has motion sensors that tell me if you fidget or flinch. The blood pressure cuff is self-explanatory. But you know what I always found the most telling?"

"I don't know."

"The finger cuffs. They measure something called electrodermal activity. Do you know what that is?"

"Something to do with skin, I guess," she answered, finding that the urge to inch away from him was getting too strong to ignore.

"Yes. Electrodermal activity is how much you sweat, Natalie."

"Oh," she said, taking a tiny step backwards.

"This is a pretty cold-ass closet we're hanging out in here, and yet your face is all shiny, and there's a little bead of sweat dripping down the side of your nose like you're on a chaise lounge, relaxing on the beach in Mexico."

"Really?" She didn't know what else to say. "Sorry."

"Sorry for what? For lying to me about losing your phone? For lying about losing your earbuds?"

"No. I did lose my stuff. I'm sorry for being so . . . so . . ." This was ridiculous. What was she even doing? She had no recollection of what had happened the first time she'd gone into the gym because she'd been zonked out on a heartbreak binge of beer, uppers, and downers, and they were going to find out, one way or another. How long could she play dumb? Natalie swallowed and finished her sentence. "I'm sorry for being so sweaty."

Ken sighed loudly and stood up. The room shrank. Natalie took another infinitesimal step backwards, and this time her back hit the door. "Well," he said casually, as if it was simply time for him to get going. "We're going to search your desk and purse and other personal items now."

"Wh-wh—" Natalie couldn't believe it. She was stammering. This was exactly what she'd warned herself not to do. "What?"

"You heard me," he said. "You signed away your right to privacy at the workplace when you took this job."

It was true, and she had no choice but to bite her tongue.

Natalie trailed a few feet behind Beth and Ken as they returned to the front office. Every few seconds she looked side to side, as if searching for a window large enough to jump through, smashing the glass, so she could go sprinting into the woods behind the stadium.

In the end, she stood there silently alongside her workstation, as Beth produced a pair of latex gloves from a pouch on her belt and began to rifle through Natalie's things.

Yvonne watched the whole spectacle from behind her desk, rapt and silent, while Rex pretended nothing at all unusual was happening. A minute later, Mr. Dilly appeared and began observing as well. First Beth went through Natalie's purse, which she kept underneath her desk with her gym bag. Eventually Beth seemed satisfied that neither contained anything of interest. Then she began to search the drawers.

Tiny white flurries like snowflakes began to sprinkle softly through the periphery of Natalie's vision, and she realized that this was a first for her: a first time for feeling woozy and "seeing stars."

In the top drawer, Beth found Natalie's planner. She turned it over in her hands curiously and then took a long look at Natalie. The notebook was Winnie the Pooh themed and Natalie did not look like a Winnie the Pooh woman, with her severely blunt bangs and a rebellious set to her jaw. After a cursory glance at a few pages in the middle of the planner, Beth said, "I'm going to need this photocopied." She looked around and spoke broadly to everyone. "You do have a photocopier, correct?"

"Yes," Mr. Dilly answered, sounding

miserable. "We do. Yvonne will help you."

It took Beth all of two minutes to work her way through the rest of Natalie's desk. Eventually she pulled out the plastic organizer tray from the top drawer. The cascade of stars became absolutely torrential as Beth discovered the necktie and seven oval-shaped pills, four orange and three white. She placed the items on top of the desk and went to the coatrack, where Natalie's fluffy, floral, 1970s-era steal of a coat was hanging. "This is what you were wearing last night in the video, I take it?" she asked, touching the sleeve.

"It is."

Beth went through the pockets and produced a few dirty tissues, three red-and-white peppermint candies, an empty candy wrapper, and a Post-it that said, "Bacon, Flamin' Hot Doritos and ice cream." Beth held it up and asked with a smirk, "Shopping list?"

"For my brother," Natalie clarified, feeling immediately like a first-class moron. Why was she bothering to tell these people that it was Jay who loved junk food, not her? They'd just found drugs in her drawer.

Beth turned to Ken. "I think that's it."

Ken looked down at the items on the desk. "So, what do we have here, Natalie? A few opioids and a few amphetamines? Is that what they are?"

Natalie nodded and said, "Yes." Again, there was no point in denying something so easy to prove.

"Do you have a prescription for these? Don't bother lying. I can find out in five minutes."

"No."

"So where did you get them?"

She was not about to tell them she'd helped herself to the student prescriptions kept under lock and key in the nurse's office. "The lost and found."

And with that, she finally had Rex's complete attention. He glanced over his shoulder, and his dark eyebrows leaped halfway up his forehead.

"Okay," Ken said. "I think I get it. You stole them out of what, backpacks? Pockets?"

Natalie couldn't look at Mr. Dilly. "Yes."

"And what about this tie? What's with the tie?"

"I stole it too," she answered. Now that she was going, it was like she couldn't stop.

"From the lost and found also?" Beth asked.

"Yes," Natalie answered. She took a deep breath, mind spinning. "It reminded me of someone. I thought maybe the tie belonged to him, and, I don't know. I just took it. No good reason."

Ken looked exasperated with her. "Are you a kleptomaniac or something?"

"I don't think I am," Natalie answered. "Maybe I am. I don't know. I don't take things very often."

After a second, Beth asked, "Who did the tie remind you of?"

At first Natalie didn't respond.

Ken cupped his hand around his ear and said, "Pardon? Who?"

"My boyfriend," Natalie answered softly. "My ex-boyfriend."

"Okay. And who might that be?" Ken asked. "Name?"

Yvonne looked absolutely confused. Natalie rolled her neck around once, and it was so quiet in the room that everyone heard it crack. "Nicholas Maguire."

Over by himself, Rex coughed suddenly and violently. Yvonne's face was scrunched up as if she were trying to work out an impossible math equation in her head.

"May I?" Ken said to Beth, and she responded by wordlessly handing over her notebook. Ken licked the tip of his pointer finger and flipped through a couple of pages. "I'm going to read you the names of the people caught on the surveillance video who were in the gym yesterday: Assistant Athletic Director Nicholas Maguire. A Falcon Academy mom named Linda Leland and her seventeen-year-old son, Reade. Reade's fifteen-year-old girlfriend, Sloane Elliman-Holt, and Sloane's mother, Brooke Elliman. There was another Falcon mom in there too, by the name of Asha Wilson. Some of these people had perfectly logical reasons to be there. And some didn't. What interested me most is you, and why you went in and out twice."

"I was looking for my —"

"I know." Ken nodded sympathetically. "The expensive earbuds." He gave her a questioning, concerned look. His brow furrowed, and he seemed suddenly fatherly. Kind. "But we're investigating a crime, Natalie. Something horrible has happened. And you went in and out of a blood-spattered gym twice yesterday. You're going to have to tell us the whole story and nothing but."

36

It had started to snow again, and Natalie was watching the flurries come down through the window. The sky was a solid, dull white, and if she hadn't been more or less imprisoned by the two detectives in the school conference room, she would have been checking the weather channel to see what sort of storm was on the way. It looked like it could be a bad one, especially since it was so early in the autumn and the salt trucks and snowplows might have been underprepared. She turned away from the window to glance at the clock that hung behind her on the wall.

They'd been done with the interview on camera for twenty minutes, and since then, no one had spoken.

Ken was scrolling through what appeared to be a barrage of messages on his own phone, while Beth continued to sit quietly at the opposite end of the table, methodically going through the photocopied pages of Natalie's Winnie the Pooh planner. While Natalie stared at the female detective, who was so emotionlessly reading through descriptions of Natalie's most intimate desires, worst impulses, harrowing fears, and destructive insecurities, Beth looked up. Their eyes met. The expression on Beth's face was clinical. *What are you? What is wrong with you?*

Natalie began to bite at a hangnail.

Ken suddenly raised his phone to his ear. "Go on," he said. "Uh-huh. Okay." He hung up and said to Beth, "Pete's ready for us."

"All right." She put the papers detailing the last six months of Natalie's life away in a slim leather binder that she then slipped into her bag.

Ken said, "Natalie, we're going to have to go down to the sports pavilion for a little bit. We'd like you to stay here."

Again, Natalie looked over her shoulder at the clock.

"Do you have somewhere urgent you need to be?" he asked, pushing his chair back to stand up.

"No," Natalie answered.

"Good," he said.

Natalie glanced at the window, and then at the door. Ken noticed and said, "I'm sure there's no need to mention this, but we're going to have a patrol officer just outside."

"Am I under arrest, then?"

"No," Ken answered.

"But . . . Is now the time that I need to get a lawyer involved?"

Ken shook his head and shrugged, looking like a disappointed dad. "If you feel that's best, Natalie, by all means, do what you need to do. I wasn't ready to head in that direction yet, but it's up to you. I thought we were just talking."

"Oh. Okay. But you made it sound like the patrol officer outside was there to stop me from leaving."

"He's there to let us know if you decide you're no longer willing to cooperate with our request to stay put, so we can speak to you later if we need to."

Natalie rubbed her eyes with the heels of her hands. "Right. Got it. Thanks."

Pete was the crime scene technician, and he had a pleasant, youthful face, black-rimmed glasses, and not very much hair. He wore his nerdiness with pride, evidently, as he had a pen in his shirt pocket, underneath which was a small ink stain.

He waylaid the detectives with an enthusiasm that added to his aura of endearing geekiness. "I've got lots of interesting thoughts to share," he said cheerfully, meeting them at the entrance to the pavilion.

Ken responded, "There's a curse that says, 'May you live in interesting times.' I guess I'd rather hear, 'Cut and dried. Open and shut case.' *Interesting* sounds complicated."

Beth laughed and gave her partner an indulgent glance. She wasn't nearly as talkative as Ken, but she appreciated his gift of gab.

"Well," Pete said, beckoning them to follow him as he walked down the hall. "There's a lot going on here. Let's just go over each thing as we come to it. We can start in the locker room."

Beth took out her little notebook.

"So," Pete said, presenting the locker room with a giant sweep of the arm as if he were unveiling a new work of art. "All of the employee locker combinations were on file, but when I tried to open Mr. Maguire's locker, his didn't work."

Taking the cap off her pen, Beth said, "Mmm." She made a note.

Pete gave them an aw-shucks shrug. "I was able to open it anyway, of course." He led them to Nick's locker. On the top shelf, there was a yellow placard with a black number one on it. Behind the evidence placard were the usual items: deodorant, a hairbrush, and a bottle of ibuprofen, but also three small, clear glass bottles with silver lids and no labels.

"I don't like that," Ken said.

"Me neither," Beth agreed.

Ken glanced at Beth questioningly. "Anabolic steroids?"

She shook her head. "Dunno. Maybe."

"I've only seen photos of Mr. Maguire," Pete said, sliding his glasses up his nose. "His physical appearance wouldn't indicate steroid use necessarily. Still, he certainly could have been dispensing them."

Beth made another note.

Pete slipped on his latex gloves and reached in for one of the bottles. He held it up to the light. "We won't know what it is until we get the lab results, but it's unlabeled, so that might be an indication it's not on the up-and-up." He said this wearing a giant grin, as if it was all incredibly entertaining, and he hoped they were enjoying it as much as he was.

"Yes, it might," Ken said, nodding.

"There are similar vials on the mezzanine floor in the trainer's room," Pete said. "We'll get to that shortly. But those up there all do have labels. Ketorolac. That doesn't necessarily mean they contain Ketorolac, of course." He laughed. "But I don't need to tell you that."

Beth was writing again. She looked up at Pete. "Ketorolac?"

"Yeah," Ken said. "I was wondering also. I'm not familiar with that drug."

"No reason you would be. It's not restricted. It's a widely used NSAID comparable to ibuprofen. Very popular in the sports world. I was a little surprised to find it in a high school, even though it's common in colleges, but then again, a school like this? Anything goes, I guess. Even pro-athlete-style shots."

"I played college basketball and took anti-inflammatories," Beth said. "But I never had anyone give me a shot."

"Yeah, well, this type of Ketorolac is administered by intramuscular injection in the hip. With a small syringe. There were some of those in the training room. I'll test those too."

"It's not over-the-counter, is it?" Ken asked.

"No. But like I said, it's not a controlled substance, and it's not an opioid. It's approved for pediatric use. A call from a doctor and a note from a parent would suffice. The nurse or the trainer would be qualified to administer the shot."

"Beth, could you add the trainer to the list of people we're going to interview tomorrow?" Ken asked.

Beth nodded and scribbled.

"So," Pete said. "Shall we start at the top? And when I say top, I mean the top floor?"

"Sure," Ken said.

They followed Pete up the stairs to the mezzanine, which was dotted with more yellow evidence placards labeled with numbers. He began to list the items that had already been photographed. "Here on this old chair," he said, indicating a stool with a ripped cushion, "are two Monster Energy drinks. We'll be testing the contents. Might be significant given the unusual array of goodies in Mr. Maguire's locker." He led them to the training room and said, "After you."

Beth and Ken went inside and looked around. Pete showed them the medicine cabinet where Coach Carmen kept her Ketorolac vials and syringes as well as bandages, gauze, antiseptics, and other first-aid items. Her glass vials looked different from the ones in Nick's locker. They had purple tops, white labels with the medicine's name in black, and purple stripes at the bottom. "These look legit," Pete said. "But you never know. Now, if you'll follow me out to the bloodstained squat rack, which is possibly the aha discovery in this particular investigation —"

"Pete," Beth interrupted as they walked out of the training room. "There's a lock on this door."

"Pardon me?" he asked, backtracking.

Beth pointed to the lock. "The training room has a lock."

"Because of the medicine, probably," Ken said.

"No." Beth took a second look inside. "The medicine cabinet has a lock of its own. I've been in plenty of training rooms, but I've never seen one with a mechanism like this. This is like a house. It can be locked from the inside or the outside."

Pete's boyish face looked flustered. "I'll go get my camera," he said. "It's downstairs with my case. I'm sorry. I never thought."

"It's okay," Beth said, patting his shoulder. "You do that while I make a quick call." After a second, she said into her phone, "Yes, hi, Yvonne. Is Mr. Dilly available? I just want to ask him why there's a lock on the training room door. It's very unusual. I'd be interested to know if Mr. Dilly approved it. Of course." She waited for a minute, all the while pacing and looking over the furnishings and contents of the training room. Eventually, she said, "Hi. Yes, I'm still here. Oh, that would be great. Are you sure you don't mind? Wonderful, Yvonne, thank you." Beth hung up and turned to Ken. "She has the work order right there on her computer and is going to run it down."

"Good," Ken said.

Pete showed back up with his camera and placards and photographed the lock, the door, the cots, and the medicine cabinet. When he'd finished, Ken asked, "So, where were we? The bloody squat rack? That's got a nasty ring to it, doesn't it?"

"Sure does," Pete said, leading them over. "One thing that the first responder picked up on right away was the injury to the back of Mr. Maguire's head."

Beth nodded, and Ken said, "Yes. That's when they called us to come out. Inconsistent with the fall that smashed up the front of his face."

"Right," Pete said. "So, I thought maybe that blow occurred here. BlueStar picked up a lot of blood on this mezzanine. Certainly, some is old. Could be training injuries, that sort of thing. But there were a few drops that appeared to be fresh, and then you have this." Pete pointed to one of the top hooks used to hold the barbell on the squat rack. "See that?" he asked.

Ken and Beth both took a look. "Yep," Ken said.

"That seemed pretty recent," Pete continued. "With a trace of hair. I'll be looking at it to see if it matches the blood downstairs on the court."

Once again, Beth was focused on making notes. Ken said, "And if it does, then there was likely an altercation of some sort up here that preceded the fall."

"My thoughts exactly," Pete answered brightly. "And on that note, should we go down and see where he landed?"

When they reached the basketball court, Pete showed them the dried blood left behind after Nick had been removed. "Mr. Maguire tried to crawl a little bit. There's an indication of a small amount of forward movement in the blood. He was probably trying to get to his phone, which was approximately eighteen inches away from his body."

The entrance on the other end of the basketball court opened and closed, and Yvonne came trotting in with a printout. Beth waved to her while Ken and Pete continued to talk.

"Wow." Ken whistled. "What bad luck. So

close. If he'd been able to reach the phone, it would have saved him an entire night of agony alone in the dark, thinking he was going to die."

"Well, actually, no," Pete answered. "His phone was inoperable. Very smashed up."

"Will forensics be able to recover any data from it?" Beth asked.

"Maybe. Depends on just how bad it is. If he had an iCloud backup or if the phone can still connect to a computer, then yes. If not and the chip was damaged or the phone needs a total rebuild job, then it's iffy."

Slightly out of breath, Yvonne arrived beside the group and smiled, waiting politely for them to finish talking to hand over the work order. She looked down and noticed that she was standing somewhat close to what appeared to be a crime scene. She made a face and took a few steps back.

"This is where Mr. Doyle was found lying next to Mr. Maguire," Pete said, indicating a spot to the left of the stain. "Looks like the custodian arrived early in the morning, found Mr. Maguire lying here unresponsive, and managed to call 911 before collapsing due to cardiac arrest."

"What?" Yvonne shouted the word so loudly that the detectives and the technician winced. "Harry! Oh my God, poor

Harry! Harry and who else?"

Beth made a calming gesture and reached out for the document Yvonne had run down to deliver. "We can't talk about it quite yet," she said. "I'm sorry. That really wasn't for you to hear. I'll need you to be discreet for the next couple of days. Okay, Yvonne?"

"Yeah." Yvonne looked like she was desperate to run out of the gym and go announce the most recent development over the school loudspeaker, but she nodded. Still, she was clearly upset. "Harry?" she asked again. "We all thought it was going to be two moms or two students or a fight between a teacher and a student."

"I understand your curiosity," Beth said. "All incidents like this are upsetting in their own way."

"Is Harry dead?" Yvonne asked.

Ken gave her an empathetic smile. "I think you need to get back to work now, don't you?"

Yvonne nodded, still off balance from the news. After she walked away, Ken said to Beth, "How's Mr. Doyle doing, by the way?"

"As of an hour ago, he was out of the woods," she answered.

"Is he already on the list for tomorrow?"

"He is."

"Okay," Ken said. "All very interesting.

Thank you, Pete. How long do you think it will be before we get a match on the blood and know what's in those vials?"

"Well," Pete said, "I've got a lot to sift through. It's a priority, but frankly, with this storm that's moving in, it could be a slow night. I might be on my own."

"Speaking of the storm, Ken," Beth said, "Rachel wants to know if I'm coming home tonight or if we're going to be stuck."

Ken checked his watch. "We better move pretty quick if we want to make it down the mountain before traffic gets tied up. Let's go speak with Natalie again and leave."

The hour she spent alone in the conference room seemed like an entire day. She found a pencil and a copy of the Falcon creative writing anthology. On the blank page at the back, she sketched her own footprints through the snow. From her car to the door and back to the car. What had she done? What had she seen? Nick was up there with Sloane. She remembered their laughter. What did Sloane know? What did Sloane do? Who was carried out on that second stretcher? For the hundredth time she tried to remember how that first trip into the sports pavilion had ended and came up with nothing but the image of the stairwell, and how she'd leaned against the wall and sunk to a seat on the bottom step, feeling as if the world had ended.

She assumed the worst.

If I killed him, I killed him.

If Sloane killed him, she killed him.

It was either her or me.

Natalie started to sketch Jackson. Jackson, she thought. Alone and confused and wondering where Dad was. There were voices outside. The detectives had returned, and Ken was telling the patrol officer that he could go. She slipped the anthology back onto its shelf.

After returning to her seat at the conference table, she lowered her face into her hands and wished that she had a pill. Any pill. Upper, downer, sideways, she'd take it.

When Ken and Beth walked in, they seemed like they were in a hurry, but not to put handcuffs on her, as she'd expected.

"Natalie," Ken said, grabbing his coat off the back of the chair where he'd left it. "That's it for the day. You can go home now."

It was all she could do to keep her jaw from dropping open. "Oh. Okay. Thanks."

"Do you know where the Falcon Valley police station is located?"

"Yes."

"The school is closed again tomorrow, and you're going to meet us there at the station at two o'clock, okay? Will that work?"

"Sure." Natalie glanced at Beth, who was busy pulling on a gray stocking cap and some matching gloves. Beth didn't acknowledge Natalie in the slightest.

"You don't have plans to go anywhere special tonight, do you?" Ken asked, zipping up his computer carrying case.

"There's a blizzard on the way," she answered. "So, no." Her voice sounded like it belonged to someone else. Someone far more timid.

"That's good," Ken said, finally pausing in his end-of-the day pack-up. He was standing just across the table. "Listen, thank you for all your help. I know it was a long interview. When I see you tomorrow, I'm hoping to have Mr. Maguire's statement, so this inconvenience to your life will be over."

"Who?" Natalie responded in astonishment. "I'm sorry?"

Beth dipped her head to hear better as she slipped her arms into her coat sleeves.

"Just saying that hopefully by tomorrow this will all be cleared up."

"Wait." Natalie looked completely lost. "Who? Who are we talking about? Whose statement did you say?"

"Mr. Maguire's."

"But he's —"

"What?" Beth asked, turning around to face Natalie as she adjusted her jacket collar. "He's what?"

"He's dead," Natalie said, standing up, her eyes huge. "Isn't he?"

Ken put his hands on his hips. His hat was charcoal gray, lined with fur, and had long flaps over the ears. He looked comical and yet still intimidating. "Why would you think Mr. Maguire was dead? Who told you that?"

No one had told Natalie he was dead. No one had even told her who, exactly, had been involved in the accident. She realized she'd made a huge mistake. "The teachers were talking, and someone mentioned Nick," she answered, staring at the floor. "I thought I heard someone say 'two bodies,' so I guess I just assumed."

"Two people went to the hospital," Ken said. "Mr. Maguire and Mr. Doyle."

"Harry?" Natalie asked, gasping.

Ken nodded. "Cardiac arrest shortly after finding Mr. Maguire."

"Oh my God. Did he — ?"

"It looks like Mr. Doyle is going to be okay."

"And Nick?" Natalie asked. "What about Nick?"

"He's in bad shape," Ken said. "Still unconscious. But the doctors expect him to wake up sometime tonight."

"Oh," Natalie said, collapsing back into her seat. "That's . . . such good news."

37

The school had shut for the day. Brooke stood in front of her living room window, which usually had a view of the river, the town, and the mountains across the valley. She could barely see the clock tower of the school down below, and everything else was a powdery blur. The enormous mountain range blended into the white sky and had become completely invisible. It was the kind of weather that would cause even a hardy Coloradan to break out the booze and start searching Netflix. Going out was not looking very friendly, and it was about to get worse.

The television was droning on behind her. A perky blonde meteorologist was delivering the local news, announcing the arrival of a statewide blizzard. "We haven't had a storm this big and this early in the fall for twenty-two years, and that one took seven lives, stranded thousands, and caused widespread power outages across the state. Denver International has already canceled a number of flights," she announced. "And we're expecting slippery streets for your commute. Take your time, folks, and when you get home, stay in and stay warm."

Sloane had not yet returned from school despite the early dismissal, and Brooke was about ready to admit herself to a mental institution. Nick had gone over the railing the previous evening and since then, Brooke had been one drink short of losing her mind.

She and Asha had escorted Sloane out of the training room and down the stairs, and left the building without the girl ever being anywhere near the gym. At one point on the way home, Sloane said, "Where did Coach Nick go?" To which Brooke had promptly answered, "The bathroom." That was it. That was the only question Sloane asked. She'd seemed sleepy but otherwise okay, and Brooke made the decision to wait and see what she might eventually remember. Brooke had thought about taking her straight to the ER, but whatever it was that Nick had slipped to Sloane — maybe one of those "roofies" she herself had been warned about in college — appeared to be wearing off. She needed to consider the consequences of showing up to a hospital claiming that her daughter had been drugged by a man whom she'd just pushed over a balcony and left for dead. When Sloane sat up in the back seat and said, "Can we swing by Starbucks for a vanilla Frappuccino?" Brooke said yes, and then took her daughter home.

Brooke couldn't stop babbling afterwards. "What do you want for dinner, hon? Should we order salads? Should we order sushi? Can I make you avocado toast? Do you want to watch something? What about the two of us go soak in the hot tub for a little? I could braid your hair. I haven't done that in a long time."

Sloane took her up on the avocado toast but nothing else. Eventually she remarked, "You're acting kind of bizarre tonight, Mom."

"I am?" Brooke asked. "I mean, yes, I think I am. You're right. I think I had too much caffeine late in the day. That's got to be it." Brooke nodded emphatically while clutching her wineglass in both hands, because just one wasn't enough to keep it steady.

At ten, Sloane had gone up to her room to do what she presumably always did in her room before bed: talk to Reade. As soon as Brooke saw Sloane's bare feet hit the top of the stairs and turn down the hall, she was out in the garage with a shot glass, standing in front of the freezer, holding the bottle of limoncello. "One-two-three-four-five-six . . ." She couldn't even manage to do a proper relaxation breathing exercise. She gave up on breathing and decided to go back into the house and pace. Pacing was therapeutic in a weird way. Once that had stopped working, she stripped naked and got into the hot tub, taking the limoncello with her.

"I killed him," she whispered to the sky. She was drunk. "I killed him," she said again. Then she thought about what he'd done to Sloane and Mia. "And I'd kill the bastard again."

In the morning, she woke facedown on the living room couch. Sloane was nudging her. "I'm off to school."

"Dad's here?" Brooke asked, half-asleep.

"No. Mrs. Green. Carpool." She paused. "Like usual?"

"Right. Yeah." Brooke sat up and tried, unsuccessfully, to straighten her clothes, and wipe the makeup and drool from her face. It was obvious that she'd passed out. Sloane didn't seem too bothered by any of it.

"Have a good day, honey," Brooke said, standing up so quickly that she nearly fell right back down. After Sloane left, Brooke grabbed a pillow off the couch, held it against her mouth, and screamed.

She tried to call Asha. No answer. She'd begun to receive texts and emails from the school informing parents about the shortened day due to "an unforeseen tragic accident." Brooke had decided she was too hungover, panicked, and borderline psychotic to drive, so she'd texted Gabe to see if he could pick up Sloane and bring her home. He'd texted back, No problem.

That had been hours ago.

Sloane was not responding to texts. Not answering. Gabe, who was usually reliable, was also missing in action. This was absolutely the last thing Brooke needed.

For the seventh time, she dialed Gabe.

"Hello?" He sounded out of breath.

"It's about time," she yelled.

"Whoa. What's wrong?" he asked. Not apologetic, seemingly not concerned about anything.

"Is Sloane okay? Is she with you?"

Gabe sounded muffled, like he was in the middle of something. "She called me and said she was getting a ride home with a friend and not to worry. Sorry, hold on, I'm just walking in. Let me finish getting my hat and scarf off."

"Gabe!"
"What?"
"Which friend?"
"Mia," he said. Brooke could finally hear his voice clearly and pictured him with ice in his hair, about to shake it out like a wet dog. She missed him. "That's okay, right?" he asked.
Brooke relaxed slightly. That was sort of okay. It was better than many other possibilities. "Why didn't you call to tell me? And why haven't you been answering your phone?"
"I'm sorry," he said. "I wasn't thinking. When the storm started coming in, Tabitha asked me to run some groceries over to her mom, and when I got back, I had to go out and salt the drive because ours is pretty steep."
These words, as innocuous as Gabe might have thought they were, almost brought Brooke to tears right then and there. He'd referred to the driveway of Tabitha's apartment as "ours" and taken food over to Tabitha's mom. It was a dagger in the heart. Brooke realized then that he had changed. He was invested. Attentive. It appeared he could be a better, happier man with a woman who needed him and treated him like he was someone important. "Gabe," she

said. "I'm really sorry."

"No worries," he said. "I should have had my phone on me."

"No," Brooke said. "I mean, I'm really, really sorry. I should have done better. I'm talking about us."

"Ohhhh," he said, drawing out the word. "Brooke. It's okay. It's fine. I should have too. And just so you know, I am going to do better with Sloane. I'm going to make sure I have her every other weekend, if that's okay with you. Now that I'm settled and stuff."

"Wonderful," Brooke said, even though she was devastated. He'd used the word *settled.* "That's great, Gabe, thank you."

"Give me a call when she gets home, okay?" he asked. "I mean, she did say they were going to go hang out at a friend's for a little bit, but I would have thought she'd have been home by now."

"Where were they going? Did she say?"

"No, she didn't. She just said —"

"I've got to run, Gabe," Brooke said, suddenly fully certain that if Sloane had left the school with Mia, it had been in the back of Reade Leland's G Wagon. "I'm sorry. Take care. Talk soon."

Ten seconds later, Brooke sent the following text: Hi Linda, extending an olive branch here. Sloane's phone must be dead. Is she with Reade at your house by any chance? If so, could you please have her call me? Thank you!

Linda texted back shortly thereafter: Hi Brooke. I've asked her to give you a call. I know we agreed to limit Reade and Sloane's time together but with the scary news from the school and the storm rolling in I just thought I would make an exception. I'm sorry. I should have checked with you.

Oh no, that's fine! I'd just like to have Sloane home with me. They're saying power outages!

Okay! But FYI, Reade has another friend over and the kids are having fun in the basement. Everyone is safe to ride out the storm. They are welcome to spend the night. We have plenty of room, generators, food, blankets, candles you name it!

Sloane was in a basement, in a snowstorm, with her horny, banned boyfriend. And this mom thought everything was great and was talking about them curling up under some blankets by candlelight.

Absolutely not.

That's so kind of you, Linda! But please

tell Sloane I'll be coming to pick her up soon. Thank you!

38

The first thing Natalie did after leaving the school was drive way too fast through town. Her heart was racing, and she was consumed with thoughts of jail, escape, and her mom, who would be so ashamed when it all came out that Natalie had either killed someone or walked away from someone who was dying and needed help. Lost in thought, she missed a traffic light change from yellow to red, and had to slam on her old, grinding brakes. She skidded through the intersection screaming in her own ears while two cars honked, passing her on either side.

As she tried to get back on the road, she felt her tires slipping. She had places to go and people to see, and it wasn't going to happen in her old Honda Civic tonight. Five minutes later, she pulled up at Jay's.

"What the hell, Natalie," Jay shouted, swinging the front door open before she could even ring. "Do you have any idea how worried I've been?"

"I'm sorry," she said. "I need your Jeep."

"What did you mean in your message, 'I did something bad'? People are starting to spread rumors on Facebook and Snapchat. What happened at the school? Does this have something to do with the coach?"

"Yes, listen, it has to do with all that, but right now I need your Jeep."

"What happened, Natalie?" Jay planted his cane and leaned on it, scowling, as if waiting for a lengthy explanation.

"I don't know what happened, and that's the problem. I need to find out exactly what I did, so I can figure out what to do next." Natalie ran around him, into the kitchen, and grabbed his keys from the Star Wars cup where he kept them along with years' worth of pennies. On her way back out, she said, "I'll explain everything later if I'm not in jail."

"What?" he asked, trying to hobble after her frantically. "Jail?"

"I've got to go! Thank you!"

"Stop!" Jay called after her. "Please, stop! I'm really mad at you right now! I don't think you should be driving in this weather! No one should!" He sighed and rubbed his beard. "Okay then, be careful! Make sure and use the four-wheel drive!"

As Natalie sped away from Jay's house, she tried to imagine all of the awful things she might have done to Nick when she had blacked out. She could have crept through the door from the stairwell unnoticed if his loud music was playing, to find him doing sit-ups in the corner. At the top of each crunch, the crown of his head would have been an easy target. Or perhaps he'd been using the rowing machine. Either way, he would have been vulnerable. She pictured herself, eyes black and empty, her whole body quivering with rage, standing above him with a round cast iron weight in her hands.

She could have cracked his skull like an egg.

It was harder to imagine how she might have then managed to throw him over the balcony.

Natalie knew where the Ellimans' house was located. People drove past it sometimes just to gawk at the size of the thing, perched up there above everyone else, now the lonely home of two beautiful, solitary females, like the premise of a gothic horror novel.

Driving on her way to the other side of the river, she passed the parking lot at Price Chopper. It was still filled with cars belonging to last-minute storm stockers, but the downtown and surrounding streets were mostly quiet. Jay's Jeep, with its raised chassis and oversized tires, gave Natalie confidence in the worsening blizzard, but the snow was blowing sideways in a frenzy. She tested the brakes, and the bright red warning sensor for icy conditions lit up on the dash.

She was just one turn away from the street that would take her up to Brooke's house when she saw a car on the side of the road. It was a buttery-colored Mercedes with a personalized license plate that read, "YUMCAKE." They were not old money, the Ellimans. Brooke was stunning and wealthy but had never been subtle. "Holy shit, that's her," Natalie said out loud, pulling over.

Brooke was in a silver parka, her long hair tangled and wet, hanging out from underneath a matching silver cap. She was pacing around and barking into her phone. Natalie rolled down the window and yelled, "Mrs. Elliman, do you need some help?"

Brooke squinted through the snow in Natalie's direction. "Miss Bellman?"

"Yes, from the school. Are you stuck?"

Brooke nodded. "They put me on hold."

"Who did you call? Triple A?"

"Highway patrol," Brooke answered, stomping through a snowdrift to cross the road. She scrutinized Natalie, who was wearing a stocking cap with a pom-pom on top, and took a long look at Jay's souped-up Jeep with the fiery emblem of Adrenaline Extreme Sports splashed across the side.

"Get in and get warm," Natalie said, pulling the cap off.

Brooke barely hesitated. After she'd closed the passenger door, she took off her gloves and held her hands up to the hot air blowing out of the vents. "Thank you," she said. "I shouldn't have been driving that car right now, I guess. My husband took the four-wheeler we usually use in the winter, and I haven't gotten around to buying myself one yet. I just wanted to go pick up Sloane and bring her home."

Sloane. Just the person Natalie needed to see. "Where is she? I'll take you to get her. This Jeep can handle pretty much anything."

"Would you do that?" Brooke asked, looking surprised and grateful. "Really?"

"Of course. Where am I headed?"

"She's at Reade Leland's house. About fifteen minutes from here. Up Devil's Canyon for starters."

Natalie began to drive. Brooke pulled

down the mirror on the back of the sun visor and began to wipe damp spots of mascara from underneath her eyes. "I was just leaving my house to go get Sloane, and Linda Leland called me, having some sort of nervous breakdown, saying she had to see me right away, right away, to come this minute. Crying. Hysterical. The next thing you know, she had me so worked up, I turned my car right into that drift."

"Well, that's upsetting. I'll have you there shortly."

Brooke shut the sun visor and sighed dramatically. "I've had a traumatic twenty-four hours."

It was all Natalie could do not to respond, *You don't say.*

Brooke turned to look at Natalie. "Thank you, Miss Bellman. For doing this."

"It's not a problem. You can call me Natalie."

"All right. In that case, why don't you call me Brooke?"

Traversing the mountain towards the six-acre ranch where the Lelands lived, Natalie tried to figure out the best way to start the conversation about what had happened to Nick.

"It's really nice of you. Especially," Brooke continued uneasily. "Because the last time we saw each other —"

"We don't have to talk about that," Natalie said, cutting her off. "I just felt bad for Asha, and I said something to you that I shouldn't have said. How you conduct your private life, I mean, it's not my business."

Brooke blinked. "Excuse me?"

"The last time I saw you, I said what I did because I know about you and Phil."

"Me and Phil?" Brooke asked indignantly. "What on earth are you talking about?"

Natalie briefly took her eyes off the swirling white mess ahead to glance at Brooke. "You two. You and Phil. Seeing each other."

"Natalie," Brooke said, "I don't know where you got that idea, but it's absolutely not true."

"His car was outside your apartment in the middle of the night a few weeks back."

Brooke considered this for a moment and then waved her hand dismissively. "Mia's been sneaking her dad's car out. Asha told me."

"Well, what about the Le Méridien in Denver?"

"What about it? He stayed there, not me."

"You never spent the night with Phil in Denver?"

"No! I —" She paused. "Actually, I did have dinner with him one night in Denver.

That's true. But I only ran into him at Ocean Prime Seafood. He was there on business, and I was as well, and we ate some oysters and drank some wine. I never told Asha about it because he was in town dealing with some business trouble that he wanted to try to sort out without worrying her. I probably should have said something. I mean, now that I know you both suspected I was sleeping with him, I definitely should have said something."

"I guess I just assumed —"

"Look. Nothing ever happened between me and Phil Wilson. I know my behavior with men over the years has been . . . inappropriate at times. I'm going to own that and change that. If I could go back in time and do things differently, I would. I lost my husband over it, and nearly my daughter, too. It breaks my heart to see how hurt Sloane is over the whole thing."

Natalie turned up the heat and made the windshield wipers go faster. She tested the brakes. The visibility was terrible. "I acted out way worse than Sloane when my dad left. I was a nightmare for my mom."

"I'm sorry," Brooke said. "I had no idea. What kind of trouble did you get in?"

Natalie hesitated, then said, "After he left, my mom got a prescription for Valium, and

I tried it, and I liked it. My brother was older, and he let me come to parties with him and drink sometimes. One night I blacked out and woke up in a boy's bedroom. There were race car and heavy metal posters all over the walls, but I didn't know whose house it was. I couldn't remember much, just the words 'it's okay' being whispered in my ear. I wasn't wearing all of my clothes. I knew something had happened, but I didn't know what. And I still don't know."

"How did you deal with that?" Brooke asked quietly.

"I stole a long sweatshirt and walked home barefoot at five in the morning. It was several miles. After that I stopped drinking. For a long time, at least. I got a tattoo on my wrist." Natalie left out the fact that the tattoo covered over a scar; the aftermath of a really bad night when she'd been trying to decide if she wanted to live or not. "It says 'self love' because I wanted to try to treat myself better. I think it's safe to say at this point that it wasn't a magic tattoo. Not the talisman I'd had in mind. It didn't protect me after all."

"What did your brother do when he found out?"

"He doesn't know," Natalie answered. "I

never told him. I was afraid he would kill the guy. Or guys."

"So, you never said anything to anyone?"

"Until just now."

"God, that's terrible." Brooke was staring at Natalie, looking deeply troubled. "I can relate. Sloane's had some very bad experiences, too."

"You're right about that," Natalie said.

Brooke shifted in her seat uncomfortably. "What are you talking about?"

"I'm talking about Nick."

Brooke began to play with the door lock.

"Which way do I turn?" Natalie asked, slowing down for a stop sign.

"Right," Brooke answered, distracted. "What about Sloane and Nick?"

"How much do you know about what happened at the school yesterday afternoon? About what happened in the gym?"

"Very little," Brooke said. "What do you know?"

"Quite a bit, actually," Natalie answered, and Brooke grabbed the door hand rest, squeezed, and waited.

"I know the following things," Natalie went on, increasing the windshield wipers to a frenetic speed, uselessly trying to help with the fog created by the snow. "I know that Nick is one of the people who was injured. I know that the police are investigating it as a crime." Natalie rolled up to a stop sign and braked carefully. She turned to look at Brooke. "I know they think I attacked him, but I don't remember doing that. I also know that he did something terrible to your daughter —"

"What? Exactly?"

"He took photos of her. Knocked her out somehow. The police know who was there. You, your daughter, a handful of others. But it probably comes down to two people. Either I hurt Nick, or Sloane hurt Nick, because of what he did to her."

"Sloane didn't do anything wrong," Brooke said.

"Are you sure?"

"Yes."

"Left here?" Natalie asked, reaching a T-stop. She glanced at Brooke, who didn't answer. "Left here, Brooke?"

"Sorry, yes." They passed several multi-acre ranches and drove through a quarter mile of forest. Brooke was quiet throughout, having placed one hand over her eyes. Her head was resting against the passenger window.

They'd reached a giant wooden gate reading "Land O'Leland." Natalie started up the snowy asphalt drive. "Well," Natalie said. "I guess that's it. I did it. It's not like it's the first time I ever blacked out and did something I regretted."

There was a heavy silence as Natalie parked the Jeep in front of the Leland ranch. The house was huge, but strangely neglected. A soggy American flag was being pummeled by the snow and wind. It was situated next to a basketball hoop that was missing its net. A white plastic bag was stuck in the bare branches of a tree, and two green beer bottles had been tossed on top of the snow in the front yard.

Finally, Brooke looked at Natalie and said, "It wasn't Sloane. And it wasn't you. It was me. It was me and Asha."

"Oh my God," Natalie said. "Are you playing with me?"

Brooke said, "No. We knew what he was doing too."

"Then you need to figure out your plan."

"We don't have a plan. We're just saying we never saw him."

"I'm sorry," Natalie said. "I left out the one other thing I know."

"What's that?"

"He's not dead. They're expecting him to wake up and tell them exactly what happened in the morning."

Before Brooke could try to speak, there

was a knock against the window. It was Linda Leland in a house robe worn over a flimsy tank top, yoga pants, and knee-high rubber boots.

"Linda," Brooke choked out, rolling down the window.

"I've been waiting for you," she said, electrified and appearing borderline manic. "I wasn't sure if you'd make it or not," she said, combing one hand through her disheveled hair.

"I wouldn't have it if it weren't for Miss Bellman."

"Miss Bellman?"

"Hi." Natalie attempted to smile at Linda, but it looked more like a sick grimace.

"My house is a mess," Linda blurted out, apropos of nothing. "I'd ask you in, but —"

"We just came for Sloane," Brooke answered. "We don't need to come in."

"No, Brooke, you do, you do," Linda said imploringly. "I told you on the phone. I have to talk to you. I don't know what to do. Please, Brooke. Just you. Just for a minute."

"I'll wait in the Jeep," Natalie interjected quickly. "I don't mind. I don't want to intrude."

"Thank you for understanding," Linda said. "I'm just not that comfortable with someone from —"

"I get it," Natalie answered, holding up a hand. "I'll be here in the car. No worries."

"Come in, Brooke," Linda said, opening the car door. "Hurry. Before I freeze."

Reluctantly, Brooke followed Linda into the house.

Natalie had a very bad feeling in her stomach. She thought maybe she was going to throw up. Brooke and Linda had been inside the ranch house for all of five minutes when Natalie opened the Jeep door and leaned out. She took several deep breaths of icy air and felt better.

A gun shot rang out in the night. And then another, and then another. Natalie fell out of the Jeep into the snow, picked herself up and went sprinting across the front yard towards the house as fast as her legs could move.

Linda hadn't been joking. Her house was a mess, strewn with clothing, dirty plates, empty glasses, and dusty balls of hair and fluff under chairs and the tables. As soon as the door was closed, Linda pulled on Brooke's arm, dragging her into the living room. She pointed to the couch. "Sit. I have to tell you something. It's bad. It's very bad."

"I'm listening."

Linda began cracking her knuckles. The sound was sickening. "I owe you an apology. Actually, a couple."

"Okay."

"It was me that sent that email with the photo of Sloane. It was an old photo, from before the 'scandal,' just a pretty picture on Reade's phone that I found, and she was dressed, wasn't she?"

"Barely," Brooke answered stonily, picturing the sports bra that had been hiked up to reveal the lower portion of Sloane's breasts.

"Nick helped me."

"What?"

"When you emailed me that article about that teenage boy going to jail for sharing photos of his girlfriend, I literally thought you were going to ruin Reade's life. It was a very scary threat. I didn't know who to reach out to, so I called Coach Nick for help, because he's been invested in Reade's future for two years, and I didn't think he would want to see my son go to detention. He told me what to do. He told me how to do it. He knew how to make the email look like it had come from somewhere else, another country, and also how to scare you without any real repercussions. We just needed you to stop causing problems. Neither one of us wanted to bring the police into the situation. You can understand that, right?"

Brooke stared at Linda. She knew exactly why Nick had not wanted the police involved. He could have cared less about Reade's future. He was worried about himself. Nick would have been found out for the liar, abuser, manipulator, and predator that he was, so he had to make sure that no one made any waves whatsoever.

"I shouldn't have done it," Linda went on. "I was wrong. I was so, so wrong about Nick and about everything. I'm afraid to even tell you . . ."

"What?"

"Do you remember last spring, when I said to you, 'It was all Sloane's idea to take those pictures'? Do you remember?"

"Yes. Of course, I do."

"I'm so sorry. It wasn't Sloane's idea."

"So it was Reade's after all, like I said." Brooke was starting to lose enthusiasm for this outdated conversation. At this point she had bigger worries than Reade.

"No. Kind of. It's more than that. Ohh . . ." Linda trailed off like the story was just too big and complicated.

"Calm down, Linda, and tell me what happened."

"Okay," she began hesitantly. "Today,

when the school let out early, Reade brought some friends back here. Later in the afternoon, after you and I texted, I called Reade upstairs. I was going to ask him to pass the message on to Sloane that you were coming to get her."

Brooke nodded.

"And when he came up to the kitchen, I could tell he'd been crying." Linda touched the corner of her eye. "I asked him what's wrong and he said, 'Craig just called.' Craig is his cousin. My nephew. He's a paramedic. And I said, 'Okay. What's going on?' And Reade told me that Craig said it was Coach Nick in the accident at the school, and that he was over at Colorado Medical, dying."

Brooke swallowed and refrained from commenting. She opted for looking appropriately devastated. "Wow."

"And I said, 'Oh, Reade, sugar, I'm so sorry.' Because maybe I'm the dumbest mom in the world, but I truly believed those two were close after spending so much time together doing the private training sessions over the years. I said, 'You must be so sad.' " Linda paused and reached for a tissue from a package lying on the coffee table. "And do you know what he answered?" Linda whispered, as if there were people listening. "He said, 'Mom, I'm crying because I'm happy. I hated him.' " Linda sat back and blew her nose.

"You're kidding."

"I was shocked," Linda answered. "And I just hugged him because I knew there must be some absolutely awful reason he would say that. He's not a mean boy. He has some problems with alcohol, and he's obsessed with your daughter, but he's not a bad boy, you know? He's just a teenage boy. But why would he be glad Coach Nick was going to die? So, I asked him, while I was hugging him, I asked him why he felt that way. And he just kept hugging me, which he never does anymore, you know? He always pulls away. But he just kept hugging me so I couldn't see his eyes, but from his voice I knew he was telling the truth. He said, 'It was Coach Nick that told me Jill's death was my fault, because the only reason she ever drank was because I drank.' Reade was so sad after Jill died, but then Nick swooped in to be his mentor and do the privates and help him 'heal.' They got close, I guess. Nick tried to be his friend. For a while, I think, it worked. Reade thought Nick was awesome. But then Nick told Reade that if Sloane loved him, she would take those photos for him. He egged him on about it for weeks. And then, when Sloane finally agreed to send him some photos, the first thing that happened was that Reade got busted with them by Coach Carmen, who stole his phone and reported the whole thing."

"That's what Sloane told me too," Brooke said. "That Coach Carmen confiscated the photos, and that Nick was trying to keep it quiet and help the kids stay out of trouble."

"Which is a lie! I know now. Nick never tried to keep those kids out of trouble. He just wanted them to be in trouble only with him! So he could control them! Reade says he wanted to *see* the photos of Sloane and was furious when he found out that Coach Carmen had gotten rid of them. He told Reade that he could still go the police and tell them about the photos, and that he had the final say on where Reade was accepted to college, and then —"

Linda threw her hands up in the air. "And then this sociopathic, sadistic piece of shit, trusted faculty member started *blackmailing* my son. He wanted Reade to tell him everything they did with the girls, parties and sex, drugs, you name it. All the info. He asked Reade to bring him drugs. Club drugs, speed, prescription stuff, everything under the sun. At his condo in town. *Blackmailing a student.* Can you believe that?"

Brooke very well remembered a night not

long before when Sloane had snuck out with Reade and the two had made a brief, middle-of-the-night night stop at an apartment in town. Probably Nick's place. "Yes, I can believe it."

A tremendous gust of wind rattled the house, and both women looked towards the windows facing the backyard, as if expecting the glass to break. The howling of the storm was deafening.

"Reade hated what was happening," Linda continued. "He kept crying, Brooke. My big boy, my big teenage son who towers over me now, was holding me and crying. I can't believe it. I gave that horrible man six hundred dollars yesterday at the gym, for Reade's private training sessions. I was paying the man who was hurting my son. I was so blind."

"We all were." Brooke put her arm around Linda. "It wasn't just you."

"I know it's horrible to admit this, but just between you and me? I'm so glad he's gone."

"Well . . ." Brooke said. "In that case, I've got some bad news." Before she could say anything more, there were three loud, cracking noises outside. Brooke tensed up and said, "Oh my God, now what?"

Linda waved a dismissive hand. "Probably

tree branches breaking from the wind." She fixed Brooke with a stare. "What's the bad news?"

The gunshots had come from the rear of the ranch house. Natalie trudged through the snow around the side of the house, and saw what looked like some animals prowling around the backyard.

Not coyotes, Natalie thought. People. One of them fell face-first, tramping towards the woods in the drifting snow. Another gunshot sounded, and then there was a disturbing squeal of laughter. The snow was still coming down, but she could see that there were three people, two boys and a girl, and one of the boys was shooting at some bottles sitting on a wooden picnic table in the woods.

"Sloane?" Natalie yelled. Her voice was nearly lost in the immensity of the stormy night. "Is that you?" Natalie called out again. "Sloane? Your mom's here looking for you! Are you okay?"

It only took a second for Natalie to recognize them as Reade and his friend Greg Woodson. Sloane was flailing, trying to pull herself to her feet in an uncoordinated way. Something was wrong with her.

"Here, Sloane," Natalie said as she approached, reaching out her hand. "You want to come with me?"

Reade stepped in front of Natalie and said, "She's fine."

"Is that who I think it is?" Greg asked in a sedated slur. "The one and only Miss Bellman?"

"Yes," Natalie answered. "That's me, the one and only." She put her hands under Sloane's armpits and helped her to her feet. "Your mom's inside the house."

"She's going to be able to tell," Sloane said. "She's smart."

"Be able to tell what?" Natalie asked.

"That we took GHB," Sloane answered. "And coke. And what else was there? There was something else too, right?"

"Jesus," Greg said. "Just be quiet, will you?"

"Sloane, come with me." Natalie was worried. "I'll take you to the Jeep, and we'll wait for your mom."

Greg took a menacing step towards Natalie, and she saw that he had a revolver in his hand. "When we're not at school, I don't think you get to tell us what to do. You're trespassing, aren't you?"

Natalie glanced towards the house, hoping to see a burst of light from the front door. *Help,* she thought, a tiny voice in her head. *Help me.* "Sloane?" she said. "Let's go, okay?"

Greg put his arm out to stop Sloane. "It doesn't look like she wants to go with you."

"Stop it, Greg," Reade said. "Give me my mom's gun."

"What? Why?"

"Just give it to me."

Greg handed it over, sulking.

Reade slipped the revolver into the back of his pants, and Natalie took a deep, shuddering breath. "Sorry, Miss Bellman," Reade said. "It's my mom's. It's legal and everything. We were just shooting some targets in the snow." He plunged his hands into his big parka pockets. "Listen, Miss Bellman, I can get your phone back for you."

Natalie had already accepted the fact that she'd never see that phone again, but she was surprised. "You can?"

"Yeah. I took it. I was hoping to get dirt on Coach Nick, so we could finally put that whole thing from last spring behind us."

"Which wasn't even that big a *deal,*" Greg said, looking cross-eyed, and as if he was about to pass out. "Because of a few photos, Jeremiah lost his car. I lost my PS5 and almost went to military school. Everyone says Alish, Alish . . ." He was slurring and couldn't pronounce Alistair. "Everyone thinks Alishter is in Grand Cayman, but he's really in some rehab place in Switzerland getting his brain hard drive erased and rebooted with some bullshit oxygen tank treatment that's going to leave him a retard. I bet Kasper's never even coming back from Poland now."

"Greg, can you be quiet for a minute?" Reade seemed ashamed. "It was dumb. We never should have taken any photos. It wasn't worth it. Right, Sloane?"

Sloane nodded and said, "No way. No way. Never again."

"But once we did do it," Reade explained, "Coach Nick held it over us like he was a mob boss or something. I saw the two of you leaving the school together a few times and it seemed like you had something going on with him. I just thought, I don't know, that maybe there would be something on your phone that I could use against him. So I could get free of him. It was a bad idea, and I'm sorry. But I hated him, and I had to try."

Natalie couldn't believe it. Reade Leland wasn't quite the monster that she'd thought. She was at a loss for words.

"I'll bring your phone back to you on Wednesday at school," Reade said. "And by the way, you should change your passcode.

1234 is no good."

"Thanks." A laugh escaped and she said, "But I don't even know if I'll be at school on Wednesday."

"Why not?" Reade asked.

Just then, a side door of the house opened, and light spilled out. Brooke yelled, "Sloane? Are you out there?"

"Here, Mom," Sloane answered, and Brooke came running, as best she could, through a lawn covered in four inches of snow.

Reade plodded drunkenly behind Sloane all the way to the Jeep while Greg lumbered back to the house. Linda's silhouette could be seen, watching, in the front window.

When they were loaded up in the Jeep, Reade blew a kiss through the window. Sloane caught it, touched her fingers to her lips, and smiled.

"Where am I going?" Natalie asked. "Am I driving straight north and over the border to Canada?"

"Why would you do that?" Sloane asked groggily from the back seat, and Brooke flashed Natalie a warning look. *Not in front of her.*

"We need to talk with Asha," Brooke said, looking at her phone. "I've texted her a million times, and she hasn't texted back."

"She was admitted to the hospital this morning," Natalie said.

"What? Is she all right?"

"I don't know. I would have checked on her, but I was being held hostage in Mr. Dilly's conference room all day."

"Go there, then. We'll make sure she's all right. Get all our stories straight."

"What stories?" Sloane mumbled from the back seat.

"Nothing," Brooke said, reaching back to put one hand on Sloane's knee. "You just go to sleep."

39

Asha had been having a beautiful dream. It was years earlier, when Mia was a slightly chubby bowlegged toddler who loved bath time and all her water toys. Asha used to line them up on the edge of the gigantic Jacuzzi tub. There were rolls of baby fat on Mia's arms and legs and belly, and her brown hair was still thin, soft, and short. Her smile was magnetic even then, and her eyes so luminous and cheerful that just looking in them brought joy. On her pudgy baby finger was a dragonfly ring, even though Asha hadn't given her that ring until she was twelve. Nick was suddenly there too, in the bathroom with Asha, watching Mia bathe, and he said, "Look at that cute little silver dragonfly ring." Then he raised his phone to take a picture, and Asha hit it out of his hand, yelling, *"No."*

That was what woke her, and she must have spoken out loud, because it woke Phil as well. He'd been sleeping upright, slumped against the wall in the corner of the hospital room, and his whole body jerked.

Nearly falling out of his chair toward the hospital bed, he asked, "Are you okay?"

"I don't know," she answered truthfully, looking around in an anxious fright. "I don't know." The memory of what happened in the gym was starting to form again, following hours of sedatives and sleep. In the back of her mind was the image of Mr. Maguire going over the balcony in slow motion. Her hands, and Brooke's, against his chest. Phil didn't appear to know what had happened. "What's going on?" she asked. She needed answers. *Who knows what?*

"I slept in the basement last night because you were snoring. One of the ladies from the carpool was just picking the kids up for school when I woke, and Mia told me you hadn't gotten out of bed yet. I found you in the bathroom. You were thrashing around. You said, 'Something's wrong with the baby,' and I brought you here."

"And is something wrong with the baby?" Asha asked, hands flying to her stomach.

"Dr. Ruiz said there's a tear in your amniotic sac. You need to stay on bedrest and let them monitor the situation. You'll either be induced eventually or be here in the hospital until the delivery. But the baby's going to be fine either way. Early, but fine."

Asha reached out and grabbed his arm. "Are you sure?"

Phil nodded and leaned down to kiss her cheek.

"You're not lying?" Asha asked.

"No, honey. No. I wouldn't lie about something like that."

Asha didn't let go. She pulled him closer. "What would you lie about?"

"I'm not sure what you mean."

"You said you wouldn't lie to me 'about something like that.' But you were happy to lie to me about something else, weren't you?"

Phil pulled his hand out of hers, wiped one of his eyes, and dragged the chair over to her bedside. "How did you find out?" he asked, sitting and looking down at the floor in a wretched way.

Asha hadn't expected an immediate confession. "I found out that you were at Le Méridien last spring. I know you were with someone. You had dinner in your room. Two meals and two bottles of wine."

Phil nodded.

"How could you?" she asked. "I've been a

good wife. I've been a good friend. I've been fun and loving, and I've been a good mom to our kids. I thought our sex life was great, and —"

"Wait," he said. "Wait, wait, wait."

"And with my friend. How could you? With her?"

"Who? What are you talking about?"

"Brooke. I know about the lies."

"Stop. There's only one lie. And I'm not cheating on you, and certainly not with Brooke. When you said, 'I know,' I thought you meant you knew about the lawsuit. Are you serious? Do you actually think I'm interested in anybody besides you?"

"I thought you were interested in anybody *besides* me. Look at me. I'm a mess. What lawsuit? Are you saying you *weren't* cheating on me?"

"No, baby, I didn't cheat on you. I love you. I would never do that. But I did lie to you. Six months ago, one of my clients lost a lot of money and sued me for mismanagement. I didn't want to tell you because I knew it would upset you, and I thought I could work it out. The whole thing stressed me out to the point where I was sick. Stomach aches. Insomnia and then fatigue, and then vice versa. The whole time I just kept thinking about how your parents never thought I was good enough for you, and what they were going to say when I lost my license and you would have to rescue me with your family money. It was horrible. I had to go to Denver on a number of occasions for meetings, some early, some late, a few requiring an overnight. I did see Brooke there once. I ran into her at that seafood place on Larimer Square, and we had oysters and drinks, but *not* sex. I did ask her not to mention it to you, and she said she totally understood about keeping business issues separate from family and, you know, she was nice about it, to be honest. Later I had dinner with Bob. Bob Bruckheimer at my hotel. We both had steak and we split a couple of bottles of merlot. We've had a few meetings like that over the last six months."

Asha closed her eyes and rested her head against the pillow. "I hate you," she said.

"But do you still love me?" he asked, smiling.

"Yes. I'm just so happy. I'm so happy that you got sued instead of falling in love with someone else."

Phil laughed. "And the best part is, I wasn't in Phoenix the other night. That was another lie. I'm sorry. I was in Denver at the Le Méridien eating steak and drinking wine without you. With Bob. Again. Good news, too. The lawsuit has been dropped."

Natalie parked the Jeep outside of the Colorado Medical. She, Brooke, and Sloane, who was still weaving a little when she walked, entered through the revolving double doors that led into the lobby. Due to the storm, it was a quiet evening. The gift shop was closing for the night. A few nurses and doctors walked the halls, but there were barely any visitors. The ones there looked like they'd scoped out a couch or a chair, collapsed, and planned to stay out the storm.

On the second floor, outside the maternity ward, was a sitting area with several couches, a big-screen television, and a table piled high with children's books. Oliver was there with Mia. He was playing on his iPad, and she was scrolling on her phone.

"Hi, kids," Brooke said, trying to sound cheerful. "How's your mom?"

Oliver looked up first. "Hi, Mrs. Elliman. Dad says she's going to be okay."

Sloane slumped down next to Mia. "I'm sorry to hear that she's sick," she said. "What happened to her?"

"Something with the baby," Mia answered. "It was scary."

"Are you okay?" Sloane asked.

"Yeah, I am now. Are you?"

"Umm," Sloane grunted. "Yeah."

"But just barely?" Mia asked, laughing, some sort of inside joke.

Sloane yawned. "Yeah, just barely." She put her head down on Mia's shoulder. Mia readjusted a little bit to make it more comfortable for Sloane, and then went back to scrolling through her phone.

Phil walked in from the direction of the rooms, looking bedraggled. "Brooke," he said, surprised to see her. "It's so nice of you to come. Jesus, and with the apocalypse storm bearing down too. You're a good friend."

"I try. Is she up for visitors?" Brooke asked.

"That would be great, actually," he said. "If you could keep her company for a little bit? I need to get these kids home and feed them before we're stuck here." He didn't seem to notice Natalie, who was trying her best to be invisible by examining a terribly boring painting in shades of brown over one of the couches.

Outside, the gusting wind rattled the windows. The hospital was surrounded by large trees, and there was a startling noise above as a branch, whipped asunder, came crashing down on the roof.

The lights suddenly flickered. Dark, light, dark. A flurry of voices could be heard barking questions and answers down the hall. After a few seconds, the power was completely on again.

"You should go now," Brooke said. "And drive safe. I keep getting notifications about pileups on the interstate. Try and stay off Devil's Canyon."

"Can Sloanie come with us?" Mia asked, throwing an arm around her shoulder and making a pretty-please pout.

Brooke looked at Phil. "I don't know. That would be up to your dad, and he's already had a hard day, so —"

"We'd love to have Sloane," Phil said. "That would cheer Mia up, I think. Can they do a sleepover? I'm going to have a whiskey when I get home, and I don't want to drive again tonight."

"That would be great, Phil," Brooke said. "Thank you. I'll come get her in the morning."

Asha's bed was next to a small padded bench at the base of a window. A television was mounted high on the wall. Underneath it was a round table and two chairs. The overhead light was off, but there was a nightlight just below the shelf on the far wall. Asha had fallen back asleep after the conversation with Phil. By her bedside was a monitor quietly reporting her vitals. In her hand was the television remote, but the volume was on mute. The only noise was the whisper of air coming and going from Asha's slightly parted lips.

"Hey," Brooke said softly, leaning down. "Asha?" After a second, Brooke cleared her throat and said more loudly, "Okay. Time to wake up."

Asha's eyes flew open, and she looked startled and a little pissed. "You scared me, Brooke."

"I'm sorry. We need to talk to you."

"Natalie," Asha said. "What are you doing here?"

"She knows everything," Brooke answered. "It's a long story."

Asha struggled to sit up and reached out for Natalie. "Come here." Natalie approached and took her hand gently. "What do you know?" Asha asked.

Natalie sniffed, trying not to be too emotional. "I know I was in a relationship with a sick man who was keeping secrets from me. I know that he was doing the private training sessions with your daughters and that he did bad things. Like giving them something to make them sleep and taking photos of them. I know he hurt them, and I hate him, and that whatever happened to him, he absolutely deserved, and I'm just so sorry —"

The sound of three quick knocks made Natalie snap her mouth shut and look fearfully towards the door.

"Just checking in on my favorite mother-to-be and real-estate magician. How are you feeling?"

The doctor standing in the doorway of the room was Elena Ruiz. She had high cheekbones and dark hair pulled back in a bun. She was even more beautiful than Natalie remembered from that day months before, when she'd seen her embracing Nick at the gas station in town. No one had told Natalie about Nick's "intervention" with Mia, and she still believed that Nick had gone to the Ruiz house for a clandestine tryst with Elena the night before. Natalie felt physically sick. She wanted, in the worst way, to get out of that room.

"I'm good, thank you, Elena," Asha answered, trying her best to sound composed. "How nice to see you. I wasn't expecting you."

"I just got here. Barely, I might add. The roads are terrible. You all should think about getting home safe and sound. But I had a look at your chart and spoke to Dr. Gordon. You and the baby are doing really well, considering. We're going to try to keep the situation very calm and under control here for a little bit longer while I do some tests. There's a slight chance we may want to look at giving you some steroids to make sure the baby's lungs are in good shape in case of an early arrival, but I won't make that decision until tomorrow. I'm not worried about you or the baby. Everything is going to be fine."

"Everything is going to be fine?" Asha repeated, looking at Natalie and Brooke. "Did you two hear that?" Asha let out a short, sharp laugh. "Everything is going to be fine. I sure hope you're right."

"Get some rest, okay?" Elena said. "I'm here all night if you need anything." The doctor tucked her clipboard under her arm and left.

Natalie watched her go. Elena was clearly a wealthy, educated, graceful woman. An older woman, who didn't look like she would play Nick's ridiculous games, or be his type. But the fact of Nick's tie crumpled on the floor of a bedroom in her house indicated otherwise.

Suddenly overwhelmed by it all, Natalie

said, "I need some fresh air. Brooke, you tell Asha the news about Nick. Figure out what the two of you want to do, and I'll be back in twenty minutes to drive you home."

She wanted to see him.

Natalie took the stairs down to the intensive care unit. It smelled of disinfectant and coffee. The lights were too bright, and the sterile white atmosphere was depressing. The nurses looked tired and overworked, shuffling from room to room pushing carts and computers.

There was a man in a uniform leaning over the central desk. Natalie didn't think he was a police officer. Whatever task he'd been given, he'd abandoned it to chat with a slender blonde nurse in hot-pink scrubs.

Natalie surveyed the hallway. Only one room had a fold-up chair placed against the wall beside the door. The chair would have been set up there for the guard. Nick's room.

The security guard was badgering the pretty blonde nurse about getting a drink sometime. Natalie passed behind them and continued on down the hall.

Nick's room was mostly dark except for a strip of light spilling through the cracked bathroom door and the flickering red lights from a myriad of machines. The door was ajar, and Natalie slipped through without changing its position. Nick was reclining on the raised back of the white bed, heavily bandaged. Most of his body was underneath a blanket, but his arms, one in a cast and one not, rested on top. Natalie took a few tentative steps inside.

"Nick?" she said softly, and the sound of her own voice chilled her, because it was eerily similar to when she said his name in the gym as he lay there bleeding from his head wound. "Are you awake?"

Nothing.

"Can you hear me?"

Nothing. She approached the bed and leaned down. He smelled like an old man, bad breath, body odor, and antiseptic.

"I know what you did," she said, close to his ear. "I know what you did to Sloane and Mia."

Suddenly the lights in the hallway went dark for the second time. Another power outage. The machines in his room continued to blip on and off. Red. White. A dinging sound, but otherwise completely quiet. Again, they were alone. She leaned down close to his face, to see him better in the pitch-black hospital room.

His eyes sprang open.

A terrified scream froze in her throat.

He made a noise. She waited, listening to his breath coming and going. It appeared he wanted to say something.

"Listen," Natalie said, her eyes boring into his one good one. "Can you hear me?"

He moved a finger and then blinked.

"Good," she said. "That's good."

Was he trying to smile? It seemed like he was happy to see her. Natalie smiled back and said, "When the police come to see you in the morning, you say you fell, okay? That's what happened. Or it's all going to come out. If you talk, we'll all talk." Secretly Natalie believed he would likely deny everything, but it was worth a try. "Do we have a deal? You fell. Are we clear?"

"Baby." His lips were parched and swollen. His hand rolled over, palm up. He wanted her to take it.

A momentary surge of pity caused her to oblige.

With her hand in his, he squeezed and said, "Don't."

"Don't what?" she asked. "Don't believe it? How can I not believe it? I saw."

"No. Don't."

"Don't what?"

"Don't — be — a bitch."

Her mouth dropped open from shock before a wave of hot fury swept through her body. For a second, she pictured herself smothering him with a pillow. She began reaching for the one behind his head.

Like an explosion, the overheads in the hall burst back on, flooding the room with white light. There was a noise and Natalie spun toward the door. A doctor in full scrubs, mask and a cap, was standing behind her. Only the eyes were visible, but the doctor's body language seemed to suggest that he or she was shocked to find Natalie there.

"I made a wrong turn," Natalie mumbled, choking back tears of anger, frustration, and fear. "I'm sorry." She ran down the hall to get away from him once and for all.

The mood in the Jeep was somber as Natalie drove Brooke back to her house. The windshield wipers were going back and forth like crazy trying to keep a half circle of glass clear. The snow seemed to be coming from all directions. Natalie came up behind a slow-moving plow and settled in to follow his taillights, like a lighthouse in the fog, for a long climb back up the mountain.

"What did you and Asha decide?" Natalie asked. "What's the story?"

"We showed up to get Sloane. Nick was acting strangely. Drunk or on drugs. We left abruptly. That's it."

"And what will you say when he says you pushed him over the balcony?"

"Remember," Brooke answered, "that he nearly died from a traumatic brain injury. He could wake up and start talking about spaceships, unicorns, and flying monkeys."

"He's going to say that you pushed him. And he's going to say that I broke his phone and left him there to die." Natalie parked the Jeep outside Brooke's house. "He's going to say horrible things about us, and your daughters. Imagine the information he has to work with. It's going to be a nightmare. It will be our word against his."

"We'll fight," Brooke said. "He's a pedophile and a pornographer. We'll expose him for what he is and what he's done."

"But the police won't see it that way," Natalie responded. "They'll say you don't get to push someone over a balcony just because *you* think he did something wrong. You and Asha will go to jail. And probably me too."

Brooke opened the passenger door and stepped out. "I don't think it will come to that."

"Are you sure you don't want to make a run for the border?"

Looking completely worn out, Brooke

sighed. "Natalie. Do you even have a passport?"

"No."

"I didn't think so. Go home and get some sleep. Tomorrow, be ready to tell the police that you walked into the gym and thought that he was dead. You panicked and left. That will cover you no matter what he says. Asha and I have our own story. That's all. Okay?" Brooke sounded ominously resigned. Suspiciously resigned. "We'll all do what we have to do."

"Okay. Good night."

"Goodbye, Natalie."

It felt very final.

When she got home, Natalie flopped down onto the bed. Her head hit something hard. She reached underneath the comforter and pulled out her landline receiver, which she had taken to sleep with her the previous night and totally forgotten about since. It was blinking. She picked it up and typed in her password, which was also 1234. "I've got to change that," she said to herself.

The machine voice said, "You have one message." It was from the day before.

The call had come in early Sunday morning after the Fall Feast. She remembered now that she'd taken her landline to bed with her and waited for Nick to check on her, like he'd said he would. After several hours, she'd taken some pain pills and finally fallen into a deep sleep.

She pressed the button to listen to his message.

Natalie had seen him drunk on very few occasions, but while leaving this message, he was clearly not in his right mind. He was whispering in a threatening way, and she was certain he was under the influence of alcohol, drugs, or both. "You crossed the line tonight. Taking my phone? You are a crazy bitch, and I'm done with you. Don't talk to me at school. Don't call or text. Pretend you don't know me and pretend you never knew me. I don't require your services anymore."

He hung up.

"I don't require your services anymore?" she echoed, staring at the receiver in her hand. A part of her wanted to throw the phone. Pound a beer. Smash a vase. Call Jay and cry. Another part of her was just disgusted and tired. What a stupid, tragic, fucked-up ending to a stupid, tragic, fucked-up fling.

40

The storm had ended sometime in the middle of the night, leaving the valley with a dazzling and blinding backdrop of radiant white snow. The tree branches dripped with sharp icy daggers, and there was that strange quiet that accompanied the aftermath of a large snowfall, as if all of nature was trying to sleep in, cuddled up in a soft blanket.

When she opened her eyes, Natalie had a clear and sudden understanding of what she needed to do. She stood in her bathroom, putting drops in her eyes and practicing. "I thought he was dead. I was going to call for help. His phone wasn't working. I was upset and felt sick, and I didn't want to be there. I panicked and left."

She repeated her statement several times in a variety of different voices and then rehearsed her responses to their possible questions.

"It was already broken," she practiced

answering. "That's not right. I think he must be confused. Understandable, given his injuries."

Asha and Brooke could tell whatever story they wanted to tell. That was up to them. Natalie had no intention of contradicting them. She had no reason to.

Natalie walked over to the kitchen counter. She found Ken's business card in her purse and sat down on her couch. After a few nervous minutes, she forced herself to pick up her home phone.

"Detective Ken Bradley here."

Natalie said, "Good morning, Detective Bradley. This is Natalie Bellman."

"You better not be canceling," he said. She could hear him taking a sip of something, probably his morning coffee.

"No, but I was wondering if I could talk to you now."

"Oh? Okay. Sure."

"Could I see you? Talk in person? Would that be possible?"

"Hold on." Ken muted her and she waited until he returned. "Listen, Natalie," he said.

"Yes?"

"I'm with Detective Larson right now. She and I are just about to pull into the parking lot of the hospital. If you drive down here to meet us, we can chat straight away."

"I'm almost ready to walk out the door," she said. "I can be there in thirty minutes."

"All right. Give me a call when you get here."

The streets had been plowed and aside from the dirty banks of sludge pushed to the side of every road, it was a clean new day. The fir trees twinkled like giant green gowned ladies in sequined dresses, and there was a crisp, bright, radiant aura hovering above the glowing horizon.

Natalie walked through the doors to the hospital and made a left turn toward the intensive care unit. The gift shop was open, a kiosk of cards, stuffed animals, and balloon bouquets out in front. Just past the lobby, by the first of several desks and a handful of nurses, she stopped and used the wall phone to make her call to Ken. "I'm here," she said, leaning against the counter. "Sure. I'll wait. I'm not going anywhere."

A middle-aged man with weary, bent posture and thick glasses looked over and asked, "Can I help you, miss?"

"I'm fine, thank you," she answered. "I'm just waiting to speak to the detectives who are back with Nicholas Maguire."

"Oh. Too bad about that," he said, his

watery, kind eyes magnified behind his lenses.

"Wait, what? What do you mean?"

"Umm . . ." He started pawing through some papers. "You didn't hear? Are you family or . . ."

"Family," she said. "I lost my phone. What's too bad?" Natalie looked down the hallway and saw Ken and Beth emerge from around a corner. They were heading her way.

"At times like this, I think it's important to mention that we have a chapel right here in the hospital —"

"What?" she demanded. "What happened?"

"He succumbed to his injuries," the man said apologetically. "Last night. But if it helps, I can assure you he didn't suffer. In fact, he never regained consciousness. He passed peacefully in his sleep."

"Oh my God."

"Maybe you should sit down."

She forced herself to pull it together. She turned around as the detectives were just approaching.

"Natalie," Ken said, pleasantly. "Good morning."

Natalie opened her mouth, but nothing came out.

Ken scowled and crossed his arms impatiently. "You wanted to talk," he prompted.

"This young lady has just received some bad news," the nurse interjected kindly, while cleaning his glasses with a tissue. "I don't think now is the —"

"This young lady," Ken interrupted, "has just gone from being a person of interest in a suspicious incident to a person of interest in a murder."

"Yes, sir." And with that, the friendly nurse stood up, looked for something to do, and began sanitizing his hands.

Ken was staring Natalie down in a menacing way.

Nick isn't going to wake up. He isn't going to talk. Maybe Asha and Brooke will be fine. Maybe no one will ever know that I left him to die.

"Why did you want to see us this morning?" Ken demanded.

"I wanted to let you know . . ." She stalled.

"What?"

"I know who has my phone. It's a student. Who is involved peripherally, but also somewhat importantly, like part of the investigation somewhat? He found it on the floor, and he's going to give it back to me tomorrow, so if you still want it, I can give it to you then. I know you wanted to see it and so —"

Beth said, not in an unfriendly manner, "You're kind of rambling. But you're saying you found your phone?"

"Yes."

"That's great, but really?" Ken asked. "That's it?"

"No," Natalie said, in a way that seemed terribly consequential. "That's not it." She looked down and took a deep breath.

"What?" Ken asked.

"There's more," she answered.

Beth gave her a quizzical look. "Natalie, please. We're busy. What else?"

"Nick's dog. Somebody has to go get Nick's dog. He's in the townhome."

"Somebody picked him up this morning," Beth said. "Relax, okay? The dog is fine. Ken, we're supposed to be meeting with Harry Doyle right now."

"Right." Ken pointed at Natalie. "Two o'clock at the police station."

"I'll be there."

Ken and Beth walked off towards the escalator, and Natalie pretended to be headed for the hospital exit. Once they were gone, she booked it back to the elevator and went up to the second floor. She ran down the hallway to Asha's room, praying she would still be there.

She was.

"Natalie!" Asha exclaimed. "You look like you stuck your finger in a light socket."

Asha was by herself, and Natalie pulled the door shut behind her before going over to her bedside. "He *died,*" Natalie tried to whisper. "Last night."

Asha slapped her hand down on the adjustable table at her bedside. "Mr. Maguire?"

"Yes, Nick!" Natalie said, shifting from side to side like she needed to pee.

"I can't believe it." Asha put her hands together in prayer, looked up, and said a few whispered words.

"Can you call Brooke?" Natalie asked. "And let her know before they interview her?"

"I'll do it right now. What time is it? Oh shit! I'm supposed to be meeting with the detectives in thirty minutes."

"Okay. I'm going to get out of here before they see me," Natalie said, backing out of the room. "You've got this?"

"We've got this. Go. Go. Brooke and I will work it out. Thank you!"

When Natalie arrived at the Falcon Valley police station, she approached the officer at the entrance desk, a grim, middle-aged woman in a bad mood. "I'm here to see Detectives Bradley and Larson."

The officer escorted Natalie down the hall and said, "Second door on the right." Natalie found herself in a featureless lobby, consisting of two plaid couches on either side of a long, low coffee table scattered with various brochures.

Waiting for a long time, she was able to read up on a variety of topics from bicycle theft to domestic violence. She tore out the number for a local law firm. About ready to ask the man sitting at the big desk at the far end of the room if she would have to wait much longer, she heard footsteps coming towards the lobby from the back of the station. Loud, clapping footsteps like a woman marching in heels.

Natalie craned her neck to peer down the hall, and she could see Brooke, walking side by side between Beth and Ken. Sloane was trailing behind them, her hair hanging around her shoulders like a Manson girl doing her perp walk. Brooke was wearing a high-waisted pencil skirt and a tight turtleneck. She looked both breathtaking and intimidating. Brooke spotted Natalie, and her expression revealed nothing whatsoever. She passed with not so much as a slight nod. If anything, she held her chiseled chin up higher to avoid any eye contact.

Natalie was immediately anxious and uneasy, which quickly turned into a chill up her neck and a twisting fist in her gut. She hunched over. This was not good. This was not good at all.

For the first time, it dawned on her that Nick's death might be the worst thing that could have happened to her. Had he woken up, the nastiest thing he could have accused her of was breaking his phone and walking away.

Dead, his words had disappeared with him. Without his story, there was only the evidence. Her fingerprints in the sticky blood on Nick's phone. Walking in and out of the gym twice. The horrible things she'd written in the planner. Then, with a shudder, Natalie considered what else there was to still to find. Whatever blood was left on her skirt, wadded up in a Target bag under her sink. A message she'd left for her brother, saying, "I did something bad."

Natalie had the urge to run, the fight-or-flight instinct kicking in, telling her that if the police thought it was murder, she was the obvious killer. Not the rich, powerful moms but the damaged girl: the outsider, the thief, drug addict, and obsessive ex-girlfriend.

She stood up and was about to leave when, at that moment, Ken appeared in front of her, blocking her path. He held out his phone, and on the screen was a photo of Nick wearing a huge, toothsome, thank-God-it's-Friday sort of smile. He was standing between Lars Jaeger and Carmen Sorella. They were hugging one another, with the Fall Feast stage as a backdrop, and he was wearing his turquoise-blue soccer-ball print Vineyard Vines necktie, the one that the detectives found wadded up in the back of Natalie's work desk.

"Natalie, I'm not even going to mention the lost earbuds bullshit lie right now," Ken said. "I'm just going to show you this photo. When I asked around for recent pics of the victim, this is one that was sent to me. Looks like this one was taken the night of the Fall Feast. The night before his accident." He stood there, phone held out, photo in her face. "Recognize the tie? Are you sure you stole that tie out of the lost and found?" Ken sounded like he was talking to a bad dog. "Care to change your story?"

Natalie glanced over her shoulder at the window: quaint ranch-style sprawling town, foothills, the mountains behind them, the canyons beyond that, and the plains, the borders, the other countries, all the rest of the world she'd so wanted to see. So many places she could have run if she'd had the guts.

"Did you lie?" Ken asked.

"Obviously," she said, finally giving in to the nervous laughter, the exhaustion, and the absurdity of the whole ridiculous situation. "I mean, obviously, I did."

"Natalie Bellman," he said. "You're under arrest for the murder of Nicholas Maguire."

KBEV 16 Breaking News:

"It's been another big day in Falcon Valley, folks. I'm Melissa O'Hare for KBEV Colorado. I'm outside the police station, and sources inside tell me that just hours after Nicholas Maguire, the Assistant Athletic Director at Falcon Academy, passed away at Colorado Mountain Hospital, police not only have a person of interest but have already made an arrest. This is pretty shocking news, given that most of the community had assumed that Mr. Maguire, a distinguished athlete in his own right as well as an administrator and coach who was admired by students, parents, and teachers, had been gravely injured in an accident in the school gym. Officials are not naming the suspect at this point, but I've learned from inside sources that this terrible crime could all come down to one of the oldest motives in the world. Jealousy."

41

Dr. Leonard Romano, the prosecuting attorney, had a PhD in law from some forty years earlier, and was half-blind, so his report was printed in oversized font. Small and wiry, with close-trimmed steel-gray hair, he wore a suit with a bow tie, as he did every weekday except casual Fridays, when he ditched the buttoned-down look for a collared shirt tucked into grandpa jeans. "I take it suicide has already been ruled out?" he asked.

"Mostly," Ken answered. "He had several guns at home, which would have been an easier way out. We doubt he purposely threw himself backwards against a sharp object with the intention of puncturing the base of his skull before then jumping over a balcony."

"Uh-huh. And no defense wounds?"

"No."

"And the girl? What was under her

fingernails?"

"Not his skin. Plus, she's barely a hundred pounds. Nevertheless . . ."

"This is an unusual case," he said to Ken and Beth over sandwiches and coffees at his desk. "My, my, my." He touched his glasses, as was his habit. "Natalie Bellman, what a piece of work, eh? Relationship to the victim. Ex-girlfriend. Fingerprints in the blood on his phone." He looked up at Ken and Beth. "Very damning."

Ken nodded, and Dr. Romano went on in his gravelly voice. "Surveillance footage showing her going in and out of the gym two times the afternoon of the alleged incident. Last person in the building. Search warrants uncovered victim's blood on a skirt hidden under her sink and a message on her brother's phone in which she stated, 'I did something bad.' She also stole drugs from students and had the dead man's tie stuffed in her desk drawer." Dr. Romano looked up again. "Not looking good for this young woman, is it?"

Beth said, "Well . . . just wait."

Dr. Romano touched his glasses again. "These excerpts are from her diary?"

"It was more like an exercise log and planner," Beth said. "With the occasional short summary of how things were going in her life."

"I see. Fits of rage, paranoia, jealousy, and thoughts of self-harm and harming others." He leaned back in his reclining office chair and put his hands behind his head. "Frankly, detectives, I'm surprised you characterized this as a humdinger. This seems more like a slam dunk."

Beth turned the page of her copy of the report and said, "At first. Keep going and see what you think."

"You've got some doubts about this, Detective Larson?"

"Actually, Doctor," Ken said, tapping his own report, "we both do. You've just read everything that we knew right before we arrested her, but as we consider going forward and making formal charges, there's more to the story."

"Talk to me," Dr. Romano said.

"Beth, would you like to go first?" Ken asked.

"Sure," she answered. "So, it turns out Mr. Maguire was a bit of an enigma."

"How so?"

"Well, he had alcohol in his system at the time he sustained his injuries. Which is not unusual in general, but he'd been working with children all day long. Also, lab results have come back on a Monster Energy drink can that had his fingerprints and DNA, as well as trace amounts of the drug GHB."

"I'm old. Refresh me about the drugs these young people are doing."

Reading from her notes, Beth said, "GHB is a drug that was originally popular with athletes as a growth hormone, but was outlawed in the early nineties. It then emerged as a club drug, and a date rape drug. People who take it say that it's an intense aphrodisiac.

"Depending on the dose, GHB can cause mild feelings of increased libido and euphoria all the way across the board to intense hallucinations and seizures. Medical vials in Mr. Maguire's locker were found to contain GHB and ketamine, which is another club drug. Ketamine is a dissociative sedative more often referred to as Special K. At one time it was used as an anesthetic during surgeries on people. Eventually it was mostly discontinued for human use. It's still considered safe and inexpensive to use on animals, so it's not that hard to get. There are plenty of these drugs here in Falcon Valley. GHB and ketamine are both Schedule III controlled substances."

"And he had these in his locker?" Dr. Romano asked. "Tsk tsk. You never know about people. Go on."

"Miss Bellman at first denied ever seeing Mr. Maguire on that Sunday afternoon, but after her arrest and a number of interviews, she revealed that she'd been afraid to tell us the truth. That she had been in the gym that evening, and that she had seen Mr. Maguire, but that she thought he was dead. Her story was that she picked up his phone to call for help, saw that it was broken, wasn't thinking clearly, panicked, and decided to leave the body, unaware that he was still capable of being saved."

"Hmm," Dr. Romano said. "I don't know about that. Didn't she have her own phone? No one goes anywhere without their phone anymore, do they?"

"She lost it the night before at a school function," Beth replied.

"Oh yeah?" Dr. Romano laughed. "Well, that's convenient."

"We thought the same thing," Ken said. "Until we spoke to a student who confirms she dropped her phone that night and he picked it up. He didn't return it to her right away. We've had a look at the phone since, and there's no suspicious activity on it."

Dr. Romano shrugged. "All right then. That's a bit of a surprise."

"Miss Bellman was eventually bailed out

by the law firm Klein & Carrol," Ken went on. "We continued to investigate with the hope of bringing formal charges. But the more we learned, the more complicated it seemed." Ken looked at Beth and said, "Sorry, Beth, please continue."

Beth turned the page of her report. "Per CCTV footage, Sloane Elliman-Holt arrived for a private training session with Mr. Maguire at 3:59 p.m. Natalie Bellman went into the gym at 4:08 p.m. Sloane says she saw Miss Bellman sitting in the stairwell when she went to the bathroom at about a quarter after. Mr. Maguire was alive and well at that time. Miss Bellman then left a few minutes later, as per CCTV. The next two people to enter were Asha Wilson and Brooke Elliman.

"Brooke is Sloane's mom. She and her friend Asha went to pick Sloane up from her training session a little bit early to go out to dinner. According to both women, they arrived to find Mr. Maguire seemingly intoxicated and alarmingly aggressive. They said he was stumbling and acting in a way they 'found frightening.' "

Dr. Romano interlaced his hands and nodded. "Hmm."

Beth read out loud from the report. "Mr. Maguire's behavior was so upsetting and unusual that the two women decided it would be best to leave. Together with Sloane, they exited the mezzanine, walked down the stairs, and turned down the hallway that led to the exit. At that point in time, Mrs. Elliman said that she heard a sound like a 'splat' from inside the gym. Mrs. Wilson said that she heard something also, but to her it sounded more like a 'thump.' She thought perhaps Mr. Maguire had thrown a gym mat or a medicine ball over the balcony. Neither one of them wanted to stay in the pavilion any longer because of Mr. Maguire's scary and threatening behavior, so they proceeded to leave without looking into the gym. In retrospect, Wilson and Elliman believe the sound they heard was Mr. Maguire either jumping or falling and landing on the basketball court."

"You're kidding," Dr. Romano said.

"No. That's their statement." Ken moved to the edge of his seat. "If we take these women at their word, then their version of events corroborates Miss Bellman's story that she went in about thirty minutes later, at which point she picked up his phone to call for help, realized it was broken, and came to the conclusion that he was deceased. And if that's the truth, then the only thing she did wrong was walk away without calling later to report what she'd seen."

Dr. Romano typed something into his computer and spun back to the detectives. "I keep expecting it to change, but we're still a 'no duty to rescue' state. Even though we probably shouldn't be, given all the people that keep ending up at the bottom of cliffs while out for a hike with spouses who don't call for help."

Beth nodded. "Agreed. But we *are* a 'no duty to rescue' state, and even the 'failure to render aid' misdemeanor only applies if you're a medic or in a special relationship with the injured, such as parent, spouse, or employer."

"A couple other things to consider," Ken said. "A third Falcon mom by the name of Linda Leland came forward later to say that she had to go the sports pavilion mezzanine much earlier in the day to pay Mr. Maguire for her son's private training sessions." Ken paused. "These private training sessions seemed to be a cash-only kind of thing, if you get my drift."

"Christ." Dr. Romano wiped his forehead with a handkerchief. "I pay my lawful taxes. Am I the only one doing it by the books?"

"Not the only one," Ken said, smiling and indicating Beth. "She's very honest too."

Beth laughed, but inaudibly.

"So, this Linda Leland lady," Ken went on. "She claims that Mr. Maguire appeared to be impaired and acting irrationally as early as noon on the day he took the big dive."

"This guy seems like a real gem, huh?" Dr. Romano said. "And this woman is credible too?"

"I mean," Beth said. "Yeah. Kind of a rich hippie. Prominent member of the community. I can't see any reason why not. Had a DUI fifteen years ago, but that's it. No record."

"And lastly," Ken said, "we spoke with Mr. Maguire's former girlfriend. She's a Canadian actress by the name of Amelie Bernard —"

"I've heard of her," Dr. Romano said. "She was famous. He was dating her?"

"Yes," Beth said. "But they had long since broken up. Miss Bernard told us that despite the fact Mr. Maguire had been telling everyone around here that they were in a long-distance relationship, she'd called it quits with him almost two years ago. The final straw was when he had a seizure in a nightclub in Toronto after taking too much GHB."

Dr. Romano looked disgusted and said, "I'm not sure I need to hear any more. I'm thinking this guy took some of these drugs he kept in his locker while he was supposed to be working with kids and got loopy and then — let's see. You say here he had an injury to the back of his head? Okay. So, he was lurching around up there on the balcony area, fell, and hit the back of his head on this weight lifting equipment thingy that's mentioned here with the blood, tissue, and hair. At that point, he fell over a railing and suffered some terrible internal injuries that led to his death."

"That's certainly one of the possibilities we're looking at," Ken said.

"Well then," Dr. Romano said, "you can be sure that's going to be the defender's case, and it's a good one. I don't think jurors are going to think this was a nice, innocent guy."

Beth cleared her throat. "No. That's for sure. Plus, we're in the process of rebuilding his phone and getting search warrants for the home computer that was put in storage after his death. I've got be honest. It's looking like the tip of the iceberg with this man. Not a nice, innocent guy at all."

"What are we going to do? Charge this young woman . . ." Dr. Romano flipped through some papers. "Who moved to Falcon Valley to look after her disabled brother, was a stellar employee at a top-notch school, no criminal record whatsoever until she stole some pills out of the lost and found, and whose story is corroborated by three other women?"

He flipped though more pages of the report. "The blood on her clothes. Here we are. She said she wiped the phone off so she could use it to call for help, only to realize it was broken. The call to her brother. 'I did something bad.' She was ashamed that she panicked and left. No DNA under her nails, and no offensive or defensive wounds. Nothing in this report indicates that all these ladies are lying."

Ken nodded. "Well. Natalie did change her story about why she had his tie hidden in her desk a couple of times. I think she was embarrassed about snatching a little souvenir from the relationship."

Dr. Romano closed the report definitively. "I think Natalie Bellman was in the wrong place at the wrong time, and I think that pursuing this case would only make us look like idiots. My opinion is that this man's debauched lifestyle led to death by misadventure, and despite the fact that you say he was a beloved faculty member at Falcon Academy, my hunch is that he won't be missed."

■ ■ ■ ■

Several Months Later

■ ■ ■ ■

42

It was a cold Saturday morning in February, and Natalie was at the Olive Diner, having breakfast with Jay and Yvonne, who were officially dating. Natalie wasn't eating much. Not because of any pills. She was done with those. She was just nervous. In an hour and a half, she had an appointment to meet with Beth and Ken, again at the Falcon Valley police station.

"It's going to be okay," Jay said, scooping up some hash browns on his fork.

"I know," Natalie answered. "I think so, anyway. I've got butterflies, but that's normal, right?"

"Totally," Yvonne said. "I still get nervous buying booze. You've got nothing to worry about, girlfriend."

Jay gave Yvonne a closed-lip smile as he chewed on his potatoes, and she smiled back while sipping on her Bloody Mary. They were happy.

Natalie hoped Yvonne was right. Since the district prosecutor had declined to press charges, she'd kept a low profile. Though she'd been prepared to crawl across broken glass to keep her job, Mr. Dilly had said, "Of course you can't come back. An inappropriate relationship. Drugs. Lies. Stealing. An arrest, for God's sake."

In the ensuing few months, Natalie had considered moving back to Denver, but decided that was a last resort. She joined care.com as a dog walker and started driving for Instacart. Lately she'd been painting for hours every night. Mostly she stayed at home, and if she did go out, she avoided places where she might run into Brooke or Asha. She knew now that the story they'd told the officers had likely saved her from a lengthy trial and probably jail, but she felt it was best to keep her distance. It didn't seem like it was safe to come out yet.

She checked her phone. It was nearly noon. "I better go, guys," she said to Yvonne and Jay, reaching for her wallet.

"I've got it, Nat," Jay said. He'd just started back at his old job at Adrenaline Extreme Sports, this time in sales rather than leading bike and Jeep tours. "Good luck," he said.

By the entrance, as she was leaving,

Natalie said, "Rex?" The big man was hunched over a bowl of berries, yogurt, and granola in the window by the door, reading the newspaper. Natalie smiled sheepishly. "Hey."

"Hey," he said back.

"I was just —" she gestured back into the diner "— having breakfast with Yvonne. It's nice to see you. How're things at the school?"

"I don't work there anymore," he said, wiping his mouth and putting the napkin back down on his lap. "Yvonne didn't tell you?"

"No." Natalie sat down in the chair opposite him. "Since when?"

"Not long."

"What happened? I mean, I know we weren't really friends, but still —"

"It's okay," Rex said. "We weren't friends. We didn't even know each other. I didn't know much about you, and you didn't know much about me. For example, you didn't know I used to be in the military police."

"We barely talked."

"That was me. I didn't want to talk to people. I wanted a nice, quiet job where I didn't have to get to know anybody. And then Dilly totally messed up what happened with that girl Sloane, interviewed all the accused boys before the victim, and then completely ignored mandatory revelation laws? I know about the laws. Christ. He should be in jail. I was very unhappy when he fired you."

"I thought you hated me. You gave me some dirty looks there at the end."

"I did," Rex said. "Some dirty looks like, why did you get involved with that jerk? I thought you were smarter than that."

Natalie nodded, looking troubled. "Yeah, I should have been. I'm sorry you lost your job."

Rex plunged his spoon into his yogurt. "Who said I lost my job? I didn't lose my job. I quit. I'm half Arapaho, and I'm working at the Black Swift Casino and getting the salad buffet every day twice a day. Good for my diabetes. Don't worry about me. Take care of yourself."

"I will. Thank you, Rex."

Natalie hadn't been back to the Falcon Valley police station since she'd been arrested and detained in a featureless and empty holding cell equipped with two cameras, an old-fashioned wall phone, a water fountain, and a stainless-steel toilet in the corner.

Today she was led to a small room in the back, where Beth and Ken were waiting for her. "Hi, Natalie," Ken said. "Nice to see you."

"Nice to see you too, Detective Bradley. Detective Larson."

"You look very well," Beth said. "Healthy."

Natalie took a seat. "I'm doing better. Thank you for noticing." Beth placed a bottle of water on the table. "So," Natalie said, pulling the water bottle closer and beginning to toy with the paper label. "What's this meeting all about?"

Beth opened a manila folder. "We wanted to follow up with you about what we've been doing these past few months."

"We completely rebuilt Mr. Maguire's phone," Ken said. "Which takes a while and doesn't always work, but we got lucky."

"This is tricky, Natalie," Beth said. "We can't tell you everything. There are minors involved."

Natalie crossed her legs nervously and waited.

"Clearly," Beth went on, "I know a lot about what went on between you and Mr. Maguire from reading your planner."

This made Natalie incredibly uncomfortable.

"Let's talk for a minute about the drugs," Beth said.

"Do we have to?" Natalie asked, and Beth

and Ken both laughed, which was strangely comforting.

"Yes, we do," Ken said. "But you're not in any more trouble. Just relax and answer truthfully. First of all, have you gotten help for your addiction? Because if not, we have resources we'd like to extend."

"Thank you," Natalie said, examining her nails as if she'd love to chew on them. She folded her fingers into fists. "But I stopped. Nick was dead. I lost my job. I spent some time in jail. I no longer had access to the pills from school, and my brother took all the painkillers that he hadn't used over the past year to some sort of safe prescription drop-off place, and I was just . . . there was nothing. I was never that person who had a phone number to call to go meet someone on the corner of you know, First and Vine, or anything. I went to some group therapy meetings at the Unity Church in Blackswift. It helped. But I really had no choice but to stop. I don't mean to make it look easy, but I did. I just stopped."

"That's impressive, Natalie," Beth said. "Not a lot of people can do that. Now, if you don't mind, I'd like to ask you some personal questions related to your . . ." She smiled encouragingly. "*Past* addiction."

Natalie took several quick breaths and

said, "I'm ready."

"Correct me if anything I say isn't right. Mr. Maguire initially supplied you with amphetamines." Beth consulted her notes. "Which you eventually began to take often."

"Yes, that's true. He provided me with a leftover bottle of Adderall that his previous girlfriend, Amelie Bernard, had left at his home during a prior visit."

"Ms. Bernard claims those pills were never prescribed to her," Beth said. "You didn't see her name on the bottle, did you?"

"I never looked. No, that's incorrect. I did look, but there was no name. It was ripped off. I thought that was, you know, for privacy. Because she was famous." *And rich and skinny and perfect-looking, all reasons why it made sense to take the same pills that she took.*

"Those pills were acquired by various other means, not by lawful prescription."

"Oh. I just — okay."

"Also, you occasionally took opioids that had been prescribed to your brother, which it appears you'd been using for some time to self-medicate a history of periodic depression."

"Depression?"

"Umm-hmm, that was my interpretation. Was I wrong?"

Natalie thought about it for the first time ever. "No, I don't think you were wrong."

"And is there anything else you took? Drug-wise. It's important we know."

"Edibles," Natalie answered. "Nick and I ate marijuana edibles every once in a while. They were legal. Bought at the dispensary."

"But you didn't ever take GHB or ketamine?"

"No. I've heard about them," Natalie said. "But never been offered. Never been interested."

"They're club drugs," Ken said.

"I know what they are," she said. "But we didn't go to clubs. Nick and I didn't even go out to restaurants. We barely went anywhere."

"I understand," Ken said. "Let me put it another way. Do you think it's possible that you might have been given either of those drugs?"

"What do you mean? Without my knowledge?"

"That is what I mean, yes," Ken clarified. "Usually, GHB is diluted in a beverage. It looks like water and has almost no taste. Ketamine is a tranquilizer and can be taken in a variety of ways. One of which is by injection."

"What exactly do these drugs do to you?"

"They might make you feel good and relaxed, and then again, they might knock you out. Make you go to sleep. Is it possible you might have ingested either of those without knowing, during your time with Mr. Maguire?"

Natalie looked away, thinking. "Did he have those drugs?"

"Yes," Ken said, nodding.

The two detectives waited while Natalie unscrewed the top from her bottle of water and took a drink. When she set the bottle down on the table, she answered, "It's possible."

Beth made a note of this and looked at Natalie with a very grave expression. "We found pornography on Mr. Maguire's phone and computer. He had some chat room acquaintances around the country that helped us piece together the events of last spring. Mr. Maguire was hoping to obtain some illegal photos of a certain underage girl via her boyfriend, but that fell through, and it was very frustrating for him given that he was in a state of pathological sexual anticipation. At that point it appears he resorted to more extreme measures to get what he wanted. While quite a few of the images we found on his computer originated elsewhere, even in other countries, there are several dozen that appear to have been taken in a location that would indicate he himself personally took the photos."

"The training room," Natalie said, closing her eyes.

"What makes you say that?" Beth asked.

"Just a bad feeling," she said, even though she knew it was the truth. "I'm right, aren't I?"

Beth declined to confirm, but went on to say, "We think that Mr. Maguire drugged two girls in order to photograph them. We know that the trainer routinely administered anti-inflammatory shots to some athletes. We also know that on two occasions, the trainer wasn't available, and Mr. Maguire administered injections to female athletes on his own."

"Is he allowed to do that?"

"No. But we understand why a predator would go to all this trouble. First of all, the ultimate motive behind getting these types of photos is not just sexual gratification, but also coercion. Blackmailing the girls to get them to do what he wanted. We think this is probably where Mr. Maguire was going, but he never made it to the finish line, so to speak. Second, why the injections? There are no more overnight tournaments in hotels, at least not with a male coach and a girls' team, so we believe Mr. Maguire had to get creative. He was never alone with anyone except for his private training sessions, and they were an hour to three hours at the most. That's not enough time to dose a person with GHB or Rohypnol. It takes too long to get those 'date rape drugs' out of the system and recover."

"So, then, what was he giving these girls?" Natalie asked.

"He used ketamine," Beth said. "Injected it right into their hips. He was able to find something that took effect almost immediately and lasted a very brief amount of time. Ketamine is often snorted recreationally, but in that case, it enters the body more slowly. Only by injecting it can you get an instantaneous reaction. It's a knockout drug that causes confusion. Not knowing who you are or where you are."

Natalie thought back to all the times she'd spent hours upon hours passed out in Nick's dark bedroom. There had been the time when she'd woken with a sore hip. She'd originally attributed it to a pulled muscle from their bike ride but had later noticed it was bruised a greenish-blue. That hip had been tender off and on all summer until they'd stopped seeing each other, and then the bruise had finally gone away. And then there was the morning she'd woken to find that her clothes were in the dryer. Why? Because she'd had an "accident" that she couldn't remember. There were so many missing moments over the past six months — not blackouts exactly, but deep sleeping — and she'd blamed herself, thinking she'd worked out too hard, or was exhausted after being too amped on the Adderall, or had taken one too many painkillers, or that she shouldn't have had that second margarita.

"Are you all right, Natalie?" Ken asked.

She nodded, and at that point, Beth continued. "Mr. Maguire administered the victims a very precise amount of ketamine, enough to knock them out for five to ten minutes. When the victim woke up, it wouldn't necessarily feel like they'd been drugged. Ketamine would make them groggy. It might have seemed like seconds had passed. Like maybe they'd fallen asleep." Beth glanced quickly at Ken, and he returned her look with a subtle nod. "It's likely . . ." Beth said, uncomfortably fiddling with the corner of one of her papers. "It's likely that it was a challenge for him to get just the right dose for his . . ." She took a deep breath and looked up, into Natalie's eyes. "His agenda."

Nick's last voice message had said, "I

don't require your services anymore." Natalie thought maybe she finally understood. She could barely believe what she was about to ask. "Was he — experimenting on me?"

Ken lowered his eyes, but Beth nodded, her face pinched in a solemn way that indicated she was either furious or sorrowful, or both. "It's not just possible, Natalie. After reading your planner, it appears that Mr. Maguire had a very unusual interest with your weight. Giving you drugs to make you thinner, taking them away when you got too small, giving them back when you started gaining again. Not interested in seeing you when you weren't the right size. I found it both puzzling and suspect that he wanted you to be exactly one hundred and eight pounds."

Natalie waited, and Beth seemed to be trying to decide whether to say more. "Tell me," Natalie said. "Tell me what you're thinking."

"A hundred and eight pounds is the median weight between the two minors who were drugged," Beth said gently. "One was a hundred and six pounds, the other, one hundred and ten. I know this is hard to hear. It's hard to even imagine. But yes, we believe Mr. Maguire was fine-tuning the toxicity of his injections by using you. He was meticulous in determining how much was just enough, and how much was too much. The lengths he went to, to make sure he had just the right dose, are criminal and obsessive. To that end, he needed you to weigh roughly the same amount as his fifteen-year-old victims."

Natalie understood then, like a slap in the face, that he'd chosen her. That day in the forest, in the middle of their hike, sitting by the lake with Jackson? It had been meaningful for her, but theater for him. She'd told him that she'd been hurt by someone in the past. "But I don't want you to think that I'm some wounded and broken person. I'm not. I'm good. I've got a little baggage, but —"

He'd answered, "Shh. That's not what I was thinking at all. In fact, the actual thought that was going through my mind was, 'She's perfect.' "

A perfect target.

During their initial flirtation, Nick had said to her, "What are you? About five-four?"

"Precisely," she'd answered, feeling playful.

He'd been sizing her up. Not even one

day of their relationship had been real.

Not. One.

43

It crossed Natalie's mind, as she drove away from the police station, that she could go straight to Jay's. He would have beer in the fridge, and though there would be no Vicodin in the bathroom, she could always smoke a bowl or eat an Indica dark chocolate sea salt edible and zone out on his couch watching something mindless and funny. She didn't have to be alone, going over and over the horrendous details of what had happened to her and those girls.

"Those girls," she said out loud. That wasn't the extent of it. Not by a long shot. It was also Reade, who'd listened to a powerful middle-aged mentor and done what he was told to do. It was Reade's friends: all punished, all tainted. Families ruined. A school scandalized. An entire town, obsessed with wealth, prestige, and winning, had been easily poisoned by a slick salesman who promised them everything they desired, at the cost of the kids. Natalie wasn't going to let him poison her anymore. She was going to rise above it.

It was difficult, but when she came to the turn that would lead her to Jay's house and the relief of beer and weed, she went the other way. Maybe later, when she wasn't hanging by a thread.

At home, she tried to stay busy. She made herself a bowl of ramen because it was the closest thing she had to comfort food in the apartment. After slurping up the last of the noodles, she put the dish in the sink and admitted that she couldn't keep from thinking about it forever. She went into her bathroom, turned on the faucet, and splashed her face with cold water. "Don't blame yourself," she said to her reflection, but who was she kidding? There was no way around it. She'd gotten involved with him. She'd seen warning signs and wanted to ignore them. As if checking her own pulse, her fingers went to her tattoo, but the words *self love* didn't help. She'd allowed herself to be used in the worst way possible.

Natalie selected a medium-sized fresh canvas and took it to the workstation in the corner of the kitchen. As she began to paint, she tried to think of happier times. Selling her first painting on Etsy. Getting a two-hundred-dollar tip from the big party at the rooftop bar at Le Méridien. Laughing so hard she choked on her pizza with Jay. Her mom and dad dancing like teenagers to electronic music after Thanksgiving dinner while she and Jay jumped on the couch the year before Dad packed a bag and left, saying, "See you next week."

Beth had said that she'd been self-medicating for depression. That was Natalie's first diagnosis, and it was the first time that she'd ever considered it, but she supposed it was true. Real joy had been missing from her life for a while after her dad left and then later, after the blackout at the party. There had been ups and downs, of course. Good times and bad, but she had gotten used to there being something missing. Nick had come along, and his attention had filled the void.

"Idiot," she said out loud, using a sponge to rub light gray paint onto her canvas to create a background the color of a snowstorm. Her plan was to paint her own footsteps across the parking lot the night she'd found him, an image that she couldn't shake from her mind.

You might have been stupid, she thought, *but you weren't the only one.* Amelie Bernard had fallen for Nick, and she was a celebrity.

Brooke Elliman had hoped to date him, and she could have had any man she wanted. Elena Ruiz was not only beautiful, but an intelligent doctor, and she'd been cheating on her husband with Nick.

Natalie stopped there, with that thought. Elena. She did not fit the profile.

Nick sleeping with Elena suddenly didn't ring true. For the first time, Natalie realized, *I got it wrong.* Nick wanted girls, not women. Nick hunted girls, not women. He used women to get to girls.

Natalie went to the sink and began rinsing out a paintbrush. Watching the water pour, rubbing the bristles between her fingers, she allowed her mind to wander.

He'd drugged her.

He drugged Mia and Sloane while he was training them.

Jill Ruiz had died shortly after being trained by him.

Nick drove Mia home that night. Natalie had assumed he'd gone to Elena's house afterward to sleep with her, but he must have taken Mia there. Why had he taken Mia to Elena's house, to Jill's room, where Natalie had found his tie bunched on the floor? Because he'd been obsessed with Jill Ruiz, as obsessed as he had been with Sloane and Mia, but Jill had been his first.

The first, the most important, the one he couldn't forget. Suddenly Natalie understood what Beth had said about his experimentations. Meticulous. Just the right amount. Not too much, not too little. He needed a guinea pig this time around, because he didn't want to make another mistake. He'd given Jill the wrong dose. Maybe too much, maybe too little? Either way, she'd woken at the wrong moment, ran, and jumped in her car. A sixteen-year-old brand-new driver with drugs in her system trying to get the hell away from a monster. Ending in her untimely death.

Your wings were ready, but my heart was not. Yet another family he destroyed.

Nick had clearly been unhappy with the result of that experimentation and had decided to do better next time.

Natalie put down her paint sponge, grabbed her car keys and headed for the door.

The doctor and her husband had put their house up for sale, but Natalie thought there was a good chance that they'd stayed in the area and that Elena would still be working at the hospital. As she drove towards Colorado Medical, she tried to organize her thoughts. If she was going to have this conversation, she needed to be prepared.

Natalie told the nurse at the front desk of the maternity ward that she was looking for Dr. Ruiz. "Is she your obstetrician?" the woman asked pleasantly.

Placing one hand on her stomach, Natalie said, "Yes." It was easy to confirm that Dr. Ruiz was still on staff. "I don't suppose she'd be here right now, by any chance?" she asked.

"No, I'm afraid not," the woman answered.

"Thank you anyway."

As Natalie left, the woman called after her, "She's scheduled for tonight, though. If you come back in an hour, you might be able to grab a quick word before she goes into surgery."

"That's great," Natalie said, waving. "I appreciate it."

Natalie went to her car to grab her stocking cap, a pair of gloves, and a scarf. There was no reason to go home and come back, and the last thing she wanted to do was miss Elena by waiting in her car. Once she was bundled up, she went and sat on the bench situated outside the revolving doors leading into the wing that housed the maternity ward.

There was a staggered parade of evening shift nurses between seven and seven thirty, and then no one at all entered the building for the next fifteen minutes. Natalie knew it was Elena when she saw her across the parking lot because the woman was so statuesque. She was dressed all in black — coat, boots, and cap — and she walked with purpose, as if she were an intrepid assassin.

Which, Natalie thought, was exactly what she was.

Intercepting her before she crossed the street to the front entrance, Natalie said, "Dr. Ruiz? Could I have a word with you?"

Elena hesitated.

Natalie loosened the scarf around her face, hoping to be recognized.

The doctor squinted and it seemed, for a second, that she had placed Natalie as the young woman from the hospital room. "I'm afraid I can't talk right now," she answered. "I'm very sorry. I've got an induction in an hour."

"This will only take five minutes," Natalie replied.

"I'll give you my card. You can leave a message with my nurse." On her black cap was an embroidered black flower. Her face was like a Modigliani painting. Doe-eyed, classic. Lined from sadness.

"Okay," Natalie said. "So, I should just tell your nurse that I want to discuss Nicholas Maguire with you?"

Elena stopped digging around in her purse for a calling card and looked at Natalie more carefully. "It's you, isn't it?" she asked. "The girl who was in his room."

Natalie nodded and said her suspicion aloud. "And you were the doctor standing there behind me, when the lights came back on."

"Come with me," Elena said. "Let's go sit in my car." She led Natalie to a nondescript gray Volvo and used her key fob to open the doors. "Please," she said, motioning for Natalie to climb in on the other side.

Once they were seated, Elena took off her hat and laid it in her lap. "What can I do for you?" she asked, looking extremely tired.

"I saw the two of you together once, in a store," Natalie said hesitantly. "He was holding you, and you were touching his face. I thought you were having an affair with him."

"I wasn't," Elena answered, and it was clear that even the thought was unpleasant.

"I know that now. I figured it out about two hours ago."

"Good then," Elena said briskly. "And with that out of the way, can I go see to my patient?"

"I mean," Natalie said, "I've got it all

figured out."

It was so swift that Natalie barely caught it, but alarm rippled across Elena's face. Composure replaced it, and she said, "Really? At such a young age? I've never 'had it all figured out,' but if you think you're there, I'm sincerely happy for you and wish you all the best."

"He spoke to me that night. He wasn't succumbing to his injuries. He was waking up. He was getting better."

Elena looked at Natalie as if trying to read her mind. "Have you told anyone else about what you saw?"

"No."

"Is this about money? I don't have anything to hide, but neither do I want any problems. I don't have anyone to leave my money to anymore, so if that's what you want, I really don't care. Just make me an offer. What will it take to just leave me and my husband alone?"

"I'm so sorry," Natalie said. "I gave you the wrong impression. I don't want money."

"Then what do you want?"

"To understand. To know, going forward. Rather than wondering every single day if any of it really happened the way I remember it, if I talked to him, if I imagined it, if I made it up in my head what he did to them.

All of them. If I'm crazy."

"You're not crazy." Elena immediately looked away and said, "I mean, you don't seem crazy."

"Did you hear us talking that night?" Natalie asked. "Did you?"

Elena shook her head. "Talking about what?"

"You were there," Natalie said. "Asha, Brooke, and I, we were all in her room, and I remember the conversation we were having. I said something like, 'I know that he was doing the private training sessions with your daughters and that he did bad things. Like giving them something to make them sleep and taking photos of them.' And then I turned around, and you were there. Standing in the room, listening to us."

"Asha was my patient. I had a reason to be there."

"Did you have a reason to be down in Nick's room in the ICU twenty minutes later?"

"I can ask you the same question."

"I was thinking about killing him. What were you doing there?"

Elena sat quietly for a moment, her dark eyes huge and calculating. Eventually she sighed. "Yes. Okay. I heard the three of you talking when I came to Asha's hospital room that night. I understood that Mr. Maguire had drugged those two girls during a private training session. That was all I needed to know. He was training my daughter the afternoon she died. My daughter wasn't perfect. But we had a good relationship. Mr. Maguire told me that against his wishes, she left her training session early to go meet some friends. Jill died in a car crash shortly after that. I never could find these friends that she'd made plans to meet. It wasn't Reade Leland. I checked. He was at a family get-together in Vail. It bothered me ever since. But after listening to you three talk, I asked myself this question. Why did my daughter leave her training session early, get in her car, and start racing home?"

"Because he did something to her."

"Yes. That was my conclusion."

"How did you do it?"

"Do what?"

Natalie said, "I know. I know what happened. You killed the man that abused your daughter and caused her death. I know it. I'd just love to know how."

"I don't admit to anything you're accusing me of. But. If I was going to do something to Mr. Maguire? Hypothetically speaking? To make him slip back into an unresponsive state just as he was emerging?

I would have simply given him a shot of potassium chloride."

"That simple?"

"The coroner did an autopsy and found that Mr. Maguire's cause of death was vasospasm. An inexplicable narrowing of the coronary artery. Basically, a heart attack. Organ failure after terrible trauma."

"Caused by a shot of potassium chloride?"

"No one will ever be able to determine that, unfortunately. Potassium chloride is naturally present in the body, and the level becomes elevated after death. There wouldn't even be any cause for suspicion or further investigation. Unless . . ." Elena paused and looked up at the roof of the car, vulnerable for the first time. "Unless, for example, someone came forward to say that he was getting better, rather than worse. That he was awake, and talking, rather than slipping away. That would be a problem. That would be a big problem. For me and what's left of my family."

"I'm not a problem," Natalie said. "I'll never tell anyone I spoke to him. And, I'm so sorry."

"About my daughter?"

"Yes."

"Thank you," Elena said. "Me too. But

let's be clear. I'm not sorry about anything else."

"I understand," Natalie said. "And in that, you're not alone."

44

Summer had announced its arrival. Jay had started to accompany Natalie on the first quarter mile of Rocky's walks, still dependent on his cane. At that point Jay would head back for home, and Natalie would take the dog another mile or so before turning around. She was just starting on her way back to Jay's house when she got the text message from Asha.

> It's been such a long time, Natalie! I would really like to talk. Can you please stop by the open house I'm having this weekend? I've attached information. I really would LOVE to see you.

Natalie opened the attachment. The "open house" was actually an apartment. She recognized the address. It was Brooke Elliman's "pied-à-terre" that she'd bought for her now ex-husband in the hopes that her generosity and civility would help lure him back to their home and marriage. The apartment that had been empty for ages except as a party pad for wayward teenagers. Who had open houses for apartments?

The invitation was questionable, to say the least.

Then again, Natalie had started questioning everything after learning that her relationship with Nick was fake. Despite the fact that she had eventually been released without being charged in Nick's death, Natalie would never, ever stop thinking about one thing: Asha, Brooke, and Elena had killed him. She felt complicit for what she'd done to his phone, of course. Asha and Brooke didn't know about Elena, and Elena didn't know about what had happened in the gym. At the end of the day, only one person knew it all. Her. How long would those women go on living their lives, wondering if she was ever going to tell anyone about their role in his death?

Natalie did, in fact, have a passport now.

She debated meeting Asha at Brooke's "open house" apartment. It felt weird, and she wasn't sure she could trust them. But in the end, she decided to go.

I'll be there, she texted back to Asha. I'm looking forward to seeing you.

■ ■ ■ ■

When the weekend arrived, Natalie drove into town and across the river to the mountain slope opposite where she and Jay lived. The Koi Creek Apartments were modern and minimalist, with a soothing waterfall and small koi pond in the lobby. Natalie buzzed the ninth floor, and an elevator arrived to take her up. It opened directly into the open plan loft, decorated in the same theme as the lobby down below. Expensive but characterless. No fish. Lots of stainless steel, white leather, and black accents.

Asha was a little plump half a year post-pregnancy, but still very cute and quicker on her feet. She came running over. "Thank you for coming, Natalie."

Natalie was reluctant to step out of the elevator. Something wasn't right.

"I know it's a little weird," Asha said. "I'll explain."

Brooke emerged from the kitchen. "Come here," she said, holding her arms out for a hug.

Natalie's eyes dropped to the floor of the apartment. She half expected to see a plastic tarp, so that they could kill her, wrap her up, and get rid of her body without a mess.

She said, "I shouldn't have come. I'm sorry. I think I might just go."

"Don't be silly." Asha motioned for her to step out of the elevator. "It's okay. I didn't tell you it wasn't a real open house and that Brooke was going to be here because I wasn't sure you would have come."

"I might not have. Why does this feel like a trap?"

"Shh!" Brooke shook her head. "You've got the wrong idea. Just come in already."

Natalie finally relented and stepped out of the elevator and into the apartment.

"What do you think of this place?" Asha asked. "It's dazzling, right?"

"It is," Natalie said automatically, and without looking around. "I'm still confused as to why I'm here."

"You seem mad. Why are you mad at us, Natalie?" Brooke asked. "We made up that story about him falling so they couldn't do anything to you. I would have thought you'd be happy."

Natalie crossed her arms over her chest. "I am. But it's also hard to forget you walking by me in the police station acting like I was garbage right before they arrested me. I thought you'd thrown me under the bus. You still could. I have some trust issues."

"That was just an act for the police, so

they didn't think we were in cahoots," Brooke said.

"Whatever you say," Natalie answered. For her, every bit of it still stung. Someone laughed in the other room and Natalie looked spooked.

"Just Mia and Sloane," Asha said. "Ever since everything that happened, they've been sort of inseparable. Brooke and I like to keep them close. They're in the bedroom watching a movie."

"Are they . . ." Natalie searched for the right words. "Doing well?"

"They're doing better than they were before," Asha answered. "Now that Mr. Maguire's not riling them up about colleges, pitting them against one another, and trying to exert so much control over them, they've both been more relaxed and happier. They're getting along great." Asha paused and glanced toward the bedroom door. Under her breath, she said, "We don't talk about him with them. Not yet."

"No more issues about UCLA between us," Brooke said. "Mia wants to stay in state for college so she can see her baby sister more, and Sloane has decided she doesn't want to go to UCLA anyway, because she doesn't want to 'spend her life in my shadow.' " Brooke threw her hands up.

"And I . . . whatever. That's fine. I'm over it. I'm proud of her for wanting to do her own thing."

"Excellent update," Natalie said.

"Yeah. So. Follow me," Brooke said. She led them over to the sliding glass door that opened onto a stupendous balcony. Asha followed, and they all gathered overlooking the nine-story drop to the ground.

Natalie suddenly pictured the two of them pushing her over it, just like they'd done with Nick. She took a step back, away from them. No matter how much they smiled, touched her arm, and threw their heads back laughing like they were lifelong close friends instead of conspirators, Natalie knew what was going through their minds.

Only one person knows what we did. This chain is only as strong as its weakest link.

"I do want to thank you both," Natalie said, grabbing onto the steel railing. "For telling the police that you heard him fall. They believed it, and here we are. Otherwise, I think I'd be, well, pretty much screwed."

"That was the least we could do," Asha said.

"Linda helped us too," Brooke said. "She lied for us. She knew what Nick was all about."

"But does she know what really happened?" Natalie asked, hoping there were no other loose ends.

Asha shook her head. "No. Nobody does, except the three of us."

"Not even the girls?" Natalie asked.

"No," Asha said. "Mia's got the bad memory of the intervention. She knows that someone took photos of her when she was unconscious, but she doesn't know who. She thinks it could have happened at one of the kids' parties."

"And Sloane says Coach Nick never did anything to her. No recollection of any of it."

"Are you going to tell them the truth?" Natalie asked.

"Of course," Asha said. "But we're working with their therapist to figure out when is the right time to do it."

Natalie glanced towards the bedroom. The girls were laughing again. It must have been a comedy. "They can still be troubled by what happened. Even if they can't remember and haven't been told."

Brooke nodded. "We know. And we know what happened to you when you were their age, and that you understand better than anyone what they might be going through. Their therapist is the best in the area."

"Natalie," Asha said. "This therapist? She's available to see you, too."

"Oh," Natalie said, waving her hand. "Now that Mr. Dilly fired me, I don't have any health insurance for the time being. But I'm happy for your daughters. I think they'll be okay."

"We'd like to pay for it, Natalie. Scratch that. We are paying for you to go and see the same therapist as Mia and Sloane." Brooke looked as if she was ready for Natalie to challenge her. "It's happening."

"I couldn't —"

"Yes, you could," Asha cut in forcefully. "Just say yes. Please. We owe you."

"Umm —" Natalie looked at each of them, and they seemed to genuinely want her to accept. "Okay. Thank you. Do you mean it?"

"We mean it," Asha said. "And, I was wondering." The breeze was kicking in, and Asha had to brush her hair out of her eyes. "Now that I want to spend most of my time with Tara —"

"Is she here? I'd love to see her," Natalie said.

"Phil's looking after her at home. He's been surprisingly excited about being a new dad. You'll get to meet her. She's a handful. As I was saying, though, now that I want to work less, I was thinking I could use an assistant."

"That makes sense."

"She's asking you if you'd be interested," Brooke said.

"Someone to help me stage, who actually has an artistic sensibility. Someone who understands composition, color, and lines, and not just pinecones in a bowl that you saw on Pinterest. I could teach you, and you could help me, and maybe eventually I could guide you through getting your real estate license."

Natalie was silent for a second. "I would love that."

"When Asha told me that she was thinking of offering you a job, I had an idea too," Brooke said. "I was wondering if you might be willing to help me out."

"In what way?"

"This is the apartment I bought for my husband when we separated. It's dusty. Someone needs to water the plants and, I don't know, all that stuff that most people do, like change filters and light bulbs and shit. I need someone to look after the place."

Natalie cleared her throat. "Who, me?"

"Would you be interested?"

"Like, for how long?"

"For as long as you want."

Natalie thought about it, looking around at the apartment that had probably cost at least a million dollars. "What would my rent be?"

Brooke considered this. "What if we said you were the housekeeper, and I didn't ask you for rent?"

Natalie felt a lump in her throat. "I've been looking into adopting a cat. Could I have a cat here?"

"Yes. Done deal then," Brooke said.

"Come to the kitchen," Asha said. "I have a tradition. We always drink champagne when we pass on a property to a new tenant." She went and grabbed a bottle from the fridge and opened it with an expert twist and pop.

Brooke placed the keys to the apartment on the counter in front of Natalie, raised her glass, and said, "One of us needs to say it. Here's to getting away with it. Here's to Asha, for figuring out what was going on. Here's to me, for that amazing right hook. Here's to you, Natalie, for stomping on his phone, because if you hadn't done it, he would have called for help, lived, and Asha and I would probably be in jail. And here's to Linda, who decided to back us up and say that he was a drunk loser by noon on the day he dived over the railing. Cheers."

Natalie clinked her glass against theirs, thinking about Elena and Jill. At some point, she thought, when any threat to Elena was long past, she would go see her and tell her the whole story.

"You know what?" Brooke asked. "I like this. Next Saturday, let's do this at my house. Brunch at eleven? Asha, you bring the baby. Natalie, you can bring bagels from the bakery, and I'll make a lox platter and mimosas. What do you say?"

Natalie smiled. "I guess I'm in."

Epilogue

KBEV 16 Breaking News:

"Melissa O'Hare here. Stunning developments in Falcon Valley in the case of the deceased Nicholas Maguire, a minor celebrity in the sports world and once a much-loved coach at the Falcon Academy private school. Startling allegations about his abuse of student athletes are trending on social media and being covered by all major news channels. There's new information that has drawn national attention to the 'Soccer Sleazebag,' who appears to have been using drugs to sedate and abuse girls under the guise of physical therapy. It turns out that Mr. Maguire now has accusers stepping forward from Arizona, California, Texas, and Illinois, which has, as you can imagine, warranted the interest of the FBI.

"In light of this new information, the Denver Major Crimes division has decided to reopen the investigation into the 'Soccer Sleazebag' death last October. According to lead Detective Ken Bradley, they now believe the coach had a number of potential enemies who likely wished him harm.

"Should be interesting. Stay safe, Colorado. We've got a storm coming in."

ACKNOWLEDGMENTS

Especially for Maddy, but also hugely for everyone else at the Madeleine Milburn Literary Agency, thank you. I have felt valued and championed since day one. I am so grateful to all of you.

For Natalie Hallak, Erika Kahn Imranyi, Stefanie Bierwerth and Jessica Lambert, my tireless editors around the world, you have been incredibly patient, supportive and brilliant. You stuck by me during a challenging project and a tumultuous period. Strange times. Thank you for seeing me through it all with such a dedication to our work and the shared belief that the future was bright, no matter how dark some days.

Emily Kerstein, Melissa Sherwood and Amy Hartman, thank you for being my first readers. Your input and encouragement meant the world to me.

Jos, Caidan and Jude — I love you more than words can express. Our fourteen months of isolation weren't easy, but also not that hard, because the three of you made me laugh every single day.

Mom and Dad, I love you with all my heart. Thank you for taking me to all those gymnastics practices and soccer tournaments over the years and repeatedly reminding me, "Anne can."

ABOUT THE AUTHOR

Annie Ward is the author of *Beautiful Bad.* She has a BA in English literature from UCLA and an MFA in screenwriting from the American Film Institute. Her first short screenplay, *Strange Habit,* starring Adam Scott, was an official selection of the Sundance Film Festival and the Grand Jury Award winner at the Aspen Film Festival. She has received a Fulbright scholarship and an Escape to Create artist residency. She lives in Kansas with her family.

The employees of Thorndike Press hope you have enjoyed this Large Print book. All our Thorndike, Wheeler, and Kennebec Large Print titles are designed for easy reading, and all our books are made to last. Other Thorndike Press Large Print books are available at your library, through selected bookstores, or directly from us.

For information about titles, please call:
(800) 223-1244

or visit our website at:
gale.com/thorndike

To share your comments, please write:

Publisher
Thorndike Press
10 Water St., Suite 310
Waterville, ME 04901